THE WHARF BUTCHER

by

Michael K Foster

Typeset in Bembo Std

Design, typesetting and publishing by UK Book Publishing

UK Book Publishing is a trading name of Consilience Media

www.ukbookpublishing.com

ISBN: 978-1-910223-56-7

Cover images:

© T. Al Nakib © Mark Bryant © Nick Benjaminsz – freeimages.com

In memory of Rita Day

Preface

Fear strikes him like never before. He is immediately drawn into a spiralling, bottomless pit that threatens to drag him ever closer towards the edge of eternal darkness. He hesitates, filled with indecision and the fabric of uncertainty. Nothing is real anymore, everything a dream. Then the voice in his head returns.

Have you taken your medication today?

Chapter One

Newcastle, September 2011

One of the many hated things in Ernest Stanton's life was the number thirteen. He could never explain why, just that it was his unlucky number. Today of all days it was Friday the thirteenth, and the thirteenth day of his trial. It was shortly after two o'clock when he finally entered the witness stand. Of course he was guilty. The whole damn world knew that. What no one knew, not even him, was that in just a few hours he would be dead.

Wearing a pinstriped suit, white silk shirt and gold silk tie, Stanton looked immaculate. Few would have guessed he was wearing Santoni black leather shoes; there again, few would have realised that this was his last grand performance. His defence lawyers were reputedly the best and the presiding Judge, Mr Justice Fowler, a firm but fair man, ran Courtroom One with an iron rod. Nothing, it seemed, had been allowed to go unnoticed.

It all started innocently enough, as most marathon court cases do. Mr John Purvis QC, counsel for the Crown, took Stanton through a series of undemanding questions before making great play of his dubious background. By the time he'd finished, everyone was in no doubt that they were dealing with an unscrupulous businessman. Throughout that afternoon, Courtroom One had offered Stanton few answers, only questions, and there were many. Good barristers need to have many roles – law makers, courtroom personalities, even private detectives. The moment Mr Purvis QC accused Stanton of conducting fraudulent business activities, the defence was on its feet. Stanton's defence lawyers were furious and so was Justice Fowler, who challenged his statement as hearsay and of little substance or value to the case. It was the turning point in the trial though, and one from which Mr Purvis QC would never recover. It was an astonishing turn of events. Even Judge Fowler's summing up speech had brought outcry from the public gallery. But to say it was a moral victory would have been a gross over exaggeration. It was the kiss of death for Ernest Stanton.

Later that evening, as the last rays of sunlight played through the windows of Stanton's luxury cottage, he turned the empty bottle in the fading light and brushed the dust from its label. Jameson, triple distilled Irish whiskey, matured and bottled in Ireland. A fitting blend and utterly deserved he told himself. Pouring another generous measure, this time taken from a crystal decanter retrieved from a large drinks cabinet, there was no mistaking his contentment. Ernest Stanton was more than pleased with the verdict; his lawyers had done well. Too well if the truth was known.

After a long time – how long Stanton had no idea – he began to relax. Beyond the breakwaters and further out to sea, a stiff easterly crosswind that had buffeted the north east coastline for the best part of the day, threatened to move inland. A storm was brewing. Closer to home, he watched as a small armada of fishing vessels ran for the shelter of the harbour. Tightly packed together as if there was safety in numbers, they were making perilously slow headway between the North and South Shields piers. He could think of much easier ways of making a living, and far less risky.

As the light began to fade, Stanton was inexplicably drawn in by the weird ghost-like reflections that twisted and danced across his cottage walls. What caused them to move as they did, he had no idea. The more he thought about it, the more he questioned their presence. Nothing could have prepared him for what happened next. Not even the good Lord. At a glance, he thought he recognised the intruder. His face looked familiar. He was tall, lean in stature, with short cropped hair and dark penetrating eyes that cut through him with an ice-cold, menacing intensity.

How long had he been there?

Startled, Stanton eased his position and made as if to stand – a friendly gesture, non-threatening. The next thing he knew he'd been stabbed, that much he was sure of. Terrified, he clutched at his side in a vain attempt to stem the blood flow. What followed next can only be described as a moment of utter madness. First his head was jerked back, and then he felt the cold steel blade of the intruder's knife as it slid effortlessly across his throat. Stanton crashed to the floor – sending the decanter and its liquid contents in every direction. In those last crazy few seconds, his whole life began to open up before him.

Nothing could stop the warm red torrent from gushing through his fingers. No matter how hard he pressed. Worst was the knowing, knowing he was going to die. Coughing and spluttering in a vain effort to breathe, he hauled himself back onto his elbows. Only then did he recognise the intruder, and that familiar gloating smile that only he could perform. But there was something else, something more sinister that was fuelling Stanton's anger.

Then he remembered.

Slipping in and out of consciousness, he reached out towards the upturned table and grabbed hold of his mobile phone. He was trembling, and his whole body was uncontrollably shaking with fear. Through sticky blood-soaked fingers, he punched in the predetermined number and waited for a connection.

Then he heard footsteps.

His business here done, the intruder turned his back on Stanton and made towards the sanctuary of the hallway. It was over. At precisely *thirteen* minutes past seven, the line went dead.

Chapter Two

The door creaked open as Lexus slipped unnoticed through the rear entrance of the old wharf building. Adjusting to the dark, he searched for signs of life. Built on two levels, the building once housed plumbing materials. Not anymore. Thick stone walls, and boarded up windows and doors had helped turn this place into a perfect drugs den. Close to the river, off the beaten track, he was confident the police would never come looking for him here.

Outside the storm had decidedly worsened, the wind was blowing in every direction; with it the rain. Wearing a black leather bomber jacket, black jeans and T-shirt and Totectors safety boots, Lexus was soaked to the skin. He preferred to dress casually, for comfort, but right now his whole body was aching with the cold.

He glanced at his watch.

It was ten minutes to midnight and the streets outside were deserted. Had Ernest Stanton been found guilty that afternoon, things might have turned out differently. But they hadn't, and the fact that Stanton was dead spoke volumes. Then in the darkest corners of his mind the voices returned.

How did he die?

'Hideously!'

Perfect, you're such a genius.

Numb with disbelief, he felt for the knife. The same one he'd used earlier that evening. The handle felt sticky, and slippery in his grasp. Stanton had died easily, too easily perhaps. The speed of his death had surprised him – even he had not realised that killing could be so easy. Watching the man grovel as he thrashed the air in a vain attempt to stave off the inevitable, had excited him. He'd felt good about it, exhilarated. There were many ways to die, the variations seemed endless. The pure act of killing someone had somehow come naturally to him, without destructive regret.

'The vile beast is dead,' he laughed out hysterically.

Did he always talk to himself, he wondered?

No. Sometimes to me, the voice in his head replied.

Then, suddenly, he stiffened. Lurking in shadows, he spotted an unmarked police car cruising along Hadrian Road and towards Berwick Street and Marine House. The Vauxhall Vectra car's headlights were dipped, and the occupants were wearing bullet-proof jackets.

Was it his imagination, or had he seen movement?

His throat tightened.

It was then he noticed the white Transit van, as it slowly approached from the opposite direction. Full of police support officers, all were kitted up and ready for action. As he stood there, he watched as the front passenger leaned out of the side window and shone his high-powered flashlight into the old wharf building. They were looking for someone, but who could it be, he wondered. He mistrusted the pigs at the best of times; nothing they ever did made any sense. At least to him it didn't.

'This is it,' he screamed.

Gripped by uncontrollable rage, Lexus suddenly took off and into the deserted back lane, and the line of parked up vehicles within it. Several thoughts ran through his head – including the Mk3 Ford Mondeo, the one he'd nicked earlier that evening. He was almost home and dry. Just a few more minutes and he'd be long gone – free from the dangers that surrounded him.

The clock on the dashboard read one minute before midnight, when beneath the bonnet the Mondeo's powerful two-litre Duratorq TDCI engine roared into action. No sooner had he hit the accelerator, when the menacing 'twos and blues' flashing police lights filled his rear-view mirror. Hoping to lose them at the next junction, he braked hard, and swung the Mondeo into the maze of back streets on the outskirts of Newcastle. He thought he'd lost them, and laughed out loud.

Then, another police car appeared, up close and intimate.

Fear surrounded him as he hit the accelerator hard and felt the seat back pressing against him. Directly ahead, he caught sight of the red traffic lights.

'Jesus!' he yelled, as he narrowly missed a white transit as it approached at speed from one of the many side streets. Then he heard the bang.

Open your eyes, the voice in his head commanded. *What do you see?*

He checked his mirrors – nothing there.

Look again.

Not more than fifty metres away, its blue spinners still rotating, he could just make out the mangled wreck of the police car. It had collided head on with the white transit van.

'Perfect,' Lexus chuckled.

Barely a mile from the village of Newburn, his attention was inexplicably drawn towards a low-pitched rumbling noise – akin to that of a low flying aircraft coming into land. He checked his surroundings. Spurred on by millions of gallons of impetuous rainwater, the swollen River Tyne had burst its banks. Fields, farms and houses alike were awash in a deluge of floodwater. Within seconds, the murky brown liquid was lapping round his ankles, ice cold and threatening.

Lexus sat motionless, his hands shaking, his fear increasing. Then without warning the car's headlights suddenly went dead and he was plunged into total darkness. Caught in the river's grasp, he felt a terrifying jolt. Swept broadside by the river's powerful currents, the stolen Mondeo was being carried along at breakneck speed. The noise deafened him, and it didn't take a rocket scientist to figure out the seriousness of his current situation. Spurred on by millions of gallons of rampant floodwater, his whole world was rapidly spinning out of control.

He gazed at the roof; the air gap had closed.

He tried the doors; nothing. The immense water pressure now pushing up against the vehicle was preventing him from opening them.

He tried the windows; nothing. The electrics were dead.

Only then did he realise the hopelessness of his untenable position. He was trapped, and there was nothing he could do about it. Disoriented and imprisoned inside a sinking steel sarcophagus, like a thousand nightmares, his whole life was slowly ebbing away before him.

Shivering and numb with uncontrollable fear, the lower half of his body was now completely submerged under water. Panic gripped him as the Mondeo took another terrifying buffeting; only this time felt different, very different. As the weight of the car engine block finally began to seal his fate, he cried out in utter disbelief. First the nose, then the roof, the Mondeo slipped effortlessly beneath the icy black depths of the raging River Tyne.

Death, it seemed, was inevitable.

In one last desperate effort, he sucked in the last mouthfuls of air and tried to embrace the darkness. All the while his pale white face and hands pushed hard up against the window.

Then he heard voices – as sirens lured sailors to their deaths.

Try the doors again.

Both hands now firmly gripped around the passenger seat, his feet shoved hard up against the car door, he pushed with all his might.

You're such a genius.

Chapter Three

Several weeks later

David Carlisle's morning wasn't getting any easier. It had started to snow, and a biting cold wind was blowing straight in off the North Sea. He'd not felt this cold in a long while. Wearing a thick woolly hat, a Nanavik black Parka Jacket, frayed jeans, scarf, gloves and a sturdy pair of leather gun boots, he was chilled to the marrow. His hat now pulled down over his ears, Carlisle arched his athletic frame against the raw biting wind, and glanced out across the River Tyne. The temperature had plummeted rapidly over the past twenty-four hours; it was now minus two. When he spoke, his warm breath condensed into tiny water vapour droplets, sending out thick clouds of white fog. Everything seemed surreal.

Earlier that morning, a police helicopter attending a road traffic incident had spotted a submerged vehicle lying in four metres of water. Close to Dunston Staithes and barely visible from the road, this was the fifth vehicle incident the police had dealt with in as many days. Although the tide was out, the River Tyne was still heavily swollen. Less than a week ago, most of the surrounding fields had been under three-foot of water and a major clean-up was now in operation. The whole area had been cordoned off from public view, with several police vehicles parked up at either end of the approach road.

Fast approaching forty-two, David Carlisle had never intended to be a private investigator: it had happened by chance. Having studied Behavioural Psychology at The Open University, he'd joined the Metropolitan Police, working his way up to Detective Sergeant. Most of his time had been spent busting drugs rings, prostitution and small-time smuggling syndicates in and around the city limits. It was nothing exciting, mainly repetitious and at times utterly frustrating work. After his selection to the Murder Investigation Team (MIT), the job came naturally to him. Starting at the bottom as a criminal psychologist, he soon found himself involved in hunting down psychopaths, serial killers and the occasional hostage-taker who threatened National Security. It was a hazardous job but he'd managed to stay focused, building a reputation as a risk-taker, which suited the senior backroom staff.

Sadly, a bunch of Westminster politicians – the infamous men in grey suits with very few brains and no respect for the subtle differences of national identity – finally put paid to it all. Within weeks, his tightly-knit team had been unceremoniously disbanded in favour of a multi-national force. Transferred to the Northumbria police, he spent his next five years stagnating. It was soul destroying, and Carlisle hated every minute of it. When voluntary redundancies came along, he was the first in the queue to apply. It was then he'd teamed up with his current business partner, Jane Collins. Having set up office together in the heart of South Shields, it was nothing ambitious, just enough to earn them a decent living – or that was the theory.

Chatting to PC Manning from Gateshead police, Carlisle suddenly spotted the reappearance of the police launch. Five minutes earlier, two divers from the River Police Team had plunged from the side of it, and into the sub-zero depths of the river. Wearing specialist breathing apparatus and blue wetsuits, they'd trawled the riverbed ever since.

Then one of them broke surface.

'Anything?' an officer called out.

The diver gave a thumb up signal, and pointed down at the murky waters below. All eyes now turned towards the large Atlas crane, as its long orange boom arm slowly swung out over the river. When its hook reached out directly above the diver's head, it stopped with a loud clunk. Suddenly, the riverbank was a hive of activity.

Drawn up alongside the Atlas crane, the driver of the Mercedes Sprinter recovery truck began positioning his two rear tail ramps. After checking the winching gear, he laid out a series of straps down either side of his truck. Dressed in their distinctive yellow high visibility jackets, several road traffic officers gazed on in anticipation. One of them, the senior officer, began dishing out instructions to the crane driver. Nearby, Carlisle picked out the portly figure of Carl Jones, the crime scene photographer. Standing beside him was the smartly dressed Sharon Dexter, a new member of the Forensics Team. As the crane-driver winched the submerged vehicle from the bottom of the river, anticipation levels heightened. Boot first: two thick yellow lifting straps had been attached to its rear axle. Suspended out above the river, murky brown water now poured out from every available orifice. The car's roof was flattened, and both passenger doors appeared badly buckled and dented.

An image formed in his head. Carlisle detested water, especially fast flowing water. Ever since his beautiful wife Jackie had been taken away from him in a tragic, freak ferry accident, he had struggled to come to terms with her loss. Only now was he coming out of the fog.

Still grappling with his emotions, he spotted Sergeant Kevin Morrison, one of the old-school Road Traffic Officers, moving towards him.

'What brings you to this neck of the woods, my friend?' the Sergeant asked.

'Certainly not the weather,' Carlisle replied.

The Sergeant flapped his arms about in a vain attempt to keep warm. Standing six-foot two, Kevin Morrison was a good four inches taller than him.

'What a mess!' the Sergeant said, pointing up at the mangled Mondeo.

'How long has it been in the water?'

'A few weeks I suspect, it's hard to say.'

As the police launch pushed back in the water, all kinds of emotions tugged at him. Trying to solve a crime scene was hard enough, but the emotional strain was even worse. Why must he always blame himself for his wife's death? It wasn't his fault, surely. Feeling sick in the pit of stomach, he took another deep breath.

'How's business nowadays?' the Sergeant asked.

'Money's tight, and I could do with a few good cases— '

The Sergeant returned his notebook to his jacket pocket, and stared up at the Mondeo. Now stationary, the car's grille was ignominiously pointing back at the river. Water now trickling out from the radiator grille, the bonnet lid clanked in the breeze.

'Does Jane Collins still work with you?' the Sergeant asked.

'Yes. Why?'

'It's just that I've seen her at Police Headquarters a lot lately.'

The Sergeant was in a talkative mood, informing him that an Automatic Number Plate Recognition (ANPR) had already been carried out on the Mk3 Ford Mondeo. Reported stolen in Gateshead, its occupant was wanted in connection with a murder concerning a forty-six year old male. Whoever Ernest Stanton was, he'd been viciously stabbed to death in a frenzied knife attack at his home in North Shields.

They chatted a while, before the Sergeant's radio crackled into life again. Answering the caller, he gave him a friendly salute and moved off towards the recovery truck. Over the years David Carlisle had got used to the dead being described as 'celebrities'– it came with the job. Yesterday's headlines were tomorrow's history as far as he was concerned. Staring up at the wreckage again, he was half expecting a body to slide out through the open passenger door. Some things never changed; he could never take anything for granted nowadays. Soon forensics would be crawling all over the place, picking up the pieces and looking for the minutest scrap of evidence. Somehow he doubted they'd find much in the way of DNA samples. The river had made certain of that.

Bracing himself against the cold, Carlisle checked his surroundings before moving back towards his parked car. It was strange how some people spent their entire lives avoiding trouble, whilst others got more than their fair share of it. That was the way of the world, life was a lottery and if it wasn't one thing, it was another. Times were hard and money was tight. Had it not been for a recent spate of petty crimes, his business would surely have gone into liquidation. It was a bizarre state of affairs, and the irony never ceased to amaze him.

It was mid-afternoon when he finally pulled his Rover P4 100 into the last available parking space at the back of the office building. It had stopped snowing, and a low wintery sun was casting long slanting shadows well into the heart of Beach Road. An observant man, Carlisle watched as a heavy roller shutter door came down on another day's trading. Like most shopkeepers around here, they were struggling just to pay the extortionate council rents that were being meted out. And that was another thing: they were already three months in arrears themselves. What a mess, he cursed.

Opening up the office, he made coffee, answered a few e-mails and checked for missed phone calls. Not that he was expecting any, but at least it made him feel wanted.

'I'm back!' the female voice called out.

Carlisle turned sharply away from the window and back towards the open door where his partner, Jane Collins, now stood.

'Ah! It's you, Jane.'

'Who else were you expecting to see?' she teased.

Carlisle looked up. 'The last thing I need right now is someone with a sense of humour. I'm chilled to the bone, having stood around all morning in the perishing cold.'

Jane slid her long elegant frame further into the office, running the flat of her hand down over the front of her dress as if to remove the creases. She was an extremely attractive woman, mid-thirties with long blonde shoulder length hair, deep blue eyes and a slim waistline that gave her the look of a model. If nothing else, her feminine touch had certainly brought another dimension to their ailing business. The clients loved her, she was a natural attraction. Single, Jane's latest admirers – two Siamese cats lovingly saved from the local cat rescue centre – were the love of her life.

'Before I forget,' said Jane, 'another client phoned, desperately in need of legal advice.'

More like the dregs of society, Carlisle thought, taking another sip of his coffee. Evading further questioning, he moved towards a large bay window and peered down at the busy street below. It was 3.46pm. Soon it would be dark. Apart from an appointment involving a false insurance claim, he had nothing else pencilled in his diary that day. There was, of course, his regular five o'clock Monday appointment with Mr Smallman, a ninety year old flamboyant bachelor who claimed his partner was having an affair with the chairman of the local squash club. He cringed at the thought.

It had been twelve months since their last major assignment. A vicious love triangle, as he recalled. Boy meets girl – girl disappears under mysterious circumstances – and doting father asks them for help. In the end, it turned out that girl left boy to live with her girlfriend. Not only did she fake her own disappearance, she did a damn good job of convincing everyone else into the bargain. Luckily, the girl's father was a rich industrialist and his daughter's timely disappearance had undoubtedly saved their business from bankruptcy.

'So, where have you been?'

'Dunston,' he replied. 'The police there have just pulled another car out of the river.'

'Did they say whose?'

'No, just that it was stolen.'

'That sucks!' Jane said. 'It was someone's pride and joy no doubt.'

'Apparently the car was involved in a murder . . . a guy called Ernest Stanton.'

Jane stopped in her tracks. 'If it's the same Stanton that I'm thinking of, he was a real nasty piece of work. Wasn't he recently acquitted for fraud?'

Then the penny dropped. Of course, Ernest Stanton had been involved in a massive fraud scam involving Flood Defence contracts. Having witnessed first-hand that morning the terrible devastation of nature's wrath, how could he have overlooked that? Nothing, it seemed, was sacred in humanity's desperate struggle against the ravages of global climate change. Whole communities were being swept away by flooding. It was a massive problem, and one in which the Government was willing to throw vast sums of money at in search of a solution. As Carlisle remembered, Ernest Stanton had made a small fortune out of other people's misery. Working for the Environment Agency, he was notoriously known for taking back handers. Everyone knew the score, but proving it was another matter. Stanton's untimely death had come as no surprise. Even to the police. No wonder they'd kept a tight lid on things earlier that morning.

Without giving it another thought, he closed down the lid of his computer and shuffled a few papers around on an untidy desk.

'Tell me,' said Jane. 'What were the police hoping to find after the car had lain at the bottom of the river for weeks?'

'Not a lot, I would imagine.'

'I wonder who killed him.'

'God knows!'

Carlisle took another sip of his coffee, and casually glanced down at the neatly folded newspaper laid across his desk. His attention was drawn to a short article tucked away in the small print, concerning the recent cold weather snap. As if he needed reminding. His legs were numb, and his back was still aching from having stood around all morning in the freezing cold.

'So how did your meeting go?' he asked.

'I was wondering when you were going to get round to that,' Jane said, looking somewhat miffed. Her eyes engaged with his for just a fraction longer than necessary, a warning signal. It was time to sit up and listen. 'A friend of mine was saying there's been an awful lot of change taking place at Police Headquarters. They're reorganising the place . . . shuffling people around.'

'Did your friend say why?' he asked.

Jane straightened. 'Seemingly, it's all down to the recent government cutbacks. My friend's husband is having a dreadful time of it. According to her, something very hush-hush is going on. They've drafted in several new faces apparently, specialist people, not your ordinary run of the mill coppers.'

'Did she say who these people were?'

Jane flushed, looking slightly embarrassed. 'No, but she believes they're part of the Met's Murder Investigation Unit. It seems the senior officers are keeping a very tight lid on things.'

'That's odd.'

'I know, especially when these people have been allocated their own separate floor of the building.'

There had to be a simple explanation, he reasoned, a training exercise or perhaps a combined force initiative. Besides, it wasn't unusual for the Metropolitan to assign a team of specialist officers to another force. He'd been there before, many times, but it still didn't add up in his opinion. There again, he thought, if something of major importance was taking place they may be trying to keep it from the media. Half-cocked stories made good headline news, but usually spelt major trouble for the police back-room staff.

But why allocate these people their own separate floor of the building?

'What else did your friend tell you?' he quizzed.

'Apparently your name is being bandied around.'

'What!'

'Well that's what the Deputy Chief Constable's secretary was saying.'

As the pen dropped from his fingers, it hit the floor with a clatter. He thought about picking it up, but chose not to do so. It had been five-years since his redundancy, so why the sudden 'U' turn?

'What the hell is going on?' he asked.

'How do I know, I— '

'Did your friend say why my name was mentioned?'

Jane shrugged as if not knowing; only adding to Carlisle's frustration.

Chapter Four

Carlisle woke with a start, his mind full of possibilities regarding Jane's new lead. Who were these new faces from the Metropolitan who could command such total anonymity? The combinations seemed endless. In the end he went downstairs, and made a mug of strong black coffee, before falling asleep the only way he could – propped up in the comfort of an old easy chair.

It had stopped snowing when he finally called in at the office on Fowler Street in South Shields. Jane was busy, but had agreed to contact the Chief Constable's secretary in the hope of finding out more about the Met's covert activities. It was a long shot, but anything was worth a try, he thought. The rest of the morning was spent dragging his heels in and around solicitors' offices. Picking up the dregs, small-time petty crime and endless hours spent snooping around the seedier side of some mistrusting partner's nocturnal activities. That was the nature of their work of late, unimaginative, predictable – *financial desperation dressed up in the guise of criminal profiling.*

Just before lunch, Carlisle met with an old colleague. A retired police officer turned local crime reporter, who worked for *The Shields Gazette.* Mark Patterson was a tall man, elegant, with wispy chestnut-brown hair swept back at the sides. He handled the headline news, and had an extraordinary talent for sifting out scandal. Never shy on sharing a good story, they had coffee together, exchanged information, and chatted over a local girl's recent disappearance. Not all of Carlisle's cases were straightforward, and he'd been warned to stay well clear of this one. As luck would have it, the young girl turned out to be a one-time budding entertainer who, having fallen on hard times was looking for a publicity stunt to rekindle her broken career. He'd been well advised, and his colleague had saved him endless hours of legwork. Before leaving, he informed Patterson about the stolen Mondeo – the one recovered from the River Tyne the previous day. His reporter friend was all ears.

After lunch, the sun appeared. Still cold, the blustery North Easterly winds that had been buffeting the coastline all day had finally subsided. Now it was a pleasant afternoon. Crossing into Fowler Street, he noticed a small group of hawkers stood huddled around the back of an open white transit van. Tightly bound together by some peculiar sense of communal secrecy, to Carlisle's trained eye they were obviously up to no good. He made a mental note of it. On another occasion, he would have undoubtedly checked them out. Not today; he had more important things on his mind.

Nothing much of interest in his in-tray, he braced himself for the worst. A few missed phone calls, a couple of e-mails and another blank page in his dairy. Wonderful! Just when he thought things were picking up again. It was then he spotted the large brown envelope. It was sitting on Jane's desk – the kind hastily put together by a frustrated admin clerk who hated her job. Barely twenty-four hours had passed since Jane's last visit to police headquarters; now this.

'I see the postman's been.'

'It arrived this morning,' said Jane.

Carlisle detected a twinge of excitement in his business partner's voice. 'What is it?' he enquired.

Jane bit her bottom lip. 'How the hell would I know, it's marked for your attention.'

A memory tugged at him. A reminder of the dreaded tax forms that regularly dropped through the letter box at the end of every tax year. Tax forms are full of endless questions, his father once told him. How damn right he was.

'Special delivery, no doubt?'

Jane appeared hesitant. 'No, it was handed to me by a rather hunky looking Detective Chief Inspector.'

'What time was this?'

'Just before lunch,' Jane replied.

He checked the label again, marked: CLASSIFIED INFORMATION. Police jargon for hush-hush material, but on whose authority he wondered. It certainly didn't look official, he was convinced of that. On closer examination, he could see the flap had been resealed with two thin strips of masking tape. Tight bastards, he cursed, it's been recycled.

'A DCI you say?' Carlisle said, trying his utmost not to sound too overly enthusiastic.

'Well that's who he told me he was.'

'Did he—' Carlisle checked himself. 'Does he have a name?'

'Yes. Detective Chief Inspector Jack Mason.'

'Jack . . . bloody. . . Mason!'

Jane pulled back as if her feet had suddenly been cut from beneath her. 'He spoke highly of you, and insists you meet up with him again.'

'I bet he did. No doubt the emphasis was on . . . *insists.*'

A stunned silence followed.

Carlisle took another deep breath, his eyes firmly fixed on the envelope. The first thing that came to mind was, how in hell's name had Jack Mason managed to reach Detective Chief Inspector? The last time they'd worked together, Mason was suspended from Special Branch duties for shooting a drunken female barrister involved in a frenzied knife attack with one of her regular clients. The barrister survived. Only just. Found guilty of manslaughter, she'd been sent down for ten-years. Mason, meanwhile, got off with nothing more than a stiff reprimand. The newspapers were full of it. Not only was Mason made the villain of the piece, the press had turned him into the people's hero. Some things never change, he cursed.

'I take it, you know one another?' said Jane.

'We worked at the Met together.'

'Ah, that explains it.'

He stood in stunned silence for moment. The mere mention of Jack Mason's name could only spell one thing . . . *trouble.* If Jane thought the contents of the brown envelope were the key to their salvation, she was sadly mistaken. He studied the disappointment in her eyes, the rejection. One thing for sure, he would need to tread carefully.

'What else did Mason tell you?'

'Not a lot.'

'Oh come on, he must have said something. Jack Mason has never been shy when it comes to conversation.'

Jane remained calm, as if retaliation was pointless.

'He's in a tight corner, apparently.'

'No surprises there then!'

Jane sighed. 'It's down to these recent cutbacks, and he's short of a criminal profiler by all accounts.'

'Ah. So that explains why my name popped out of the hat?'

Jane stared at the flickering computer screen. 'He seemed genuine enough. He's here to investigate a recent spate of murders apparently, and believes there could be a connection.'

'Really . . . and what else did he tell you?'

'Not a lot.'

Carlisle leaned forward with interest, both elbows on the table. Jack Mason was no fool. The man was obviously looking for a way out. A spate of murders, possibly linked, could only mean one thing. He thought about it, still trying to come up with a rational explanation as to why Mason would want a criminal profiler. His biggest concern right now would be the media. Headline news never excited Jack Mason at the best of times. Although he did have his media critics – more than a few – he knew how to handle them.

'I take it he's looking at the nature of the crimes?'

'Not in as many words, but he did express his concerns as to the psychological aspects of the case.'

Carlisle fumbled the envelope, straightened, and moved back to face the window. Mason was an arrogant sod at the best of times, in more ways than one. Besides, everything had to be done his way, which left little room for anyone else to manoeuvre around in. But why was he clutching at straws? Surely the police would have plenty of forensic evidence to link these murders. Unless . . . of course. He paused, took another sip of his coffee, and tried to get his head around it. The case sounded tempting enough, but was it the right move, he asked himself. There again, he'd been so wrapped up in his own personal grief lately. Jane was right: he needed to snap out of it, move on, and find a way of coming to terms with it.

Their eyes met.

'I know I can be irritable at times, but I know what's right for us. Mason's thick skinned, he's a difficult beast to work with at times. Hard-hitting coppers usually are. Never underestimate their tenacity to succeed; beneath the surface there's always an underlying mean streak. They'd rip the skin from your very back, sooner than look at you. Our problem is this,' he said, pointing back down at the envelope. 'The minute we tear back the flap, is the minute we step into Jack Mason's world.'

'If you feel so strongly about it, why not tell him to sod off?'

'It's not about the money, Jane, it's all about the principle. I don't want our business to be run by some arrogant, hot-headed copper. Those days are over I'm afraid.'

'But we're strapped for cash, David, and up to our eyes in debt.'

There was an uncomfortable silence between them. Then he saw reason. If Jack Mason was assigned to the case, then it had to be something special. Mason wasn't the sort of copper to be involved in routine murder.

He fumbled the envelope again.

'What if I opened it?' said Jane. 'You can always blame me.'

'I'm——'

Jane stared at him with her big blue eyes, leaving him in no doubt what she was thinking. Tearing open the flap, she removed a DVD and several neatly folded documents. From what he could see, someone had gone to work with a yellow highlighter marker pen, besides adding copious notes to the side column of each report.

'This is awful!' said Jane.

As the story began to unfold, Carlisle's attention was instinctively drawn towards the nature of the crimes. The killer, whoever he was, was extremely proud of his handiwork by all accounts. Charles Anderson, who ran a high-end legal practice in Newcastle, had been murdered in broad daylight. Two Northumberland farmers had been bludgeoned to death. Two separate crimes, both intrinsically linked, and both carried out within a six week period of one another. Whoever was responsible for this type of violent crime was usually a very dangerous person to deal with. Solving their murders was all too often like working in a minefield; you trod carefully or you got yourself blown to pieces in the process. Right now Carlisle could think of a dozen reasons why he shouldn't accept the case, but couldn't bring himself to say it.

'Were any valuables or money stolen from the property?' he asked.

'There's no mention of it.'

'Sexual motives, then?'

Jane shook her head again. 'Nope, nothing of that nature mentioned.'

'But that may have been the killer's initial intentions,' he said, staring across at her.

'I thought this case would interest you. Take a look for yourself.' Jane handed him the files. 'In the meantime, I'll make the necessary arrangements.'

'Hold it . . . young lady,' Carlisle said, raising his arms as if he were holding back a large steel door. 'We're going nowhere until I've spoken with Jack Mason.'

'That could be difficult,' Jane replied.

'Why?'

'Because Mason insists he has his answer by ten o'clock tonight.'

Carlisle drew back, but the urge to accept was too great. He peered down at the case files, and felt the hairs on the back of his neck stand on end. In his mind, it was already a done deal.

'Where do we go from here?'

Jane looked across at him and winked. 'I see what you mean about Jack Mason.'

'Oh, and what is that?'

'When Mason says jump, everybody jumps . . . feet first by the look of things.'

Chapter Five

January 2012

The first thing that struck David Carlisle was the bleak isolation. Nestling between the foothills of Cold Law and Harden Hill in Northumberland National Park, Dove Farm was barely a ten minute drive from the picturesque village of Netherton and fifteen miles from Morpeth. By eleven o'clock the sun had burned away most of the lingering mist that had persistently clung to the valleys that morning, but there was still a hint of a breeze. The views from up here were spectacular, a mixture of mosaic heather land and rolling hills, sprinkled with ancient settlements, castles and fortified buildings; reminders of Northumberland's tempestuous and rich history. Many of the rural farmsteads were widely dispersed, often located on higher ground, or at river crossing points. In his opinion, Dove Farm was no exception.

At a glance the farmhouse looked to be 18th century, although parts of the existing east wing probably dated much earlier. It had thick walls built of random rubble, with irregular window openings on two levels. The adjacent farm buildings consisted of barns, stables and shelter sheds, and a south facing row of stone built cottages. Death, it seemed, was no stranger to the farm. Built on the site of a bastle or fortified farmhouse, down the centuries the region had played a central role in the border wars between Scotland and England.

Like most murder scenes that Carlisle had ever attended, the place was a hive of activity. Beyond the yellow barrier tape marked: CRIME SCENE – DO NOT CROSS, he spotted the slightly built figure of Peter Davenport. Camera poised at the ready, the SOC photographer was busily snapping away at anything and everything in sight. Nothing was taken for granted. Everything was being meticulously recorded and taken down. Further afield, a group of forensic officers were hard at work. Their mood appeared relaxed, but Carlisle knew otherwise. Fingertip searches were a painstakingly slow process, as there was always a slim chance the perpetrator had left a vital piece of evidence behind.

No sooner had the car engine shut down, than the familiar thick-set figure of Jack Mason appeared in the doorway of the mobile Major Incident Room vehicle. Wearing white paper coveralls, latex gloves and paper overshoes, he descended the short flight of stairs and approached with an air of casual confidence. He wasn't a conspicuously tall man, five-nine, with powerful shoulders and a large moon-like face. His nose had been broken several times, and appeared to be stuck back on a face that had seen more than its fair share of trouble.

'I'm glad you could make it,' Mason said, extending out a hand. 'I had a hunch this case might interest you.'

Behind a narrow lipped smile was an unbending ruthless streak. The last time they'd worked together, Mason was having marital problems. It went with the territory. Major crime investigations usually meant long periods spent working away from home. That was the nature of the beast; it played havoc with family and social life.

'What have we got?' Carlisle asked.

'Nothing certain yet, but it looks like we have another vendetta killing on our hands.'

'Vicious?'

'I'm afraid so.'

'Mind if we take a poke around?'

'There's not much to see,' said Mason, stepping aside to allow Jane to slide her long slender legs out of the passenger seat. 'It's mainly down to forensics, I'm afraid.'

Sensing Jane's awkwardness, Carlisle came to her rescue. 'Miss Collins will be working with me on this one, Jack.'

'OK by me,' Mason shrugged, 'but I'll need to run it past the Acting Chief Commissioner all the same.'

Carlisle nodded, but offered no reply.

They were joined by Stan Johnson, the Crime Scene Manager. Late forties, with an unruly mop of curly black hair, the man had a touch of the eccentric about him. He bred budgerigars for show, and was the honorary president of his local Morris dancer's society – whatever that meant. He knew Stan vaguely, enough to know that he was a stickler for detail. Any evidence left by the perpetrator, such as DNA, fingerprints, footprints, fibres, and even tyre tracks had to be preserved untouched for the forensic teams.

'You'll need to suit up,' Johnson said. 'There are a couple of spare suits in the ops truck.'

Wriggling his way into the fresh white paper over-suit, Carlisle slipped on a pair of disposable overshoes and moved towards a large wrought iron gate. On closer inspection, he noted the whole area had been cordoned off, including many of the adjoining out-buildings. Dove Farm appeared a remote location, secluded, and off the beaten track. The wind up here seemed to be blowing in all directions. It was then he caught sight of several yellow crime scene evidence flags fluttering on the breeze. Each carried a number, each an important piece in the forensic jigsaw puzzle. Nothing, it seemed, was being left to chance. Everything that could be done was being done.

'Let's deal with Derek Riley's murder first.' Mason's jaw was clenched tight as he stared at them. 'I take it you've both read Charles Anderson's case files?'

They nodded in unison, but neither spoke.

Not the best of starts, thought Carlisle, as they made their way through thick, heavily congealed sheep droppings. Nearing the west barn – a large stone building set back on the west wing of the courtyard – they stopped for a while, and between them managed to drag open the huge timber door. As the daylight poured into the building, he could see the interior had been built on two levels. The upper floor, slightly set back, was used as a hayloft. The ground floor – recently covered in a fresh layer of straw – had a strange pungent odour.

Mason turned to face them again. 'It all begins here. This is where Derek Riley first met with his killer.' There followed a quick check of notes. 'Early Post-mortem results confirm he was struck a massive blow to the cranium, puncturing a fifty-millimetre diameter hole through the skull parietal bone. The force of the blow probably rendered irreparable damage to the cerebellum, but it did not kill him at this stage.' Mason pointed to the heavily congealed bloodstains splattered across the inner timber walls of the barn, an index finger following the blood trace. He appeared on edge, and the veins on his neck stood out like a roadmap. Every now and then, he would pause to point out where the victim had attempted to stem the blood flow. 'Take a look at this,' Mason went on. 'This is where Derek Riley finally met his ending. From here, his body was hoisted up into the rafters and then he was crucified. It wasn't a pretty sight, I can tell you.'

Sometimes it was easier to say nothing.

For one frightening, incomprehensible moment, Carlisle imagined they were dealing with a copycat crucifixion killer. All the signs were there . . . the arms outstretched, six-inch nails driven through the wrists and feet, and the body posed for maximum effect.

Mason turned to face them again. 'Not fifty metres from here, we recovered a two-metre heavy steel jack lever. DNA traces and body flesh tissue match those of the victim's blood group. In other words, we now have our murder weapon.'

'And fingerprints?' asked Jane.

'I'll come back to that later.'

Jane glanced at Carlisle, but said nothing. Mason had lost none of his pragmatic bullishness, it seemed.

'To call this a *frenzied* attack . . . would be an understatement. Derek Riley's facial features and the top of his skull had been pulverised beyond all recognition.' Mason drew breath, as if reliving the moment. 'This was a brutal attack as you can well imagine, and we found extensive traces of cerebral matter spread over a wide area.'

'Who discovered the body?' Carlisle asked.

'The farm's General Manager, a man called Eugene Briggs.'

'When was this?'

'Six thirty the following morning.'

'And the estimated time of death?'

'Between six and eight the previous evening,' Mason replied.

That meant the victim would have been dead twelve hours, thought Carlisle, ample time for the killer to carry out his business. He cupped his face in his hands, and tried to imagine the scene. Thirty feet up, nailed to the rafters and the victim's face staring down at him. The profiler's eyes suddenly shot open again. Without an accomplice it would have been an almost impossible act to perform. Unless . . .

'What kind of person commits such atrocities?' Jane asked.

Mason rolled his eyes. 'What makes him tick? Now that is an interesting question.'

Distracted by the rapid fire shutter of Peter Davenport's digital camera, they made slow progress across the farmyard. On reaching the farmhouse, a large north facing building, Carlisle took stock. The entrance, guarded by two ornate pilasters supporting a heavy scalloped lintel and carved from solid stone, had a look of stately grandeur. To each side of a solid oak door stood a large earthenware plant pot; the shrivelled unattended remains of a previous summer still lying lifeless in damp soil.

Herded along a stone floored hallway, they swung left and down a steep flight of stone stairs. The kitchen had that familiar whiff, a sweet coppery metallic smell reminiscent of death. To one corner stood a large black open-range fireplace, its huge mantel and fender now void of any warmth. All that remained were the burnt ashes lying in the bottom of the fire basket, discarded, and frozen in time. Unlike a dozen other crime scenes that Carlisle had attended, this one felt different. The room had an eerie presence, whitewashed walls and a low beamed ceiling. Pots and pans of every imaginable shape and size hung in profusion from smoke charred rafters. Slung by their handles, they reminded him of a medieval army ranked in tight formation and about to do battle.

'We found Mrs Riley's body slumped beneath this table,' Mason explained, pointing to the floor.

'How did she die?' Carlisle asked.

'She was bludgeoned to death. The manner in which this bastard mutilates his victims ranks amongst the worst I've ever come across. It disgusts me to think that such vile crimes can still be committed in a modern civilised society.'

Jane flinched. 'I take it her wounds were extensive?'

'Death would have been instantaneous.'

No attempt had been made to clear away the congealed bloodstains where the victim had fallen. The press would have a field day, he thought, but that would come later. In his notebook, he scribbled down *Serial killer* and underlined the words.

'Any particular side?' he asked, rasping a few days' stubble.

'The right side, along the suture line midpoint between the frontal and parietal bones.' There was bitterness in Mason's voice. 'She was struck with such tremendous force, she suffered multiple skull fractures. You would normally only anticipate seeing this type of injury in an automobile accident, or someone who's fallen from a high-rise building.'

'What do we know about her attacker?' Carlisle asked.

'He's male; around six-two, and of medium build. Early indications confirm the angle of entry makes her attacker left-handed.' Mason stepped back as if to enforce a point. 'In answer to your previous question, Miss Collins, we found heavy latex deposits on the jack lever. We also found transfer blood on the cooking pot handle. It was Derek Riley's.'

'So he came prepared?'

'Let's wait for forensics before we go jumping to any conclusions,' Mason replied.

At last a physical description, thought Carlisle. Not much, but at least something to work on? From what Mason had told them so far, none of this made sense. Why the killer had made every effort to avoid personal detection and yet, audaciously display his victim's body as art forms was clearly a conflict of interests. Surely a more natural reaction would have been to dispose of the evidence, bury, or even burn it. Somehow the pieces didn't fit.

Mason hesitated. 'If you ask me, this whole damn business reeks of another vendetta killing.'

'Feudal killing,' Carlisle nodded. 'Now that *is* an interesting consideration. At least it would account for his wanting to avoid personal detection, whilst allowing him sufficient time to display his artistic talents.'

'We agree on that point then?'

'I'm not convinced,' Carlisle replied.

'So we're still at odds?'

'It's not a clear-cut case . . . I wish it was.' Carlisle paused in thought. 'Suppose this was a retaliatory crime, one carried out by a hired assassin; call it what you must. The motives would be straightforward, and they'd have followed a logical pattern. However, if we're dealing with a multiple personality disorder such as paranoid schizophrenia, that's an entirely different matter.'

Mason's eyes narrowed. 'Here we go; surely you're not suggesting that this is the work of some deranged psychopath?'

'And why not?' Carlisle shrugged.

'I agree he comes prepared, but that's a bloody ridiculous statement.'

Carlisle looked at Mason before he answered. 'In that case you'd better prepare yourself for a few more sleepless nights, Jack.'

'How can you possibly say that?'

'Because this one's organised, I'm absolutely certain of it.'

'Planned executions, eh?'

'It certainly wasn't his first,' Carlisle confirmed. 'People who commit ritual mutilation on their victims are usually making a serious statement.'

The DCI stepped back as though he'd been hit a sledgehammer blow. Mason was a creature of habit; he disliked bad news. It always rubbed him up the wrong way.

It had turned cold again; there was a distinct nip in the air. At over three-hundred feet above sea level, Harden Hill formed a formidable backdrop to the local farming community. Carlisle watched as a tiny pocket of sheep began to traverse well-worn trodden tracks, high up on the peaks.

'It's such a tranquil setting, Jack. Not the kind of place you'd associate with such violent crimes.'

'We need to talk,' said Mason.

Chapter Six

Jack Mason clenched his fist and gave the General Manager's cottage door a short, sharp, authoritative rap. Four days into his murder enquiry, and Dove Farm was surprisingly peaceful again. Having scaled down his operations at the farm, all that remained was a small uniformed police presence tasked with guarding the place.

As the door drew back, Mason was immediately confronted by a sixty-year old gaunt faced male whom he took to be Eugene Briggs. Thrusting his warrant card under the occupant's nose, he announced his intentions, although not before habitually wedging his left foot up against the open door. It was then he spotted the Border Collie. It was staring up at him and baring its teeth.

'Eugene Briggs?' Mason asked, sliding his foot into safer territory.

'Yes, I am. What can I do for you?'

Mason gave him a well-rehearsed frown. 'I'm sorry to trouble you again, Mr Briggs. This is Police Constable Jackson, and we're here in connection with the Riley murders. May we come in?'

The minute they stepped into the room, Patches, a three year-old Border Collie, made her presence felt. The dog's piercing, alert eyes following the young constable's every movement.

'Fine young animal,' Mason announced. 'Is he a working dog?'

'He is a *she*. Unless I'm mistaken,' said Briggs, pointing towards the hearth rug where the dog obediently flopped down in front of a roaring log fire. The Farm Manager dropped back in his chair, took off his glasses and began cleaning the lenses with a grubby handkerchief. The shock of finding Derek Riley's horrifically mutilated body had obviously left a lasting impression on him. Briggs looked physically drained, thought Mason.

'I understand you've already made a statement to the Alnwick police,

Mr Briggs?'

'That's correct, Inspector, so why are you here?'

'Just following up on our enquiries,' Mason said, opening his notebook.

'In that case, do you mind telling me what this all about?' demanded Briggs.

Mason held eye contact. 'If you must know, our purpose here today is to establish your relationship with Derek Riley.'

'Surely I'm not a suspect?'

'Everyone's a suspect until they've been eliminated from our investigations, Mr Briggs. That's the law of the land, I'm afraid.'

Briggs eyes widened. 'Thank you for reminding me, Inspector.'

Mason detected a hint of sarcasm in the old man's voice. His eyes were red-rimmed, glazed as though lacking sleep. He was probably a good guy, but right now he remained a vital witness and he was determined to get the bottom of it.

'It's my understanding that you were employed here at the farm. Is that correct?'

'Yes, I am, lad.'

'May I ask in what capacity?'

'I'm *still* the farm's General Manager, until I hear otherwise.'

Mason lowered the tone of his voice for effect. 'This is a very sad affair; what was Derek Riley really like to work for, Mr Briggs?'

Briggs eyes welled, as if full of morose sorrow.

'Derek was a gentleman. There was never a wrong word between us in all the twenty-five years I worked for him. Why someone would want to kill him beggars belief.'

'Do you know of anyone who would want to harm him?'

'None that I can think of,' Briggs replied.

'What about the people he mixed with?'

'That's insane,' insisted Briggs.

They spent the next fifteen minutes going back over Briggs' position on the farm. What he did, his hours of work, and his relationship with Derek Riley. As though reliving the memory, Briggs struggled with his answers.

Mason made a few more notes, before moving in closer. 'Unfortunately, Mr Briggs, this type of crime is never nice to talk about, particularly when the person is known to you. Murder always leaves a nasty impression on other people's minds, and in most cases, it's the police who are left to pick up the pieces.'

'I appreciate your concerns, Inspector.'

God, Mason thought, do you. He paused to consider his next question. 'Take your time, Mr Briggs. I'd like you to tell me in your own words how you stumbled upon Mr Riley's body that morning.'

Briggs lowered his head, and spoke through cupped hands as if gaining some comfort from it. 'I never want to go through anything like that again,' he said. 'The man responsible for such heinous crimes is a monster. I cannot think of any other words to describe him.'

There followed a short pause, a checking of notes.

'When did you last see Mr Riley, *alive?*' Mason asked.

'Like I told you people before, that would be Thursday, around four o'clock,' Briggs replied. 'We were organising some fencing repairs up on yon top fields. We'd planned to do them at the weekend, but the weather wasn't up to much at the time. In the end, we agreed to put the job back a week.'

Mason caught the look of concern in the Constable's glances. Having taken a sudden disliking to uniforms, Patches was baring her teeth at him. The old man made a point of discouraging her, much to the young Constable's relief.

'And *where* exactly are these top fields?' Mason asked.

'They are over in Scrainwood. There's a footpath that runs alongside the burn; the fences stop the sheep from wandering onto the roads,' Briggs replied.

'Uh-huh. So when was the last time you saw Mrs Riley?'

'That same evening I'd called in at the farm to drop some worksheets off for Derek.' Briggs' stare hardened. 'Mrs Riley was preparing dinner, as I remember.'

'What time would that be?'

'Around five o'clock.'

Mason moved towards the window, and peered out across the farmyard. He had been over this ground before, so many times. Briggs must have entered the building through the main farmhouse entrance, as the kitchen was at the far end of a long hallway and left down a flight of stone stairs. There were so many imponderables, so many possibilities. In the end he made a mental note of it, and then said. 'The night you and Derek Riley were discussing these fence repairs, I take it you were alone?'

'Yes, apart from a passing drifter.'

Mason cocked his head in interest. 'What can you tell me about him?'

Reluctantly Briggs went on to explain how at three o'clock that afternoon, a lone drifter had wandered into the farmyard in search of casual work. There were far too many of them according to Briggs. They mainly came from East Europe, young men in their mid to late twenties, looking to improve their situation. Everyone knew the score, a day's work for a day's pay and all you got in return was a half-finished job.

'Tell me, what happened next?' Mason said, keeping up the pressure.

'He headed north,' Briggs replied. 'We never saw him again.'

That certainly wasn't picked up in Briggs' previous interview, Mason suspected. Although just a minor detail, it could have a major bearing on the case. Understandably traumatised, he had to coax rather than force the information out of Briggs. It wasn't his style. He felt uncomfortable about it, but he was getting results all the same.

'On the night of the murders,' said Mason. 'What were you doing?'

Briggs fidgeted in his chair, as though reliving a bad memory. 'After finishing work, I came back home, changed and had tea. We stopped in all evening, and watched TV.'

'You say *we* . . . would that be Mrs Briggs?'

'Yes, it would.'

'You mentioned taking Patches for her walk, what time would that be?'

'Around ten o'clock, and before you ask, we were only gone ten minutes or so.'

'I see,' said Mason.

There was nothing to be gained by questioning his wife, thought Mason. Briggs' alibi was watertight. Mason looked at his watch. 'One further question, if I may, Mr Briggs. Did Derek Riley ever mention the name Lowther Construction to you at all?'

'No. I can't say as he did. Why do you ask?'

Mason supressed a grin. 'I assume you knew of Derek's involvement in such a company though?'

'No. That's the first time I've heard that name mentioned before.'

'Are you sure?'

'Of course I'm sure, Inspector. Besides, why would Derek Riley want to get involved in a construction company . . . he was a sheep farmer goddammit?'

Mason smelt a rat. He knew Derek Riley certainly had shares in Lowther Construction; previous police investigations had already established that. If Briggs was telling him the truth, then it was a damn good question. He stood for a moment, hands in pockets, shoulders hunched slightly forward. Perhaps he should have been more forceful, attacked the question from a different angle. There again, he doubted Briggs would have stood up to such a gruelling. He checked his notes; had he missed anything?

Then he remembered.

'I understand Derek Riley had a son.'

'I presume you mean Selver,' Briggs mumbled.

'Ah, yes, that's the name I was looking for,' Mason confirmed. 'You wouldn't happen to know his whereabouts would you?'

Mason jotted down some details, and stood as if to leave. The moment the young Constable reached for the front door, Patches lifted her head and growled. Hesitant, the two officers exchanged glances. Undecided as to who should go first, it was time to pull rank.

Seconds later, Jack Mason burst out laughing as the rookie policeman took flight across the farmyard. It was precious little moments like these that brought a rare smile to the senior detective's face.

It was 2.30pm when he finally pulled up outside the Market Tavern, a traditional pub in the centre of Alnwick market town. Close to the castle, just round the corner on Fenkle Street, the place had a great atmosphere. Standing at the bar, Mason ordered steak and ale pie and a pint of Maften Magic real ale. Most likely, he thought, Briggs had nothing to do with it. The person responsible for these crimes undoubtedly knew his victims. There again, if the old man wasn't involved, then the killer had to be someone local. But why crucify Derek Riley? What the hell was all that about?

Then there was the question of Briggs' previous interview, the one held at Alnwick police station. Why hadn't the desk Sergeant picked up on the lone drifter? How could he have missed that? The timing made perfect sense, even if nothing else did. And another thing, apart from watching TV that night, what was Briggs doing around the time of the murders? It had just turned six o'clock; surely he must have heard something that night, a scream, a cry, or even a plea for help. And yet he heard nothing.

Mason sat aimlessly staring out of the pub window. Why a farm owner would want to get involved with a construction company, he no idea. It didn't make sense. None of it did. Unless, of course . . .

His steak and ale pie arrived.

Chapter Seven

David Carlisle hated the long drawn out, dark winter nights; alone, behind closed doors, and faced with countless sleepless nights. Having spent the best part of the evening browsing through the Charles Anderson case files, he'd woken with a start. It was dark, and the street lighting was casting a strange ominous glow over the bedroom walls. Ever since his wife's untimely death, he'd been struggling to cope with his loss. The house was so quiet nowadays, as if the heart had been ripped out of it. There were times, and there had been many of late, when he thought of what might have been. Somehow he didn't think it was humanly possible to miss another person as he missed Jackie. She was such an amazing woman, and so full of life.

Suddenly, the day ahead seemed full of doom and gloom. At two in the morning, his was a black, silent world, full of memories. And another reason to feel miserable was the feeling of guilt. Why must he always blame himself for Jackie's untimely passing? Surely it wasn't his fault. How fickle and fragile life really is, he thought. Nothing is for certain. It didn't take much to alter the course of another person's life – a small gust of wind, a lapse of concentration, a mistake. How such a thing could happen, was beyond him. Why hadn't they stopped at home like everyone else that morning? Gone swimming, or even spent time out shopping together. One minute she was there, the next, she'd been tragically torn away from him.

Staring aimlessly at the globules of rain now trickling down the bedroom window pane, his mind was all over the place. The chilling manner in which Charles Anderson had met his untimely ending wasn't helping either. Over the years, Carlisle had spent many a sleepless night trying to unravel the reasoning behind such senseless killings. It was his way of dealing with it, his way of solving a problem. Whoever was responsible for Anderson's murder clearly had a Dr Jekyll and Mr Hyde personality. Trying to unravel what went on inside these people's minds was incredibly difficult, if not impossible at times. Most psychopaths he'd ever dealt with were ruthless manipulators, and would go to extreme measures to get what they wanted. Charles Anderson's brutal murder was no exception. His killer lacked empathy. He was a callous predator, who would stop at nothing. Whoever it was they were looking for was a very dangerous person. He realised that, but the real Mr Hyde had yet to surface, and that worried him.

Feeling sick in the pit of his stomach, his mind flashed back to Jackie's clothes again. What to do with them. Her wardrobes were crammed full of the stuff, summer dresses, winter coats, dozens of pairs of shoes, and a handbag for just about every occasion. Sooner or later he would need to deal with it, but the act of giving them away always seemed too final to him. He'd always imagined it would be easy donating her clothes to a charity shop. Not anymore. Now it felt different, as if he was closing out another chapter in her life. He wasn't, of course. He knew that, but it still made him angry.

Then there was the question of a small teddy bear called "Bertie". Now sat staring across at him from the bedroom window ledge, they were like two lost souls. Adopted from an airport in Greece, Jackie had simply adored him. He had his own passport, organised his birthday parties, and accompanied her wherever she went. *The two of us are inseparable,* Jackie had once told him. How bizarre was that?

By the time he'd finished his breakfast cereals his head was in bits again. He showered, got dressed, and checked his mobile phone for any missed calls. Suddenly, the day ahead seemed full of the things to do, and none of them pleasant. Even the TV breakfast channels were playing out Dove Farm's brutal murders – so called experts hypothesising over possible motives. They didn't have a clue. None of them did.

After firing off a couple of text messages, he poured himself another mug of black coffee, and slumped back into his favourite easy chair. The thought that a bunch of school children could stumble across Charles Anderson's badly mutilated body incensed him. It was broad daylight, mid-afternoon, and Anderson had been stripped naked and found strapped to a warehouse door. If that wasn't bad enough, six-inch nails had been driven through his upturned wrists and feet.

Who could have done such a thing?

Carlisle sat for a moment, the car engine ticking over and his mind still at sixes and sevens. He watched as the neighbours opposite said their goodbyes, and took off in different directions. It was Thursday, nearing the weekend, and the streets were busy with people heading for work. What if this was a grudge killing? What then, he suddenly thought. The act seemed deliberate enough, as if there had been some kind of logical correlation behind the killer's thought processes. Whoever had killed Charles Anderson sure knew how to draw other people's attentions towards his handiwork. That much he was certain of.

Turning into Laygate, he pulled up in front of the temporary traffic lights and waited for the lights to change to green. No wonder the local residents were up in arms over the number of roadworks taking place. The whole area resembled a bomb site – war torn Lebanon sprang to mind. Nothing seemed straightforward anymore. Everywhere was madness; unplanned chaos with a few little extras thrown in.

The lights changed to green.

Peering down into the great bottomless abyss that ran the entire length of Laygate, Carlisle sat gobsmacked. Not exactly his favourite tourist attraction at the moment, he cursed, as his foot hit the accelerator. It was then he noticed the poker-faced workman, glaring down at him from the seat of his dumper truck. Dressed in a Hi-Vis vest, yellow safety helmet and mud spattered work boots; he was shaking his head in despair at him.

Then Carlisle did what he always did when frustration had got the better of him.

He hit back.

'Digging for victory?' he shouted.

That had done the trick, and suddenly his day ahead felt a whole lot better.

Chapter Eight

Northumbria Police Headquarters, home to the sixth largest police force in England and Wales, was a twenty-minute drive from Newcastle city centre, located on the outskirts of Ponteland. Carlisle was already thirty minutes late for his appointment with Jack Mason. Clearing security, he was met by DI Archie Swan, a suave, regional counterterrorist officer in his late thirties. Having recently returned from a joint police training venture in Afghanistan, Swan still carried that untrusting look in his glances, as if a bad man was lurking round every corner.

Leaving the lift together, they moved at pace down a long central corridor and towards the rear of the building. Security was tight. Intrusion detection, access control, and video surveillance were all in evidence. On reaching the Operations Room, DI Swan punched a four-figure code into the unlock keypad, and waited for the security door to swing open.

Inside, the room was 'L' shaped. One side was laid out as a meeting area; the other was home to some twenty police officers employed in providing a front line service in the hunt for the killer. Every desk had a workstation, electronically linked to the Police National Computer (PNC) system, offering instant access to millions of police records. Three large conference tables served as a focal meeting place, providing seating accommodation for thirty officers. Close to the back wall, several logo boards, an overhead projector and drop screen offered visual communications. Like most ops rooms Carlisle had ever worked in, the place was a hub of activity.

Taking stock, Carlisle was directed towards a glass-fronted office tucked away at the back of the room. He hated uncertainty; the not knowing what was coming next. Taped onto the back of the glass door panel, an A4 sheet of paper identified: DETECTIVE CHIEF INSPECTOR J. K. MASON. Someone had drawn a large smiley face in one of the corners; obviously not the occupant's handiwork. Peering through the office glass partition walls, he found Jack Mason hunched over a laptop computer. Wearing a blue denim shirt, black casual trousers and white trainers, his shirt was drawn tight under the armpits by the cross strap of his shoulder holster. The handle of a nine-millimetre Smith & Wesson Model 36 revolver nosed from its housing; a full cartridge box laid open on the desktop in front of him told Carlisle the handgun was probably unloaded.

Mason forced a smile, and beckoned him inside.

'You finally found us—'

'No problems. I simply followed the fresh trail of sheep shit,' Carlisle replied.

'Spare me the embarrassment. That damn farm cost me a bloody good pair of shoes.'

Mason's phone rang. Seconds later, he put his hand over the receiver and asked him if he would like anything to drink.

'Coffee, black, no sugar,' Carlisle said, dropping back into the comfort of an old battered leather chair.

Mason repeated the order down the phone, leaned over, and closed the lid on the laptop computer. Late night boozing sessions were beginning to catch up on his old workmate, Carlisle thought to himself. Mason looked haggard, as though he'd been dragged through a hedgerow backwards. There again, who the hell was he to go round criticizing other people's drinking habits? Having sat up half the night listening to a *JJ Cale* concert, he'd managed to drink his way through another bottle of red wine. Lindeman's Shiraz Cabernet, his favourite, and one he'd been saving for the weekend. God, that was the third bottle in as many days; he was drinking far too much himself lately. Not a good sign!

He watched as Mason shuffled a few papers around a cluttered desk, clasped his hands in front of him and slid his elbows onto the desk top. Mason's body language appeared relaxed, but that could change in an instant.

'What did you make of the Charles Anderson murder files?' Mason asked.

'They certainly made interesting reading.'

'And the crucifixion bit?'

'Well, it proves he's not squeamish, Jack.'

'I got the distinct impression these were vengeance killings,' Mason said smugly. 'It's as if the killer is taunting someone. The sooner he's brought to justice, the better.'

Still fresh in his mind, the Coroner's report had made pretty gruesome reading. Carlisle loved profiling work, getting inside the mind of the suspect. Whoever had killed Charles Anderson was making a serious statement. It wasn't an everyday occurrence to find a half-naked corpse nailed to a warehouse door, especially in broad daylight.

Mason broke off to acknowledge a familiar face now peering in through the office window. Following a cursory thumb up, he watched as Vic Miller melted back into the operations room again. Seconds later the drinks arrived. Mason lost no time. Leaning over, he grabbed a digestive biscuit and took a huge bite out of it.

'Sorry about that, it's a bit manic at the moment.'

Carlisle sighed, and shifted his position. 'These new developments that everyone's talking about, I've—'

'Ah, yes,' Mason interrupted. 'It seems our suspect has what's known as a short leg syndrome. Have you heard of it before?'

'No. I can't say as I have. Is it common?'

'God knows!'

'So, what's the significance?' he asked.

'Well, it certainly narrows the field down,' said Mason, brushing the crumbs from his mouth. 'If nothing else, it's allowed me to open up a whole new line of enquiries.'

'Anything of interest show up?'

'Early days, I'm afraid. We know our suspect wears a corrective right boot which has a two-inch lift, or addition to the sole. It's certainly not a recent affliction.' Mason leaned back placing his hands behind the back of his head. 'We've got Hedley looking into it. No doubt he'll soon get to the bottom of it.'

'That wouldn't be, Tom Hedley, would it?'

Mason raised an eyebrow. 'Do you know Tom?'

'We once used the same golf club.'

'It's a small world, eh.'

As Carlisle recalled, Tom Hedley had married his childhood sweetheart, Doreen Pearl, a studious type, brainy, nothing stunning, nevertheless a decent looking woman. They'd grown up together, lived on the same council estate, and gone to the same school. Hedley was a stickler for detail, a natural selection for forensic work but an extremely boring person to socialize with.

Mason pushed back in his seat, but didn't stand.

'Whatever it was that caused this bastard to limp, it certainly didn't happen overnight,' Mason sighed. 'What's more, footprint impressions left at both crime scenes indicate his right boot is well worn on the heel.'

'What about hospital records?'

'No, nothing of interest showed up. Our prime candidate is serving a six year sentence in Durham prison, and was a right pain in the arse. The other has Alzheimer's disease. He is eighty-seven, goddammit.'

'Not exactly a fruitful outcome?'

'You can say that again. The old guy couldn't even tie his bloody shoe laces.' Mason lowered the tone of his voice. 'Not a good start, I'm afraid. If the truth be known, our killer is still out there and probably preparing his next grand performance.'

'What about private clinics?'

Mason gritted his teeth. 'I barely have enough ground troops to keep this place ticking over, let alone any for checking out private clinics. Take a look around, my friend; this is my so called Operations Room. There's barely room to swing a cat in here, let alone run a murder investigation. If this is what modern day policing has come down to, then God help us all.'

He watched as Mason opened the top drawer of the nearest filing cabinet, and took out a thick file marked: FRYER'S WHARF. With the exception of a small computer table, the rest of the office was untidy and cluttered.

'I had these brought over from Gateshead police station.'

'More witness statements?'

Mason looked at him sceptically. 'I was rather looking forward to some feedback on the previous case files I sent you, but hey—'

'I'm still working on it, Jack.'

'So is everyone else round here, it seems.'

There was something in Mason's tone that caused him to sit back. He needed more time, but the Chief Inspector was pushing for answers. Fresh leads had a nasty habit of vanishing quickly; he realised that, but this was ridiculous. He reached over, and opened the folder – a mixture of witness statements, and police interviews involving some of Charles Anderson's close business contacts. Skim-reading through the first few pages, he recognised the suspect's MO. It had a familiar pattern to it – a swift death, followed by heartless mutilation. Nailing your victim's body to a warehouse door was one thing, but to carry out crude disfigurement as an afterthought took a special kind of mentality. The case was deeply disturbing, and bore an eerie resemblance to that of the Riley murders. Just as Jack the Ripper became the archetype lust killer, this one enjoyed showing off his artistic talents. His methods were unnerving, if not demoralising.

Mason stared reproachfully across at him. 'My hunch says he's vengeful.'

'Hmmm, that's questionable.'

'But we can agree it's the same person?'

'His behavioural patterns are uncannily similar—'

'Forget the psychology crap,' said Mason. 'I've said all along these were gangland killings, and I'm sticking to it.'

Carlisle's heart sank; Mason's was a thoughtless reply.

'I'm still trying to understand why he chooses to display his victim's bodies like something out of a chamber of horrors,' Carlisle said. 'There's no logical reasoning behind his brutality; it's unnatural in my opinion.'

Their eyes locked.

'We've ruled out drugs, blackmail, and sex,' Mason shrugged. 'What other alternatives are we left with?'

'Don't rule out selective group killings.'

'Argh . . . so we're back to this damn serial killer theory of yours.'

'And why not, tell me?' Carlisle replied.

'I'm not the one who needs convincing here. Besides, you still haven't persuaded me these aren't gangland killings. In my book, they fit the bill perfectly.'

'Surely you're not suggesting these were planned executions?'

'Tell me why not.' Mason screwed his face up, as if the matter was already decided. 'Someone out there is spreading fear around. It's an age-old practice, my friend. It's called payback time. It's what these people do best.'

'It's one way of looking at it I suppose,' said Carlisle. 'But I'm still not convinced.'

'Fear, David. This whole damn business smacks of fear.'

Carlisle elected to stay clear of Jack Mason's intimidation, preferring a more subtle approach. Fear was an option, but it certainly didn't fit the bill. Besides, gangland warfare was usually more clinical, decisive and much more direct. This wasn't the case here, which is why he was intrigued by the singularity of it. Vengeful brutality with a subtle psychological twist, that's how he now saw it.

Mason eyed him with suspicion. 'We clearly have a difference of opinion here, my friend. Tell me, which one of us is misreading the facts?'

'It's not a straightforward case, and I wish it was.'

Mason's sighs grew increasingly louder. 'Let's turn this on its head . . . what can we learn from the victims' backgrounds?'

'Better still, what are his selection criteria?' Carlisle questioned.

'Bollocks,' Mason snapped. 'That's a typical psychologist's remark.'

'But it stands on firm ground.'

Mason held his hands up in despair. 'Then convince me otherwise.'

The room fell silent again.

Mason was clutching at straws, challenging his every statement. There were two ways of looking at this, thought Carlisle. Either the killer was trying to mentally poison someone's mind by killing those around them, or he was purely fulfilling his own fantasies. Whatever he was trying to do, he was certainly going out of his way to achieve it.

Carlisle dug his heels in.

'He's a loner, Jack, and he's targeting a specific group of people.'

'So why does he mutilate them after they're dead and not when they're alive?'

'Perhaps the reality of the murder never completely fulfils the fantasy, and he feels let down by it. What follows is always more stimulating than the actual crime itself? It's a typical mindset of this type of person.'

'It's an interesting theory, David, but it is what it is . . . a theory,' said Mason.

In turning to Ernest Stanton's murder, they were both agreed. There had been no witness statements, no CCTV coverage at the victim's cottage, nothing. According to Dr Pamela Wilson – the home office pathologist – post-mortem had revealed very little about the weapon used; only that she believed it to be a large kitchen knife. Stabbed in the left side, Stanton's throat had been slit, severing the carotid artery, jugular vein and windpipe. The blood loss and lack of oxygen alone would have certainly weakened the victim. Whoever killed Stanton knew exactly what he was doing. That much they were agreed on.

The more they talked it over, the more convinced they became. Yes, Stanton's death had been quick, but no mutilation or theatrical exhibitionism had taken place as it had in the Anderson and Riley murders. Ernest Stanton's death, it seemed, had certain inevitability about it. Stanton was hated.

Mason ran the flat of his hand over the top of short-cropped hair, and expelled another long drawn out breath. Thumbing through the pages of his notebook, he turned to face him. 'This lone drifter, seen in the vicinity of Dove Farm,' Mason said. 'It has a nice ring about it, and I need you to take a look up there for me.'

Mason explained.

'Where the hell is Alwinton?' Carlisle asked.

'Not far from Rothbury, I'm told, and within spitting distance of Dove Farm.' Mason grinned. 'There's an Inn there ... called The Hanging Tree.'

'Blimey, that's aptly named.'

Their conversation was interrupted by the lone figure now staring in through the office glass partition wall. Mason raised two fingers and mouthed the words *two minutes.*

The officer disappeared.

With thoughts now elsewhere, the DCI reached over and handed him a well-thumbed document. There was another awkward exchange of glances, before Carlisle leaned over and peered at the label: CHARLES ANDERSON – PATHOLOGIST REPORT.

'It's a real horror story,' Mason said, shaking his head. 'But this time I need to know what your thoughts are.'

Carlisle nodded.

And with that, Mason took off in a hurry.

Chapter Nine

Looking far from relaxed, DCI Jack Mason stood before the assembled team in what was now the tenth briefing of *Operation Appletree*. Even the weather seemed to echo the team's sombre mood. It had rained incessantly that morning, with no signs of abating.

Fresh out of police training school, the late arrival of a windswept female Probationary Constable brought the usual friendly banter.

'Jesus,' said Mason. 'I was worried you might not make it, Constable Ellis.'

'Sorry, boss, I've only just finished duty.'

Mason shook his head.

They sat around three central tables hurriedly pushed together. A drop-down projector screen and two white boards were now the dominant features in the room. Scribbled across the top left-hand corner of one of the white boards were the words: KILLER STRIKES FEAR INTO THE CITY.

Mason shuffled a few papers together, and waited for the noise levels to die down.

'Today's headlines,' Mason groaned, banging the flat of his hand against the whiteboard. 'I can well imagine what the Chief Constable will say when he reads this crap in his morning newspapers.'

Carlisle, sat huddled around the middle table, listened with interest as Mason ran back over the past few days' events. Not for the first time, the nature of the crimes had certainly attracted more than the media's attentions. Grotesque killings and badly mutilated bodies made good press. It's what sold newspapers, it was part of society's bigger picture. Even so, the local radio channels were pushing out regular bulletins at an alarming rate. Someone was feeding them insider information. If not, the news teams were damn good at their jobs – too good in Carlisle's opinion.

'It's a well-known fact that most murder victims in the UK knew their killers,' Mason explained. 'So what does that tell us about our killer? Two of his victims were strung up like wild beasts in a hunter's trophy room. Charles Anderson's naked corpse was found strapped to a warehouse door. Arms outstretched, legs straight, and six-inch nails driven through his wrists and ankles. It was broad daylight, close to the main street, and there was no CCTV coverage.'

Now the DCI had mentioned it, it seemed pretty obvious, thought Carlisle. But how would the others react? Vic Miller raised his hand in a request to speak. A member of Northumbria's Armed Response Team – or NART as it was better known – DS Miller had a keen eye and a cool head for detail.

'Pathology found minute strands of car seat fabric in Anderson's right hand,' said Miller. 'Could a cadaveric spasm have taken place, in which case death would have occurred inside the killer's vehicle . . . and not as we first thought . . . outside of it?'

'Good point, Vic. In other words, after killing Anderson, did the killer drive to Gateshead where the body was later discovered?'

'It's plausible,' Miller nodded.

'OK,' said Mason, sounding a little more upbeat. 'What do we know about Anderson's business partner, Leo Schlesinger?'

Miller checked with his notes. 'We know that Schlesinger had a major stroke four years ago, and that's when he sold out his half of the business to Charles Anderson. Apart from that, we have very little else on him.'

As thoughts gathered pace, Mason's cold eyes toured the room.

'Yes, Luke,' said Mason, pointing to a middle aged, balding detective who had positioned himself at the far end of the table.

All eyes now craned towards a tall black officer, mid-forties, with strong facial features that Carlisle took to be of Afro-Caribbean origin. Having spent the past fifteen years working with the London Metropolitan's Special Investigation Branch, Luke James seemed a natural selection to Mason's team.

'CCTV coverage points towards a black Mk3 Ford Mondeo seen in the vicinity. Used in the Anderson murder, it was stolen from the Gateshead Council offices car park on the twenty-fourth. Two days later, it was found abandoned close to Walkergate Metro station.'

'Remind me of the car used in the Riley murders, Luke,' Mason said.

'That was another Mk3 Mondeo, only that one was silver.'

'And was that stolen too?'

'Yes, boss.'

'And where was that from, exactly?'

'The Malting House car park in the Felling,' James confirmed. 'It was later found abandoned by a passing police patrol car on Shields Road. That's near Chillingham on the north side of the river, for those not familiar with the area.'

'Anything else we should know, Luke?'

'There was no CCTV, but tyre tracks left at Dove Farm match those of the stolen vehicle.'

'So, he's partial to Mk3 Mondeos,' said Mason, thoughtfully stroking a thickset jawbone. 'What about DNA and fingerprints?'

'We believe he wears disposable rubber gloves. They're a common brand, sold mainly to the medical and domestic markets. With well over two-million pairs sold last year, I'm not holding my breath on this one.'

'And the six-inch nails,' Mason muttered. 'Where are we with those?'

James appeared hesitant. 'I'm a bit disappointed about our enquiries into that, boss.'

'Disappointed . . . disappointed about what?' Mason insisted.

'Having concentrated our efforts on reputable hardware outlets in the North East, we now find they're being sold in huge quantities on the internet.'

Carlisle sensed the mood change; this was no pushover. The killer, whoever he was, was well organised and extremely devious.

'Just a thought, boss,' said Miller. 'Could this be the work of a religious freak?'

'Meaning—'

'It's the way he displays his victim's bodies?'

'I'm still not with you, Vic,' Mason shrugged.

'Well, the act always appears sacrificial, similar to that of a crucifixion homicide.'

Mason petulantly pushed out his bottom lip as though carefully balancing the facts.

'What's your take on it, David?'

Carlisle breathed out slowly, as he stood to address the team.

'The person we're dealing with here is a loner, someone who can move in and out of society at will. He's single, probably local, and has a fairly good knowledge of the area. Never underestimate him. He's cunning, extremely dangerous and can kill at the blink of an eye. He's certainly not the spontaneous type,' he said, to hushed audience. 'The crimes he commits are carefully orchestrated, long before they are ever committed. And yet, his thought patterns are totally illogical, which makes him an extremely complex person to analyse. Believe me, subjects who can keep one step ahead of us are no fools. Whilst you are investigating their latest murder, they're planning their next. It goes without saying that nobody should underestimate this man's capabilities; these people are craftsman at their work.'

'Just a thought,' said James, referring to his notes. 'Could he be working with an accomplice?'

'I very much doubt it,' Carlisle replied.

'What makes you say that?' said James.

'Of course I can only base my findings on the evidence; supposition must never overcome facts, especially when you are dealing with a serial killer.'

Gasps rang out around the room.

'Your statement surprises me,' said DC Manley, better known as 'Humbug' to the rest of the team. 'You've said we're dealing with a serial killer, and yet, we're being told not to rule out feud killing.'

'One thing's for sure,' Carlisle said, collecting his thoughts. 'His victims are all connected. That's why they were targeted.'

'So why assume he's a serial killer?' Manley questioned.

'Past experience and the complexity of his crimes tell me so,' he replied. 'The behavioural profile of fantasy, his exhibitionism and his notoriety seeking traits are the trademarks of a serial killer.'

'And how exactly would you describe a serial killer?' PC Phillips asked.

Although Constable Phillips was an expert diving instructor, much to Carlisle's relief his explanation was well received.

'So this one strikes selectively, like prostitutes, college students or the gay community?' said PC Philips.

'That's correct,' Carlisle nodded.

Jack Mason took the floor again.

'Regardless of what he is, will he strike again?'

'If he is who I suspect he is, his current murders are merely the tip of the iceberg.' Carlisle paused in an attempt to gauge the rest of the team's reactions. 'Until your subject eliminates the source of his problem . . . his final solution, he'll not rest.'

'So he's not a hired man?' said DC Manley.

'Assassins, hired guns, call them what you like, these people generally eliminate their subjects for monetary gain or revenge.'

DC Manley took another humbug out of its wrapper, and annoyingly popped it into his mouth. The man was addicted, and seemed to carry an endless supply of them in his pockets.

'So what brings him to do it?' DC Manley questioned.

That's a bloody good question, he thought.

Carlisle spent the next fifteen minutes broaching the subject of unstable backgrounds, and how as young children, most serial killers' had experienced some form of child brutality or childhood abuse in their lives. Despite all his best efforts, he was still being bombarded by questions.

'More to the point,' said Mason, cutting in. 'What's his current state of mind?'

'He probably sees himself as the only person who can resolve his own problems,' Carlisle replied. 'To him it's a personal crusade, a compulsion he'll endure until he reaches the final solution. Nothing will get in his way, and he will tear down every barrier to accomplish his aims.'

The room fell silent again.

Constable Ellis held her hand up. 'You're losing me, sir.'

'Oh, in what way?' said Mason.

'Please tell me who I'm looking for?'

Everyone fell about laughing. Even Mason saw the funnier side.

'Vic,' said Mason, wiping the tears from his eyes.

'There's been another development, boss,' said DS Miller, flicking through his notepad. 'Both Anderson and Riley were active members of the Green Party. In Riley's case, he relinquished his membership six months prior to his being murdered.'

'But they were both active members?' queried Mason.

'Yes,' Miller nodded.

'Good work, Vic. We need to get uniforms to run a few discreet checks into these people's social activities. I'm looking for a connection . . . what brought these people together.'

As the briefing came to a close, Mason made a special point of reminding everyone about the next meeting time. 'That's ten-thirty tomorrow morning, Constable Ellis.'

'I'm on it, boss,' Ellis replied.

Mason shook his head despairingly as he returned to his office.

Chapter Ten

Locking the car door, David Carlisle stood for a moment and took in his new surroundings. The inn had appeal, and an hour's long drive from South Shields had given him a thirst. There was nothing to suggest why the inn was named – The Hanging Tree. Even the sign above the door offered few clues. Locals preferred to tell the tale of a notorious murderer called William Winter, a hardened criminal who was caught, tried and executed in Newcastle in 1791 for the murder of Margaret Crozier. Winter's body was purportedly hung from a gibbet not too far from the inn. It was that kind of place.

It was with no surprise that Carlisle found the innkeeper an obese, middle-aged self-appointed voice of the community. The locals fared little better. Steeped in petty prejudices delivered in low whispers, they formed part of the inner sanctum of matters of unimportance. To Carlisle's approval, free drinks readily opened up minds and soon tongues began to wag. The ringleader, a man in his late sixties, had a dry sense of humour and cynical, darting eyes filled with curiosity. He wore a grubby threadbare jacket, buttoned down shirt, and a pair of baggy brown trousers slung low at the waistline. Every now and then he would bang the table with the flat of hand, and raise his empty glass as if to attract attention towards it. Nobody paid much attention, which annoyed him intensely.

'And what of this stranger you talk of?' Carlisle said.

The innkeeper stared at him quizzically. 'He wasn't exactly the friendliest chap around the village, that's for sure.'

'Was he aggressive?'

'Nah, he was more withdrawn, I'd say.'

'What did he look like?' Carlisle asked.

'He was scrawny looking, with a pockmarked face and dark inquisitive eyes. He always wore black gumboots, a knee length coat and wool Beanie hat pulled down over his ears.'

Carlisle watched as the Innkeeper continued to wipe the top of the bar down with a stained wet beer cloth. He was determined to get to the bottom of it, find a way of teasing the information out of these people. Theirs was an isolated community, full of suspicion and mistrust. It was precious moments like these, that he wished he was a fly on the wall.

'So where was he living?'

'Rumour has it that he was sleeping rough,' the innkeeper shrugged.

'Do you know where?'

'Yeah, a place called Barrow Burn. It's North of here, near Shillhope Law.'

'Did he speak to anyone?'

'Not to me he didn't,' the innkeeper replied. 'From the moment he set foot in the bar, I knew he was going to be trouble. There was something about him, if you know what I mean.'

'Menacing?'

'Yeah, menacing. That's the word I was looking for. He had those horrible shifty eyes, spooky looking. Mind, he never caused any bother.'

'It sounds like he was a bit of an unsociable sod.'

The innkeeper eyed him with suspicion. 'He was more than that, mister. This one definitely had a chip on his shoulder.' Arms unfolded now, both hands firmly placed on the bar top in front of him, his story began to unfold. 'It was the same routine every night; you could almost set your watch by him. He would arrive at seven, and leave dead on the stroke of eight. Same order every night, a pint of Foster's lager and packet of salted peanuts . . . this one never failed.'

Carlisle stood for moment, and tried to get his head around it all. Whoever this stranger was, he was undoubtedly the talking point of the village. How much of the innkeeper's story was pure fantasy, he had no idea. But he guessed most of it was.

'What about you guys?' said Carlisle, swinging on his barstool to confront the inner sanctum. 'Did he talk to any of you?'

The ringleader glanced at the others.

'What is it you're after, mister?'

'Netherton, that can't be far from Barrow Burn,' Carlisle said.

'Barrow Burn covers a lot of ground, mister,' said the man in the threadbare, blue jumper.

Carlisle's eyes narrowed as the ringleader banged the flat of his hand on the table, and raised his empty glass. There was mischief in his face, as if another free pint of beer was in order. 'Out there is hostile territory, mister, especially in winter. Besides, it all depends on which direction you're travelling from.'

'Not an easy place to get to?' Carlisle acknowledged, feeling somewhat pressurised.

The ringleader breathed more quickly, and his face had grown pale. 'Not from here it ain't, especially on a dark winter's night. A person can easily get lost.'

'But that's where this stranger was living rough . . . Barrow Burn?'

There followed an awkward silence, a coming together of the inner sanctum.

Fast running out of ideas, and conversation, Carlisle was desperate to break the deadlock between them. But how? That was the question. These people were far too set in their ways. Perhaps the stranger never existed in the first place, he reasoned. It was then he noticed the pub had no CCTV, only an alarm.

'This stranger you talk of, did he have a car?' Carlisle asked.

'Nobody said he did,' the innkeeper replied, fervently.

'But it's logical, especially if he was living rough out there.'

'How would I know?'

'So he must have walked here every night,' Carlisle shrugged.

He watched as the innkeeper began to pull another fresh pint of beer, the froth tumbling over the side of the glass and down into the catch tray. Seconds later, he placed the half-filled glass on the bar and moved to confront him.

'For a stranger, you ask an awful lot of awkward questions.'

Carlisle hunched his shoulders, a defensive stance. 'I'm just making conversation, that's all.'

A faint hint of a smile crept across the innkeeper's face. 'Well, if he didn't have a car, then yes, he would have had a bloody long walk home every night, wouldn't he.'

Laughter broke out over his shoulder.

Fast losing his patience, the innkeeper began to clear a few empty pot glasses from the corner of the bar. There was suspicion in his glances. 'So tell me, mister, what's your interest in Netherton; you're not a reporter by any chance, are you?'

'No. I'm not.'

'What then?'

'There's a rumour doing the rounds that two farmers around here were viciously murdered in the middle of the night. Just wondering if there's any truth in the story?'

'I wouldn't know, you're asking the wrong person,' the innkeeper said, guardedly.

Carlisle shoulders slumped. 'It's not a problem.'

The innkeeper stared at him, the distance between them as great as ever. 'The next time you go poking your nose round these parts, try asking questions at the local Post Office. Not here.'

That had done it. The mere mention of murder had changed everything. Perhaps there was some truth in the lone drifter after all. Stepping out from behind the bar, the innkeeper began another tour of empty pot glass collecting. Stacking them one inside the other, he purposely made towards the inner sanctum. Now deep in discussion over matters of monumental unimportance, they had decided to turn their backs on him.

Left in the cold, Carlisle finished his pint and slipped out of the building through the side entrance. Glancing round, the man in the threadbare, blue jumper was staring out of the pub window at him. Smiling to himself, Carlisle unlocked the car door and clambered into the front seat. Why on earth, he wondered, would someone walk twenty miles every night, to stand in a bar full of miserable morons?

It was time to make tracks.

★

No sooner had the Riley murders hit all the headlines, than shock waves reverberated throughout the city. The very nature of the crimes had captivated the attention of even the most cynical press reporters. To a packed media gathering, and representing the Northumbria police force, Jack Mason was about to embark on yet another consummate performance. The public's insatiable demand for answers was unrelenting. TV cameramen, sound engineers with long boom microphones, reporters and photographers with powerful satellite transmitting cameras, were all crammed into the tiny interview room. Up close and intimate, the atmosphere was electric.

As the noise levels heightened, a young female TV reporter moved forward and towards a solid bank of microphones set up in front of the broadcast table. After making some final adjustments with her sound engineers, she returned to her seat. Broadcasting live across the networks, the DCI did not disappoint. Skilfully using the power of the media to his greatest advantage, he waited for the shuffling to die down before reading a brief statement.

Mason's face had remained expressionless throughout.

Gathering up his notes, the DCI thanked everyone, and coolly slipped from the room. It was that kind of meeting, the bare facts and nothing more.

Chapter Eleven

The address on the envelope read: Companies House, 4 Abbey Orchard Street, Westminster, London. Two blocks south of Victoria Street and within easy walking distance of Victoria tube station, it was Jack Mason's old stamping ground. He knew the area well. Too well if the truth was known. Not the best neighbourhood to patrol at night, Mason thought, but at least he still had some fond memories of the place. However, for a small fee and in the relative comfort of his office, he'd purchased a DVD ROM Directory direct from Companies House. The only thing he knew for certain was that listed amongst the directory's central archives was the past ten-year business accounts for Charles Anderson's legal practice. A very useful tool, and one Jack Mason was slowly getting to grips with.

He soon discovered that Charles Anderson, operating from Grainger Street – within close proximity of Newcastle's city centre – had been joined by his lifelong colleague and fellow member of the European Law Society, Thomas Schlesinger. Together they'd formed *Anderson & Schlesinger Law Firm,* an upmarket legal practice serving the North East of England. He hadn't given too much thought to it, but within a two year period of starting up, their legal practice had moved from rundown premises on Scotswood Road, to an upmarket property block in the heart of Newcastle's prestigious business sector. No doubt Thomas Schlesinger's professional influence had something to do with it. Nevertheless, the company's meteoric rise to success was remarkable. On the surface everything appeared in order, but the deeper he dug, the more Mason began to uncover. Ninety-six per-cent of Charles Anderson's business, it seemed, had been tied in with a conglomerate called Gilesgate Construction. To make matters worse, its Chairman, an articulate self-made multi-millionaire and ruthless local politician called Sir Jeremy Wingate-Stiles, immediately set alarm bells ringing.

Not the most trustworthy person to do business with, Mason reasoned, Sir Jeremy was a renowned Machiavellian type. Mason hated bureaucrats at the best of times, but the contrast between the imaginary world of virtues, and the real world of vices, couldn't be plainer. Clouding the issue was the fact that Gilesgate Construction was Europe's leading company in the building of national sea defences. Six billion pounds, as Vic Miller had said, was an enormous sum of money. But that's what the UK's Environment Agency had spent on climate change initiatives in 2010. The figures were mind blowing, let alone the potential business opportunities that were slushing around in the system. Vast fortunes were being made out of other people's misery, and Sir Jeremy was a central figure in all of it.

Mason clicked the keyboard, and suddenly felt an adrenaline surge.

There, jumping out at him, were the answers he'd been looking for. Charles Anderson and Derek Riley were not only major shareholders in Lowther Construction; they were listed on Gilesgate's Board of Directors.

How convenient was that.

Scribbling down the details, he decided to call it a day. At least for now, that is. Spring had arrived, and after weeks of continuous bad weather, things had changed for the better. Pleased with his findings, the sun was shining when Mason finally drove south towards the outskirts of Newcastle. The traffic wasn't particularly heavy, but at the roundabout with the A69 he swung east into West Road and suddenly ground to a halt. Typical, he cursed. Not the best of places to be stuck in traffic.

Fingers tapping the steering wheel, he mentally ran back over Charles Anderson's last known movements. The truth, all of them said, was hidden in the detail. This had to be a vendetta killing, and not as David Carlisle had predicted – the work of a serial killer. The day Anderson was murdered, he'd met with a fellow business client and lifelong friend, Bert Lawson. After outlining plans for a new £260M innovative flood development system in the heart of Newcastle's banking sector, four hours later he was dead.

Had the Profiler got it wrong? Misread the facts? He wondered. Whatever it was that was going on inside David Carlisle's head, it didn't make sense anymore. There again, ever since the reorganisation, things hadn't quite turned out as Mason expected they would. Everything had been cobbled together, disorganised, make do and mend. What's more, his old workmate wasn't the same person anymore. Not since the tragic loss of his wife, that is. In his opinion, Carlisle was far too emotionally withdrawn nowadays, and there wasn't a damn thing he could do about it. Maybe he should never have taken him on in the first place – gone it alone, and done things differently. He hadn't, and he was now under enormous internal pressure himself. The mechanics of a murder investigation could be quite overwhelming at times, but something had to give. If not, he could soon find himself with another dead body on his hands, and that prospect didn't bear thinking about.

What a bloody mess!

As the traffic eased forward, two things were preying on Jack Mason's mind. The first was Gilesgate, and the second, Lowther Construction. Past experience had taught him that where huge sums of money were involved, it usually meant trouble. With that amount of money slushing around in the system, someone would usually get greedy. Whatever it was that Anderson and Riley had been mixed up in, it certainly wasn't good. Maybe they'd been lured into some kind of dodgy transaction, a deal gone wrong perhaps? If not, then he couldn't think of another plausible explanation as to why they'd been murdered.

Then he had another inspiration.

Chapter Twelve

Deep in thought, David Carlisle pulled his Rover P4 100 into the overgrown car park and switched off the engine. The Sat Nav coordinates were right, but the location was all wrong. This wasn't the operational headquarters of Lowther Construction, surely not. To one side and dominating the skyline, he noticed the ruins of a derelict warehouse building. Its boarded up windows, collapsed roof and broken drainpipes told a story of abandonment and neglect. Having suffered extensive fire damage, the heat generated from the fire had caused one of its walls to collapse inwards. All that remained was little more than a heap of rubble.

To the left of the car park, behind a high security fence marked, WARNING – GUARD DOGS, a huge mountain of scrap metal stood. It was then he spotted the ferocious looking German Shepherd Dog as it peered out at him from behind the steel metal fence. Its collar, attached to a long thin steel hawser wire, gave it the full freedom of the compound. This was no pet, this dog meant business – best stay clear, thought Carlisle.

Then, directly ahead, he picked out a series of portable steel cabins. Set back behind a large pile of earth, their roofs had been covered with heavy-duty plastic sheeting and tied down at the corners with rope. In search of life, he pushed on regardless, even though his instincts were telling him otherwise. How he hated the uncertainty, the not knowing what was coming next. He checked the nearest cabin and from the darkness within, the air had a putrid smell. Someone was barbecuing horseshit, he told himself. God, it smelt awful.

'Is anyone at home?' he yelled.

Peering through the gloom, Carlisle suddenly felt the cold muzzle of the gun as it pushed into the base of his skull. Panic gripped him, and his legs turned to jelly. This wasn't the first time he'd landed himself in a tight corner, only this time it felt different.

'Don't move another muscle,' the stranger's frail voice demanded.

Carlisle tried to turn, but the muzzle of the gun pressed harder into the base of his skull. 'I'm Car . . . lisle . . . David Carlisle—'

'Are you now?'

'Yes. I'm a private investigator.'

'Keep your hands exactly where I can see them, Carlisle.'

His ten years with the Met had taught him many things, above all, obey the stranger's demands. Flinch, and that itchy finger might squeeze the trigger and he would join the long list of statistics. Still trembling, Carlisle placed his hands on the cabin door, just as the training manual had taught him to do. How many times had he read it – a million perhaps, maybe more? The paragraphs now firmly imprinted in his brain – *win over your adversary's confidence – remove the tension barriers – talk it through.*

Where the hell did it mention heart rate?

'I'm here to investigate a murder,' Carlisle said nervously.

'And whose murder might that be?'

'A man called Derek Riley.'

The voice behind him hesitated, and he sensed the indecision.

'That's odd,' the stranger replied. 'I've already had a visit from the police today. Tell me, Carlisle, what exactly are you doing around these parts?'

'I'm not a police officer, I'm a private investigator. I work freelance.'

'Do you now.'

'Yes.'

The voice sounded a little shakier now; could there be doubt in the stranger's mind? Then to Carlisle's relief, he felt the cold muzzle of the gun being pulled away.

'You should have said so in the first place,' said the old man, now confronting him.

'I did, and I—'

The stranger gave him a once over, then pocketed the heavy metal torch. He had a high wrinkled forehead, slicked back silver hair, and sported a large walrus moustache. The ends had been coated in a thick mixture of grease and grime, giving him a bizarre appearance.

'You scared the living daylights out of me old timer.'

'Did I now?'

'You certainly did,' said Carlisle. 'I genuinely thought that was a loaded shotgun back there, and you were about to blow my brains out.'

'The name's Duke,' the old man said, extending out a hand. 'The next time you go poking your nose into other people's property, Carlisle, make sure you announce yourself good and proper.'

Duke retreated back inside the portable steel cabin. From a makeshift wooden table, grabbed a handful of fat greasy sausages, and tossed them into a pan full of hot burning oil. Fat flying everywhere, Carlisle suddenly felt as though he'd been transported into another world.

'Feeling hungry?' Duke asked.

The thought made Carlisle retch. 'No thanks. I've just eaten, and I'm—'

'Suit yourself; the dog will eat the leftovers,' Duke interrupted.

He watched as the old man prodded the sausage skins with the precision of a neurosurgeon, and gummed his bottom lip. They talked a while, about everything and nothing, but Carlisle was eager to push on. 'I'm looking for a Lowther Construction Company,' he said. 'But I must have missed my turning back there.'

Duke shook his head and eyed him with suspicion. 'This is the old Lowther Engineering site; but there's never been a construction company around these parts, Carlisle.'

And yet, he thought, this is where his Sat Nav had brought him. Of course he would occasionally get it wrong, punch in the wrong coordinates, or press the wrong information button. Once he'd even ended up on the wrong side of the country, but that was a genuine mistake. Not this time. He'd checked and double checked the postcode before leaving, and this was definitely the right address.

'Are you sure?'

'Of course I'm sure,' said Duke. 'Tell me again, what was the name of the construction company you're looking for?'

'Lowther Construction,' Carlisle replied. 'One of the shareholders, a guy called Derek Riley. He's the murder victim the Northumbria Police are currently investigating.'

'Umm . . .'

'I'm obviously at the wrong place,' shrugged Carlisle.

'Hold it, young man,' Duke said, looking somewhat confused. 'This is old Bert Riley's place, and he did have a son called Derek.'

Carlisle sensed uncertainty in the old man's voice. No doubt there would be a dozen Derek Riley's in the local telephone directory, and he guessed he was getting his wires crossed.

'How long ago is this?' Carlisle asked.

'Five years back, maybe more.' Duke gummed his bottom lip again in concentration, and then said. 'Old Bert's son certainly wasn't into engineering. As I recall, he ran a farm up in Northumberland. Somewhere near Alnwick, I believe.'

Carlisle stood shocked.

'A farm you say?'

'That's right.'

'That wouldn't be *Dove Farm*, would it?'

'The name sounds familiar, but I could have sworn it was called Netherton, or was that the name of the village?' Duke stood for a minute, motionless. 'Sadly my memory ain't what it used to be, Carlisle. Age creeps up on all of us, unfortunately.'

'Netherton—'

Duke grinned. 'You look like you've seen a ghost, Carlisle.'

'What else can you tell me about this place?'

He listened with interest as Duke explained how Lowther Engineering was once a thriving manufacturing business. Involved with the local shipyards, when the UK's shipbuilding industry went into decline, old Bert Riley foresaw a grim future. A shrewd businessman, he sold off his company assets, and held onto the land as a future security investment. Sadly, he never lived long enough to reap the benefits of his ambitious plans and his inheritance fell to his only son. Thirty years on and the massive regeneration programmes now sweeping the River Tyne made this a prime redevelopment site.

'Tell me, Duke, how long have you been keeping an eye on the place?'

'Ten years, maybe more,' Duke replied, looking somewhat bemused.

'And nobody's ever questioned as to why you're still here?'

'After old Bert passed away, I made a couple of discreet telephone calls . . . but they kept sending me the cheques.'

'Cheques, what cheques are these?'

'They come from a solicitor's office in Newcastle,' Duke replied.

'That wouldn't be "Anderson & Schlesinger Law Firm" would it?'

There was only a short pause. 'Uh-huh, they're the people.'

Carlisle recognised the guilt, but ignored the reasoning behind it. He watched as the old man heaped the last spoonful of potatoes onto his plate, and smothered them with a thick layer of black, greasy gravy. If Duke was telling him the truth, and he had no reason to doubt him, then Lowther Construction and Lowther Engineering were one and the same companies.

'How often do these people send you these cheques?'

Duke scratched his temple and gave him a quizzical look.

'Monthly. Why do you ask?'

Something was wrong. This had to be the place; even the address matched that with Companies House. Then the penny dropped. What if Charles Anderson had managed to fiddle the books – after all he was a legal adviser, wasn't he? Carlisle smelt a rat, and knew then he was onto something. He also realised that there was probably nothing more to be gained from listening to Duke, and responded diplomatically. The old man smiled meekly as Carlisle pushed on towards the overgrown car park. Gathering his thoughts together, he climbed back into his Rover and sat for a while. Not a bad start, Carlisle reasoned, but that's how these things usually panned out.

Twenty minutes later, he pulled up alongside one of the many Tyne Tunnel toll booths, dropped some loose change into the pay toll bucket, and waited for the barrier to rise. The minute the lights turned green, he slipped into second gear, and joined the steady stream of traffic heading south. It was weird, the images that sometimes came into Carlisle's head. Maybe it was the pub chalkboard that had set him off laughing: FREE AIR GUITAR WITH EVERY PINT. Customers hoping to pick up a free air guitar with every pint could soon find themselves leaving empty handed.

When he was younger, he'd always fancied himself as a bit of a budding guitarist. Carlisle loved nothing more than a decent guitar riff; Eric Clapton, Brian May, Pete Townsend were all part of his checklist. The nearest he'd got to ever becoming a rock star, though, was miming in front of his mother's wardrobe mirror with an old broom handle.

Some things never change, he grinned.

It had turned five when he eventually arrived back at the office. The place was in total darkness. Then he remembered: it was Jane's night out – a once a month meeting with friends, touring the quieter bars in South Shields. Letting himself in, he made a mug of black coffee, fired up his laptop, and checked his e-mails.

It was time to give Jack Mason a call.

Chapter Thirteen

It hadn't been the greatest weekend of his life, though Carlisle, as he drove north towards the Police Headquarters and his morning briefing with Jack Mason. It was ten o'clock, and his brain was now stuck in overdrive. Mason had certainly done his homework; his investigation into Companies House was a pure stroke of genius. Having unearthed a darker side to Gilesgate's activities, much to everyone's surprise, the DCI had decided to keep Sir Jeremy on tenterhooks. Despite the evidence being heavily stacked against the Gilesgate Chairman, there probably wasn't enough proof to lay charges against him at this stage. To go in heavy-handed now would only open up another bag of worms. There again, what if the killer was one of the Gilesgate directors, what then?

Carlisle had thought long and hard over that. All weekend in fact.

Earlier that morning, at a place called Shillmoor in Northumberland, two police undercover officers had stumbled across an abandoned Mk3 Mondeo. Close to the River Coquet, barely three miles west of the village of Alwinton, it had sparked off a major manhunt. Recovered from the boot of the vehicle were three-dozen boxes of live ammunition, a spare change of clothing, and enough food to last a fortnight. Whoever had stolen the vehicle was obviously intending to hole up in the area.

Entering the operations room, Carlisle was immediately hit by the smell of Indian takeaway. Something was afoot, and by the state of the place, the team had worked all weekend by the look of things. Not ten feet away, several police officers sat huddled around a large computer screen. Heads buried deep in some thought or other, they appeared oblivious to his presence. A telephone warbled in the office, but no one answered it. Eventually, the person on the other end of line gave up and the phone went dead. Even Jack Mason seemed to have lost all track of time. Decidedly jaded, as if he'd spent the whole weekend cooped up inside his office, he was staring aimlessly down at a large map spread out across his desktop. Planning never was his forte; especially well orchestrated plans. Jack Mason's arrangements were more spontaneous affairs – spur of the moment tactics – the kind written on the back of a fag-packet. This time felt different though, more organised, more controlled.

Mason lifted his head and yawned. 'Your drifter fits the bill perfectly.'

'Let's hope it's him, Jack'

'It is, and its time he was brought to heel.'

The timing made perfect sense, Carlisle reasoned, and something had to be done. If not, the DCI could soon find himself with another dead body on his hands. Even so, the local TV channels were pushing out news bulletins at an alarming rate. The general public's insatiable demand for answers was relentless. What was he to do? Too much publicity and the media would simply blow his cover. Too little, and the case would go cold on him. It was a fine balancing act, and one that most senior police officers had to deal with from time to time.

Carlisle spoke with caution. 'It's a large area, Jack. Are you sure you have adequate resources?'

'Fortunately the Northumbria police have a mutual arrangement with other police forces, which means I'm able to draft in reinforcements as and when I require them.'

Carlisle nodded, but refused to be drawn in. Lowering his eyes, and with Mason's words still ringing in his ear, he gathered his composure. There were times when tactful diplomacy seemed the only real answer to combating Mason's spontaneous actions. Now wasn't the time for confrontation. After weeks spent trying to convince him they were dealing with a psychopath, had the penny finally dropped?

'Do we have a description?' he asked.

Mason swung to face him. 'Yeah, he's lean, six-two, and thirty-something with short cropped hair. We know he's stolen a Mondeo, and sleeping rough in the foothills around Barrow Burn. Need I say more?'

Carlisle took a step back, holding his hands up. 'I rest my case, milord.'

'It's him all right, and he's now my number one priority.'

Oh dear, Carlisle thought. Mason's commitment was unparalleled, but there were times when he lacked subtlety in his approach. Besides, the ammunition found in the boot of the suspect's car still puzzled him. This wasn't his style; he wasn't that kind of killer. His was a more controlled approach; guns were direct, instant.

'Do we know what type of weapon he is carrying?'

'I've no idea, but the search team's recovered three-dozen boxes of .22 LF rim fire cartridges from the boot of the stolen vehicle. That's as much as we know?'

'That's an awful lot of ammunition, Jack.'

'If he intends to finish it in a shootout, then so be it.'

The room fell silent, a stony silence that commanded a time of reflection. The strain was beginning to tell, and Carlisle detected uncertainty in Mason's voice. His killer was still out there somewhere, and it was slowly eating away at the detective's patience.

'Let's hope the weather holds.'

'Yeah,' Mason shrugged. 'But I don't need reminding about his will to succeed. If I'm reading this right, this bastard is about to get his comeuppance.'

'It won't be easy, Jack.'

'Nobody said it would.'

'Be careful, he'll resist you all the way.'

Mason swung to face him. 'Stopping him is one thing. But stop him I will.'

After what felt like an eternity, Mason stormed towards the open office doorway. His mood was explosive, and Carlisle could not remember the last time he'd seen him in such a state as this.

'Wallace,' Mason shouted. 'You need you to organise the dog teams . . . first light tomorrow morning.'

'How many teams, boss?'

'Two, that should be enough, anymore and it will all get out of hand.'

'Leave it with me,' Wallace replied.

Mason thought for some moments, and then said. 'We'll need air reconnaissance to cover the Barrow Burn area. Make sure they understand what's required.'

'Let's hope the bastard doesn't drag us into the marshlands,' Wallace replied.

'Possible,' said Mason, 'but highly unlikely, don't you think?'

Wallace nodded, but did not reply.

'Remind everyone that my briefing starts in five minutes,' said Mason.

Seconds later, Carlisle could hear tables being hurriedly dragged into position. Now on auto-pilot, Mason's eyes toured the rest of the room. Things were moving at a pace, and everything that could be done, was being done. Under the terms of a voluntary agreement between the Association of Police Officers and the media, Mason had requested a total news blackout. How long it would hold was anyone's guess. But at least it gave them some comfort.

'It's a pity you'll not be joining us tomorrow,' Mason groaned.

'I wish I could,' Carlisle replied, 'but I'm a key prosecution witness in an embezzlement trial. Not the best timing, I'm afraid, but these things happen unfortunately.'

'What a shame. Let's hope it's all worth your while, eh.'

The moment they stepped into the ops room, Carlisle felt the tension. Mason's powerful presence exuded authority, as if sucking the rest of the team into a deep black hole – a central vortex full of unknown. He watched as the senior detective unfurled a huge map across two adjoining tables. Leaning over, he picked out several features with a red marker pen and stepped back.

'OK. Listen up everyone. At first light tomorrow morning two dog handler teams will move into position north of Alwinton. Everyone else is to take up their respective positions by 6.0am. The main assembly point is close to the village. Here . . . and here,' said Mason, pointing to two pre-marked positions on the map. 'Directly after this briefing, those officers assigned to team ALPHA are to check with Luke James, and those assigned to team TANGO, report to George Wallace. Anyone got any questions?'

Nods of approval gathered pace. Everyone understood what was required of them – or so it appeared. Mason moved freely now, almost robotic. 'At midnight tonight, all roads within a twenty mile radius of our suspect's last known position will be closed to the general public. Without transport, our suspect's only hope of escape is to move around on foot.' Mason paused for effect. 'Three teams, each made up of thirty officers, are to block any potential escape routes. At first light tomorrow morning, that's 4.30am, two dog handler teams will begin their sweep of this area.' Mason brushed an index finger across a large section of the map. 'Their objective is to flush him out of hiding. Once out in the open, the rest should be pretty straightforward.'

Vic Miller raised his hand, and then said, 'The Armed Response Teams, Jack. We still haven't received our instructions.'

Mason stroked his chin in a sort of dutiful disapproval. 'I was coming to that, Vic,' he replied, as if quick to dispel any notions that there were flaws in his plans. 'Every team will be accompanied by an armed response officer. Remember, we're dealing with a crazed psychopath here, so no one is to take any unnecessary risks.'

'Like what?' said Harry Manley, annoyingly sucking on another Humbug.

'You're to work as a team, Harry. The last thing I need is gung-ho-heroes.'

Looking somewhat confused, Vic Miller scratched his forehead.

'So what's our brief on this one, Jack?'

'Armed police officers are under strict instructions to use only the minimal of force. Unless a police officer finds himself or herself in a life threatening situation, only then will my "Shoot to kill" policy be implemented. Do I make myself clear on that?'

Nods of approval all round. No one spoke.

'What about backup?' DS James asked.

'Good point, Luke. For that I've organised two rapid response teams, each made up of twenty officers. These will be placed at strategic positions . . . here and here,' said Mason, pointing down at the map again.

As notes were taken down and opinions exchanged, a nervous fervour gripped the team. Mason raised a hand as if to draw their attention towards a more important issue.

The room fell deadly silent.

'On this occasion it seems I've drawn the short straw, gentlemen. I'll be directing operations using the services of the North East Air Support Unit's helicopter. My call sign, should you require it, will be 'Roger One—'

A loud jeer broke out around the room.

As the briefing drew to a close, Carlisle felt a hint of disappointment in his total lack of involvement. In turning to leave, Mason pulled him to one side. There was a glint of devilment in the Chief Inspectors eyes, as if sensing victory.

'With any luck, by tomorrow night we'll have this bastard behind bars.'

Carlisle said nothing, still full of grave doubts.

Chapter
Fourteen

Close to a stone bridge that crossed the River Coquet, a lone undercover police car pulled discreetly into a roadside lay-by. Stepping from the vehicle and wearing a green bomber jacket, blue jeans and a black casual jumper, Jack Mason checked his bearings as he moved towards the yellow Mobile Command Truck. It was 5.45am, and the whole area was swarming with police officers, many of whom had been drafted in from specialist units from up and down the country. In what had been a well-guarded secret, Mason's voluntary press agreement was still holding firm. But for how much longer was anyone's guess.

Shortly after six, a lone helicopter could be heard approaching the village of Alwinton. Equipped with a Nite Sun 30 million candlepower searchlight, earlier that morning the aircraft's powerful video and thermal imaging cameras had been put to good use. With a top cruising speed of 130 knots per hour, it was ideally suited for the work in hand. At a pre-arranged rendezvous point – a grassy knoll not more than sixty metres from the stone bridge – the helicopter finally came to rest. With its rotor blades still turning, Jack Mason climbed into the back seat of the helicopter, fastened his seat-belt and put on his communications headset. As the door slid shut, the pilot increased his rotor blade speed and began a vertical climb.

Airborne at last, Mason caught his first glimpse of the unfolding police activity below. Two miles north of Alwinton village, a mountain rescue team could be seen heading north towards the base of the Cheviot foothills. Following in their wake, two armed police officers looked distinctly at odds in such a picturesque setting. Mason was taking no chances: a potential serial killer was at large and he was determined to finish it.

Further north, after climbing out of Shillmoor, the first of the three man dog handler teams were making steady progress into the neighbouring foothills. Thick overcast skies threatened rain. It was 8.0am, and 'Razor', a five year old German Shepherd, was already showing early signs of fatigue. The dog was panting heavily, and his huge head was lolloping ever closer towards the ground. Too close for the man in charge of the dog handler teams. Recognising the animal's distress, Sergeant Manton pointed towards a large wooden gate set back some thirty metres up ahead.

'Let's rest these mutts, or they'll not last the distance,' the sergeant ordered.

As the last of his men settled down into the long grass, he reached into his backpack and retrieved a large aluminium water bottle and green plastic bowl. Unscrewing the water bottle cap, he poured the contents into the green plastic bowl and gave the signal. Obligingly, 'Razor' pushed his long snout towards the inviting clear water.

It was gone in seconds.

'Five more minutes, lads,' the Sergeant ordered.

Pleased with their progress, the sergeant removed his police cap and wiped the beads of perspiration from his brow. At least the men were bearing up to the intolerable conditions, if not the dogs, he thought. Gathering his bearings, the climb ahead looked reasonable. Only the middle ground appeared tricky. Ahead lay a small ridge, along which ran an extensive meandering track leading to the summit of Inner Hill. With any luck, the dogs would soon pick up the suspect's scent and they'd be home and dry by lunchtime. Turning to face his companion, there was an air of reassurance in Sergeant Manton's voice.

'The son of a bitch is still out there.'

'I'm not convinced,' Constable Smart replied.

The two men had been good friends, for as long as anyone could remember. A few days shy of his fortieth birthday, Constable Dick Smart was still living in hope of getting his foot on the first rung of the promotion ladder. Having spent the last six months working with the Police Firearms Team, things were looking up. Beaver, his four year old Belgian Malinois, was an expert in sniffing out and detecting explosives. They worked well together, and his dog's reputation was second to none. Having taken part in several recent counter-terrorist operations – including work with the North East Border Agency – they'd forged a formidable partnership together.

The sergeant shifted his position.

'I say he's still out there.'

'Nah, the humidity getting to you, Tom,' Constable Smart chuckled.

Then, to everyone's astonishment, the sergeant suddenly pointed to the valley below. Barely visible to the naked eye, and in extended line, a group of police officers were closing in on a series of derelict outbuildings. Had they spotted something?

Twenty minutes later, having reached the summit of Shillhope Law, the team began its long winding descent towards the village of Barrow Burn. The ground underfoot was treacherous, made worse by the damp slippery undergrowth. As the mountain dropped away, their final approach was met by the unexpected presence of the police helicopter, as it swooped low over their position.

Acknowledging with a thumbs up signal, the sergeant adjusted his communications headset and spoke directly with DCI Mason.

'We're moving north,' Sergeant Manton shouted, through cupped hands.

'Do we know where?' asked Constable Smart.

'No. But '*Roger One*' has picked up a heat trace.'

'Is it static or mobile?'

'Mobile, and heading in a northerly direction by all accounts,' the Sergeant replied.

Brushing down the dust thrown up by the downdraft of the helicopter's rotor blades, the sergeant consulted his map. Spurred on by the noise of the advancing helicopter engine, there was a new sense of urgency in their stride. On dropping down into White Bridge, set back some two-hundred metres from the footpath was a narrow wooden footbridge.

'That water looks inviting,' the lead handler said, pointing the way ahead.

Caught in the moment a thin smile swept across the sergeant's face. It wasn't what Constable Taylor had said that had made him grin; it was the way his colleague had said it. Harry Taylor was reputedly the most experienced dog handler in the County. Well known to the criminal fraternity, his faithful companion, 'Oscar', had been setting a cracking pace that morning. Too fast if the truth was known.

Ten minutes later, after crossing a fast flowing mountain stream, the ground suddenly gave way and they were facing a more difficult challenge. Rising some eight hundred feet above their position, a steep vertical gully – lined on either side by exposed rocks – ran centrally towards the summit. It was a formidable climb, the sergeant thought, and one that involved tired dogs. Anxious, he turned to the others and gave out a new set of instructions. Then, to everyone's astonishment, the advancing helicopter suddenly swung left as it cut a northerly path between two distant rolling hills.

'It looks like they've spotted something.'

'And moving towards the summit by the look of things,' said Constable Smart.

'This bastard certainly knows how to pick his ground,' another cursed.

Raising a hand in acknowledgement, the sergeant cast a critical eye over the surrounding slopes. Progress was slow, painfully slow. The heat was unbearable, made worse by the low-lying clouds forming an impregnable barrier between land and sky. No one spoke, each preferring to suffer his own torment in silence.

Then gunfire broke out.

'Man down!'

'Take cover,' someone shouted.

As another bullet ricocheted perilously close to his position, the sergeant crawled towards a steep overhang. Outwitted, and hopelessly pinned down in the gunman's deadly crossfire, he could only watch in horror as Constable Smart struggled to keep his dog in check. Fit as he was, the slightest movement and they'd both end up as tomorrow's headlines. Drawing comfort from a large projecting boulder, Sergeant Manton readjusted his binoculars and reconsidered his options. To his left lay a steep central gully. Guarded on two sides by a sheer vertical rock face, its steepness surprised him. Like a lot of other demanding climbs he'd encountered, the higher up you went the more challenging it became. He realised that, but there were no other options left open to them. It was their only route of escape.

Exhausted and cut to pieces by falling rocks and debris, they clawed their way to the summit. As far as Sergeant Manton could see, the crest was a long flat plateau – running north to south for about one-hundred yards, and ending in a sheer vertical drop on two sides. Then, as his eyes rolled sideways he spotted some other movement. Barely forty metres separating them stood the gunman. He was a small man, lean and feeble looking, not as he'd imagined him to be. Then, to everyone's astonishment, the gunman shifted his position, and with lightning reflexes dropped to one knee.

Death came quickly and mercifully to Beaver – a well-aimed bullet to the dog's upper torso. Scattering in every direction, police officers now dived for cover. With little or no time to think, the sergeant unleashed his dog and hit the ground heavily in front of him. In that split-second judgement, it felt as if the whole world had suddenly turned against him. What to do next? Rounds were falling perilously close to his position, much too close for comfort.

'Take cover,' he shouted.

Everyone heard the screams; the blood curdling pleas that rang out across the mountain top. No one dared to move. Even the wind held its breath. As the surge of adrenaline died away, the sergeant popped his head above the long grass and peered towards the gunman's last known position. Nothing could have prepared him for this. Hit on his blindside, Razor had lunged into the gunman's upper torso, sinking his huge teeth into his upper forearm. From what he could see, the gunman was bleeding heavily with the dog now standing guard over him.

It was over.

The helicopter's rotors still turning, Jack Mason hit the ground running.

'Check him for weapons,' the DCI yelled.

Jack Mason wasn't the sort of person you wanted to get on the wrong side of, especially in tight situations. Within seconds, the sergeant was joined by a dozen armed police officers, all eager to assist. Unconscious and still bleeding heavily, the gunman was unceremoniously rolled over and onto his back and his legs spread-eagled. Taking stock, the sergeant knelt down and checked for hidden weapons.

'He's clean, boss.'

'Nice work, Sergeant,' Mason acknowledged. 'Your dog did a fine job.'

Glancing up, the sergeant watched as Jack Mason bent down and rolled back the gunman's trouser leg. From what he could see, the injuries to his face were superficial. Apart from the upper forearm, which had been terribly mauled by his dog; everything else seemed fine. Then, as Mason checked the suspect's footwear, he caught the look of concern on his face. Something was wrong, and whatever it was they were about to find out.

'It's not our man, George.'

'It must be, Jack,' Wallace replied, as a dozen fellow officers crowded forward to get a better look.

'I'm telling you, George. This isn't our man.'

Uncertainty spread like the plague.

'If he isn't our man, then who the hell is he?'

His face as black as thunder, Mason took a deep breath as he turned to the nearest plainclothes police officer. 'Lock this bastard up, and whilst you're at it throw away the key.'

Everyone stood gobsmacked as Mason turned and stormed off towards the waiting helicopter. No one spoke. Whoever the gunman was, Jack Mason was far from happy.

Seconds later, the helicopter took off in a northerly direction.

Chapter Fifteen

Dave Carlisle sat in the hospital waiting room, his patience severely tested. It was two in the morning, and the long hours spent hanging around for Jack Mason to show had left him irritable. Clinging to the memories of his mother's last few months of life, Carlisle detested hospitals at the best of times. The familiar smell of disinfectant, clean linen sheets and the long nights of empty conversation all flooding back. Alone by her bedside, slowly wasting away, until in the end the gaunt figure of a woman that he once called mother, had changed beyond all recognition.

The hospital décor was modern, impersonal, he thought. To one corner, a green plastic sign bore the inscription: EAST WING RVI – STAFF ROSTER. The clock on the wall – now stuck in time – was already three hours slow. Part way down a narrow corridor stood an armed police officer. Motionless, with arms folded tight across his chest, he was barring the entrance to another part of the building. Then, through the main entrance admissions doors, Carlisle caught sight of yet another yellow NHS ambulance as it drew up alongside A&E. As the vehicle's back doors swung open, an old lady strapped into a wheelchair was placed onto the tail-lift of the vehicle and carefully lowered to the ground. Christ, thought Carlisle, how many more patients do these people have to deal with tonight?

Slowly, the commotion died down.

Opposite him, the duty night nurse sat propped against a large admissions desk. Her long gaunt face buried deep inside a pile of hospital records, she scribbled through patients' ailments with the conviction of a judge passing sentence. Despite constant interruptions, she somehow appeared impervious to distractions. Suddenly it dawned on him, what the hell was he doing sat in a hospital waiting room in the middle of the night anyway. Two o'clock in the morning wasn't exactly his favourite time of the day; he could certainly have done without this.

Then, through tired eyes, he spotted a white-coated figure approaching from one of the side wards. He was young, late twenties, short in stature with long blond hair neatly tucked beneath a blue surgical cap. From a side coat pocket hung the ends of a stethoscope – crammed there in a moment of haste.

'I'm sorry to have kept you waiting. Mr Carlisle, I presume?'

'Yes. That's me.'

Carlisle staggered to his feet. In what had been a long three hour wait, his mouth was dry and the back of his tongue felt like coarse sandpaper. 'I'm here on official business, Doctor, but I'm waiting for DCI Mason to show. I'm sure he'll be along shortly.'

The doctor looked at him in surprise. 'DCI Mason left four hours ago, Mr Carlisle.'

Thinking more clearly now, Carlisle tried to get his head around the doctor's statement. The anger surfacing, he took another deep breath and tried to steady himself.

'I'm instructed to serve you with a court order, Doctor.'

The young doctor was quiet for a moment.

'Ah! Yes. Detective Chief Inspector Mason did warn me about this.'

'Did he now— '

'Yes,' the Doctor interrupted. 'What does it entail exactly?'

'One of your patients has been charged with attempted murder,' said Carlisle. 'The South Shields' magistrates have refused bail on the grounds of a previous bad record of absconding. This one, apparently, has a nasty habit of breaching his court orders.'

'Ah, I see. I take it he already has a police record?'

'In legal jargon,' Carlisle went on. 'That means your patient is technically here under house arrest, and that's why there's a heavy police presence.'

Carlisle pressed a large brown envelope into an outstretched hand, the official court crest boldly stamped across the top. Tearing back the flap, he watched as the doctor moved towards the reception desk where the light was much brighter.

'Are you able to confirm the patient's name?'

Damn, Carlisle cursed. What the hell was Mason playing at?

'Is there a problem?' he asked.

'There could be.' The doctor paused in thought. 'His name's John Matthew, by the way—'

'Yes, I know.'

The doctor stared at him. 'It appears the police have not been forthcoming with their information, Mr Carlisle.'

'Oh, and in what respect?' said Carlisle after some moments of thought.

'Well,' the doctor replied. 'What are we to do in the event of an emergency?'

'I'm quite sure the police will have made their own contingency plans for that.'

The doctor shook his head. 'Yes. You're probably right.'

And that was another thing, thought Carlisle, who was John Matthew anyway? He knew very little about the man, or what he even looked like, come to think of it. If this wasn't the killer, then what the hell was he doing here? Then it struck him. It wasn't curiosity that had caused him to get involved in the case, it was the intrigue. From the moment he first got involved with criminal profiling, he'd always been fascinated by the mind-set of vicious criminals. What made them tick? And yes, he admitted, it was the very nature of the beast that had drawn his attention towards these people.

'It's been a long night,' the doctor smirked. 'I'll get you Matthew's medical details.'

Carlisle watched as the night nurse handed the doctor a sealed hospital envelope. Noting her eavesdropping on their conversation, he gave her a filthy look. She blushed, and buried her head behind the computer screen again.

'What's Matthew's current condition?' Carlisle queried.

'I doubt you people will be able to speak to him, if that's what you mean. We've managed to save his right arm, but it's still touch and go.' The doctor gestured towards the official hospital document. 'These next thirty-six hours are critical in my opinion.'

Hospital jargon that meant he was barely alive, Carlisle assumed. He tilted his head back still unconvinced. 'I take it he'll survive?'

'This patient's a fighter, his type usually are. They never give in easily.'

Carlisle's ears pricked up. 'So when can we see him?'

The doctor shuffled awkwardly; hospital body language for uncertainty. 'He needs rest. At least another ten hours, I'd say.'

'Ten hours!'

'Don't worry. I'm sure your armed police officers will take good care of his welfare,' the doctor replied sarcastically.

'Is he conscious?'

'No, he's still heavily sedated, I'm afraid.'

'At least another ten hours you say?'

The doctor nodded. 'Do you have any contact details, Mr Carlisle?'

From an inside pocket he took out a business card out and handed it to him. 'Call this number any time, but I must warn you that your patient is now police property. Any information regarding John Matthew's medical condition is strictly classified information, and that,' said Carlisle, raising a finger as if to emphasise a point, 'means no statements . . . and certainly not to the press.'

The doctor puffed out his chest.

'You're forgetting I'm a doctor, Mr Carlisle. We too are bound by certain ethical rules.'

'Thanks for reminding me . . . just call me the minute Matthew pulls round.'

It had been a long night.

Chapter Sixteen

The sound of the phone jarred Carlisle from a deep sleep, but the caller hung up long before he could reach it. Fumbling for the light, he threw back the blankets and checked his watch. He'd overslept. It was 9.10am, and he should have been in Newcastle goddammit. On lifting the receiver, he punched in the last caller button and watched as the digital display ran through its laborious memory sequence. The moment Jane Collins' number popped up on the tiny digital display screen; there was no mistaking his relief. Skipping breakfast, he showered, got dressed and checked for any other missed calls. There were none.

The rush hour traffic had eased, but the roads were still relatively busy as he drove north towards the Royal Victoria Infirmary, a journey he made in record time. Parking his car, he made straight for the waiting room. The same dismal building he'd spent the previous evening in. Night security had long gone, replaced by a pokerfaced porter whose lecherous eyes mentally undressed every female who came within ten feet of him. Behind the administrations desk sat a large buxom blonde, who dished out instructions to anyone and everyone who happened to call her way. Not the friendliest of people to deal with, he mused. He made himself known, and managed to find a quiet corner away from the sick and wounded.

Twenty minutes later, Carlisle was joined by the diminutive but attractive figure of Detective Carrington. Fresh out of police training school, and newly appointed member of the team, Carrington was dressed in a dark blue suit, white blouse, black leather shoes, and wearing a thousand-watt smile.

Not at a bad looker either, thought Carlisle.

'You got my message,' the young detective said, glancing round warily. 'When did you get here?'

'Fifteen minutes ago.'

Carrington swung to face him. 'I know this is awkward, but Jack Mason told me to contact you the minute that John Matthew pulled round.'

'So that's why you called my office.'

'I tried to call you earlier, but your phone went straight to voicemail.'

'What time was this?'

Carrington checked her iPhone, as if to mentally reassure herself.

'Eight-thirty . . .'

Carlisle recognised the signs, the fluttering of eyelashes and the suspicion in her glances. She was far too eager, far too excitable for his liking. Recently assigned to Jack Mason's ground troops, outwardly she appeared composed, but beneath the surface he sensed her inquisitive mind had to work in overdrive.

'What do you know about John Matthew?' Carrington asked, unable to hide the enthusiasm in her voice.

'Not a lot, I'm afraid. I know he was brought here under armed escort, and that he attempted to kill a police officer in the line of his duty.'

The young detective threw her head back in surprise.

'There have been a lot of new developments since then, David.'

'Developments, what developments are these?'

'Are you aware that Matthew was out on prison licence when the police finally caught up with him?'

Carlisle felt his jaw drop. 'No I wasn't?'

'It seems one of the Strangeways prison officers was tipped off that someone wanted Matthew silenced.' Carrington's voice mellowed slightly. 'He's a nasty piece of work by all accounts.'

Carlisle fell silent again, hands deep inside his trouser pockets staring down an empty hospital corridor. He admired Carrington's enthusiasm, but struggled to cope with her questioning. Besides, it was far too early in the day. Then he remembered. 'I had an inkling that something wasn't right, prisoners' seldom talk – do they?'

'More to the point,' Carrington said warily, 'John Matthew isn't our man.'

'I already knew that.'

'Oh!'

Carlisle paused to let his statement sink in. 'I'm a profiler, Sue. That's what I do.'

There. It was said. He removed his spectacles and began massaging the flesh around his eyes. If Jack Mason wasn't so damn arrogant, he could have warned him too. Matthew carried guns; it wasn't the killer's style.

His was a more subtle approach; the killer's more grandiose, and decidedly sensation seeking. It was then the young detective brought him up to speed on the rest of the previous day's events.

'Nevertheless, Matthew is still a very dangerous man,' Carrington went on. 'Apparently he has connections with Newcastle's criminal fraternity, which may be of interest to the case ... and Jack Mason of course.'

Carlisle drew back. 'So, why am I still involved?'

'That's Jack Mason's call, not mine,' Carrington shrugged. 'But let's not get hung up on it.'

Carlisle leaned back and fixed his gaze on the white plastic wall clock. Its batteries replaced, the red second hand had begun another circuit of the clock face. Across the corridor, the armed police officers had changed. This one was younger; athletic looking, fresh out of training school. Always nice to see a young copper; he smiled. Young police officers were becoming a bit of rarity nowadays. Recruitment was down, and the financial squeeze wasn't helping either.

Then, through the large double glass doors, Jack Mason appeared. Accompanied by a tall middle-aged doctor, wearing green hospital scrubs and carrying a clipboard in his right hand, they approached them at speed. Mason looked relaxed – outwardly at least. After short introductions, they were ushered along a corridor that stank of a combination of disinfectant and waxed floor polish. Despite the doctor's talkative mood, on reaching a small side ward, he suddenly took off in another direction as though his presence elsewhere was the difference between life and death.

It was then Carlisle noticed the huge white cradle covering the right side of Matthew's body; an IV tube taped to the back of his only visual hand was feeding a clear liquid. Hooked to an electrocardiogram machine, every now and then it sent out a monotonous bleep across a tiny plasma screen. Not a good sign, he thought.

'I'm DCI Jack Mason and these two are colleagues,' Mason announced.

Heavily sedated, Matthew wasn't in the best of shape. The man had a pallid look, ghostlike, as if he'd just been paid a visit from one of death's messengers. The flesh around his upper right cheekbone had been fused back together again, and a large white sticking plaster hung over a swollen right eye. His movements were lethargic, almost computerized, and the suspect had difficulty in talking.

'Aren't you the detective from the Met?'

'It's called question time, if that's what you're trying to tell me,' said Mason.

Carlisle caught the pain in Matthew's unshaven face. His eyes sockets were black, and the whites bloodshot as if he'd been up all night. At least he was alive, if barely.

Matthew swallowed hard, as though suffering a sore throat from the insertion of the endotracheal tube during his surgery. 'You're coppers, Goddammit?'

'I could be the man from the moon if you care to ask me nicely. There is a subtle difference, of course.'

'Maybe, but you all stink of the same shit to me,' Matthew croaked.

'Shit smells sweet, John, especially when you're up to your neck in trouble.' Mason took a step back. 'We're here to ask you a few questions, and I need you to cooperate. It's as simple as that.'

Matthew's eyes fixed on the young female detectives blouse, and the corner of his mouth lifted. 'Nice pair of tits, lady. Not bad for an undercover copper.'

Detective Carrington stiffened, but still kept her composure. 'Don't tell me something I already know. Try telling me something I don't,' she said, firmly.

'Like what, lady?'

Mason nodded his approval for Carrington to continue.

'What do you know about Dove Farm?' she asked.

'I know my rights, young lady; I'm entitled to legal advice, and—'

'Maybe,' Mason interrupted. 'But you're forgetting, John, you shot dead one of my police dogs besides attempting to murder a police officer in the line of his duty.'

'What a pity I didn't shoot the fucking lot of you.'

The brittle smile reappeared on the young detective's face. 'Dove Farm, what do you know about it?'

'Not a lot. I—'

'Let me remind you,' Mason said, cutting Matthew short. 'It was owned by a Derek Riley.'

'So?'

'Three weeks ago, both and he and his wife were brutally murdered there,' Mason explained. 'Some callous bastard had it in mind to nail her husband to the rafters. Tell me, John, who would do such a thing?'

'I prefer listening to the young lady.' Matthew croaked. 'Although she too talks a lot of crap, it sounds much nicer coming from her lips.'

Mason stepped closer, his eyes shone like daggers. 'Don't push me, John. You were picked up near Barrow Burn which isn't too far from Derek

Riley's place. In my books, that makes you my number one suspect.'

'Thanks for the tip off, Jack.'

Mason drew breath. 'You're up to your neck in trouble, my friend, so don't dig yourself into a deeper hole. Besides, you were spotted drinking in The Hanging Tree Inn.'

'That sounds like a good idea to me.'

Mason's expression grew cold. 'Outside this door there's a heavily armed police presence. Further down the corridor there's a dozen more. Now I'd say that's an awful lot of protection for a little piece of shit like you.'

'Sure, but just how far do you think I can get?'

Mason pursed his lips and leaned back. 'I'm not trying to keep you in here, John; I'm busting a gut in trying to keep your enemies from doing what they do best.'

Matthew's eyes suddenly shifted in their bloodshot sockets, the concern on his face now showing. 'That sounds like a threat to me, Jack.'

'Don't push me—'

'I'm still listening,' Matthew croaked.

Mason was selecting his words carefully, playing around the edges.

'Someone doesn't like the way you operate, my friend. Maybe you had nothing to do with these Riley murders, but someone believes you did.'

'Like who?'

'My contacts tell me these people are itching to cut your tongue out.' Mason shuffled awkwardly. 'So if you want my advice, you'd better start cooperating.'

There was a long silence between them, broken only by the blip of the heart monitoring machine as it sent out another set of meaningless signals.

'What's it to be?' asked Mason.

'I'm thinking—'

Carlisle sensed the fear; he could almost reach out and touch it. Matthew's face twitched and contorted with Mason's every word. He watched as the hitman ran his tongue over his lips, as if crossing a burning desert without a single drop of water. He was drowsy, laconic, and fighting back the effects of the drugs.

'Play it your way, John,' said Mason, 'but you're fast running out of time, my friend.'

'These Riley people, I didn't—'

'Go on,' Mason urged.

'I was working for Henry Fraser, he had . . . ah—'

'Stay with me, John.'

Suddenly, it felt as if the spotlight of life had been extinguished long before the show had ended. It was over, thought Carlisle; nothing would happen now until Matthew regained consciousness again. Whenever that would be? Still there were alibies to check, and reports to write up. Even so, the outcome was still depressing in Carlisle's mind.

At the reception desk Mason picked up Matthew's possessions, including a bundle of blood-stained clothes – all neatly bound and labelled with white plastic hospital ID-wraps. Tossing a pair of muddy Nike Blazers into the plastic bag provided, Mason swung to face them. 'He's holding back on something.'

'I got the same impression,' Detective Carrington nodded.

Carlisle, who had said very little so far, was quick to signal his thoughts. 'You do know he's not your man, Jack.'

'Tell me about it,' Mason shrugged. 'The son-of-a bitch is still out there somewhere. Even I know that.'

Each nodded in agreement, each sensing the DCI's disappointment. Carlisle could almost smell the failure clinging to the senior detective, but he was still refusing to lie down. Defeat, it seemed, wasn't a word in Jack Mason's vocabulary.

A memory tugged him.

'He's getting to you, Jack. I warned you he would play games with your mind.'

Mason turned sharply towards the hospital main entrance, and away from the high security wing. 'We know where he killed them, when he killed them, and how he killed them. The question is . . . *why*?'

'That's always the ten million dollar question, I'm afraid.'

'Even so,' Mason said, thoughtfully. 'Why is he killing them to order?'

'He's local, and it's his way of dealing with it. This one's geographically stable and intent on tearing his world apart – brick by brick if needs be.' Carlisle sighed. 'He's out there and his mind's racing, but the trouble is he's so caught up in his own fantasies that he can hardly breathe.'

Mason swore. 'Goddammit, I could have sworn John Matthew was our man.'

'Matthew is undoubtedly dangerous, but it's not his style of killing. The person we're looking for is a loner, someone who can mutilate his victims for the sheer impact of spreading fear into someone else's world. His is a game of elimination, a world full of hate and fear where his victims are mere pawns in a reign of terror against someone he utterly despises.'

Mason grinned. 'Someone you wouldn't like to meet in the dark, eh.'

'Not if you were his next victim. No.'

The three of them fell silent.

Chapter Seventeen

Lexus was hungry. He had not eaten in days now and he was running on pure adrenaline and catnaps. He felt cold inside and yet, the room temperature was overpoweringly humid. High up on the nineteenth floor, in one of Newcastle's notorious tower blocks, he had found sanctuary. He had made this place his own, and for the past six-weeks had been able to come and go as he pleased. He was alone here, isolated, free from the distractions and demands of the cruel outside world. Behind heavily bolted doors, he sat cross-legged on the cold concrete floor and pondered his next movements. A light flickered in the darkness, a solitary candle flame that cast eerie shadows over graffiti filled walls. He had no electricity: that had long since been disconnected.

Then, the voices returned.

What do you think of your new place?

'It's perfect,' Lexus replied.

No one will ever find you here.

The flat was unfurnished, and filled full of black polythene bin liners and other junk. To one corner, an unmade makeshift bed was cluttered with rubbish and discarded food wrappers. The air reeked of decay and a rotten stench of human squalor. It played on his nostrils, a rancid smell, but it still didn't excite him. Only the dead could do that.

There was nothing here of value, except for his laptop computer, and that went with him everywhere. He seldom let it out of his sight. The batteries had run flat, and it annoyed him intensely. He was going to recharge them, but then remembered.

There was no electricity, was there?

Don't you prefer the darkness?

'You have two minutes, get to the point.'

Lexus paused for a moment, and glanced down at the black and white photograph now positioned at his feet. He'd memorized every single one of these people; closely, and without prejudice. Why shouldn't he? Hadn't he studied them for as long as he can remember? Didn't he say these people were important? At least to him, they were. Dressed in their best attire for a very special occasion, every single one of them carried an air of arrogance on their faces. Lexus shuddered at the thought, and wondered what it would be like to be dead. Was there such a thing as life beyond the grave . . . ?

'I'm scared, mama.'

What are you scared of, my son? The voice in his head questioned.

'Do the dead ever come back?'

Why should they? These people were scum, all of them. How dare they call themselves Good Samaritans when all they did was to make vast fortunes out of ordinary people's misery? Didn't they deserve to die?

Not all were dead of course, Lexus was certain of that. But hey, wasn't he the chosen one, the only person who could rid this world of this so called evil . . . Gilesgate?

Spread around his feet was dozens of newspaper cuttings. Each meticulously catalogued, each an important record of his unbelievable achievements. He never once watched TV, preferring instead to read about his exploits in the daily tabloids.

After all, wasn't this his story?

Absolutely—

Plagued by uncertainty, Lexus searched the darkest corners of his mind for that one piece of inspiration that had made him famous. His next would be spectacular. It was important to him, if only for his fans.

And there were many.

Oh. You're such a genius, Lexus.

Rocking back on his haunches, his head struck another resounding blow against the wall. His eyes rolled back in their sockets, and the whites protruded as though invisible fingers had pulled the lids apart. His mouth open, not from convulsions; this was pure euphoria. Then, as he moved towards the trapdoor of perpetual delusion — a spiralling abyss that threatened to drag him ever closer towards the edge of eternal darkness — he reached out towards the image of a young woman. She was beautiful, with long golden locks that hid her face from view. She cradled a small child, wrapped in a thin white cotton shawl and held close to her bosom. Panic gripped him, as the ghost-like vision continued to shimmer in the flickering candlelight.

Was this a dream?

He watched in astonishment as the young woman's lips moved as if to answer, but her pitiful voice was too weak to grasp. He cried out to her in the darkness, but the image slipped from view and all that he was left with was the fearful reminders of a childhood and a mother he never came to know.

Then, just as Judas Iscariot had betrayed Christ, his evil father appeared. Gripped by unimaginable hatred, he lunged out, and towards the apparition that dared to call himself Father. Plucked from the depths of hopelessness, the voices returned—

Do not despair, my son. The monster that created you was never a match for your genius.

Drawn in by an act of pure sadistic defiance, Lexus stared down at the photograph again. His pen circled a face, a young woman's face. He had played out this ritual before, yes, many times. This wasn't his first, nor would it be his last. He knew that. These people were close to him, all of them, and why shouldn't they be?

His pulse quickened as he reached over, and kissed the photograph and the fourteen familiar faces within it. His next would be spectacular, and he was certain of that. Then, quite unexpectedly, a feeling of calm surrounded him. He clicked his tongue, softly, and hissed as a viper would attract its prey.

Deep inside his twisted inner mind, Lexus reached out – towards the outstretched hand. Both arms fully extended now, he lovingly called out her name again. His voice echoed through the darkness – a haunting sound – but there was no one there.

There never had been!

Chapter Eighteen

Mark Patterson's telephone conversation was brief. They usually were. For the next few hours, David Carlisle pondered over his contact's intriguing proposition. A local crime reporter working for the *Shields Gazette,* Mark Patterson had a gift for sniffing out a good story. If his intelligence was correct, and Carlisle had no reason to doubt otherwise, then any information regarding John Matthew would be a valuable boost to the team's morale.

The light was beginning to fade when he eventually called by the Northeast Press offices in Sunderland. At the reception desk, he picked up the sealed envelope that his friend had left for him. Inside he found a compliment slip and two free admission tickets for the Pelaw Grange Greyhound Stadium. His contact's unconventional approach to doing business never ceased to amaze him. It went with the territory. Press reporters usually had to work hard to grab a good headline story. Freebies and backhanders came with the territory. It opened doors that otherwise would have remained shut.

Returning to his car, Carlisle phoned the office and moments later his business partner answered.

'It's me, Jane,' he said. 'What are you doing tonight?'

There was a long pause at the other end of the phone.

'Is that a proposal, or a hypothetical question?'

He thought about it, and then went on to explain his friend's bizarre arrangements.

'So, what do want *me* to do about it?' Jane Collins replied.

Carlisle sensed bad vibes; he was obviously not in her good books.

'My contact at the Shields Gazette has booked a table for four, seven-thirty at the Pelaw Grange dog track, and he's bringing a female partner along with him. I thought it would be an ideal opportunity for the two of us to sit back and relax a little.'

'Oh, come on,' Jane sighed, over the phone. 'Surely you can do better than that.'

'I take it that's a no?'

There was another long pause.

'So you're inviting me to the dogs?'

'That's the bottom line. I—' His voice began to crack.

'OK, be at my place for seven.'

The phone went dead.

Wearing black designer jeans, a low cut blue silk blouse and ankle boots, Jane looked simply stunning. They met in the bar, and after short introductions Patterson led them to a premium table overlooking the dog race track. According to the race programme, the Pelaw Grange Greyhound Stadium in County Durham is home to some of the most exciting racing action in the country. Not that he knew anything about greyhound racing, or how the betting system operated come to think of it. No, Carlisle was there for another reason.

With the two women holding a central gambling kitty, the action-packed race card soon had them on the edge of their seats. The first race, a 590 metre sprint, got off to a flying start. With odds of 2-1, the blue dog was picked out by Jane whilst Patterson's partner, Jennifer, had chosen the red dog at odds of 4-1. Amidst the razzmatazz and hype, the race was over in less than 40 seconds. Nudged out on the final bend, both women's dogs were sent crashing into the hoarding boards; along with their money. By nine o'clock, they'd lost the entire betting kitty and desperate measures were called for. Between placing bets, ordering drinks, and dashing to and from the monitoring screens to work out the betting odds, Jane was in her element.

Billed as the climax of the evening, a loud fanfare announced the arrival of the next six runners. Down at the trackside, the bookies were doing brisk business. With everything to play for, the atmosphere was electric. With all six greyhounds now loaded into its chosen trap, the hare was sent running.

'A word in your ear, if I may,' Patterson said, pulling Carlisle to one side.

What made Mark Patterson stand out above the rest of the crowd was his ability to lure people into a false sense of security. It was all about timing, and Patterson was a master at his game. "*Timing is everything when you act,*" he'd once told him. "*Always remember that the past no longer exists in life, it is just what it is . . . The Past!*" If Mark Patterson's life was governed by timing, then he couldn't have chosen a better moment to have caught Carlisle off guard. Pushing their way through the crowd, they soon found a quiet corner.

Patterson's mood had changed – along with the humour. As his story began to unfold, it soon became apparent that John Matthew was well known to the local authorities. Brought up in one of the poorer neighbourhoods of Newcastle, his parents were incapable of managing their son's unruly behaviour. Ordered into foster care, Matthew soon built himself quite a reputation for sorting other people's problems out. He was good at it and nasty with it by all accounts. Amidst countless other problems, it wasn't long before Matthew began to graduate to the more serious crimes. Gaoled for killing a notorious pimp by the name of 'Benny the Bracelet', Matthew always swore his innocence. Not just content with knocking his victim down, according to CCTV footage, he intentionally reversed his car back over Benny's already broken body. Charged with manslaughter, Matthew was found guilty and given a fifteen-year prison sentence.

Carlisle racked his brains.

'And this all happened ten years ago— '

'John Matthew has contacts – he knows how to work the system. That's how he managed to get early prison release.'

'That's ridiculous.'

'I know, but that's how the system works unfortunately.' Patterson folded his arms, a defensive pose. 'Within days of his release from prison, he was back to his old tricks again.'

'So what was he doing up at Barrow Burn?'

Patterson stared at him, his hard face pinched. 'That's when this all starts to get a little messy, I'm afraid. Prior to his recent capture, John Matthew was involved in an armed robbery on a petrol station in the Bensham area of Gateshead. At the time, he was working for a guy called Henry Fraser.'

Carlisle cocked his head to one side, his interest levels heightened. 'Henry Fraser. Now there was a name from the past!'

'Yeah, he's better known as Newcastle's Mr Fix it.' Patterson paused in thought. 'Fraser's got form. He owns half of Newcastle, and runs a heavy muscle service besides acting as Sir Jeremy Wingate-Stiles' publicity manager.'

They exchanged glances

'What, the local politician!'

'That's the guy, and he's not exactly everybody's cup of tea by all accounts.'

Already ahead of the game, Carlisle's mind was filled with a thousand questions.

'So it was Fraser who got Matthew to rob a petrol station for him, is—'

'No.' Patterson cut in. 'This petrol station robbery was Matthew's own idea. When Fraser got wind that he was out on prison licence, that's when he hired Matthew to do a hit for him.'

'So tell me, what was John Matthew doing up at Barrow Burn?' Carlisle asked again.

Patterson grinned. 'He was running away from the police. When Fraser found out, that's when he contacted his friends in Strangeways. It was the inmates who spread the rumour about that someone wanted Matthew silenced. Sadly, the Prison Service and the Northumberland police both fell for it.'

Carlisle's felt a sudden surge of adrenaline. 'I should have known. I had a hunch that something wasn't right. Besides, prisoners seldom break their own code of silence.'

'It certainly fooled everyone.'

Patterson's eyes narrowed as he went on to explain Fraser's involvement in Sir Jeremy's wheeler-dealer style of politics. Not the best of people to deal with, the man was a political thug in Patterson's opinion. Those who asked awkward questions, or demonstrated a negative attitude towards his policies, could expect to face the consequences. That was Henry Fraser's role, that's what he was paid to do. Sir Jeremy, it seemed, had it all worked out and even the press were in his pockets.

The stadium noise levels heightened as the next event got underway.

'So, what kind of contract did Fraser have in mind?'

Patterson looked down at his shoes. 'Rumour has it that John Matthew was sent to go after someone, but that's as much as I know.'

Carlisle felt his friend's answer was loaded.

'You mean take someone out?'

'Fraser's well connected; he knows people and it wouldn't surprise me if he didn't know who's responsible for this recent spate of killings.'

Patterson's face had remained expressionless throughout. Surely his friend didn't think these were gangland killings – surely not. Carlisle's mind was suddenly at sixes and sevens again.

'So how did you come by this information?'

'That would be telling,' said Patterson, tapping the side of his nose.

Suddenly the pieces of the jigsaw puzzle were beginning to come together. There was more to this than had first met the eye. Whoever killed Charles Anderson had obviously ruffled Sir Jeremy's feathers. But why had the killer selected Gilesgate to carry out his artistic talents.

'So what do I owe you, Mark?'

Patterson whistled through his teeth. 'I need a big favour, old boy.'

'Try me.'

His friend stared out across the dog track, as the next race reached its climax. 'I'm under a lot of pressure from my editors, and desperately in need of a good story. You know me, David, it's all about timing. Everything I've told you is kosher, but it's worthless as it stands.' Patterson turned to face him. 'When you do eventually catch up with your killer, and no doubt you will, I need to be amongst the first to know.'

'*Quid pro quo?*' Carlisle said.

'That's the kind of deal I'm looking for.'

Carlisle nodded. Not a good idea, he thought.

'When we return to our seats,' said Patterson. 'Check out the big guy sitting alongside the loud mouthed blonde with the big tits and low cut leopard skin dress.' His friend paused for effect. 'That's Henry Fraser.'

Carlisle felt his jaw drop. '*What!*'

'I thought that might perk you up.' His friend grinned. 'Rumour has it that Fraser is working with Gilesgate's Board of Directors, but don't quote me on that.'

'When did you find this out?'

'Think about it,' said Patterson. 'When the police arrested John Matthew, he wasn't too far from Derek Riley's place . . . was he?'

'So what's the connection?'

Patterson looked on in surprise. 'I would have thought the police would have known the answer to that.'

'They do, but I was—'

'So why ask?'

'Believe me, Sir Jeremy and his cronies have been under police surveillance for weeks now,' said Carlisle, lying through his back teeth.

Patterson shook his head glumly.

'I always knew those bastards were up to no good. And now I know.'

If nothing else, Mark Patterson certainly knew how to weed vital information out of people. With Matthew out of the frame, Henry Fraser would undoubtedly be of major interest to Jack Mason. It took Carlisle all of two-seconds to pick out the big man. Everything about him exuded trouble. Greasy slicked back hair, swarthy complexion and sporting two day stubble, Fraser was no bible reader – he probably did not own one. Then it dawned on him. Why would Sir Jeremy employ a notorious thug like Henry Fraser, unless of course he wanted someone silenced?

As the evening wore on, Carlisle's mind drifted back towards more important issues, and it had nothing to do with greyhound racing. His biggest concern, right now, was Jack Mason. If the DCI continued to put the squeeze on Matthew, then every criminal in the North East of England – including Fraser – would simply go to ground. One thing for sure, the killer certainly knew how to stir up a hornet's nest. No wonder Sir Jeremy and his cronies were running scared.

Amongst the last to leave, Carlisle climbed into the front seat of his Rover P4 100 and sat for a while. Not twenty feet away, he watched as Fraser's henchman stubbed out his cigarette with his foot, and fired up the Jaguar XJ engine. Seconds later, just as Henry Fraser appeared, the car's headlights flicked on and off. A signal no doubt. People like Henry Fraser, who took the law into their own hands, always worried him. Invariably the dregs of society, they were difficult people to deal with.

It was 11.30pm, and time to make tracks.

After jotting down the car's registration number on a spent betting slip, he popped it into his wallet. Jane said nothing, but her eyes were all over the place.

Not a bad night's work, he thought. It was time to make tracks.

Chapter Nineteen

Annie Jenkins, dressed in a cream floral dress, tights and white trainers, sat impassively on the edge of the bar stool. She was a slim built woman with hazel eyes, a ruddy complexion, and long brown curly hair swept back from her face and tied back. A confirmed alcoholic, just three months short of her thirty-sixth birthday, Annie had worked tirelessly with every organisation in the land to rid herself of her drink addiction. None had succeeded. Not even the Probation Criminal Justice Service. Placed on a detox treatment program using chlordiazepoxide, even that had failed miserably.

Come rain, come shine, Annie was a creature of habit. Every morning at ten, she would stand at the top of Gateshead High Street and await the first pub door to open. Today was the turn of 'The Grove' and Annie was its first customer. Eight hours later, after staggering into her favourite watering hole on Bensham Road, she looked decidedly the worse for wear. Now amongst friends, no one gave a damn about Annie's inebriated condition. It was that kind of pub: all were welcome and not judged.

'Same poison?' The barman said, in broken English.

'Yeah,' Annie replied, fumbling in her purse to grab a handful of loose change.

Nowadays, alcohol was the only remedy that could mask Annie's panic attacks. It gave her false courage, helped her to sleep and, above all, allowed her to cope with everyday life. Little did she realise just how much damage it was doing to her health. Not that she cared. Looking back, things had not always been this way, at least not until the depression kicked in. Nowadays, Annie's entire life seemed to revolve around her comfort zones. They were the only mental boundaries that Annie felt safe in. Depression and drink were inseparable in Annie's crazy upside down little world. Both were evil, and both utterly debilitating. Besides, who gave a damn that her husband had walked out on her, or that she'd lost her job because of it. Nobody! Even close family and friends had deserted her. But hey, did anyone really understand what she was going through? The emotional battles, the drink demons, and her divorce problems with Luke? Now that was an episode in Annie's life that she could never quite come to terms with. It was the beginning of the end, a desperate downward struggle that had driven her to the very depths of despair.

Through bloodshot eyes, Annie's attentions had inextricably been drawn towards a tall, dark stranger now playing the gaming machine. He was scrawny looking, and wore a black open neck shirt, black trousers and a stylish black leather bomber jacket drawn tight at the waist. His hair was cropped short, and he was sporting a three-day stubble. It wasn't the ridiculous Totectors safety boots he was wearing or the cold steely glint in his eyes. No, it was something else that had drawn Annie's attention towards him.

At a glance, he wasn't as old as Annie had first made him out to be. He was younger, much younger. Not handsome, just scrawny, perhaps a little jaded around the edges. Amused by the stranger's antics, she sat spellbound as the four large chance wheels tumbled into free-fall again. What followed was an endless cacophony of jingles, thumps, bangs and pulsating coloured lights.

Then it struck her.

The stranger was wearing a leg brace.

The room was extremely busy tonight, two deep at the bar; standing room only. Annie recognised a few regular punters in the crowd, *The Stay Clears* as she liked to call them. These were the local drug pushers, the no-goods who plied their evil trade on the vulnerable and brought nothing but misery to the rest of the local community. Not all were bad of course; there were a few decent people amongst them, including her drinking partner Scrumpy Jack. Everybody's friend, Scrumpy was a bit of an oddball. He always wore a black Pork Pie hat full of badges, and had a great sense of humour. There again, he could be extremely violent at times, especially when drunk on cheap cider. Like so many of Annie's so-called drinking partners, the majority had ended up in the gutter of life.

'Hi,' the stranger whispered.

'Piss off.'

'You okay?' he asked.

Annie dug her heels in on the bar stool and spun to face him.

'Lost all your money, pet,' Annie slurred.

There followed a moment's hesitation, a recovering of balance. When the stranger spoke, his words were lost in the general noise of the room. It unsettled her. Devilment shone in his eyes, as he temptingly slid a large double whiskey towards her. It was already too late. Without thinking she leaned over and grasped tight hold of the whisky tumbler as if her whole life depended on it. Her head was swimming, and the drink wasn't helping any either. Leaning over, she playfully tugged on his coat lapel and caught the strong whiff of garlic on his breath. It was weird, the notions that sometimes came into Annie's head. If he wasn't a vampire slayer, then who the hell was he?

'I don't remember asking you for this.'

'You didn't.'

They stared long and hard at one another.

'I don't take drinks from strangers,' Annie mumbled.

'Not even from Lexus?'

Annie wasn't sure what she wanted at this moment, and that name certainly didn't mean anything to her. Should she end it now – before it all got out of hand? What the hell, she cursed. She was beginning to enjoy herself and the stranger seemed fair game.

'Don't push your luck, I'm no whore.'

'You're Annie Jenkins – aren't you?'

Annie drew back. 'Everyone around here knows who I—'

'But do they know you once worked for Gilesgate?' the stranger interrupted.

How could he have possibly known that? She never talked to anyone about her private life; it was her one golden rule. Her past was sacrosanct, and she cherished it beyond everything. Drawn by an irresistible magnetism, Annie sat spellbound by the stranger's alluring antics. He reminded her of an unfinished chapter in a book; incomplete, wanting and yet intriguing. She tried to think logically, anything but this. Then, as another large whiskey tumbler fell into her grasp, she suddenly felt vulnerable.

Twenty minutes later, and the room began to spin. She steadied herself, reached out, and grabbed tight hold of the bar rail. It was then she noticed the deep scar running diagonally across the stranger's brow. Its ugliness fascinated her.

'Tell me about this,' Annie said, teasingly running her finger along the scar line.

The stranger pulled back, brushing her hand aside.

'Don't touch!'

'And why shouldn't I?'

'Cos,' the stranger replied. 'It's not for you to touch.'

Overcome by an overwhelming sense of uncertainty, fear gripped her like never before. Hit with a sudden wave of panic, she lurched for the bar rail, slipped, and fell awkwardly to the floor. Her brain cells were no longer functioning, and the roof of her mouth felt numb. Not for the first time in her life Annie Jenkins had drunk herself into another semi-conscious stupor – she was no longer in control. Amidst the confusion the barman telephoned for a taxi, but it was already too late. The stranger had taken over.

★

There were no other cars in the car park that night, except one. And that was a Mk3 Mondeo. Well it had taken him long enough, hadn't it? This was the perfect end to a perfect evening, Lexus thought. Both arms firmly wrapped around Annie's slim waistline, he bundled her into the back of the stolen vehicle. This was his moment, his part of the bargain, and nothing could stop him now. Camera-free and dimly lit, the car park was the ideal location for what he now had in mind. As he slid in behind the driver's wheel and fired up the engine, he checked his surroundings. Perfect.

Then the voices returned.

Who would have thought of that?

'You're beginning to annoy me – I know what I'm doing.'

You're ever so clever.

'I know. So why must you keep reminding me?

Just checking—

Chapter Twenty

July 2012

The tide was on the ebb as David Carlisle pulled into St Peter's Wharf. Along the marina wall the receding waterline had left its damp tell-tale mark behind, evidence of another high tide. Black mud slime ran steeply down from the wooden jetty to be met by a narrow central water channel. A small flotilla of fishing vessels lay low in the water; the day's catch now in North Shields fish market. Still hung over, Carlisle felt terrible. Rubbing weary bloodshot eyes, he glanced at his watch. It was 7.25am.

'You'll need to suit up,' the familiar voice rang out behind him.

Carlisle straightened in anticipation of what was about to follow. A stickler for detail, any contamination such as minute fibres from his clothing or soil from the soles of his shoes could lead to a false trail. It was Stan Johnson's responsibility to ensure that didn't happen. Not at any cost. Returning to his car, Carlisle struggled into the hooded white paper coveralls, which he'd purposely kept in his boot for such an occasion.

Ducking beneath the police cordon tape, Carlisle was met by the SOC photographer, Peter Davenport. A slightly built man, of average height, with a shock of long blonde hair, Davenport had huge inquisitive eyes that protruded from their sockets like a bubble-eyed goldfish. Above all, it was the little man's exuberance that irritated him most. He was intelligent, with an overpowering sense of enthusiasm that Carlisle found difficult to comprehend.

'What can you tell me?' he asked.

'I believe he's struck again, Mr Carlisle.'

'What do we know about the victim?'

'Young woman, early-forties, slightly built, around five-six. She was found earlier this morning by an old guy walking his dog,' said Davenport, pointing towards a short wooden jetty. 'The dog found her first, but she'd been dead a few hours by all accounts.'

'Any indications as to how she was murdered?'

'It's difficult to say at this stage,' Davenport replied. 'From what I can make out, she'd been badly mutilated.'

'Mutilated?'

'Well, she'd certainly been knocked around a bit,' the SOC photographer said, his huge eyes scanning the marina. 'From the marks on her neck and by the colour of her skin, there's a twenty-quid note says she died choking.'

Carlisle took a step back. His day had started badly; rude awakenings never did put him in a good frame of mind. Out across the river he caught sight of a large gull as it raked close to the water's edge in search of food. He knew the feeling; two paracetamol and a mug of strong black coffee was as much as he could handle himself that morning – *nothing comes easy my friend* – he cursed.

Davenport moved at a canter, and Carlisle had difficulty in keeping up with him. He had a peculiar walking style, unsynchronized, reminding him of an agitated chicken in search of food scraps. Scurrying along the wharf, the police photographer's digital camera continuously thudded against his narrow waistline.

'Do we know who she is?' Carlisle asked.

'Good question.'

'I take it that's a no?'

'Yes, but we're working on it.'

'What time was she found?'

Davenport stopped in his tracks, and then turned. 'According to George Wallace, it would have been around five-thirty.'

'Where's Wallace now?'

'He's assisting the police surgeon, a Doctor Hindson.'

Gathering his bearings, Carlisle stretched his arms and gained some mobility into stiffened limbs. Clambering down a steep wooden ramp, they reached the first of a series of wooden walkways leading out onto the marina. On either side a large array of sailing boats were moored, their halyards clattering against tall metallic masts as a stiff westerly breeze cut directly across their path. It was then he noticed a white tent, standing at the end of the jetty. Following closely in Davenport's footsteps, he approached the last few yards with trepidation. It was little moments like this that always sent his adrenaline racing.

The outstretched gloved hand felt sincere, and the face had a familiar look.

'In here,' said DS Wallace, holding back the flap of the forensic tent. 'It's not a pretty sight, I'm afraid.'

'Where's Jack Mason?' he asked.

'He's on his way.' Wallace grinned, glancing back along the empty jetty as if to confirm his statement. 'That should give us plenty of time before the shit hits the fan.'

Stepping aside, Carlisle caught sight of the young woman's half naked body. She'd been strung up like a ship's figurehead. Arms extended, the palms upturned and hammerhead nails driven through both wrists. Her dress, torn away from the upper torso, revealed a small pair of white breasts. Deep lacerations ran diagonally across the soft fleshy tissues, suggesting a blunt instrument had been used. He stood for a while, staring at her face. She had an understated beauty, as if posed in freeze frame. Her head had fallen forward, tilting slightly right; the chin pressed heavily against the breastbone keeping the mouth firmly shut. All the warnings were there. The sickening egoistic signs of ritualized mutilation, systematic crucifixion violently displayed as an artist's brush strokes.

Who are you, he asked himself? *What has he done to you?*

Whoever she was, she had met an untimely ending. Of that he was certain.

'How long has she been dead?' Carlisle asked.

'It's difficult to be precise,' said Wallace. 'Not more than six hours, I'd say. No doubt the doctor will fill you in on the details, but I fear the Coroner will insist on a full investigation.' Wallace shuffled awkwardly. 'Which means it'll take much longer.'

Carlisle squeezed past the doctor's portly figure, but said nothing. He studied the victim's eyes, wide open, frozen and staring into emptiness.

'Any indications as to how she was murdered, Doc?'

The doctor glowered. 'Asphyxiation . . .'

'Was she strangled?'

Ignoring him, Dr Hindson continued to run a wooden spatula beneath the young woman's fingernails, placing his findings in a small flat plastic dish. 'Had you looked closer, you would have found no sign of garrotting. The throat bruising, especially around the region of the trachea is typical with throttling. There's also heavy bruising at the nape of the neck, consistent with concentrated thumb pressure.'

Taken aback by his clinical abruptness, Carlisle was immediately put on the defensive. Dr Hindson's professionalism was unquestionable, but his arrogance unforgivable. Turning to face him, Carlisle refrained from retaliation.

'I take it she was attacked from behind?'

'Yes,' the Doctor grunted.

'Any trace evidence?'

'Ah. Now that should have been your first question,' Dr Hindson replied, truculently. 'It appears your killer wore gloves. He came prepared in other words, which suggests to me we're dealing with a pretty shrewd cookie here.'

The doctor made a little grimace as he bent over to examine the dead woman's hands.

'I would have anticipated seeing more blood—'

'She wasn't killed here,' interrupted Wallace.

Carlisle stood to face him. 'You mean she was deliberately brought here before he carried out his handiwork. Is that what you're saying?'

'It rather looks that way,' Wallace nodded.

The sound of heavy footsteps along the wooden jetty signalled Jack Mason's timely arrival. His approach was direct, and straight to the point.

'Anyone know who she is, Wallace?'

'No. Not at this stage.'

Mason brushed past him, peering inquisitively at the woman's body. 'Well, it certainly looks like his handiwork,' said Mason, pulling out his notebook. 'And he's definitely gone to town on this one.'

'It would appear so.' Wallace nodded.

Mason turned to Carlisle. 'What do you think, David?'

Carlisle recognized the signs, and chose his next words carefully. 'He definitely likes to display them with a certain artistic panache. It's not your everyday kind of murder.'

'He's persistent; I'll give the bastard that,' Mason retorted.

'Predictable more like,' Carlisle sighed. 'And it's fast becoming his trademark.'

Mason turned sharply towards where George Wallace was now standing. 'I want this whole area sealed off. No press, no cameras, and no budding TV presenters spouting off unnecessary panic. Do I make myself clear?'

'Yes, boss,' said Wallace, now pinned up against the tent wall in an attempt to avoid Mason's flaying arms.

'And you can—'

'I would concentrate some effort around the new development area, Jack,' the doctor interrupted. 'She was dragged here after she was murdered – you'll need to establish where.'

'Did you hear that, Wallace?' said Mason.

'I'm on it, boss.'

'Report to the Crime Scene Manager, I want this place run over with a fine tooth comb . . . no stones unturned. Nothing moves in and nothing moves out of here, until you're completely satisfied that you've covered every inch of the ground.'

George Wallace's complexion had turned a jaundiced colour.

'I'll see to it, boss.'

Pen poised at the ready, Mason's look was stern.

'What else do you have for me, Henry?'

The doctor flicked an annoying strand of silky white hair away from a wizened face. He looked late fifties, chunky with an overhanging belly that suggested he was fond of good living. His movements were methodical, deliberate as though speed was an intolerable word in his personal diary. 'There are no physical signs of a struggle, and the heat generated from the brain suggests she's been dead around five hours. That would place the time of death around . . . one, one thirty,' the doctor said, pausing to recover his breath. 'She'd been brutally beaten about the head and body before manual strangulation took place, I'm convinced of that. There's also heavy loss of skin tissue on the backs of both heels, which suggests she was dragged here after he killed her.'

Carlisle watched as the doctor ran his spatula over the deep lacerations on the young woman's breasts, before continuing. 'Any visible mutilations such as the ones seen here, and here, were carried out post-mortem interval. In other words, the time that elapsed after he strangled her to the time of her being brought here.'

'Anything else I should know?' Mason asked.

'One thing's for sure, Jack, your killer's no surgeon.'

'Any indications as to where this could have all taken place?'

'Where he practised his surgery,' the doctor sighed. 'He probably did it within thirty minutes of killing her. Exactly where, you'll need to talk that over with forensics. By the loss of skin tissue on her heels, I'd say she'd been dragged here over a considerable distance. Find her shoes and you'll not be far away from the scene of the crime.'

Mason checked his notes.

'And you're convinced she never put up a struggle?'

'I'm certain,' the doctor replied.

'That's strange; they usually put up some form of resistance. Surely, she must have known that she was about to meet her death?' said Mason.

The doctor nodded thoughtfully. 'Perhaps she was unconscious through drink, or smacked out of her mind on drugs. Under either of those circumstances, the victim is usually in no fit state to put up a fight. There is of course the use of Rohypnol, but I doubt your killer used that method. He's far too advanced to stoop that low.'

'Not much to go on, eh?'

'I'm afraid not, Jack. We'll need to bring her in and open her up. Let's see what the Coroner's investigation throws up.'

Mason pointed to the side of the young woman's head. 'The bruising and lacerations to the face?' he asked.

'Like I say, she'd been knocked around a bit before she was strangled.'

'Any sign of a weapon being used?'

'No. The wounds are pretty consistent with physical blows, in my opinion.'

'It sounds like her exit was a horrific affair.' Mason shrugged.

The doctor removed his surgical gloves, tossing them into his medical bag. 'For her sake, let's hope it was quick.'

Mason shook his head. 'What a fucking mess!'

'Murder is never pleasant at the best of times, I'm afraid,' the doctor replied.

'Unfortunately I'm left with another stiff on my hands – and, a whole lot of explaining to do,' Mason conceded grudgingly.

'You'll think of something, Jack,' the doctor grinned. 'You always do.'

Stepping aside, the doctor closed the lid of his medical bag and made to leave. Amidst the mumbling, Mason turned to face him. 'It's ironic to think that it would take another murder to bring us a little closer to the truth, Doc.'

Dr Hindson shook his head. 'It's always the case, Jack. By the look of things, this one's methods are pretty consistent.'

'Damn!' Mason cursed. 'What kind of a monster are we dealing with here?'

Carlisle sensed the unease. This was no vendetta killing; this murder had all the hallmarks of another psychopathic killing. At times such as these, the strange intricacies and bizarre fantasies of a serial killer's mind didn't bear thinking about. Their victims, nearly always hapless pawns in a wicked world of reverie, were regarded as mere instruments of pleasure to satisfy their warped minds. Sadly, and to make matters worse, there was the chilling factor of their rational and calculating approach to their work. Yes, he'd faced plenty of it before, but this murder was brutally different.

'He's acquired a taste for it,' said Carlisle, 'and that bothers me.'

Mason scowled, raising his finger and stabbing the air at him. 'Then he must be stopped, and quickly.'

'I know, but *how*, is the problem.'

'Surely he's left something behind for us, a small scrap of evidence perhaps?'

Carlisle fell silent, thinking. 'I'll admit they normally become complacent and forget the detail. Their irrationality always surfaces one way or another, and hey presto . . .'

'Yeah, but this bastard's cunning with it.' Mason shrugged.

Carlisle recognized the hurt, the deflated ego. Somehow Jack Mason looked older, much older. His eyes were withdrawn, bloodshot, as if the lights had suddenly been switched off. Removing his spectacles, the profiler breathed heavily on the lenses before giving them a quick wipe. The fact the killer still had a mission to accomplish, worried him. Serial killers started slowly, built up their confidence, until reaching a point where the killings become more frequent. All the tell-tale signs were there, the little idiosyncrasies that this one seemed to use. He stood for a while. Hands in pockets, shoulders slightly slouched towards the ground. The early morning chill had lost none of its edge, but he still felt the warm rays of the sun as it played on his cheeks. Beyond the steep ramp, the wharf was now a hive of activity. Fanned out in extended line, a group of uniformed police officers were carrying out a fingertip search. Close to the water line, he watched as a small team of forensic experts gathered up anything and everything of interest. Sometimes they would get lucky, he thought, come up trumps with a small scrap of evidence.

Suddenly he felt the knot in the pit of his stomach tighten.

'His victims are all connected, Jack,' Carlisle said. 'It's as if they belong to the same shopping list. One at a time, calculated, cold premeditated slaughter. It's the trait of the Missionary killer . . . they see it as a gradual process of elimination.'

'The son of a bitch,' Mason responded excitedly. 'You make it all sound so bloody simple. Don't tell me he's working through some sort of human inventory.'

'He probably is, and he won't stop until he's totally eliminated everyone on it.'

The silence between them felt strange, uncomfortable, as though Mason was deliberately ignoring the heated signals now passing between them. Was this Jack Mason's way of dealing with it, he wondered.

Replacing his spectacles, Carlisle's attention was suddenly drawn towards the end of the jetty, where the appearance of the coroner's body bag party was making heavy work of a steep wooden ramp. Dressed in white coveralls and wearing green rubber gloves, the four-man team was struggling to keep in time as they conveyed a large wooden casket towards the end of the jetty. Carried by the handles, waist height, they progressed as one. On reaching their destination they turned smartly inwards, at the foot of the corpse. Their leader, a grave faced standard-bearer, removed a crumpled document from an inside pocket and thrust it under Mason's nose. His voice, sombre, was tinged with authority.

'The victim's body has been cleared with the Home Office pathologist, Chief Inspector.'

Mason shook his head, as though resigned to the finality. It was an undignified, needless ending, and a pitiful waste of life, thought Carlisle. Once they knew the woman's identity, it would be a simple case of legwork. Until then, it was a painful process of elimination.

Turning on heel, together they made their way back along the wooden jetty.

'It sounds daft, I know,' said Mason. 'But I do feel much closer to him now.'

Carlisle nodded. 'You're getting to know him, Jack.'

'Is that what it is?' Mason replied, turning sharply to face him.

On their reaching the little Bistro Bar, beyond the police cordon tape, Carlisle caught sight of the local TV crews. Cameras poised at the ready, they surged forward in anticipation of yet another headline breaking story.

He stood for a while, and took one last lingering look at St Peter's Wharf and the haunting activity surrounding it. Normally a peaceful community, this was the last place he would have anticipated to find a serial killer hanging around in. Within easy walking distance of Newcastle's city centre, it certainly offered a different kind of lifestyle to the everyday bustle of the city. Not today, Carlisle shrugged. Today it was different.

Chapter
Twenty-One

The Home Office pathologist, Dr Jillian King, put the cause of the woman's death as – *asphyxia by manual strangulation*. Although horrifically mutilated, she had suffered little at the hands of her attacker. Damage to the thyroid cartilage and a broken hyoid bone supported the findings of a quick death. The report also confirmed the early stages of sclerosis of the liver, a condition that had little bearing on the murder, but one which enabled the investigating team to reach a swift conclusion. Jack Mason's ground troops had moved swiftly, uncovering a notorious alehouse barely a stone's throw from the River Tyne. The victim, a local alcoholic called Annie Jenkins, was the former personal assistant to Sir Jeremy Wingate-Stiles. How convenient was that?

Of course, Jenkins' insatiable drinking habits had been well documented. Sadly, her decline and loss of social respectability within the community had ended in tragic consequences. And, needless to say, the case had taken on another twist. Considered a weak link in Gilesgate's organisation, Jenkins still had access to some highly sensitive documents. The question was now: did she know her killer?

The morning chill had quickly given way to warmth, as David Carlisle drove into the carpark at police headquarters in Ponteland. He was met by a hostile group of reporters – Annie Jenkins' brutal murder had unquestionably caused a major stir amongst the media ranks. Fear, it seemed, had spread like wildfire, and people were demanding answers. Now calling the killer *The Wharf Butcher,* the press were having a field day.

Clearing security, Carlisle shared the elevator with DS Wallace. Struggling with a pile of case files, he reached over and pressed the lift button. As the doors slid open, Carlisle instinctively took off towards the operations room.

'The venue's been changed,' Wallace said.

'Changed, changed to where?'

'It's now being held in the Conference Suite.'

'That's an odd place to hold a team briefing.'

'I know,' said Wallace, the cop inside him surfacing, 'but the senior brass are now involved.'

Following in Wallace's footsteps, he strode at pace along a narrow central corridor passing numerous laboratories and anterooms along the way. The place reeked of forensics, a mixture of antiseptic and volatile cleaning fluids, which immediately attacked Carlisle's sense of smell.

'I see Sir Jeremy's made all the morning tabloids,' Wallace grumbled. 'The guy's a bloody menace, if you ask me. He's never out of the headlines nowadays.'

'What's he up to now?'

'Not a lot, but he certainly knows how to drip feed the media with all the right kind of information. In return, he gets primetime coverage,' Wallace said, pointing the way ahead. 'I never liked the guy from the moment I first clapped eyes on him.'

'It's called politics, George,' Carlisle grinned.

'Whatever?'

Wallace's statement made sense. The idea that a mainstream politician was able to poke his nose into police affairs didn't sit well with a lot of top senior brass. A notorious public critic, Sir Jeremy had spent his entire political career exploiting other people's weaknesses. Renowned for his associations with the more unscrupulous paparazzi, Sir Jeremy's dubious methods of scoring political points was frustrating to say the least. Grave news and obnoxious politicians sold papers, regardless of how many people's lives it destroyed. Having outlasted three prime ministers, five by-elections and countless courtroom writs, it spoke volumes about Sir Jeremy's integrity. How he'd managed to remain in public office beggared belief. But he had.

Moments later they entered a large circular building known as THE CARLTON SUITE. It was brightly lit, with laminate flooring and cream walls, and three large north-facing windows overlooking rolling open countryside. Freshly decorated, the room smelt of emulsion paint, Carlisle thought.

'What took so you long, George?' Mason asked.

'I got here as fast as I could, boss. The press isn't helping any either.'

'Where's the rest of the team?'

'They're on their way over, boss.'

Glancing up from behind a large glass fronted lectern, Mason made no reply. Three rows of chairs neatly set out in front of him, gave the impression he was about to head up a tribunal hearing. It was that kind of briefing, calculated and far from informal. As the room began to fill, the odd strangers amongst them were obviously the senior back room staff; the variety seldom seen in broad daylight. The late arrival of the Assistant Chief Constable brought with it a sombre reticence, broken only by the whirr of the closing window blinds as the room was plunged into semi-darkness.

First, Mason took them through the forensic evidence, followed by key eyewitness accounts leading up to Annie Jenkins' murder. According to the events timeline, around nine-thirty on the night in question, she was last seen sprawled out across the back seat of a stolen Ford Mondeo, being driven at speed from the Phoenix public house in Gateshead. The vehicle's driver was described as a tall, thin set, white male Caucasian. Dressed all in black, his age was given as twenty-five to thirty.

'Vic. What's the latest feedback on the pub's CCTV?' Mason asked.

'There wasn't any,' Miller shrugged.

'What do mean, there wasn't any?'

'On the night in question, the pub's CCTV system was switched off.'

'That's a fat lot of good. What did the landlord have to say?'

Miller braced himself. 'Earlier that evening the punters had been watching a European football match. Milan verses Arsenal. It was a great game, but a crap result if you were an Arsenal fan. They got hammered four-nil. Anyway, after the match the landlord simply forgot to switch the system back on again.'

'More likely the tight bastard didn't have a Sky Sports Box Office licence,' jested PC Dobson.

A few titters of laughter broke out, but it was short lived.

'That means we lost our best chance of getting a positive ID on the driver,' said Mason, still holding the young constable's glances.

'Sorry, boss. I was merely raising a point.'

'And a bad one at that,' said Mason, turning to face the rest of the team. 'OK. What other CCTV coverage have we managed to secure, Kev?'

DS Morrison clenched his jaw. Having attended just about every type of road traffic accident there was to see, nothing surprised him anymore. The Sergeant's only pet hate was attending fatal road traffic accidents where young children were involved. With six grandkids of his own, he detested the emotional stress involved.

'There were fifteen live cameras operating in the area that night. All but four have been accounted for. The rest were none operational.'

'Do we have a fix on the type of vehicle used?'

'Yes,' said DS Morrison. 'It was a Mk3 Mondeo.'

Mason shuffled awkwardly. 'A Mondeo . . .'

'I know, and there seems to be a general pattern building here.'

'Remind me of the car used in the Riley murders?' asked Mason.

As he spoke, Morrison kept referring to his notes. 'There was no CCTV coverage available on that murder enquiry, boss. However, tyre treads left at the crime scene matched those of a Mondeo found abandoned on Shields Road in Chillingham.'

'In other words . . . the same vehicle,' said Mason.

'Yes, but I think we may have another small problem here.'

'Problem?' said Mason.

The sergeant raised an eyebrow. 'Our suspect seems to have found a method of disarming this type of vehicle's security system. He's clever with electronics, by the look of things.'

'Good work, Kev. Let's run an Automatic Number Plate Recognition on every Mk3 Mondeo in the area. I believe the A1M motorway is still covered by a number of fixed cameras, is it not?'

The Sergeant nodded.

'Let's start by covering both directions between Gateshead and Cramlington.'

'That's one hell of a stretch of road,' the Sergeant added.

'I don't care. I want round-the-clock surveillance on this one.'

'It's just an observation,' said George Wallace. 'In the event of any vehicle pursuit, unmarked patrol cars tend to give us better results . . . you may wish to consider it.'

'Good point, George. Let's go with that and see what results it brings in.'

The tension was building.

Turning to the Coroner's report, Mason outlined the deep lacerations to Jenkins' upper torso, as being drawn from left to right – the hallmark of a left-handed attacker. Described as six foot two, slightly built, and exceptionally strong, the killer was thought to be local. Things were coming along nicely, thought Carlisle. They had a few solid leads, forensic on the footwear, and a clear description of their suspect's physical characteristics. Now that Ernest Stanton's murder was back in the frame, Mason was concentrating on the kill zones. Not a bad idea, he though, as he scribbled down some ideas and put them to the back of mind.

They spent the next fifteen minutes running back over the possibilities. Times, locations, the latest forensic developments; nothing was left to chance.

'Vic,' said Mason. 'Where are we with these new investigations of yours?'

The DS checked his files, and made a point of standing. 'We've had an interesting breakthrough involving a Baltimore clipper called *Cleveland*. Commissioned by Gilesgate to carry out its coastal survey operations, it's currently registered with the Port of Tyne Authorities. The point I'm making is this,' said Miller, holding up a well-thumbed document. 'We are now able to monitor her comings and goings, besides keeping a regular check on her passenger lists.'

Mason gave him a quizzical look. 'OK. So what's the connection?'

'Well,' Miller said, scratching the side of his face, 'that's an interesting question. As it turns out, the majority of Gilesgate's board are using her as a regular meeting place.'

A loud cheer rang out around the room.

'Nice one,' Mason said approvingly. 'Anything involving Gilesgate has to be of major interest to us. There's a link here somewhere. If not, then why is the killer targeting only Gilesgate board members?'

The noise levels heightened.

'Does anyone have anything to add?' Mason said.

'Yes, boss,' Luke James answered, holding up an arm. 'We've had a stroke of luck with our low-key surveillance operations.'

Mason gave James a long-suffering look. 'Nothing to do with this corner shop lead, has it?'

'No boss, it's better than that,' said James. 'Lunchtime yesterday, Henry Fraser checked into the Copthorne Hotel on Newcastle Quayside where he met with Trevor Radcliffe—'

Mason cut in. 'For those not aware, Trevor Radcliffe is a senior board member and has major financial interests in Gilesgate. He's clever with numbers, apparently.'

'Cheers, Jack,' said James, frantically unloosening his tie. 'As I was saying, late yesterday afternoon they were joined by Thomas Schlesinger. He was the other half of Anderson & Schlesinger law practice.'

'Hold on,' said Mason. 'I thought Schlesinger sold out on his half of the business after he had a major stroke?'

'He did, boss.'

'Any idea what he was doing there yesterday afternoon?'

James shook his head. 'No. That's the puzzling bit.'

'Isn't he still mates with Sir Jeremy?' asked Mason.

'And Henry Fraser,' said Miller. 'If you ask me, the three of them are up to no good. It could be coincidence, of course, but I'm not convinced.'

Carlisle had an inkling of where this was all heading.

'Do you think the killer may have spooked these people?' said Mason.

'There could be an element of that, I suppose.' James rolled his eyes as he glanced around at the others. 'Mind, this Henry Fraser runs half of Newcastle and is well known to the police.'

Mason didn't respond immediately. He just stood there and thought about it.

Luke James continued. 'Like I say, Fraser's a muscle man. That's why he hired John Matthew to go after this Wharf Butcher in the first place. Now that Matthew is out of the equation, it wouldn't surprise me if Fraser wasn't planning something very similar.'

'That sounds plausible,' said Mason, through tight lips. 'Let's keep this operation low key, and see what develops. The last thing we want to do is to ruffle Fraser's feathers.'

James remained standing, and it was making Mason uncomfortable. They discussed it some more, before the Sergeant finally sat down.

'Right then,' said Mason. 'It seems avarice is the common denominator in all of this. Derek Riley's murder was a straightforward case of opportunist investment gone wrong, whereas Charles Anderson's death was one of pure greed. What does that tell us? We know that every board member has invested heavily into Gilesgate, and there's an awful lot of money slushing about in the system. In which case we must ask ourselves the question, is our killer one of them?'

'It's possible, but where does that leave Ernest Stanton's murder in the grand scheme of things?' Wallace commented.

Mason was quick to respond. 'Having made vast fortunes out of criminalizing flood defence contracts, he'd obviously gone a step too far? This is all about money, George. I'm convinced of that.'

The room fell silent.

Carlisle put his writing pad down, and chewed over the DCI's last statement. Mason had got it all wrong. Nothing unusual there, he thought. Besides, serial killers seldom kill for monetary gain. And another thing, there was nothing to indicate that Annie Jenkins' murder was financially driven. No, this was about retribution; someone with a grudge. As far as he was concerned, the killer could be suffering from severe dissociative identity disorder – a condition in which two or more distinct identities or personality states alternatively take control of a person. It made more sense, at least to him it did. There again, how was he going to convince everyone else?

As the morning wore on, the raising of the window blinds finally brought the meeting to a close. It was Thursday, close to the weekend, and Carlisle was looking forward to some quality time off.

Caught unawares, Mason approached him on his blind side.

'We need to talk.'

'Talk, talk about what?'

'I need to run a few things past you.'

'Like what?'

Mason suddenly glanced at him as if they'd been lifelong friends. 'There's a little Mexican restaurant on the Promenade in Whitley Bay, it's called *Tortilla*. Meet me there, seven-thirty, Monday night.'

Something was afoot, and it didn't exactly fill Carlisle with confidence.

Not a good move, he thought.

Chapter Twenty-Two

Sitting on the banks of the River Coquet, enjoying the breathtaking views, David Carlisle could not think of a more enjoyable way to unwind, relax and retreat from the stresses of everyday life. It was a beautiful location and one full of fond memories. Earlier that morning, both he and his father had pitched their tent on a flat, grassy spur overlooking a long, gentle bend in the river. After a quick bite to eat, his father had settled down in his favourite spot, to fish for sea trout. They'd fished this same stretch of water together for as long as Carlisle could remember. With runs of salmon and sea trout and an excellent population of wild brown trout, the river offered anglers excellent sport amongst some of the most spectacular scenery in Northumberland. From early February until late October the salmon season runs, but anything caught before mid-June had to be released back into the river. There was one fish, though; a gigantic sea trout named *Herman,* his father had spent a lifetime trying to catch. Somehow it had always eluded him, but today felt different.

Out in the middle of the river, wearing a fawn RT Fly vest, green Bib 'n' Brace waders, fawn tee shirt and matching baseball cap, his father looked the part. He watched as the old man, now standing in two-feet of fast flowing water, overhead cast for the umpteenth time. Without warning, his rod suddenly bent double. Oh dear, he thought, it could only mean one thing. Herman? As another minnow was about to turn into a Moby Dick, Carlisle braced himself for the inevitable.

'She's a whopper, Davy boy,' his father called out excitedly. 'Make sure you have the landing net ready.'

'Give him a little more slack,' Carlisle shouted.

'I am.'

'He needs more, Pop.'

Picking up a large landing net, Carlisle moved quickly towards the water's edge and closer to where his father was now standing. Experience had taught him that along this fast flowing stretch of water, it was much safer to use a net. Without one, it was almost impossible to land a fish, as simply reeling them in usually ended in disaster.

As the fish ran for the cover of deeper water, he studied the confidence in the old man's hands. His father's reflexes were excellent, but his brain was far too slow to react to fast changing situations. As the tip of the rod bent double, Carlisle's heart sank. Locked in mortal combat, they were pitting their wits against one another.

'I know your game, you sly little tinker,' his father yelled.

The moment the fish reached safer water, Carlisle smelt trouble. Then, without warning, his father unexpectedly yanked on the rod.

'He's snagged, Pop,' Carlisle hollered.

'I've got him this time, Davy boy.'

'No! You need more slack on your line.'

The old man hesitated.

Like the crack of a ringmaster's whip, the line suddenly gave way, spilling his father into the fast running water. Carlisle had always tried to prepare himself for moments such as this, but the truth be told, his father's pride had taken another severe knock. Landing flat on his back, he had somehow managed to keep a tight hold of his prized fishing rod – but only just. This wasn't the first time he'd fallen into the river, and it certainly wasn't the last. Now in his late-seventies, he still had the enthusiasm of someone half his age, but time was fast catching up with him, sadly.

'Did you see that, son?'

'You're not suggesting it was him?'

'Of course it was him. Who else could have done that?'

Carlisle shook his head in bewilderment.

'Look how he took that fly down?' his father went on. 'It takes a special kind of fish to do that, son.'

'He certainly got the better of you this time.' Carlisle grinned.

'Maybe, but he won't pull that little stunt on me again.'

A memory tugged at him. Private thoughts of a small boy and a caring father who had taught him all there was to know about the good things in life. Changing into a spare dry shirt, his father returned to the edge of the riverbank – a high spot – where they could dangle their feet in the cool, fast flowing water. Theirs was an ideal location, and one in which they'd spent many a memorable day together. Snapping open the lid of the hamper basket, it appeared his father had brought enough food to keep them alive for a fortnight. Sandwiches, cheese, cakes, even a homemade sausage-meat pie, wrapped in a white cotton napkin; the aroma was delicious. Regrettably his father's pastry wasn't up to much. It always gave him chronic indigestion, but he never complained, accepting it as part of their little ritual.

'The first time I brought you here, you were a young boy of six,' his father chuckled.

'I know, Pop, you never stop reminding me.'

'Is that so?'

'Yes. You tell me at least once a month.'

His father chuckled away to himself, brushing aside an annoying wasp that was trying to get at his sandwich. He studied his father's weather beaten face; still full of enthusiasm.

'Did I ever tell you about the time I bought you a new fishing rod, son?'

'No, I don't believe you did. Why?'

He watched as his father wiped the crumbs from his chin, opened up the napkin, and went back into deep thought again. 'It only cost me a tenner, but it was the best ten quid I ever spent. It wasn't one of those cheap bamboo rods either; this one was made out of carbon fibre.'

'Carbon fibre—'

'Uh-huh. It was the best rod that money could buy in those days.'

'You've never told me this story before.'

The old man's face lit up. 'You never asked until now.'

Carlisle thought about it, but held back. His father's memory wasn't all it used to be. There again, he did have a nasty habit of repeating himself at least a dozen times or more.

'Carbon fibre – no wonder I was the envy of the school,' said Carlisle, prodding his father's thoughts.

'It was a cracking rod,' the old man said, shaking his head as if reliving a memory. 'Times were hard back then, people didn't have the same kind of money they throw about nowadays. Your mum and I had a hell of a struggle to make ends meet. Everything was expensive, even the price of food . . . imagine that!'

'So how did you manage to pay for the rod?'

His father's face fell, a guilty look. 'Fortunately your Uncle Bert worked in a city warehouse; he knew a few people, and was forever bringing stuff back to the house.'

Carlisle grinned. 'You're not telling me you bought it on the black market, surely not?'

The old man chuckled to himself. Turning, he pulled on the broken fishing line, and began wrapping it around a small twig. Every now and then the line would snag, but his strong withered hands quickly pulled it free again.

'It was definitely him—'

'Who, Pop? Who are we talking about now?'

The old man puffed out his cheeks again and expelled a long drawn out breath. Seconds later he removed his baseball cap and scratched the top of his head with his long fingernails.

'You know who I'm talking about, son.'

'Herman!'

'Who else could it have been?'

'Are you sure it was him,' Carlisle teased.

'It was him all right, and I'd swear he's getting careless.' The old man tilted his head back as if to jog another memory. 'He's never snatched at my bait like that before. No, he normally likes to tease me. He's getting up to his old tricks again, and we'll need to keep an eye on him, son.'

'If Herman was still alive, he would be at least fifty years old by now.'

'Poppycock,' his father replied. 'That son of a gun is getting up to his old games again. One thing's for sure, he's lost none of his cunning.'

Carlisle sat stunned. Five months into their hunt for the killer, and they were no further forward in catching him. Whoever he was, it took a special kind of nerve to recreate death, if that's what he was trying to do? And yes, all of his murders were staged, a macabre theatrical performance of grotesque exhibitionism. First he would draw them in, and then he would tease them on. Catching a serial killer was not unlike catching an imaginary fish called Herman. There was a subtle difference of course: catching the Wharf Butcher would take more than a stroke of pure genius. He realised that. *Nobody said it would be easy.*

'What makes you think it was Herman, Pop?'

'Of course it was him.'

'How can you tell, you never saw him?'

'Cos,' his father replied. 'Over time I've come to know all of his little mannerisms. The way he moves, his cunning behaviour, he won't fool me next time.'

He had heard that story a thousand times, but never tired of hearing it. For the past thirty years, theirs had been a personal crusade; a true love-hate relationship, and one that his father would take with him to his grave. Unscrewing the lid off the metal thermos flask, Carlisle poured the last of the coffee into two large plastic mugs. They both took it black, the stronger the better. He studied his father's reactions as he stared out across the river. He still had a good head of hair; it ran in the family, passed down through the generations from father to son. Although a little thin on top, its colour – refined silver – gave him that distinguished look that can only be acquired with age.

As the light began to fade, they packed their fishing tackle in the boot of his father's old estate car and prepared to leave. Having bagged a few trout and a half a dozen eels, the afternoon had flown by. There was no more mention of Herman; a fish that was neither perch, bream, pike, or carp. Herman was purely a figment of his father's imagination – or so Carlisle believed.

Forty minutes later, they approached the outskirts of Cramlington. It wasn't despair that was dragging Carlisle down; he had no time for the dark side of the soul. No. It was his inability to uncover the Wharf Butcher's reasoning; what made him tick?

Then it suddenly dawned on him.

Chapter Twenty-Three

David Carlisle leaned back against the bar and closed his eyes. He was having a bad day. First the fridge door had collapsed on him, spilling milk all over the kitchen floor. Then his accountant had phoned, warning him that his business was in grave danger of folding. If that wasn't bad enough, earlier that morning, he'd dropped Jackie's clothes off at the local charity shop and was now having grave doubts about it. He took another deep breath, knocked back the rest of his lager and tried to shrug off his woes.

Intentionally late, it was eight-forty when Jack Mason nonchalantly breezed into Tortilla Mexican restaurant on the Promenade in Whitley Bay. His mood seemed relaxed. Wearing a bright red Hawaiian shirt, blue jeans, sneakers, and sporting Ray Ban sunglasses, the DCI looked every bit the star in a 'Hawaii Five-O' movie.

'I thought we'd chill out tonight, without the usual distractions,' Mason said.

The moment the floor manager spotted him, they were ushered to a prime table overlooking the North Sea and offered a round of free drinks. Minutes later George Wallace joined them. The Detective Sergeant's unruffled demeanour always gave Carlisle the impression he never suffered stress. Not pushy like the rest, it was the one quality that Carlisle admired most about the man. He watched in amusement as Wallace's eyes darted inquisitively over Jack Mason's gaudy shirt. God it was awful, reminding him of Blackpool illuminations: pillar-box red, and decorated with large olive green palm trees and white birds of paradise.

'That's a real snazzy shirt, boss,' said Wallace.

'I'm glad you like it, George, cos it's one of my favourites.'

'Nice one—'

Mason shuffled awkwardly. 'How long did it take you to get here, George?' Mason asked, desperately trying to change the subject.

'Just under fifty minutes,' Wallace replied. 'I caught the Metro to Whitley Bay and walked the rest of the way on foot.'

'So tell me, how's your golf handicap doing nowadays?'

'I'm still off eight, but I don't seem to have the spare time to play nowadays.'

'Why not try out one of the local driving ranges?'

Wallace thought for a moment, unbuttoned his top shirt button and adjusted his position. 'Nah, it's not my scene, Jack.'

After what seemed an eternity, Mason peered authoritatively down at the menu.

'Don't worry about ordering lads; I'll get the chef to knock us up one of his specials.'

Wallace nodded his approval, but said nothing. When the starters did eventually arrive – carried shoulder high on a large pewter platter – they were placed in the centre of the table. Wine glass in his hand, Jack Mason leaned over and did a quick mental check. 'If you like your food mild, these are fine,' he said, obligingly pushing his fork into one of many side dishes now covering the table top. 'But if you want your arse to glow like the cosmic universe, try these little devils.'

Without warning, the hot chilli sauce suddenly hit the back of Carlisle's throat as if his whole mouth was on fire. God it was hot, hellishly hot. Reaching over he grabbed a jug of ice water, and took a huge swig from it. He could barely breathe.

'As I was saying,' said Mason, staring quizzically across at him. 'I'm seconding George here to help in our investigations into Gilesgate. In return, I need a big favour of you.'

He'd been conned, big time. He should have realised that the minute he stepped into the restaurant. This was no social gathering; this meeting was planned, meticulously, right down to the very last detail. Even the setting was Mason's choice. God, Carlisle cursed, how could he have been so gullible?

'What kind of favour are we talking about?'

'Let's push that to one side for a moment,' Mason said. 'I've been thinking about John Matthew, and his connections with Henry Fraser.' Mason stared into the bottom of his empty glass, his face expressionless. 'Now that Fraser's declared his intentions, there's a good chance he'll lead us to the Wharf Butcher. But there lies a problem: how much does Fraser actually know?'

Wallace shot him a sideways glance. 'That's a difficult one. He could be bluffing of course. On the other hand—'

Mason shook his head despairingly. 'My gut feeling tells me there's a lot more to Fraser's partnership with Sir Jeremy than first meets the eye. Fraser's got form; he's well known to us, and has a criminal record as long as your arm. That's why I've decided to put a twenty-four-seven surveillance team on the two of them.'

'So,' said Wallace. 'What happens to John Matthew now?'

'We let him stew a while, George . . . let him think about his future,' said Mason. 'When he does eventually recover from his injuries, he's probably facing a twenty-five year stretch anyway.'

'Bugger me!' Wallace grimaced.

Carlisle stared at the two of them. 'So what are your plans for me?'

'I've been giving that a lot of thought lately.' Mason tapped a finger on the side of his forehead, as though about to unearth another well-kept secret. 'I need you two to run a health check over Gilesgate's senior management for me. We need to get closer to these people, find out what we're really up against.'

'Fine by me,' said Wallace. 'But do we know where Sir Jeremy's interests lie?'

'One thing for sure, it's not legitimate. No, George, this whole operation needs to be kept low-key. The last thing I need is the media getting hold of it.'

Carlisle rolled his eyes. 'I hope you're not asking me to work undercover?'

'WHAT?' Mason's face darkened. 'You're a private investigator – that's what you're paid to do, isn't it?'

'Like hell it is.'

Mason flapped his hands up and down as if to cool the atmosphere.

'At least hear me out first. If I leave it to my chaps, they'll only go in heavy-handed and we'll lose the initiative. No, we need a more subtle approach.'

'That's absurd,' said Carlisle. 'This has nothing to do with criminal profiling?'

The DCI looked fit to explode. 'My first priority is to catch the Wharf Butcher, put a stop to his killing. But that gives me a major headache; we have absolutely no idea why he chooses to target only Gilesgate's board of directors.' Mason pushed back in his seat. 'One thing's for sure, wherever money's concerned it usually brings out the worst in people.'

'I couldn't agree more,' said Wallace, chewing on a piece of chicken.

'Let's put ourselves in Sir Jeremy's shoes,' said Mason. 'There's this maniac out there who is hell bent on tearing your boardroom apart, but you can't go to the police. Why not? Because they'll only go poking their noses into your business affairs, and that's the last thing you want them to do. So what alternatives do you have?' Mason bent over and recharged his glass. 'You can, of course, get someone take care of your problems for you.'

'Henry Fraser!' Wallace smirked, wiping the crumbs from his chin.

Mason waved his hands about as if to ward off any further distractions. 'I've thought long and hard over this one; you being a private investigator, my friend, you're better placed to open a lot more doors than any PC Plod would ever do.'

Carlisle managed a weak smile. If nothing else, George Wallace was an excellent choice. He was level headed. Besides, he had long suspected that Jane had a soft spot for Wallace, which meant the two of them would get on admirably together.

Mason emptied his glass, and replenished it from another bottle sent over with the manager's compliments. 'If I ever write my memoirs,' said Mason expelling a long drawn out breath. 'Remind me to leave this bloody mess out of them.'

'Surely you're not thinking of retiring, boss?'

'The day I retire is the day I'm on the plane to Mexico, George. Cozumel, Cancun, all the faraway places where the food burns the back of your throat, and the Tequila hits your stomach like rattlesnake's venom.'

'Never fancied the States?' Wallace nodded.

'Nah, I can't stand those Yanks. They're too much in your face for my liking. I prefer Mexico; the people are far more laid back.'

'If America was all that bad, then why are so many Mexicans fleeing across their borders and into America?' Carlisle smirked.

For one brief moment Mason looked pensive.

'Each to his own, I suppose,' Mason said deferentially.

Yes, thought Carlisle, the night was turning out just as he imagined it would. He watched as Mason wiped the corner of his mouth with his napkin. His face had that anxious look, as if holding back on something. When the main course arrived, the back of his throat was on fire again. God the food was hot.

'I'd planned to retire at fifty . . . take up a part-time job where I didn't have to do any thinking. Sadly the ex-wife put a stop to all of that,' said Mason. He fumbled his glass then stopped. 'The last time you and I worked together, David, I was going through a bad patch in my marriage. You know how it is; every copper's nightmare, late nights, heavy drinking sessions and problems at home with the kids. It was all getting too much, and the ex-wife and I needed a break from it all. That's when we should have gone someplace in the sun together . . . straightened things out. We never did, there was always another case to solve. In the end we just stood our ground and slogged it out. When the *bitch* finally slapped a court order on me for possession of the kids, that's when the shit really hit the fan.'

Carlisle tried his best to sound sympathetic. 'It sounds like a bitter experience, Jack.'

'Yeah, that's women for you.'

'How long ago was this?' asked Wallace.

The crushed look on Mason's face told him he was reliving a bad experience. He sounded different: sad, beaten and ground down. No anger, only resentment. 'She left home around six years ago, and it's taken me all of that just to straighten my life out again. I still see the kids, of course; they've all grown up now, and doing really well for themselves.'

'That's nice,' Wallace acknowledged.

Throughout the evening Mason's body language had shown signs of agitation. Something was afoot. Even so, there was no way of telling what was going on inside the DCI's head. Even if he asked him outright, he still wouldn't get a straight answer. No, whatever it was, Mason was playing his cards close to his chest.

'No thanks to Sir Jeremy, this case is drawing on the media's attentions for all the wrong reasons,' Mason went on. 'We've spent weeks now trying to find a connection to Gilesgate. Now that we've found one in Sir Jeremy, you would have thought the Assistant Chief Constable would have been more supportive towards us. Apparently not; the man seems indifferent to it all, and at times off-putting.'

Carlisle couldn't understand the logic. 'That's odd, Jack?'

Mason's look was stern. 'I've been doing some digging around; searching the archives so to speak. Not surprisingly, Sir Jeremy is not all he's cracked up to be. Amongst other things, I'm convinced he's leaking confidential information to the press. Where he gets his information from is another thing. But he's well informed.'

Mason held back until the waiter had exchanged the empty wine bottle with another house red. It was a little too bitter for Carlisle's liking, so he ordered another fresh pint of lager. Waving a gesturing hand towards the manager, Mason recharged his glass as if there was no such thing as drink driving laws.

'Where was I?'

'Sir Jeremy, boss,' Wallace reminded him.

'Oh! Yes. That slippery toe-rag . . .'

'I take it you don't like the man,' Wallace replied.

'I detest the little bastard, why?'

'He's not exactly my favourite politician either,' Wallace admitted.

Mason mouth tightened to a thin line. 'The last time I crossed paths with him, was over that damn schooner of his.'

'Would that be 'Pelican'?' said Carlisle.

Mason shot a glance at him, 'God, you've got a bloody retentive memory.'

'Wasn't it impounded for drugs trafficking?'

'That's only half the story,' Mason insisted. 'Sir Jeremy has good lawyers. That's why the crafty bastard renamed her Cleveland and turned her into a weekend adventure training ship for underprivileged children. Of course, the story made all the headlines for all the wrong reasons and the case was thrown out of the courts.'

Carlisle shook his head despairingly. 'You're too well informed, Jack.'

'Not really,' Mason replied. 'I simply Googled it after Vic Miller mentioned it at the last ops briefing. That's when I checked on the ACC's private finances.'

'You're not inferring he's in cahoots with Sir Jeremy, surely not,' said Carlisle.

'Tell me why not?'

'But he's a highly respected copper.'

Mason pondered his statement. 'Maybe, but the man has his fingers in an awful lot of pies – a lot more than some people would like to make out. I bet you didn't know he's made large investments into Gilesgate's global warming initiatives?'

Carlisle hit back. 'So what? It still doesn't mean he's in collusion with Sir Jeremy.'

'One thing's for sure,' said Mason, shaking his head. 'I'm not convinced it's a legit business they're running. Proving it, of course, is another matter.'

On the surface, the Assistant Chief Constable seemed a decent guy; he certainly wasn't the crook that Mason was making him out to be. Besides, there had to be thousands of people involved in global warming investments. That aside, was Mason trying to ride roughshod over them? After all, that was the nature of the beast. With limited resources at his disposal, the pressures were certainly mounting on the DCI. There again, if the killer was a member of Gilesgate's boardroom, then Mason's new proposals had leverage. It was a fine balancing act, and one he was gradually warming to.

'So how do you propose we approach this?' Carlisle asked.

Mason's eyes narrowed. 'In my books it would be impracticable to put a twenty-four-seven surveillance on every Gilesgate board member.'

'Why not?' interrupted Wallace. 'Surely they're all potential targets.'

'They may well be, George, but do the maths. Six men to cover every single Gilesgate board member, factor in support, and that's the number you're looking at.'

Wallace blew through his teeth. 'Bugger me, its eighty-odd men.'

'Now you know why I want this operation kept low-key, George,' said Mason, thoughtfully. 'Tell me, David. How would you handle this?'

Carlisle put down his glass.

'Our killer's no professional, I'm convinced of that. He's an opportunist who stalks his victims in their own environment. His mind's deranged, and he's using physical not mental violence. But there lies a dilemma: is he displaying his victims for pure self-gratification, or simply getting back at someone?' Carlisle fell silent for moment, searching a memory. 'Whatever he's trying to do, he's searching for a way to do it and in my opinion he's still on a learning curve, practising his art – and building towards a climax.'

Mason raised his eyebrows. 'God, sometimes you scare the living daylight out of me.'

'If we're dealing with a serial killer here, someone with a hate campaign against a specific group of people, then we're all in for the long haul, I'm afraid.'

He watched as Mason leaned over and recharged his empty glass again. His expression had darkened. 'I'm concerned more about the ACC's integrity in all of this,' said Mason. 'It's beginning to get to me . . . big time.'

The truth at last, thought Carlisle.

'So, what are you intending to do about it?' he asked.

Mason lowered his voice, realising he was attracting attention towards them. 'Let's park that problem to one side for a moment. Before I go sending in the heavy troops, I need you two to carry out a discreet undercover investigation into Gilesgate board members. If our killer happens to be one of them, then you two are best suited to flush him out.'

Carlisle thought about it. At least they were both on the same wavelength at last.

'It's a very dangerous ask,' Carlisle grimaced.

'I realise that, but what other options do we have?'

'None I suspect.'

A muscle in Mason's neck pulsed. 'It would be nice if we could get our hands on a few Gilesgate documents, medical records, personnel files, that kind of stuff. In the meantime, I intend to run a few discreet checks into employee background details, criminal records, that sort of thing.' Mason gesticulated by running his fingers across his throat. 'Let's put the cat amongst the pigeons, and see what materialises.'

'Sounds good to me,' Wallace nodded.

'One more thing,' said Mason, lowering the tone of his voice to a whisper. 'If you happen to drive a Mondeo, then my advice is to stay well clear of Gateshead tonight.'

The three of them fell about laughing.

They left Mason to pay the bill; he seemed in no hurry to leave.

Chapter Twenty-Four

Another horrific night spent studying photographs of the Wharf Butcher murder victims had left Carlisle in no doubt about the state of their suspect's twisted mind. What he saw and what he now felt were two different things. Their killer had remarkable vision, and was capable of creating an entirely different profile to that which others now saw. A ruthless psychopath, he would stop at nothing to get what he wanted. Whatever happened to Annie Jenkins was now firmly locked away deep inside the killer's traumatised head. His were dangerous mind games, a test of intellect that only he could perform. Gift-wrapping his victims' bodies as an artist presenting his latest masterpiece to the world, took a special kind of mentality. And another thing, the element of power and control over his victims' deaths, and the staging of the victims' bodies, was very much part of the killer's MO. The Wharf Butcher, whoever he was, was a dangerous predator who was becoming more predictable.

Carlisle shrugged off that line of thought and got down to the business in hand. Close to the Millennium Bridge, Gilesgate's Operational Headquarters sat amidst some of the finest architectural structures on Newcastle's quayside. His first impression was one of opulence and success, which made him think he'd definitely chosen the wrong profession. He should have been an architect, it seemed, as that's where the money was being made.

Lewis Paul, Gilesgate's Director of Operations, had the look of an athlete, but the walk of an orang-utan. His clean-cut features and swarthy complexion suggested he was of Mediterranean extraction, more Greek than Italian. Carlisle normally enjoyed investigative enquiries, but there were times when he felt awkward about it. It was a temperament thing, but right now he felt on top of his game. The moment he introduced his business partner, he caught an instant sparkle in Paul's eye. Bingo, just as

Jack Mason had predicted.

'I hope this is nothing serious, and we can quickly get to the bottom of it,' said Paul.

'It all depends on what you consider to be serious,' Carlisle replied.

'You can always try me.'

'Let's start with murder?'

'That is serious,' said Paul. 'In which case, you'd better step this way, Mr Carlisle.'

Paul ushered them along a long central glass walkway, full of potted plants and wall mounted pictures of Gilesgate's achievements. The meeting room had a modern feel, spacious with two sides fronted by tall glass windows overlooking the River Tyne. In the centre of the room, a quaint, ancient-looking water pump, sat on a rough stone plinth. It reminded him of some exhibit or other in a museum. It was then he spotted the coffee pot.

These people were obviously expecting this to be more than just a social visit.

His first impression of Lewis Paul was a man suffering from an obsessive-compulsive disorder. His attention to detail was mind-boggling. Pouring coffee into bone china cups that appeared far too expensive to drink from, Paul meticulously checked and double-checked that everything was in its rightful place.

'I take it that this is your first visit to Gilesgate's Operational Headquarters, Miss Collins?' said Paul.

'Yes,' Jane replied, giving Paul another admiring glance before settling back in the comfort of a large leather armchair. 'It's certainly a beautiful building.'

'Have you visited any of our other regional sites?'

'No. This is our first port of call.'

'I see.'

'I'll be frank with you,' said Jane. 'We prefer to visit by appointment.'

Paul reached for the sugar bowl. 'Security informs me your people have been checking on our flood construction sites.'

'I can only . . .' Jane's voice tailed off.

Typical, thought Carlisle. His business partner had really gone and put her foot in it – big style. But he didn't care. He still had an ace up his sleeve.

'Perhaps you would prefer the police deal with the matter, rather than us,' he said.

'Do I have an alternative, Mr Carlisle?'

'Yes, of course,' he replied, brushing the biscuit crumbs from his trousers.

'But is there a difference?'

'I believe so. Besides, we have absolutely no interest in the criminal aspects of this case. That's strictly down to the police to deal with. Of course, there's always the off chance they might treat this matter somewhat differently.'

Paul's eyes narrowed. 'It's all about trust . . . eh?'

Carlisle nodded, and took out his notebook.

Just as he thought they would, Gilesgate had done its homework. If not Lewis Paul, then someone else in the organisation with a personal interest in the case had. They should have approached this differently, gone for the jugular instead of pussy-footing around. They hadn't, and now they were on the back foot.

There followed an awkward pause, a repositioning of the sugar bowl.

'I believe you were acquainted with Charles Anderson, Mr Paul?' Carlisle said.

Paul squirmed in his seat, as if taken aback. 'That name's not familiar – no – why?'

'Let me remind you,' Carlisle said, eying up another biscuit. 'Up until his death, Charles Anderson had conducted well over eighty-million pounds of legal agreements for this organisation. Surely you must have come into contact with him at some stage or other?'

Paul's reply was blunt. 'That may well have been the case, but I still don't recollect the name.'

'You don't sound very convincing. I'm—'

'Let's be clear on one thing, Mr Carlisle. This site is strictly an Operational Headquarters; here we deal with overseas clients and our European counterparts in the supply of consumables to the construction industry. Legal matters, and in particular financial affairs, are of little concern to us here. May I suggest you take this matter up with Sir Jeremy, or even one of the Board of Directors? Not me.'

Paul was lying; the strained looks on his face had told him so. Carlisle took another sip of his coffee, a brand he did not recognise. 'You mentioned, Sir Jeremy—'

'Yes, Sir Jeremy Wingate-Stiles, he's the Chairman of the Board. He doesn't work here; he operates from Lakeside House in Northumberland.'

Carlisle made a note of it and flashed Jane a puzzled look.

'And what about Annie Jenkins,' he asked. 'What can you tell me about her?'

'In what respect?' asked Paul.

'How would you describe her?'

Paul clasped his hands, and lowered his head in thought. 'Annie was a good-natured person, but she did have her difficulties of course. She was a big miss. It was such a shock.'

'Yes, it must have been.'

There was an exasperated sigh, followed by a repositioning of the milk jug.

'Of course,' Paul went on. 'Annie's drink problem was no secret to anyone in this organisation. Try running a business when one of your key members of staff has an alcohol problem, it's not the easiest matter to deal with. I can assure you of that.'

'I can well imagine,' he nodded.

Carlisle detected a hint of nervousness in Paul's voice, and decided to exploit it. 'Before she resigned her position from Gilesgate, am I correct in saying that Annie was Sir Jeremy's Personal Assistant?'

Paul drew back looking somewhat stunned. 'You surprise me; Annie never resigned – she was dismissed for gross misconduct. I thought you people were aware of that.'

Jane's dark eyebrows raised a fraction, as she took down the details.

'Are you able to say *why* she was dismissed?' Carlisle probed.

'Certainly not, that was strictly between her and Sir Jeremy.'

The atmosphere in the room had suddenly changed.

'Can you think of any good reason as to why anyone would want to kill her?'

Paul puffed up. 'That's outrageous. How can you possibly say such a thing?'

Carlisle sat silent for some moments, thinking, absorbing this. Newcastle had seen its fair share of murders over the years, but this one was totally different. 'Tell me,' he said. 'Was Annie ever threatened in anyway?'

'No. Definitely not,' Paul insisted.

'What about workmates?' Jane asked.

Paul waved her aside. 'This is not the place to ask those types of questions, Miss Collins. You need to talk to her ex-husband about that. Not me.'

Carlisle pulled back, knowing full well the police had already eliminated Annie's ex-husband from their enquiries. As more information began to unfold, the sheer scale of their investigations soon became apparent. This was a massive undertaking, the scale of which Jack Mason had grossly underestimated. His eyes shifted to a pile of folders sitting on a small side table. Written across the top of one of the files were the words: FLATLAND FLOOD BARRIER. He made mental a note of it, and decided to dig deeper.

'I presume you keep medical records of all your employers?'

'Jesus!' said Paul sitting bolt upright in his chair, clutching a half-empty cup of tea. 'What kind of enquiry is this? I thought you people were private investigators – not the police.'

Carlisle collected his thoughts, and narrowed his eyes towards Paul. 'I was merely asking if you kept medical records, Mr Paul. That was all.'

'Then the answer's *yes*, but where is this all heading?'

'The police believe the killer has connections to your organisation, Mr Paul. That's why I raised the issue.'

Paul gave a nervous twitch of his head. 'What makes them think that?'

'You need to think carefully. I'm sure we can handle these matters with far more discretion than the police ever would.'

'That may be true, but—'

'This shouldn't be taken lightly,' Carlisle advised. His tone was calm and controlled, despite the fact that he was angry. 'You do realise we're dealing with murder here.'

'I appreciate your concerns, but I need a little more time.'

Carlisle held Jane's gaze as he leaned over and set his coffee cup down on the table. His suspicions were well founded; Paul was floundering, and it was time to press home his advantage. If the killer was a member of the organisation, which he now very much doubted, then his medical condition would surely have followed him. If not, then it would prove his theory was correct. It was a win-win situation, in his opinion.

'You mentioned that Sir Jeremy operates from Lakeside House,' Carlisle began. 'How does that tie in with his political interests?'

Paul's jaw dropped. 'Surely that's the Chairman's business. Not mine.'

'But wasn't Annie Jenkins, his Personal Assistant?'

'I'm not sure where you are coming from, Mr Carlisle.'

He watched as Paul squirmed awkwardly in his seat, and desperately tried to compose himself. The director was trembling, and his breathing was sporadic. 'You mentioned earlier that this site was strictly an Operational Headquarters. And I quote . . . *we deal purely with overseas clients and our European counterparts.*' Carlisle paused for effect, and then closed his notebook. 'Unless I'm grossly mistaken, there seems to be a conflict of interest here.'

'Tell me, what are your concerns?'

'Five people are dead, Mr Paul, that's my concern.'

'I hope those accusations are not aimed at anyone in particular; if they are, then I strongly refute them.'

'Well I wouldn't let it—'

'I know my employees,' Paul interrupted. 'None of them are capable of committing such despicable atrocities.'

'What about sub-contractors, I suppose you can vouch for them too?'

'I ... err ... believe—' Paul's voice tailed off.

'Perhaps we should start by me interviewing everyone in the organisation, Mr Paul.'

'That's preposterous.'

'But is it?'

'You know it is. Besides, I doubt you understand the implications of such a request. In order for me to sanction that, I would need to speak to someone in higher authority.'

'I see,' said Carlisle. 'And while you are at it, perhaps you might care to mention that a serial killer is at large and targeting your board of directors. That should do the trick ...'

Feeling pleased with himself, they exited the building into bright sunshine. Lewis Paul was no fool; the young executive was obviously under no illusions as to the seriousness of the situation, but would he cooperate?

Probably not, he thought.

Chapter Twenty-Five

The day of Annie Jenkins' funeral, Jack Mason had all but turned Saint Oswin's church in Wylam into an impregnable fortress. Ten miles west of Newcastle, Wylam village, the birthplace of the famous railway pioneer George Stephenson was now in a state of mourning. Not that it concerned Jack Mason; his main objective was to catch the Wharf Butcher, and he was determined to do that.

The skies, overcast, a light freshening breeze was throwing the occasional splodges of rain on the pavement when David Carlisle stepped into Saint Oswin's churchyard. Further south and close to Wylam railway station, DC Harry Manley sat guarding the southern approach over the River Tyne. A few miles further north, Sergeant Morrison had parked his unmarked police vehicle in a small overgrown lay-by close to the A69 – an east-west dual carriageway that ran between Newcastle and Hexham. Intrigued by a cluster of journalists sheltering under umbrellas, Carlisle recognised one or two plainclothes detectives mingled amongst them. Nothing had been left to chance, or so it appeared.

Just after eleven o'clock, the slow moving cortege finally came into view. The hearse, carrying the small oak coffin, was adorned with white and yellow flowers and messages of sympathy. All along Church Road, the streets of Wylam – where Annie grew up – were lined with people wanting to pay their respects. It was a large turnout, including a strong contingent of past and present Gilesgate employees. Minutes later, as the four black limousines drew up alongside the ornate wooden lych-gate, close family and friends solemnly filed into the church. High up on St Oswin's south tower, a lone police photographer was merrily clicking away at anything that took his fancy. If the killer's curiosity had got the better of him, there was every chance he was now amongst them.

The minute the coffin was carried into the church, Carlisle slipped unnoticed through the east wing vestry door. Never the religious type, he felt uneasy from the moment he first set foot in the place. He loathed funerals at the best of times, believing they were always long drawn out affairs with an abrupt anti-climax. Now a hive of activity, this bat ridden haven had been turned in a temporary operations centre. Packed to the rafters with computers and high-tech electronic recording equipment, the tech boys had done themselves proud.

'The man in the black shirt and jacket,' Mason said.

With the speed and dexterity of a top court stenographer, the young police technician sat at the computer keyboard ran a quick facial recognition check over the suspect's features. Shrouded by dark sunglasses worn across narrow features, the dubious facial image that suddenly exploded across every computer screen in the building sent a shiver down Carlisle's spine. If this was their man, there was every chance of detaining him.

'How's that, boss?'

'What do we know about him, Parker?'

'He's six foot two, weighs around two twenty – late twenties—'

'*Damn!*' said Mason, slumping back against the back vestry wall. 'Even I can see that – does he have form?'

'I'm on it, boss,' Parker grimaced.

Mason mumbled something inaudible, and began rubbing his right calf muscle. This was their first real breakthrough, and the pressure was mounting. The moment the young technician's fingers danced across the keypad, a ripple of excitement ran through the room.

'*There!*' said Mason, ceasing the moment.

Everyone froze.

Finally, and to everyone's dismay, the tiny monitor screen flickered, wobbled, and then stuck in freeze frame mode. Something was wrong, but nobody could put a finger on it. Then, from the back of the room, a printer began to spew out a long list of would-be candidates. Impossible odds at the best of times, thought Carlisle, but how would Mason react. To move now would be to blow their cover, to do nothing was unthinkable.

'It's got to be him!' said Mason through clenched teeth.

'He's certainly shifty looking,' DS Wallace acknowledged.

'And the right build, George.'

'Yeah, a little over six feet I'd say.'

'Try zooming in,' said Mason.

Startled, the technician's long skinny fingers punched in another series of commands before he finally sat back and waited for the computer to respond.

'*There!*' Mason said excitedly. 'The bastard's limping.'

Everyone just stood there as if some deadly virus had struck their midst. As a dozen pairs of eyes bore down in anticipation, the DCI instinctively wavered. In an odd way, Carlisle felt relieved that it wasn't him now calling the shots.

'What's it to be, boss?' said Luke James anxiously.

Mason's voice sounded like a dark rumble. 'Easy, lad's, let's not rush it.'

Before David Carlisle had even reached the vestry doorway, their suspect had long gone. Having squeezed his tall lanky frame through the thick undergrowth at the rear of the churchyard, he'd managed to slip the net.

'He's heading for the village!' a voice rang out, from high up on the church tower.

It was Carlisle who spotted him first, the moment the suspect clambered over a tall garden fence and disappeared from view down the other side. Within seconds a dozen police officers had made a bee-line for a long row of terrace houses set back from the village green. After fifty yards they stopped, and peered into the hedgerows and gardens. The light drizzle had now turned into a heavy downpour. Drenched, and knackered-looking, a young policewoman staggered out from one of the side gates. Her uniform, covered in mud, her face flushed.

'You see him, Constable Ellis?' Mason asked.

The young Constable shook her head. 'No. He's not come this way, boss.'

A voice crackled over a nearby detective's radio.

'Suspect heading for the Ship Inn,' a voice boomed out.

Gritting his teeth, Carlisle sprinted as fast as he could towards the far end of the street. Following in his wake, barely ten paces behind, Mason was breathing deeply and struggling to keep up with him.

'The bastard's gone to ground!' a police officer yelled, pointing to the pub car park.

'Check under the vehicles,' Mason shouted.

The rain, now lashing down, was bouncing off the tarmac. The gutters were a river of water, and the pavements full of puddles. Soaking wet, Carlisle followed Mason in through the pub door and into the warm lounge. As a dozen plainclothes police officers stood motionless in the centre of the room, the lounge doors suddenly burst open.

'He's not in the bogs, Jack,' Wallace shouted.

For one brief moment, they could have heard a pin drop.

The rain dripping down Mason's face, he checked out the clientele. Given the seriousness of the situation, there was every chance he would grab a couple of statements – but he didn't. It was lunchtime, and the majority of people were still tucking into their meals and completely oblivious to their surroundings.

Outside, the rain was still bouncing down, and another rumble of thunder could be heard. Then the radio waves fell silent. Even the sky continued to grow ominously darker. The only obvious explanation, when it came, was that the suspect had gone to ground. Reluctant to admit defeat, Mason shook his head in disbelief. Whoever it was they were chasing, had simply vanished into thin air. If not, then he would probably be miles away by now.

Carlisle saw the helicopter before he heard it. A couple of miles to the north of them, moving east, its thin white spotlight beam cutting through an overcast sky with such intensity that it created a strange vaporous glow over the tree tops. Nobody moved, but a quiver of excitement stirred the team. A few feet away, Sergeant Morrison's voice suddenly boomed out over a radio handset. '*Oscar Five, I'm in pursuit of a red Lotus Élan sports car – heading east along the A69 dual carriageway.*'

Jack Mason's foresight had paid off. The suspect was attempting his escape through the back door – east, towards the city. If anyone had doubts as to the suspect's intentions, they were quickly dispensed. Then the sudden wail of police car sirens. Moments later, blue lights flashing, as three patrol cars tore past him at speed.

The chase was back on.

Chapter
Twenty-Six

It had stopped raining when Carlisle finally arrived at the crime scene. Traced to a row of terraced houses on the outskirts of Newcastle, it would be big news locally, of course. He sat for a while, and weighed up the situation. Skewed across the entrance to a mini supermarket, two police officers in an unmarked Volvo were busy turning traffic away. Even forensics had beaten him to it. Garbed in their white sterile paper suits, overshoes and rubber gloves, they were examining an abandoned red Lotus sports car. Alongside it stood Sergeant Morrison's empty patrol car. Its driver's door open, blue flashing lights in stationary mode, the Sergeant was nowhere to be seen.

Carlisle climbed out of his old Rover and stood for moment. After several frustrating minutes, he watched as four members from the Armed Response Team moved down into Woodbine Road. Dressed in their familiar black flack suited body armour, black police caps and traditional high leather boots, they carried with them the familiar Heckler & Koch MP5SFA3 semi-automatic carbine. It was a long, straight, narrow road, with cars parked on both sides. Close to a Medical Centre, a group of journalists had been joined by a couple of out-side-broadcast vans. Huddled in a doorway, a news presenter appeared to be checking her notes. It was then Carlisle spotted the two technicians sat operating what he judged to be a long distance listening device; its parabolic microphone pointing at a house some fifty metres away.

Then he heard Mason's voice.

Gathered round him, and looking like drowned rats, were George Wallace, Luke James, and an elderly gentleman whom he took to be a trained negotiator. They were accompanied by a tall blonde woman, mid-forties, smartly dressed wearing a dark green jacket and clean-cut black trousers. Standing alongside her was the tall, suave figure of DI Swan and another well-dressed gentleman whom he judged to be the Scene of Crime Officer.

'You eventually made it,' said Archie Swan cheerily.

'I got delayed,' Carlisle nodded.

'This is George Hill; he's the man in charge of the situation.'

They shook hands, and exchanged pleasantries.

'We've reached a bit of a deadlock,' said Hill. 'Our suspect refuses to answer the door, and has barricaded himself inside the property.'

'Do we know who he is?' Carlisle asked.

The SOC manager grimaced. 'We're running a few discreet checks on the address. The red sports car, the one used in his getaway . . . it was stolen. That's as much as we know at the moment, but we'll keep you informed of any new developments.'

Oh dear, Carlisle thought. This wasn't his style. The Wharf Butcher preferred to do his business in a Mondeo, and this was a red Lotus Élan? Gathering his bearings, he noted that Woodbine Road ran in a north-south direction, approximately two-hundred metres long with terraced houses on either side. Both ends of the street had been cordoned off, as were the nearby approach roads. According to the latest intelligence reports, one of the adjoining houses was occupied by a young Asian woman with two small children. The other, thankfully, was empty. With this amount of firepower available to the police, Carlisle reasoned their best chance of recovering the situation would be one of stealth and surprise. Storming the property was too fraught with danger; even a snatch and grab approach would be difficult. But how Mason would deal with it, was anyone's guess. Even so, it was a tricky one and not the easiest of stalemates to bring to a close.

Someone spotted movement, and a dozen gun sights homed in on a large black wheelie-bin. Barely ten feet away, Jack Mason had already brushed his jacket aside and unclipped the holster flap of his Smith & Wesson. After some moments the wheelie-bin lid flew open, and out popped a big fat ginger cat.

The look on Vic Miller's face was priceless.

Approaching from the blind side, two police officers and highly trained explosive experts began to apply breaching explosives to the suspect's front door frame. At the same time, a dozen red laser pointers from the NART's Heckler & Koch zoomed in on the ground floor windows. As the door blew inwards under a cloud of white-hot vapour, there followed a second explosion – much louder than the first. As a dozen screaming police officers piled into the building, smoke bellowed out from inside of it.

It was over in seconds, the incapacitating effects of the stun-grenade having effectively disoriented their suspect. Lying face down and handcuffed. Mason had wasted no time. In one swift movement he flashed his badge of authority under the assailant's nose, and reminded him of his rights.

'Detective Chief Inspector Mason of Northumberland CID, you're under arrest.'

Still confused, the suspect shook his head as if he had water in his ear.

The DCI took a step back. 'I want this whole area sealed off. Nobody comes through that door until Tom Hedley has finished here. Do I make myself clear?'

'Yes, boss,' the nearest officer replied.

The situation now strained, Mason grabbed Vic Miller by the arm. 'As soon as the Scene of Crime Manager gives you clearance, I want this whole building turned upside down.'

'What are we looking for, boss?'

'Whatever,' Mason replied. 'I need answers, and this place is holding them.'

'I'm on it,' Vic Miller replied.

'Good man.'

Carlisle followed Mason in through the tiny, smoke filled hallway, and out onto the street. The air inside was oppressive, and his eyes were still smarting from the gas released from the stun-grenade. And another thing he noticed, the noise from the controlled explosion had set off dozens of car and burglar alarms. With all the media hype in the case, it wouldn't be long before one of the news reporters appeared on the scene and began interviewing one of the local residents. There was always someone willing to tell their story, thought Carlisle, even if the truth was heavily distorted.

Mason squinted. 'Ah! The very man,' he said, pointing out DS Wallace.

'Me?' said Wallace, as if taken aback.

'Yes, you George,' Mason replied. 'You're to escort our suspect back to Gateshead Police station. As soon as I'm finished here, I'll join you there.'

'Where is he now?'

'Follow me . . .'

Moving through a throng of police officers, they were met by the Specialist Dog Unit teams. Muzzled, the police dogs appeared agitated. Undeterred, Mason spoke to one of the handlers before re-entering the building. Now back in control, the DCI was in his element, which was more than Carlisle could say for his suspect's appearance. Completely disoriented, eyes all over the place, he had somehow managed to stagger to his feet. Smoke still filled the building; it hung in the air, a bitter taste.

Carlisle watched as Mason's eyes swung resolutely left. 'This cockroach needs suitable accommodation, George.'

'The luxury suite, I presume?'

'That'll do nicely.'

Wallace stepped forward and took a firm grip of the suspect's right arm. 'You heard the nice gentleman, you're nicked.'

'And while you're at it,' said Mason. 'Tell the desk sergeant to turn up the cell heating. I want this bastard to feel as uncomfortable as possible.'

'How does deep fry sound, boss?'

'That'll do nicely, George.'

The suspect stared at them as though they'd arrived from another planet. His eyes full of hate, the veins in his neck stood out as if he were about to kick off again. Wallace was having none of it, and the moment he protested his handcuffs were too tight, the detective forcibly dragged him outside and bundled him into the back of a waiting police car.

Carlisle's phone, on silent, vibrated in his pocket. He checked the display screen and returned the call. The stand-off had lasted a little over three hours, but there was no point in him hanging around anymore. The day had flown by, but there was still a nagging doubt over the suspect's identity. If this was the Wharf Butcher, then why had he chosen a Lotus Élan? Experience had taught him that serial killers seldom stray into unfamiliar territory. So, why the sudden change of mind, he asked. Besides, the suspect's gait was all wrong, and he looked far too immature. Even so, the cock-sure grin on Jack Mason's face said otherwise.

Oh dear, Carlisle thought.

Chapter Twenty-Seven

The following morning

Ignoring the lift, Mason stormed out of his office taking the steps two at a time. On reaching Forensics he threw back the door, a record journey of thirty-two seconds flat.

'My DNA results,' he demanded. 'Are they ready, Chris?'

Doctor Chris Brown was a lean, long-backed, medium-built, balding man, with a stern flushed face and thick bushy sideburns. In all his years he'd worked on forensics, he'd probably never witnessed such a dramatic entrance as this before. Looking distinctly the worse for wear, like a thousand hangovers, Jack Mason edged closer. Dressed in a crumpled white open neck shirt, brown corduroy slacks and white trainers, it was as though he'd slept the whole night out in them.

'Well! Are they ready?'

The doctor lifted his spectacles onto his brow, and from a large brown folder removed an official looking document, placing it on the workbench in front of him. The look of anticipation on Mason's face had surely warned him there could only be one outcome.

'It's – err—'

'Good man,' Mason grinned.

The doctor shuffled awkwardly. 'It's not good news, I'm afraid.'

'What do you mean!' said Mason, with a face like thunder.

'We've taken blood-samples from your potential suspect, and compared them against the killer's genetic marker code—'

'So what are you saying?'

'We can't find a DNA match,' the doctor replied. 'It's all laid out in my report, Jack.'

'Who needs a match,' Mason shrugged. 'It was me who arrested the bastard.'

The doctor looked at him with suspicion. 'That may be the case, but he's not your man. I can assure you of that.'

Mason backed away, as if a million volts had suddenly passed through his body. His suspect behind bars, it meant he could only detain him for twenty-four hours. After that, he would need to request an extension through the magistrate's courts – a prospect that didn't bear thinking about. What's more, if he didn't lay charges soon, the press would be all over him like a rash. Too many imponderables, he thought. The pressure was mounting, and people were demanding answers. He needed to find a way out of this, and quickly, before it all got out of hand.

'According to David Carlisle,' said Mason, 'most serial killers operate within a five-mile radius of where they live. It's called their hunting ground. So tell me, why don't we DNA every male between the ages of twenty and thirty who live within a five-mile radius of Gateshead?'

'It sounds a good idea, Jack, but how do you propose we get over ten-thousand volunteers to come forward and eliminate themselves from your enquiry? And, another thing,' said Dr Brown. 'How do we know he lives in Gateshead? Derek Riley's murder was carried out over forty-miles away from here, as I recall.'

Mason's body language had turned decidedly aggressive. 'I'm still not convinced. There must be something we can pin on this bastard?'

'Sorry, Jack. I would like to think it was him, but it isn't, and the results are conclusive. What's more, your suspect's blood group is 'B' negative and blood traces found on Annie Jenkins' body were 'A' positive.'

'What does that mean?'

'It means your killer is an entirely different blood group, Jack.'

'So who the hell do I have locked up in Gateshead police station?'

The doctor shrugged, as though not knowing. He was standing now, as if trying to evade further questioning. 'I've talked this over with Tom Hedley in some detail, and we're both agreed. Footprint casts taken from your suspect's footwear certainly don't match with those taken from the Wharf Butcher's crime scenes. The evidence is convincing, Jack.'

Mason nearly choked on the doctor's words. This was the last thing he wanted to hear. He was furious. 'If it's not him, then why did he run away from the police?'

'I have absolutely no idea.'

In all his years on the force, Mason had never come across anything like this before. He was fuming. 'I've got an ex-wife who gives me grief, a daughter who's never out of my bloody wallet, and now you're telling me this lanky piece of shit isn't the Wharf Butcher. Give me a break, Chris. Where's the justice in this world?'

Now sat astride a small stool, the doctor placed a fresh glass slide beneath the microscope lens. Closing one eye, he made some pretence adjustment to the viewfinder.

'There are some positives, of course.'

'Like what?'

'Well . . . we've managed to recover a few of Annie's personal belongings from your suspect's property. I know it's not a lot, but I'm certain you'll find it of some interest. If nothing else, it may warrant his current arrest.'

Still trying to come to terms with his disappointment, there wasn't a lot Mason could do right now. He thought about it – but not for long. Then he began to wonder. What if the doctor had overlooked some vital piece of evidence, a minute piece of fibre from the suspect's clothing? It was a longshot, but right now anything was better than nothing.

'So what are we looking at, Doc?'

There followed an infuriating wait, and Mason was almost beyond himself.

'If you must know, we found a black cardigan, an empty lipstick holder and a couple of shopping receipts in your suspect's rented property. None of them had traces of the killer's DNA on them.'

'Is that it?' Mason said, pacing the floor. 'Not a fat lot to get my teeth into . . . eh.'

The doctor flinched from the cutting edge of Mason's ranting. 'I'm sure you'll find it of some interest, Jack,' the doctor said, pointing down at the sealed plastic evidence bag.

Mason glanced at the package.

'Well, well, we finally get to the bottom of it. It seems there were some promiscuous activities taking place after all. What do we know, Doc?"

The doctor gave Mason a curious look. 'Stop trying to make a silk purse out of a sow's ear, Jack. It won't get you anywhere. The evidence is conclusive, and that's the end of the matter.'

'Was this asshole shagging her, Chris?'

'I doubt it. Besides, presumptions and factual forensic evidence don't always go together. Even you know that.'

Mason blew out a long sigh. Things were rapidly going from bad to worse, and he could barely contain himself let alone think straight anymore. The palms of his hands felt clammy – a sure sign of frustration.

He managed a rare smile. It wasn't all bad he reassured himself, surely not.

'There's not a fat lot going for me, is there, Chris?'

The doctor's brow furrowed. 'If it's of any consolation, Annie Jenkins' bodily presence was spread over a very small area of your suspect's property. She certainly wasn't sleeping there, if that's what you're trying to get at. Let's face it, he was obviously running away from something or he wouldn't have barricaded himself inside his property in the first place.'

'Right, well, like I say, it's not looking good, is it.'

'Perhaps something might come out of the interview, Jack.'

Mason's face contorted. 'I very much doubt it. If you ask me, he's beginning to sound like a frustrated parrot. The only answer he gives me is . . . *no comment.*'

'This one obviously knows the system by the sound of things,' the doctor said, shaking his head.

Mason mumbled a few utterances under his breath, knowing full well he was getting nowhere fast. It was a well-known fact that a suspect is under no obligation to answer any police questions. Besides, police interviews were usually a no-win situation at the best of times. And another thing, he wasn't feeling particularly proud of his own performance either. Just because the evidence was heavily stacked against him, he'd flown off the handle again. It was moments like this, and Mason had experience far too many lately, that he wished he could control his temper.

Even so, he would need to re-visit the video footage of Annie's funeral, find out what had spooked their suspect in the first place. Then there was the question of the stolen Lotus Élan – it wasn't the Wharf Butcher's style. He should have known that the moment he first clapped eyes on the vehicle. God, what a mess!

'Just when I thought I had the killer in the palm of my hand, he slips through my fingers again.'

'You can only work with the facts, no matter how much pressure other people are putting on you, Jack.'

'Try telling that to those upstairs,' Mason said. 'It's like standing in the middle of a graveyard . . . nobody in there listens to you anymore.'

The doctor lowered his head. 'If your suspect was acquainted with Annie Jenkins, then he's bound to know which pubs she hung around in.'

'We've already checked that one out, Chris. Needless to say, there's not a bar in Gateshead that Annie Jenkins didn't frequent.'

'So why is your suspect still refusing to talk?'

'God knows!'

'He's obviously hiding something.'

'I know, but what do I charge him with?' Mason shrugged. 'Apart from stealing a Lotus Élan, there's very little else we can pin on him.'

'For God's sake, Jack, I'm only trying to be helpful here.'

Mason slumped back against the lab wall, and finally came to his senses. 'Sorry, Chris,' he said, holding his arms up. 'This Wharf Butcher is doing my fucking head in.'

'And he's still out there,' said Dr Brown as Mason walked towards the door.

Mason paused and turned. 'I know, but where do you start looking for him?'

'Rather you than me.'

'Thanks a lot, mate.'

Just when he thought things couldn't get any worse, they had. Taking the lift, Mason was more confused than ever.

Chapter Twenty-Eight

Sir Jeremy Wingate-Stiles was in no mood for questioning. Still seething over Jack Mason's recent investigation into Gilesgate's business affairs, the chairman's look was grim. As the last of Gilesgate's board members took up their positions around the large oak conference table, they appeared ill at ease. He'd chosen this venue carefully, with purpose: it was the perfect setting. Deep inside the bowels of Lakeside House and divorced from the rest of the building, Sir Jeremy felt in control. If nothing else, it signalled his intentions. News of the suspect's arrest had travelled fast: the media were hot on the trail of yet another headline story. It was a time for engagement, a time for ratification.

'Gentlemen,' Sir Jeremy said, in words little more than a whisper and lips that barely moved. 'We seem to be stuck in the middle. On one hand we have the police looking into our business affairs, on the other, a monster who threatens to wipe every single one of us from the face of the planet. What is to be done?'

No one spoke, each avoiding eye contact with one another. Except for one that is –Henry Fraser. Unknown to everyone, Sir Jeremey and Fraser were now under police surveillance. Even so, there wasn't an area in Newcastle that Fraser didn't control. All organised – down to the very last money laundering deal.

'Snuff out this maniac first, and deal with the police later,' Fraser said.

'I appreciate your veracity, Henry. But the man now held in custody at Gateshead police station isn't the Wharf Butcher.'

Gasps rang out around the table.

'Did your contact say who he is?' Fraser asked.

'No, the police are keeping a tight-lid on his identity.'

'To hell with the police,' said Fraser, flamboyantly brushing Sir Jeremy's comments aside. 'Let's give them a run for their money.'

Sir Jeremy was a shrewd and educated man, and well aware that many around the table were mere pawns in the grand scheme of things. His beady eyes shot to Fraser and then to the others. 'Perhaps you have another cunning plan, Henry?'

Fraser's face dropped. 'I could have.'

'So what are you proposing?'

'I'm still working on it.'

Sir Jeremy thoughtfully stroked his greying moustache, pondering his next words carefully. His look was pallid, withdrawn. He spoke with a soft Irish accent; its pureness tinged with a hint of the West Country. 'Lewis Paul informs me that our aggregate quarries are already experiencing serious problems. Yesterday, I'm informed, the Bloxter site was crawling with plainclothes detectives.'

'Paul's a wimp!' said Fraser, showing little concern.

'Rest assured Lewis Paul has nothing to hide. I agree he's naive, but he's certainly not privy to affairs around this table.' Sir Jeremy paused for effect. 'Jack Mason's the person we should all be worried about. He's the one who's probing into our business affairs.'

'To hell with Mason,' said Fraser. 'What are our lawyers saying?'

'Not a lot at this stage.'

Fraser stared back at him icily. 'In which case, let me deal with him.'

'I'm not sure if that approach will work either,' said Sir Jeremy. 'What if Mason doesn't find the answers he's looking for: what then, Henry?'

'Does that idiot ever know what he's doing?'

Laughter broke out round the table.

The Gilesgate Chairman blew out a long stream of air from his lungs, and waited for a sense of order to return. Fraser's words were hard hitting; they usually were. Sir Jeremy braced himself, and caught the look in Henry Fraser's eyes. The big man was slowly taking over, and there was nothing he could do about it.

'What are you doing about this Wharf Butcher?' Sir Jeremy asked.

'In my books, it's Jack Mason who's calling all the shots here. Not this maniac.'

'Are you aware that Jack Mason has brought in a criminal profiler?'

Fraser pulled back in his seat, and shook his head in disbelief. Sir Jeremy's coercive words had obviously taken the sting out of the big man's huge ego.

'A profiler—'

'That's right, Henry.'

'What do we know about him?'

'I'm told he can read into other people's minds.'

A mischievous grin suddenly swept across Fraser's face. 'Let's hope he doesn't look into Mason's thick skull, cos there's bugger all in there.'

More titters of laughter broke out around the table – nervous laughter.

It was Trevor Radcliffe, another long serving member of Gilesgate's board who now took up the reins. 'His name is David Carlisle, and none of us should underestimate the guy. He's good at what he does, so we need to tread carefully. I've heard the police are struggling to track this maniac down, and Carlisle's been brought in to assist them.'

A short lived silence followed.

'Lewis Paul seems to think the profiler may offer us an alternative solution,' added Sir Jeremy. 'With Carlisle on our side, it may give us a little more room for manoeuvre.'

'Well, that's useful to know,' Fraser shrugged. 'Can he be bought off?'

'It's a consideration, but not at this stage,' Sir Jeremy replied.

'So what are we doing about it?' asked Trevor Radcliffe.

'We sit tight, gentlemen,' the Gilesgate's Chairman said. 'Before we make any more rash judgements, let's see what this profiler brings to the table. After all, this could work in our favour.'

Fraser's eyes narrowed. 'Even if Carlisle agrees to your terms, what guarantees do we have that Jack Mason won't come poking his nose into our business affairs?'

'Nothing's guaranteed, Henry,' insisted Sir Jeremy.

'But with Carlisle on board,' said Radcliffe, 'it may keep the police off our backs.'

Fraser pushed back in his seat, and performed an elaborate stretch. 'It's time we put an end to Mason's demands.'

The room fell silent again except for the boardroom clock, as its second-hand began another monotonous circuit. Curious as to what Fraser was really thinking, Sir Jeremy held back, knowing full well that many around the table were barely on speaking terms, let alone prepared to give way to each other's demands. He watched as Fraser tapped the table with an index finger. His was a perfectly aimed proposal, and one that everyone understood – all except Fraser, that is.

'Henry's solution makes perfect sense,' said Trevor Radcliffe, addressing the rest of the board. 'It's not what we know about Mason, it's what Mason knows about us. That's the problem here.'

'Trevor makes a good point,' another agreed.

Radcliffe nodded his approval, but chose to stay silent.

'Why don't we run it past the Assistant Chief Constable?' another asked. 'Let's see what he has to make of it all.'

'Which one is that?' Fraser questioned.

Sir Jeremy froze in his tracks. 'Irrational judgments will get us nowhere, gentlemen. The reality is none of us can sleep in our beds until this monster is either dead, or behind bars.'

Radcliffe leaned closer, his words barely a whisper. 'Why, I keep asking myself, is this maniac targeting only board members? What does that tell us?'

Fraser shrugged. 'That's a bloody good point. I'm—'

Radcliffe cut him short – a big mistake. 'He could be any one of a dozen people; even someone sitting around this table for all—'

'Enough,' Sir Jeremy demanded. 'I'll have none of that talk in my boardroom.'

'Hold on,' Radcliffe insisted. 'I'm entitled to my opinion, surely.'

Radcliffe's sudden outburst had stirred up a whole hornet's nest. It was Fraser who broke ranks, his huge fist thumping the table with the force of a sledgehammer striking an anvil. 'Oh. Yeah! Take my advice, Trevor. Button it before I do it for you.'

The silence was short lived.

'Who's handling the police investigations?' another questioned.

'Jack Mason is, I thought we'd already established that,' Sir Jeremy replied.

Fraser's temper was surfacing – another bad sign. 'Yeah, and why Jack Mason, why not the Assistant Chief Constable? You're talking out of your ass again.'

Sir Jeremy could barely contain his anger at Fraser. The big man was imposing bullying tactics, putting the others under pressure. It was time to take back control. 'It's moved on since then, Henry. Jack Mason was specifically brought in to tackle the Riley murders. Let's face it; he's probably as determined as we are at catching this Wharf Butcher.'

'So why not buy Jack Mason off?' Radcliffe insisted.

Fraser smacked his forehead with the flat of his hand, and laughed. 'You dumb bastard, we've already discussed that issue.'

Sir Jeremy came between them again. 'That's enough, gentlemen. If the Northumbria police continue to go poking their noses into our business affairs, then we *all* need to think carefully about our futures.'

Fraser reached over, grabbed the water jug from the middle of the table and poured the contents into an empty glass. His lips were quivering, his eyes bulging in rage. He was a huge man, a man of few enemies. Those who were would soon be joining the countless lists of silenced opponents. That's how Fraser dealt with his problems, no questions asked.

'I'm pitching my lot in with you, Sir Jeremy,' said Fraser, suddenly shifting his allegiance. 'I say we let Lewis Paul deal with this criminal profiler. With any luck, Jack Mason may lead us to the Wharf Butcher anyway. In which case, I'll deal with it personally.'

Sir Jeremy made a mental note of it. Even though John Matthew had failed miserably in his attempt to hunt down the killer, he had every faith in Fraser's ability to finish the job.

'Those in favour,' said Sir Jeremy.

There followed a show of hands.

The decision was unanimous.

'Rest assured, gentlemen, the police will listen to a sane man before they'd listen to a mad one. Besides,' Sir Jeremy grinned. 'I doubt Jack Mason knows anything about our organisation anyway.'

His words offered them small comfort – the killer's unpredictable actions had unsettled them. Who would be his next victim?

Only the Wharf Butcher knew the answer to that.

Chapter
Twenty-Nine

Through the glass fronted entrance panels at South Tyneside Magistrates' Court, beyond security, the court ushers could be seen taking down details of late arrivals. Amidst the confusion, solicitors, court officials, witnesses and clients were hurriedly preparing for another afternoon's onslaught. With two half-day trials in the mix, it meant for a busy schedule. The moment the diminutive figure of a repeat drug offender homed in on him, Carlisle's heart sank. Dressed in blue track suit bottoms, grey hoody jacket and white trainers, if nothing else, he appeared stereotypically turned out for the impending occasion.

'Nice day, Davy,' the drug offender grinned.

Carlisle cringed. Some things were far too predictable, he cursed. He liked nothing more than dealing with serious crime, the grislier the better. This work was different. Dealing with low-life was the pits. Unlike most decent people, these despicable cockroaches brought nothing but misery to other folk's lives. They were a plague on humanity – pushing drugs as if it were an accepted way of life. Carlisle watched as the drug offender stubbed out his cigarette with the sole of his shoe, and casually ambled towards the court waiting room.

'One of your mate's . . .' Mason chuckled.

Carlisle gave a thin, wintery smile. 'You must be joking!'

Greeted by the court clerk, she spoke briefly to them, but not before handing Mason a batch of freshly signed search warrants. Within seconds she'd disappeared back into the bowels of courtroom-one.

Mason shook his head in bemusement. 'Fancy a quick pint?'

'Love one,' he replied.

The Dolly Peel, a real ale pub on the corner of Commercial Road, was busy, but not overly crowded. Inside the bar they ordered two pints of Black Sheep, and found a quiet corner away from prying ears. Both casually dressed, much to Carlisle's amusement, they blended in well. Too well if the truth was known. How someone could habitually spend their entire lives stuck inside a pub all day was beyond him. But they did, and in large numbers by all accounts. Above the bar, a large plasma TV screen was playing out a national news bulletin in silent mode. He recognised the anchor-man as Jeremy Thompson, who was running an interview on the state of the nation's economy. Somehow, the whole depressing episode seemed much better without sound.

'What a bloody mess,' Carlisle cursed.

Mason grabbed his arm. 'Don't take it personally, but you're spending far too much time climbing into other people's heads to understand what's going on inside your own. Whatever it is that's troubling you, it's eating away at you, my friend.'

'That's politicians. They're only in it for what they can get out of it.'

'It's not that, is it?'

'Oh. What then?'

'It's Jackie,' Mason said. 'And don't try to hide it from me.'

He caught the look on Mason's face, and felt the hot flush. 'Yes, if you must know.'

'I thought as much.'

'It's the little things, I—'

Mason's grip on his arm tightened. 'No one ever said it was going to be easy, my friend. Every time you lose someone, it feels like a failure. That's life, I'm afraid.'

There were times, not too many sadly, when Jack Mason displayed a compassionate side. Six long years had passed since they'd last worked together, but things had moved on since then. His colleague was right: Jackie's untimely death had changed his whole outlook on life. He knew that, but he still felt physically and emotionally drained by her passing.

Christ, he needed to get a grip of himself.

'Have you talked it over with anyone? I mean—'

'No,' he replied.

The hurt welling up in him, an image formed in his head. It was Jackie, and she was staring at him from across the room. He closed his eyes and tried to blot out the image. Then he saw reason. Mason was right; he was only trying to be supportive towards him. He realised that, but he still felt riddled with guilt.

'Take my advice,' said Mason, pointing towards his empty glass. 'You need to snap out of it before it completely destroys you. I've been there, worn that T-shirt, and it's a horrible experience, believe me.'

Having spoken his mind, Mason shrugged as if that was the end of the matter. At least he'd aired his views, which was more than a lot of other people had done lately. Glancing in the mirror, behind the range of spirits and wine bottles, he watched as Mason screwed his face into submission. His mind elsewhere: like the tall young blonde now standing in the pub bar doorway – tarty looking and far too young.

As the afternoon wore on, it wasn't long before their conversation got down to the real matter in hand. Annie Jenkins' sad demise was an inevitable occurrence, it seemed. Had the Wharf Butcher not killed her, then the drink demons most certainly would have. According to the autopsy report, Jenkin's was suffering from the final stages of cirrhosis of the liver – a debilitating condition that would have finally put an end to her life.

Carlisle's phone rang, and went straight to voicemail: '*Hi, David, I'm getting a copy set of CCTV tapes run off from Manors Metro station. Talk to you later.*'

Mason shot him an inquisitive glance. 'Anyone I know?'

'George Wallace,' he replied.

Mason took another swig of his beer. 'What's he up to?'

'We're working on a new of line enquiries involving the Metro System.'

'Oh!'

'I'm convinced these murders were planned,' he replied.

Retrieving a crumpled Tyne and Wear Metro map from an inside pocket, he opened it out on the table in front of him. Mason said nothing, but his eyes were all over the place. 'I've seen this type of pattern before,' Carlisle went on. 'It's indicative of the way that these people's minds work.'

'This isn't going to spoil a good afternoon's drinking session, is it?' Mason said.

'What makes you say that?'

'It's the serious look on your face, my friend. It concerns me.'

'Hold on . . .'

'Listen, my friend, I'm up to my neck with senior management issues at the moment, besides a whole pile of bad ass press. I could dearly do with a break. To tell you the truth, I was beginning to enjoy myself.' The young blonde at the bar threw a cursory glance, enough to attract Mason's attention. 'Besides, never look a gift horse in the face.' Mason grinned.

'Yeah, but you're old enough to be her Granddad.'

'Christ's sake!'

That had done the trick. Five minutes later they were back down to business again.

'You were right,' said Carlisle, 'our killer leaves few clues and yet he offers his victims up like sacrificial lambs.'

'Hmm,' Mason grunted.

Fresh drinks arrived, with the crisps. Mason popped the packet open, and dug into them. 'I understand the pressures you're facing,' Carlisle went on. 'Like me, you need to rise above it. Let's face it, our killer's trying to gain celebrity status here, and wants his public to recognise him for it. Hence the theatrical way in which he displays their bodies. Four separate crimes, and on each occasion he's stolen a Mondeo to carry out his mission. What does that tell us about the killer's MO?'

Mason shrugged. 'He genuinely likes Mondeo's?'

'I'm trying to be serious, Jack.'

'Yeah, so am I.'

Carlisle thought for a moment as he engaged Mason in another staring match. 'Take a look at this,' he said, pointing down at the map. 'The kill zone is rarely ever the drop off zone. In other words, he always steals his cars from the South side of the river and abandons them on the North side . . . and, all within a one-mile radius of a Metro Station. '

'Well I'll be damned!'

'I'm convinced he's working to a plan,' said Carlisle, suddenly feeling far more relaxed. 'There's a distinct movement pattern taking place here, Jack.'

'Bugger me, I—'

'Close to the river, all within easy reach of a Metro station.' Carlisle paused for effect. 'And another thing, I'm convinced he's holed up here somewhere, between Manors and Tynemouth Metro stations.'

'So why Mk3 Mondeo's, what the hell is that all about?'

Carlisle sighed. 'It's all part of his comfort thing, and he probably feels at ease with it. There's nothing wrong with that, unless of course, you happen to own one.'

Mason winced as the barman turned the TV volume up to watch the horse racing channel. 'If you turn that thing up any fucking louder, I'll shove that remote control up your arse.' The barman stared at him, and quickly thought the better of it. Seconds later, the volume was turned back down again.

'How would you describe him?' Mason asked bluntly.

'Retaliatory is the simple answer.'

Mason took a huge gulp of his beer, and wiped the froth from his lips.

He ordered a fresh pint, as though to state his intention. 'We need to get our hands on a list of Gilesgate's employees. Run a cursory check on anyone who lives within easy walking distance of Manors and Tynemouth Metro stations.'

Carlisle drew back. 'It's only a theory at this stage, Jack.'

'Nevertheless, a damn good one,' Mason said, thoughtfully. 'Tell me, what's Wallace up to nowadays?'

'He's checking out CCTV coverage.'

'What the hell for?' said Mason, bluntly.

He pointed to the map. 'I'm convinced the killer is using the Metro system to stalk his victims, and it's fast becoming his signature.'

'Don't hang your hat on CCTV coverage,' said Mason, leaning heavily back in his seat. 'Most of the footage I've ever come across is crap.'

'George is a good operator. He's thorough with it. Let's see what his investigations throw up before we go making rash judgements about him.'

They left the Dolly Peel into bright sunshine. Apart from a few minor distractions, Mason was in an incredibly agreeable mood. There again, the DCI wasn't the only one who wanted results. Right now Carlisle would have given anything to see their killer behind bars.

'Who the hell is Dolly Peel?' Mason asked, pointing to the pub sign.

Carlisle wracked his brains. Then he remembered. 'She was an old fishwife back in the eighteenth century. The story goes that her husband and son were both press-ganged to serve in the Royal Navy.'

'Just curious . . . that's all.' Mason shrugged. 'It's a queer name to call a pub all the same.'

'If you're still interested, Jack, there's a life-size commemorative statue of her over by River Drive.'

'Best not go there . . . eh.'

'Why not—'

'You're forgetting,' Mason said breezily, 'Isn't that Wharf Butcher territory?'

Chapter Thirty

It was just another routine call that brought PC Harper back to the high-rise tower block in Gateshead. It was three-fifteen in the afternoon, and he was responding to an urgent call concerning complaints about rowdy adolescents playing pranks on vulnerable old folk in the community. The presence of his blues and twos police car lights must have temporarily frightened them away, but Harper knew otherwise. A notorious melting pot, Bethel Court was riddled with drug dealers, pimps, racketeers, and young adolescent troublemakers who had no ambition to conform to the rest of society. The grownups around here bred like rabbits and fought like rats within the confines of this concrete sarcophagus. Harper was well aware of the dangers that lay within. Two days earlier it had been the turn of the Community Police teams to sort things out; today it was his. It was that kind of community: the adults who lived round here were the product of a forgotten society – no jobs, no money and no future prospects. It was a legacy they passed on to their children.

Stifling a yawn, on reaching the nineteenth floor Harper noticed a steady stream of water escaping through the bottom of one of the flat doors. Some idiot had left a sink tap running, he cursed. Having cut its path along the narrow corridor walkway, a steady trickle of water was now cascading into the bowels of the building below. Reporting his findings to the local authorities, he was soon joined by a distraught caretaker – a cantankerous, lumbering, overweight hippopotamus whose rubbery pug face oozed flab. Not the brightest bulb in the box. There were food slops all down the front of the caretaker's T-shirt, and his clothes stank of cigarette smoke. Stepping aside, Harper observed the warden's frustration as he fumbled his way through the huge bunch of keys.

'Do you not have a master key?' asked Harper.

'Nah, they keep changing the locks.'

Rapidly losing patience, Harper brushed him aside and placed the flat of his hand on the central door panel and gave it a gentle push. Taking a pace back, he employed a forceful well placed kick – close to the side of where the lock was mounted. After several attempts at kicking the door open, the lock finally gave way and the door crashed inwards with a loud bang. Stumbling blindly into pitch darkness, the eerie silence that followed caught Harper unawares.

'Stay exactly where I can see you,' said Harper.

'I'm right behind you, Constable.'

'OK. I want you to move back to the walkway.'

Adjusting to the dark, Harper caught sight of a small shaft of light penetrating through a chink in the window blinds. The air inside was hot, repressively hot, tinged with an overwhelming stench of urine. It hung in the back of his throat reminding him of a CS gas training session. It had a distinctive odour of ketones, overpowering and incredibly strong. Whoever lived here sure had a poor sense of smell. If not, they had massive health issues.

Extending one foot in front of him, Harper shuffled towards the light source. On nearing his goal, he fumbled in the dark and tugged what he thought was the window blind cord. There followed an almighty crack. Seconds later, the blinds fell down on top of him.

'Are you all right in there?'

'Yeah, stay back.'

Adjusting to the light, Harper shielded his eyes from the bright sunlight that now poured into the room.

'Holy shit!' the caretaker shrieked. 'What the hell is all this about?'

'Stay where you are,' Harper insisted.

Wiping the sweat from his brow, the Constable replaced his police cap and gave his uniform a quick dust down. Nothing had prepared him for this; it had all happened so quickly. Reaching towards his waist-belt he unclipped the radio handset, pursed his lips, and gently blew into the speaker.

Dust flew everywhere.

'PC Harper, Sarge. I'm responding to a call to Bethel Court. I need backup.'

Swearing quietly, Harper took a step back and began to take stock of the situation. Inexplicably drawn towards the strange matchstick figures and macabre illustrations of death that covered every wall, he tried to focus his mind. Confused, he reached into his pocket and pulled out his mobile phone and began taking pictures. Whatever these images represented, they certainly had a sinister feel. He stood for a brief moment, unclipped his radio handset, and spoke directly with the sergeant again.

'We need forensics down here, Sarge. I'm sure they'd want to see this,' he whispered.

'*I'm dealing with it!*' the voice on the other end of the handset boomed out.

All in all, PC Harper was having a good day. Whatever it was he'd stumbled across, he was certain it would appeal to the experts. His thoughts now were to secure the building. Touch nothing, seal off the flat and await the arrival of the forensic team.

Without warning his handset suddenly sprang into life again; it was the control desk. Whatever it was Harper had uncovered, the sergeant was certainly excited about it. His voice sounded strained, high pitched and he was talking at ten to the dozen.

'*You're to touch nothing; DCI Mason is on his way.*'

Acknowledging the caller, Harper replaced his handset back into its case and closed down the flap. 'Nobody is allowed along that corridor,' said Harper. 'Do I make myself clear?'

'Why . . . what's happening?'

'Just do as I say.'

The caretaker's bright red face contorted as though he'd reached condition critical. Turning on his heels, his battered slippers made a squelching noise as he trudged towards the balcony. It was time for action. Removing a handkerchief from his pocket, Harper placed it over the water mains stopcock and slowly shut off the supply. At least the water had now stopped pouring over the top of the sink. Curious, his eyes returned to the wall sketches. Apart from the bizarre complexity of inhuman suffering, young children could have drawn them. There was, of course, a subtle difference. Only a madman could have drawn them – someone with the warped twisted imagination that only a madman could possess.

'What's happening?'

'Nothing, until I've taken down your statement.'

'*Statement!*' the caretaker gasped. 'What the hell is going on?'

Removing his police notebook, pencil poised at the ready, Harper returned to the balcony. His voice now in official mode, his questions came thick and fast.

'When was the last time you were up here?'

'I . . . can't remember, I—'

'Was it, days . . . weeks . . . months?' The puzzled expression on the caretaker's face told Harper all he wanted know. 'Well man, what is it to be?'

'This part of the building hasn't been occupied in months, Constable. Nobody ever comes up here.'

'Well, when was the last time *you* last set foot up here?'

'Maybe three months, I—'

The caretaker started to say something, but Harper raised his hand as if to stop him. Three months seemed an awful long time, and a lot of things could have taken place during that period, thought Harper. He would need to get the bottom of it.

'So, who lives here?'

'I don't know, it was—'

The sound of a police siren wail broke Harper's concentration. Peering over the balcony, he saw the whole area was now swarming with police. Minutes later he was joined by a half-dozen plainclothes detectives, who moved in haste along the nineteenth floor walkway.

This was no ordinary investigation, Harper told himself.

'Who's in charge here?' the lead figure called out.

The knot in Harper's throat tightened. Turning, he immediately recognised the stocky figure as he brushed purposefully past him. It was the Bulldog – Jack Mason.

'That would be me, sir,' Harper replied nervously.

'And who might this bag of shit be?' asked Mason, glowering down at the bedraggled looking caretaker.

'This is Arnold Tomkinson, sir.'

'Really,' said Mason, brushing him aside to poke an inquisitive head in through the open doorway. 'Tell me, Constable, who occupies this place?'

PC Harper felt his jaw drop. There were times, and there had been many of late, when he wished he'd taken up a desk job – this was one of them.

'That's what I'm trying to establish, sir.'

Mason looked up at the broken doorframe and tugged at a loose piece of wood splinter. 'Was this broken before you arrived?'

'No. It was me who gained a forced entry. As far I'm aware, I'm the only person to have entered the building since.'

'And no one else has set foot inside these premises?'

Harper shook his head. 'No—'

'What about this bag of —' Mason checked himself.

There followed a tense few moments, a gathering of thoughts.

'You did a good job, Constable, but don't let it go to your head. If it is the person we're looking for, he's probably miles away by now.'

Harper was feeling the pressure. What had started as a routine enquiry had now turned into a major crime investigation. Surely this couldn't be the Wharf Butcher's hideaway, surely not, thought Harper.

Chapter Thirty-One

David Carlisle stood in numb disbelief. Sixty years had passed since this concrete jungle had forged itself onto Gateshead's skyline. Built to answer a housing crisis in post-war Britain, the ideologically inspired dreams of cheap, quality, high-rise housing was quickly neglected and demonised by the middle classes. Little more than a concrete ghetto, maintenance was abysmal, lifts seldom worked, rubbish chutes were always blocked, and garages regularly burnt down by vandals. These were dispiriting surroundings to live in, and the decent people who lived here hated it with a vengeance.

Ducking beneath the police line tape, Carlisle flashed his ID at an irate police officer and made his way towards Bethel Court high-rise tower block. Around the forecourt, there was plenty of evidence to suggest a major crime investigation was now under way. At the foot of the stairwell, to the left of the building, were two marked police cars, each occupied by uniformed officers from the Tactical Firearms Unit. Further afield, he caught sight of several figures in white coveralls, moving between the floor levels with a purposeful conviction. As ever, a strong contingency of media was busily snapping away at anything that took their fancy. Security was tight, but not tight enough, thought Carlisle. How little these people understood the workings of a serial killer's mind – the behavioural patterns and different levels of intellect. This was no ordinary individual they were dealing with; did they not realise these people nearly always camouflaged themselves into contemporary anonymity?

Up on the nineteenth floor, he found Jack Mason grilling a blubber faced witness. He barely gave him a second glance. Like most crime scenes he'd ever visited, Carlisle never felt comfortable entering a killer's lair for the first time. It was the not knowing that he could never quite get his head around, even though he'd done it a thousand times before. In the past he'd learned to live by his first impressions. This time felt different — much more sinister.

Poking his head in through the open doorway, he began to take in his first real images of the Wharf Butcher's world.

Who are you, and what makes you kill?

The room had a musky smell, and was damp underfoot. Graffiti adorned every wall, macabre child-like sketches of death and horrific torture. It reminded him of something out of the Chamber of Horrors, unnatural, wicked and vile. He closed his eyes and searched for a moment of inspiration that would bring them ever closer. This was the nearest he'd come to actually confronting his killer, and his mind was all over the place.

'Most of the evidence has been bagged and taken away,' Mason said. 'He's been gone twenty-four hours by the look of things.'

'How secure is the building?'

'Water tight, from top to bottom, why do you ask?'

'It's the press I'm worried about, Jack. They are everywhere!'

'Those cockroaches can sniff out a headline a thousand miles away,' Mason frowned.

Carlisle frowned in a sort of dutiful disapproval. 'What if he's posing as one of them?'

'Rest assured,' Mason sighed. 'If the killer is amongst us, we'll have him on camera. This tower-block has twenty-four seven CCTV monitoring. It's a notorious drugs neighbourhood, and well known to us.'

Drawing in the air, Carlisle could still smell the suspect's sweat. Stripped of all physical evidence, the room had a hollow sound and void of any character.

'What about personal effects?'

'Everything's been bagged and taken away for further forensic examination.' Mason made a little grimace. 'Before anyone moved in here, I made pretty damn certain a video camera was run over the place. Believe me, this building has been stabilised from top to bottom.'

'Anything show up?'

'Not yet, but Hedley's examination was thorough.'

Mason had a tendency to rush things, thought Carlisle. The man had very little patience. He was impulsive. His eyes toured the room, as he began to take in the detail.

'Your suspect's confident; you've got to hand him that.'

'Tell me about it,' Mason sighed. 'The Computer Crime Unit has taken away a laptop, so I'm hoping we'll uncover more about him.'

The CCU's search will be thorough, Carlisle reasoned. They usually were. If he did have any electronic secrets to hide, these were the people to find it. Was this a big mistake – had he been careless? In the silence that followed, Carlisle began to take in his new surroundings.

'Do we have a name?'

'Not yet,' Mason replied.

'You mentioned contamination?'

'Forensics' had a field day. They have bagged enough trace evidence to fill a bloody transit van. Let's hope we finally have something on him.'

'Hedley's a good man,' Carlisle acknowledged. 'He's thorough with it. Did anything else show up?'

Mason pointed at the walls. 'Apart from these sketches, a dozen photographs, and several boxes of personal junk, that's about it I'm afraid.'

Carlisle swung on his heels. 'What kind of photographs are these?'

'Group gatherings ... black and white, professionally taken I'd say. Some loose in boxes, others blue-tacked to the walls.'

'They could be relevant, Jack. I'd like to see them.'

Mason jotted down his request, as if it were some kind of shopping reminder. So much was churning through Carlisle's mind, whilst everything else around him seemed to be moving at a snail's pace. Turning from the window, he noticed a damp patch in the corner of the room and dabbed his finger in it. It smelt of fish – sardines. Was this the suspect's last meal? It could well have been.

'You can almost reach out and touch him,' said Carlisle, pointing to the sketches.

'They mean bugger all to me,' Mason shrugged.

'Take another look, Jack.'

The DCI stepped back a pace and fixed his gaze on the walls. 'If you want an honest opinion, they remind me of the drawings my five year old daughter used to bring home from school. It's kid's stuff, basic, the kind you'd expect to find pinned to a child's bedroom wall.'

'I'd admit he's no artist.'

Mason's eyes burned like embers. 'Spare me a thought—'

'And yet they reveal so much about his personality.'

'To you maybe, but they do bugger all for me. As far as I'm concerned, the Wharf Butcher has the intellect of a five year old child.' Mason raised an eyebrow looking far from convinced. 'He was in such a bloody hurry; he forgot to turn off the sink tap.'

Only too pleased that Mason still had some appetite for conversation,

Carlisle drew breath. Usually by now, the DCI was ranting and raving at everyone. He lifted his spectacles onto his forehead, and cast a critical eye over a small section of wall.

'He lives in a world of fantasy, which certainly fits the component makeup of a serial killer. Forget revenge or any other theories, this one's serious about his work. In fact I'll stand by my first impression of him, he's a sensationalist.'

Mason barely glanced at him. 'He might well be, but he's spreading a lot more than the gospel about the place.'

The adrenaline racing, Carlisle delicately ran an index finger back over a series of sketches, only this time tracing their contours. There was a definite childish mentality about his style, but the subject matter was distinctly that of an adult nature. He'd witnessed its evil before – the characteristics were predictably repetitive. Deep down he found the killer's state of mind to be insidiously different from those he'd ever come across before. There was a definite arrogance in his style, decidedly unsettling.

'These sketches are sending out all the wrong vibes, Jack.'

'How do you come to that conclusion?'

'The person behind them has more than a few emotional issues.'

Mason glowered at him. 'Don't tell me you can read into this sort of crap?'

'Isn't that what you pay me to do?'

'OK. So what is he telling you?'

'He's re-enacting his childhood, but he's fighting it. It shows in his mental state, hence the childlike way in which he presents his images. Even kids would find difficulty in drawing this kind of stuff.'

'I would bloody well hope so, goddammit,' Mason asserted.

For a brief moment the room fell silent again, broken only by the wind, playing against the window latch. Dropping to his haunches, Carlisle studied the sketches from a different angle. In places the hand had been steady, in others erratic. He sensed mixed emotions. Standing now, he took another look at the subject matter. Only this time, his nose was almost touching the wall. 'He's dominant . . . and likes to express his powers of achievement.' Carlisle paused in reflection. 'And that would account for his exhibitionism.'

Mason stuck his hands deep into his trouser pockets, and looked on in bewilderment. It was as though the mental cogs were working at full stretch, but his brain still wasn't functioning.

'Don't tell me these sketches represent his victims?'

'I'd say so,' Carlisle nodded.

'Tell me you're joking—'

'Here we see Riley . . . the blow to the head. Over there . . . crucifixion, which bears all the hallmarks of Anderson's horrific ending.' Carlisle drew breath. 'Notice how the killer sees himself; he always draws himself twice the size of his victims. He's the dominant figure, commanding power over everyone else.'

'*Unbelievable!*' Mason said, shaking his head in disbelief.

'You see. Even you can reach into his world.'

They spent the next fifteen minutes going over the possibilities, Mason hanging on his every word. As the dangerous psychological cat and mouse game began to unfold, the innermost workings of a serial killer's mind slowly became more apparent. Then, Mason pointed down towards a small strip frame of sketches in the corner of the room. The victim's throat had been torn open, the head falling back, and blood spurting out of it. Carlisle caught a hint of excitement in Mason's voice, as a child discovering his first magic trick.

'What sort of person are we up against here?'

'He's mentally unstable, that's for sure.'

'Hell man, even I know that,' said Mason. 'How many of these people are dead?'

'It's hard to say.'

With the eye of a hawk, Carlisle began to take in the detail again. Every now and then he would home in on one of the sketches, but he still found the images distracting. Then it struck him. What if these sketches were unfinished thoughts?

'What the hell is going on?' Mason said, sounding even more nervous.

'Look carefully, Jack. What do you see?'

Mason took a step back in search of an answer.

'A crane mechanism, the kind found in a boat yard. Why?'

'These are more than just mere thoughts, I'm convinced of that. These are a pictorial record of his past achievements, and his future aims.'

'It will take more than a few sketches to convince me,' Mason insisted.

Mason had a point, but only a trained eye could see through the fog. Suddenly it felt as if the rug had been pulled from under him. 'Our suspect is proud of his work, and dedicated to the point of showing off. If all these murders had already been committed, then I'd suspect we'd have found a lot more bodies by now. No, the person we're looking for is a pure exhibitionist who likes to display his work as if the world was his public art gallery.'

'What worries me,' Mason sighed, 'is that he's improving with practice.'

Carlisle shuddered inwardly, sensing its vulgarity. Inside the tiny room he felt a new affiliation with his subject, as if he was closer to him than ever before. Not with-standing his motives, their suspect's style of killing were consistent. 'He's methodical, Jack, systematic to a point of being organised. His victims, all members of a specific group, Gilesgate, are the perfect fit of the missionary killer. The question is – could he be one of them?'

'God knows.'

'These black and white photographs you mentioned, they could be of major significance,' Carlisle confirmed. 'They're part of his modus operandi. Pictures are memorabilia, events of the past. I need to take a look at them.'

His request was greeted with another shake of the head. Even with the windows fully open the room still stank of urine. It played on their nostrils, a foul bitter odour.

'I've already made a note of it. I'll arrange to have copies sent over.'

'Did Hedley give any indications as to when he might have something ready?'

'Tonight with any luck—'

'Our suspect's had a very troubled past, and may well have been abused as a child.' Carlisle was thinking aloud now, as he often did. 'Whatever happened to him in the past, it's left a deep-rooted impression on his mind.'

Mason shot him a sideways glance. 'Could that have triggered him into killing?'

'It's possible, but it's hard to say at this stage as his mind is fuelled by fantasy. In our discovering his hideout, it may have sparked off all kinds of mental warfare inside his head.'

Mason paced the floor.

'I'm considering stepping up my 24-7 covert operations on Gilesgate, but I don't have the available resources.'

'Why not run it past the Assistant Chief Constable? After all, he's the one who insists you to protect, rather investigate Gilesgate's board of directors.'

'To hell with the ACC,' Mason said.

Carlisle's mind was racing now. Gripped by the suspect's movement patterns, sadly an empty room offered him few clues. Stripped of personal belongings and sparse of comforts, the flat felt cold, detached, without any personal feeling. Stepping from the room, he drew in the fresh clean air. Nineteen storeys below, he watched as the media circus surged forward – cameras at the ready, sound recorders held high above strained heads. There was no mistaking the glaze in Mason's eyes, firmly fixed ahead and staring into empty space. The veins on the backs of the detective's hands stood out, the knuckles predominantly white. He appeared troubled, and whatever it was, it was deep-rooted.

They moved towards the stairwell, and Carlisle felt the cold stiff breeze sweeping in off the river. 'The Wharf Butcher is stretching us, Jack. It's his way of dealing with it.'

'He's got us exactly where he wants us, if you ask me,' Mason sighed. 'But you were right about one thing: he's definitely using the metro rail system as part of his murder plans.'

They exchanged glances, and under the cover of a tight security ring Carlisle slipped unnoticed from the building. The rain was drumming down when he eventually drove south along the Western By-pass. Late afternoon and the rush hour traffic was nose to tail. Then, close to the Gateshead Metro Centre, it finally ground to a halt. Minutes later, the radio presenter announced that a major police incident had closed many of the approach roads in and out of Gateshead's town centre.

'Well,' he said softly, 'I wonder what that's all about.'

Chapter Thirty-Two

Earlier that morning

Even a genius feels pain.

Those words had hung around inside Lexus's head for days now. His mind was in turmoil, and it annoyed him intensely. It would be good to be rid of the voices, just for once. He could barely think straight, let alone plan anything anymore. But there lay a problem. Not more than a stone's throw away, close to the edge of reality, his tiny flat was meticulously being torn apart. It was a weird sight, but he bears no grudges, not today at least. Lexus has more important things on his mind, and more interesting!

Then the voices . . .

What do you see?

'Only the darkness,' he replied.

Can you reach out and touch it?

'No. Not today.'

Beyond the edge of the world lies a space, where emptiness and darkness collide. If you reach out and touch it, you will surely witness the light.

'Is it real?'

Of course, the voice in his head replied.

Lexus was not deterred, why should he be? The street lighting was on, and the tiny memory stick – the one he'd placed in his pocket earlier – it was still there. It was a lifetime's work, a masterpiece creation, and everything he had strived for . . . and more, of course.

Taken your medicine today?

'Do I need to?' he shrugged.

Maybe not, but do you have a plan?

'Only a genius would know that.'

Without a doubt, the voice replied. *And I bet it's a good one?*

All these questions annoyed him, intensely. Besides, he had other things on his mind – more important things. Set back in the shadows, he watched as another plainclothes detective ducked beneath the police cordon tape. There was despair on the officer's face; it reminded him of a frightened rabbit caught in the headlights of an oncoming car. Wait a minute, wasn't that the Profiler, the very man brought in to hunt him down? Surely not! Yes it was, and wasn't he much shorter than he had imagined him to be?

How exciting is that?

These people are so disappointing.

'I know,' Lexus sneered. 'I'm such a genius.'

Well then, shall we get on with it?

Moments later, he watched as David Carlisle climbed into a battered old car and sped from the crowded courtyard. He wasn't happy anymore. Not today he wasn't. He'd always imaged the profiler to be an intelligent man – calculating just like him. Then, quite by chance, people pushed past him. Everywhere pandemonium – even the television crews had difficulty in jostling for a position. Still smarting from the loss of his beloved flat, he hid in a doorway and waited.

What to do next?

He had absolutely no idea of time; time meant nothing to Lexus. It was an unnecessary nuisance. Then, at the bottom of the stairwell, Jack Mason appeared. Panic gripped him, and his pulse quickened until he could barely breathe anymore. Jack was an astute cookie, unlike the rest. Only Mason could slip in and out of delicate situations at will. And yes, it was a frightening thing being invisible. He knew that, but it still drove him mad all the same.

Then the voices again . . .

What a cunning move. How did you spot that?

'Yeah, but what to do next?' he asked.

You will think of something, you always do.

'I know, so why must you keep reminding me?'

The chaos inside his head was building now, and there was nothing he could do to stop it. Lexus could never understand the complexities of uncertainly, it meant absolutely nothing to him. At least today it didn't. As the light began to fade, he slipped unnoticed into the bowels of Gateshead Metro station. Calm overcame him. The dark was awesome. He loved it down there; the rush of hot air on his face, the hiss of the train doors, and the maze of dark tunnels, gloomy passageways and flashing coloured lights. This was his Shangri-La, a mystical paradise, set in such beautiful surroundings. Lulled into false security, he fell into another light sleep. He barely had time to relax nowadays. How crazy was that?

Then, as the train pulled out and onto the Queen Elizabeth II Metro Bridge, his eyes shot open again. He loved up here, high up above the water's edge where everything was unflustered and so peaceful. Didn't he know every twist and turn in that river? Of course he did; that was his hunting ground, his peace of mind. He once dreamt he could fly.

'Is that possible?'

Every genius can fly, Lexus.

'Including me?'

Indeed . . .

Lexus breathed in heavily. 'I always thought I could fly,' he replied. *You're such a genius.*

Chapter
Thirty-Three

The drive to Corbridge took them a little over forty minutes. Detective Carrington took the wheel; Carlisle was too busy catching up on the latest Coroner's report. On nearing the village of Dilston, Carrington turned right at the T junction and dropped down into Linnets Bank. Through a gap in the hedgerow, Carlisle caught his first glimpse of the beautiful rolling landscape. Winter here was a challenge: bleak isolation, with heavy snowfalls and bitter cold winds that cut through you as if you were naked. As the young detective pulled up in front of a small coppice, she switched off the engine and ambled round the front of the vehicle. It was late morning, yesterday's rain had gone and it was a beautiful summer's day.

Together, they made their way down a long winding footpath, until reaching a short bend in the river. Opposite stood a white stone cottage. Guarded at the rear by dense woodlands, its front was protected by cultivated blackthorn. From the outside, the place looked deserted. If they were being watched, it was from a distance. On crossing a small footbridge, Carrington pointed towards a thin plume of white smoke drifting out from one of the chimney stacks.

'Try peeping in through a window,' Carrington said.

This had to be Bradley Jenkins' place, thought Carlisle. There were no other buildings for miles. Taking the easy option, he stepped up to the door and rapped the iron knocker. It seemed to go on forever, but when the door finally opened they were met by a slender man with wispy ginger hair and mouse like eyes. Bradley Jenkins looked much older than Carlisle had imagined. He was lean, with barely an ounce of spare fat on his body.

Carrington introduced herself.

'Police,' she said, thrusting her warrant card under Bradley Jenkins' nose.

'Yeah, what do you people want now?'

They stared at one another for a few seconds, before Carrington explained the purpose of their visit. Jenkins glowered at them through the open doorway, before finally allowing them inside. The modern furnishings seemed at odds with the rest of the building. The sitting room was tiny; low wood beamed ceilings and whitewashed walls gave it a claustrophobic feel. Neatly laid out in one corner stood a large plasma television screen, next to a tall bookcase crammed full of DVDs. An anorak lay over the back of chair, left there in a moment of haste. What's more, there was rustling coming from the rear of the cottage – Jenkins wasn't alone.

Focusing on the suspect's eyes, Carlisle tried to read into Jenkins' mind. Not the best of circumstances to conduct an interview, he thought, especially when close family and friends were now locked in a bitter dispute over the rightful ownership of the cottage. If nothing else, Annie Jenkins' untimely demise had certainly sparked off more than its fair share of family trouble.

'We are here to ask a few questions,' Carrington explained.

'What is it this time?' said Jenkins. 'I've already told you all I know.'

'It's about Annie,' the young detective replied. 'It will only take a few minutes.'

Jenkins finished off the last of his drink. 'That's what you sods said the last time.'

'In that case we'll be brief.'

Jenkins scowled at her. 'So what do you want?'

'We're keen to establish Annie's last known movements,' Carlisle said, trying his utmost not to sound too overbearing. 'Tell me, does the name Lewis Paul sound familiar to you at all?'

There was another long pause before Jenkins unfolded his arms and relaxed his pose.

'Yeah, I've heard that name mentioned before. Why?'

'Two days ago,' said Carlisle. 'I put it to Lewis Paul, that Annie may have been threatened after she left her position at Gilesgate.'

'And what was Paul's reply?' Jenkins asked.

It wasn't exactly the warm welcome that Carlisle had hoped for. He watched as the sunlight played through the small bay windows, making Jenkins squint. All the while rustling continued to come from another part of the building.

'Well,' said Carlisle calmly. 'Paul gave me the distinct impression that Annie was a very amicable person to work with. But in fairness to him, he did advise we speak with you first.'

Jenkins hesitated. 'Did he?'

'Uh-huh,' Carlisle nodded. 'Did Annie ever mention anything to you about feeling threatened in any way?'

'I can't say as she did. Why?'

'What about workmates?' Detective Carrington cut in.

Jenkins just stared at her looking annoyed. 'You do realise we were separated, young lady?'

'Yes, I'm aware of that,' Carrington acknowledged.

Jenkins' face clouded over. 'I'll admit Annie could be a bit Jekyll and Hyde at times. It was always a matter of how much drink she'd had. She wasn't the easiest of persons to get on with. She was an introvert by nature, but once the drink demons took over she could be a very obnoxious woman.'

'What about her friends?'

'Nah, most of them were alcoholics.'

Carlisle was quick to react. 'Is there anyone else we can talk to?'

'I'm not sure that's a good idea either,' said Jenkins, scratching the tip of his pointed chin, as though it were an unusual question. 'As you know, Annie and I were never on good speaking terms at the best of times.'

'What about close family?' Carrington asked.

'What family! She had no family, they all buggered off the moment she hit the bottle.' Jenkins looked Carrington in the eye, and swore quietly. 'Annie drank herself into some sorry states at times. I'd even go as far as to say she drank—' Jenkins checked himself.

The young detective nodded, but did not press the matter further.

They talked openly for a while, but he told them nothing they didn't already know. However, the minute Carlisle mentioned Sir Jeremy's name, Jenkins' body language turned aggressive. 'Don't mention that little weasel's name in my house,' Jenkins retorted.

Carlisle just stared at him, not expressing any interest in the details.

'Those are strong words, Bradley,' answered Carrington.

'Look,' said Jenkins. 'It's not just me; nobody I know likes the little bastard.'

Carlisle let him rant on a bit, before cutting him off in mid-sentence. 'It's obvious you don't see eye to eye with Sir Jeremy, and I can't say as I blame you,' Carlisle shrugged. 'But how did Annie get on with him?'

Jenkins took a few seconds to compose himself. 'She didn't,' he replied bluntly. 'She never liked him. How he gets away with running Gilesgate's operations beggars belief. But he does, and that's the problem.'

Carlisle raised an eyebrow. 'Gets away with what?'

'Now hold on a minute—'

'I'm confused, Bradley.' Carlisle confessed. 'I was under impression that Lewis Paul was in charge of Gilesgate's operational sites, but your reaction tells me otherwise.'

'You're mistaken, Carlisle,' said Jenkins, shaking his head. 'Paul's just a front man. It's Sir Jeremey and his cronies who run Gilesgate, not Paul. He's a mere puppet.'

Carlisle probed deeper. 'What do mean by that?'

'For God's sake . . . Annie was Sir Jeremy's PA; she had access to some highly confidential documents. Think about it, she handled all of Gilesgate's contracts.'

The room fell silent for a few seconds, a gathering of thoughts. Had Annie stumbled across something she shouldn't have, he wondered. Was she murdered because of it? There again, they were dealing with a serial killer and that theory didn't hold a lot of water either. Carlisle felt as though he was onto something, but what, he had no idea. Somehow or other, he would need to get to the bottom of it.

'These so called cronies, what can you tell me about them?' Carlisle asked.

Jenkins looked down, examining his watch strap. There was scorn in his voice. 'It's just what I picked up from Annie, you know how it is. She always liked to talk these things over when she'd had a few drinks. From what I could gather, these people were not only guarded about their activities and their identities, they were shrewd businessmen by all accounts. And another thing . . . why would you want to hold your meetings in the dead of the night, and behind closed doors?' Jenkins puffed out his cheeks and expelled out a long drawn out gasp. 'Annie may have been a lot of things, Mr Carlisle, but she certainly wasn't daft. If she knew something wasn't right, she would stop at nothing until she got to the bottom of it.'

'And did she?'

'I've absolutely no idea.'

Detective Carrington flashed him a quizzical glance.

Carlisle thought a moment. Jenkins was scathing, but that was understandable. A confirmed alcoholic, his ex-wife had not only lost her dignity and her position at Gilesgate – what followed was a bitter marriage breakup, a major family rift, and finally murder. Maybe Jenkins felt the need to blame someone else for his wife's tragic downfall, and Sir Jeremy seemed the perfect person. No, there was something else, something more sinister that he couldn't quite put his finger on.

'Did Annie ever say who these people were?' he asked.

'Nah, as far I'm aware they were professional people, financial brokers, police officers, bankers; people with influence.'

Carlisle studied Jenkins body language. 'People with money perhaps – financial investors?'

'People with power more like.'

'Did she mention any names?'

'No. Not to me she didn't.'

'You mentioned police officers were in attendance at these meetings.' Carlisle stared back at him, looking for signs of hesitation. 'Did Annie say who these people were?'

'She did mention the Assistant Chief Constable's name, but that's as much as I know.' Jenkins screwed his face up and swore. 'I could never understand what a copper was doing getting involved with those arseholes ... unless?'

Carlisle caught Detective Carrington's glances.

'Is that why Annie became suspicious do you think, because police officers were involved?' said Carrington.

'How would I know? Annie was many things to many people, but she was never one to take it lying down.'

Detective Carrington wrinkled her nose. 'Including, Sir Jeremy?'

'Oh yes, including Sir Jeremy,' Jenkins said, spitting his words out.

They chatted a while.

'Listen!' said Jenkins. 'What are the police doing about finding Annie's killer?'

'That's why we're trying to establish her last known movements,' Carrington replied. 'The people Annie mixed with, family, friends, that kind of thing.'

'It's Gilesgate you people should be talking to. Not me.'

Carlisle thought about this, but refused to be drawn in by Jenkins' utter resentment towards Sir Jeremy. He stood to leave. 'We're grateful for your time, Mr Jenkins,' he said handing Jenkin's one of his business cards. 'If you can think of anything that may have a bearing on our enquiries, please don't hesitate to contact me.'

'I've told you all I know,' Jenkins shrugged. 'It's Gilesgate you people should be investigating. Not me.'

Carlisle whistled through clenched teeth. Bradley Jenkins had a point. Had his ex-wife uncovered a darker side to Gilesgate's operations, and if so, had she placed herself in a vulnerable position? Then, more importantly, there was the question surrounding the Acting Chief Constable's involvement in Gilesgate. Was Jenkins overreacting, venting his frustrations out on Sir Jeremy – laying the blame for his wife's sad decline firmly at the Chairman's door? He had his suspicions, of course, but refused to be drawn in by them. Besides, he would need to talk it over with Jack Mason first.

Carlisle felt a headache coming on. It had been one of those meetings, and they were leaving with more questions than answers. On reaching the coppice, Detective Carrington fished in her handbag and took out a pair of sunglasses. Leaning back against the undercover pool car, she began taking in the sun's warm rays. They'd made some progress, not a lot to report, but at least it was something.

Carrington turned to face him. 'What did you make of Bradley Jenkins?'

'He certainly has no time for Sir Jeremy.'

'No prizes there then,' Carrington smiled.

'I suspect Bradley Jenkins has told us everything he knows. Unfortunately, most of the hidden detail lies buried with his ex-wife.'

'Those were my thoughts,' Carrington said, peering over the top of her designer sunglasses. 'At least we can eliminate him from our enquiries.'

He watched as the young detective brushed an annoying strand of hair from her face.

'There's something I've been meaning to ask you,' Carrington said coyly.

'What's that?'

'Are you still single by any chance?'

Caught unawares, Carlisle felt his jaw drop. 'Why?'

'Just curious, that's all,' she shrugged.

Her voice had a mischievous tone. Sure he fancied her. Who wouldn't, he thought. He quickly pushed those thoughts to the back of his mind, knowing full well he could never get involved with another woman. Jackie had been his life, his only love. He could never dishonour her memory.

Chapter
Thirty-Four

The ten-thirty briefing trumped up all the usual faces, thought Carlisle, and the operations room smelt of fear and sweat. Owing to the vast amount of physical material recovered from the Wharf Butcher's flat, Forensics was struggling. Whilst most of the evidence had been meticulously logged, packaged and labelled, it still required considerable laboratory effort to sift through the mountains of detail. It was painstaking work, but one that could not be rushed.

Jack Mason had kept his media statement brief that morning. The national television networks were out in force, most of them running live news bulletins. The public's insatiable demand for answers had ensured the Northumbria police were kept constantly on their toes. As usual, Mason gave very little away. Dressed in a blue pinstripe suit, white buttoned down shirt and blue polka dot tie, the moment he entered the operations room, he looked more like a television presenter than a senior police officer heading up a major murder investigation.

Taking centre stage, the DCI removed his jacket, and stood to face the team. In what was promising to be a long drawn out meeting, the next fifteen minutes were spent running back over the last twenty-four hours' events. When they came to the discovery of the suspect's computer, true to form, Mason dug his heels in.

'John,' said Mason, pointing to a dour-faced member of the police Computer Crime Unit. 'What information have you managed to recover?'

From what Carlisle could make out, John Cutmore was a thirty-something year old computer geek who carried a huge chip on his shoulder. Unquestionably an oddball, what Cutmore lacked in dress sense he certainly made up for in intellect. He had one of those annoying, high pitched squeaky voices, and spoke in snatches as if his words wouldn't come out fast enough.

'Your suspect was operating a high-end Lenovo's fourteen-inch ThinkPad X1 Carbon Touch computer,' Cutmore said, oozing computer jargon. 'It was part of a large consignment, stolen from a lorry park in Leeds. None of it was ever recovered, until this one turned up.'

The noise levels heightened.

'When was this?'

'Last August,' Cutmore replied.

'Where from exactly?' Mason asked

'The Tingley Lorry Park, it's near junction twenty-eight as you head west along the M62 towards Lancashire.'

Mason jotted down some notes. 'What else can you tell us?'

'Not a lot. He's not registered with any of the usual social networking sites. If you ask me, he seems a bit of lone wolf in my opinion.'

'What about chat rooms?'

'No, nothing,' shrugged Cutmore, as if it was another stupid question.

'Did he ever use Skype?'

'Not to my knowledge.'

Mason checked with his notes. 'Does he search any particular websites?'

'He's addicted to American crime reporting, if that's what you mean.'

He watched as Cutmore leaned back heavily in his seat and yawned, as if bored by it all. Not the best of moves, Carlisle inwardly groaned.

'And that's it?' Mason said, staring at him, eyes like daggers.

Cutmore sat bolt upright as though a thousand volts had suddenly passed through his chair. His face now bright red, he put his mug down and tried to gather his composure. 'I ... err ... no, I'm not sure.' Cutmore was silent for a few moments, looking around, and eyes like a frightened rabbit. 'He seems to have downloaded an awful lot of material involving notorious serial killers. His computer was crammed full of the stuff.'

'Anyone in particular spring to mind?'

'Not really, but he does seem to have a morbid fascination with Ted Bundy's trial.'

'I see. What other things has he stored?'

'He shows a lot of personal interest in his own murder crimes.'

Mason raised an eyebrow. 'Such as—'

'Newspaper reports, YouTube clips, that kind of stuff. It starts with the Ernest Stanton trial, and progressively carries on from there.'

'If you ask me, he seems to be interested in what other people are saying about him?'

'Yeah, I suppose you could say that.'

'What about login passwords?' Mason asked.

'He uses several, boss. But the main one is *devilsmypal.*'

Carlisle's eyes narrowed as Mason moved towards a large whiteboard and tapped it with the back of hand. Now covered in photographic evidence taken from the suspect's flat, it made chilling viewing. Taking everyone by surprise, the DCI stopped short, changed his mind and smartly turned to face the team again.

'Vic. What's the latest on Trevor Radcliffe?'

Caught unawares, a spray of coffee exploded from Vic Miller's lips. 'We're still running with our 24/7 surveillance, Jack,' Miller said, wiping the dribbles from his chin. 'Nowadays, Radcliffe spends most of his spare time at the boathouse. That's the one nearest to the North Shields Fish Quay.'

'Have there been any more sightings?'

'Apart from Henry Fraser's occasional visits, it's been relatively quiet.' Miller shuffled awkwardly, as if feeling the pressure. 'I should also point out that 'Cleveland' is due back into the Tyne on Friday.'

'Just to pick up on that,' Mason cut in. 'Cleveland is a one-hundred foot schooner commissioned by Gilesgate to carry out its coastal survey operations. She's been involved in drugs trafficking in the past, and is known to have slipped under the coastguards' radar on several occasions. So we need to stay vigilant. When is she due back, Vic?'

'Early that morning, boss. She's taking the six-twenty tide,' said Miller, staring down at his notes.

Harry Manley raised a hand as if to speak. 'Any chance of getting me fixed up with a cheap happy baccy weekend cruise, Vic?'

The team fell about laughing; even Jack Mason saw the funnier side.

'OK,' Mason said eager to press on. 'Any sign of the suspect showing up at the Bethel Court flat?'

'It's all gone quiet, Jack,' Vic Miller replied.

Mason thanked him, and then turned his attention to other matters. 'Luke, what's the latest on Lakeside House?'

Luke James stared into the bottom of his empty plastic coffee cup, before turning to face them. 'We've seen an upsurge of activity, but I'm a bit miffed that Thomas Schlesinger still hasn't shown up,' said James. 'I'm convinced he was involved with John Matthew in the Barrow Burn affair, and—'

'I take it Fraser is still in regular attendance?' Mason muttered.

'Fraser and Sir Jeremy are as thick as thieves, boss.' James lowered his head. 'They're up to no good, I'd wager.'

'Wait a minute!' said Mason. 'What's happening about Fraser's car?'

'We've now fitted it with one of our new GPS tracking devices,' said James, looking smugly upbeat.

'Nice one!' Mason acknowledged. 'That means we can now keep track of his movements.'

For some minutes, they ran back over dozens of Ford Mondeo sightings – ninety-six in total – none of any interest. The killer, it seemed, was refusing to take the bait.

Mason looked at his watch. 'Sue, how did your interview with Bradley Jenkins go?'

Apart from Mary Holt, a backroom forensics scientist, Detective Sue Carrington was the only other female present that morning. Not surprisingly, thought Carlisle, the young detective gave a very confident account of their findings and seemed determined to pull no punches. The moment she sat down, it took Jack Mason all of three seconds to make the connection.

'So,' Mason said, weighing up the facts. 'We know that Annie Jenkins was Sir Jeremy's PA, and had access to some highly confidential material.' Mason paused for effect. 'Are we now suggesting that Gilesgate are using Lakeside House for some sort of dodgy business activities?'

'That's my understanding,' Carrington nodded.

Mason paced the floor again.

'OK. Apart from a possible cover up, is there a case to suggest that someone wanted Annie Jenkins silenced?'

'I wouldn't discount that theory either,' Carrington advised.

Mason allowed himself the suggestion of a smile. 'These late night meetings, did Bradley Jenkins give any indications as to who might have attended them?'

Detective Carrington referred to her notes. 'He described them as prominent people, stockbrokers, politicians, bankers, police officers . . . people in high office,' she said, nervously chewing the end of her pen.

'Do we know who these police officers are?'

The young detective lowered her head. 'Yes, he did mention the Assistant Chief Constable's name.'

In all his years on the force, Carlisle had never witnessed an operations room fall so deadly quiet before. At this point, someone would usually make a snide remark. Not today. He could have heard a pin drop. The mere mention of the ACC's involvement had knocked everyone for six.

All eyes now strained towards Jack Mason.

'Good work, Sue. Unfortunately the only person who can verify Bradley Jenkins' statement is now dead.' Mason seemed rapt in some thought or other. 'Do you have anything to add, David?'

'No. Not at this stage,' Carlisle replied. 'If nothing else, it confirms our suspicions about Gilesgate and the difficulties we are now faced with.'

'What's your take on these Lakeside House meetings?'

'Annie Jenkins had close ties to these people, which undoubtedly placed her in a very precarious position. Nevertheless——'

'Could she have been singled out?' Mason questioned.

'It's possible, but highly unlikely. The person we're dealing with has already outlined his intentions. Annie Jenkins wasn't murdered for what she knew; she was murdered because of who she was. I'm convinced of that. In my opinion, she was always an integral part of the killer's plans, and that's why he killed her.'

Mason perched on the edge of the table. 'In other words, we now have two possible strands running here. One involving a serial killer, the other involves Gilesgate's Board of Directors. Find the link, and we may find our killer.'

Carlisle glanced at Carrington.

'Dave,' said Mason. 'What's the latest on your Metro station investigations?'

A relatively new member of the team, Constable Dobson was slowly working his way through George Wallace's Metro CCTV footage – two-hundred and forty hours to be precise. Not the best of tasks, thought Carlisle.

'We've managed to narrow it down to eighty-six possible suspects,' said Constable Dobson. 'All are male between the ages of twenty-five and thirty-five, and all used at least two Metro stations on the day of Annie Jenkins' murder.'

'How many stations are we talking about here?'

'Ten, boss.'

Carlisle did a quick mental calculation. With sixty stations in the system, he wasn't exactly holding his breath. Maybe he should have thought of that in the first place. Even so, they were starting to make progress.

As the meeting drew to a close, Mason made a bee-line towards him.

'It seems we now have a major problem on our hands,' said Mason, pulling him to one side. 'How do we deal with the delicate matter of the Acting Chief Constable?'

Several thoughts crossed Carlisle's mind, but he chose to ignore them. This was an internal issue. Any accusation aimed at a senior police officer was the Northumbria force's concern, not his. Besides, outsiders were usually frowned upon when it came to internal disciplinary matters.

Carlisle gave a faint smile. 'It's a difficult one, Jack.'

'I've got a bad feeling about this one,' said Mason. 'Before the shit hits the fan, let's hope we can quickly get to the bottom of Gilesgate's illicit activities. Even so, my primary objective is to catch this maniac regardless of any outside distractions. But catch him I will.'

Carlisle leaned back and cocked his head to one side. 'By you uncovering his flat, it may have sparked him into killing again.'

'In which case, I need to step up my surveillance operations.'

In more ways than one, Carlisle concluded.

Chapter Thirty-Five

Shortly after two-thirty, Carlisle locked the office and drove north through the Tyne Tunnel. At a pre-arranged lay-by near Cramlington, he picked up George Wallace who was waiting for him in front of his undercover blue Peugeot 308. The rain that had threatened yesterday had now arrived, making driving conditions hazardous. Ten miles north of Morpeth, they pulled up in front of a pair of wrought iron gates leading to a long tarmac driveway. Lakeside House, a nineteenth-century stately manor and now the family home of Sir Jeremy Wingate-Stiles, was nowhere to be seen. On the surface things appeared normal, but Carlisle knew otherwise. High security fences and a heavy presence of surveillance cameras gave the place a Fort Knox feel.

Joined by a gum chewing security guard who stank of cigarette smoke and stale sweat, DS Wallace flashed his warrant card under the security guard's nose.

'Police,' said Wallace. 'We're here to see Sir Jeremy . . . he's expecting us.'

The security guard gave them a cursory once over, tipped his peak cap, grinned, and waved them through. 'Continue straight on ahead, sir. I'll inform them of your arrival.'

The drive took them along a series of long narrow lanes, surrounded by woodlands on either side, with a mix of rolling countryside and well-kept landscaped gardens. Then, at the turn of a sharp bend, Lakeside House came into view. It wasn't the stately grandeur that had attracted Carlisle's attention towards it; it was the Cyclops eye of the CCTV camera perched high on the manor roof. They were being observed.

At the reception desk, they were met by a tall skinny redhead, with bright red lipstick and an overpowering stench of cheap perfume. She appeared on edge, as if she'd had previous run-ins with the police. Seconds later, they were ushered along a narrow palatial hallway, high ceilinged with magnificent oak panelled walls and luxurious carpets underfoot. Inside a dimly lit lounge, lavishly furnished with stunning views overlooking beautiful rolling parklands, they were shown to their seats. Carlisle sat opposite Wallace, across a large walnut conference table which took centre stage in the room. Neither spoke.

Then, from a side door, Sir Jeremy appeared.

Wearing a grey, pin-striped suit, pink shirt and crimson polka dot blue tie, the Gilesgate Chairman carried a sombre look. 'I'm reliably informed you've been snooping into our financial affairs, Mr Carlisle?'

Wallace took up the gauntlet. 'That's correct, Sir Jeremy. The police have found it necessary to open up a new line of enquiries, it's— '

'It would have been courteous of them to inform me first,' Sir Jeremy interrupted. 'Let's hope your people have found what you were looking for.'

The Detective Sergeant sighed, but did not reply.

Easing back in his seat, Sir Jeremy stared inquisitively down at them. It was then Carlisle noticed the diamond studded gold cuff links. Everything about the man reeked of success, or so he would have them believe.

'I hope today's visit finally brings an end to the matter.'

'I'm afraid not,' Wallace replied grimly.

'What is it now, Sergeant?'

Wallace cleared his throat. 'We've recently had cause to reopen our enquiries into Charles Anderson's death. I believe he once worked for you, Sir Jeremy?'

The Gilesgate chairman looked at each of them in turn. 'The tone of your voice tells me you already have a suspect in mind,' said Sir Jeremy, shifting awkwardly in his seat. 'Perhaps I may be able to assist you gentlemen?'

'That won't be necessary,' Wallace replied.

'Oh and why not?'

'I must warn you that anyone remotely connected with your organisation is now a suspect.'

'Really!' gasped Sir Jeremy. 'And what brings you to that conclusion?'

'Three of your board members are dead, isn't that enough?'

'You don't think for one minute that anyone in my organisation is remotely connected with these murders, surely not?'

'We're certain of it,' said Carlisle.

Sir Jeremy hesitated for a second. 'You sound convinced, Mr Carlisle?'

'I am.'

'And what brings you to that conclusion, may I ask?'

Carlisle turned to George Wallace. 'We believe that another murder, one which took place last November . . . may be connected.'

'May be connected—'

'We can only deal with the facts,' Carlisle conceded.

'I knew it!' said Sir Jeremy, launching into them. 'You people never cease to amaze me. Do you ever get anything right?'

It was anxious moments like these, and there had been many in Carlisle's long undistinguished career, when he enjoyed a challenge. Ignoring the Chairman's outburst, he opened his briefcase and took out a large green folder, placing it on the table in front of him. He ran another minute in silence, just enough to heighten the chairman's curiosity.

'Do you recognise any of these people?' Carlisle said, handing Sir Jeremy a large monochrome photograph taken from the folder.

Sir Jeremy extracted a pair of silver half-eye reading spectacles from an inside pocket and sat them on the tip of his nose. He stared at the image for a few seconds, before giving it a long-suffering sigh.

'When was it taken?' Carlisle asked.

Turning it in the light, the Chairman brought it up to his face until it almost touched the tip of his long nose. 'If I'm not mistaken, this is the Nottingham Flood Contract.'

'What can you tell me about it?' said Wallace, eager to join in.

'That's not too difficult, Sergeant. At the end of every contract we hold a small social gathering. It's our way of thanking everyone who has taken part in the project. You might say it's an informal handover ceremony, between Gilesgate and the client.'

Wallace gave him a thin wintery smile, but said nothing.

'And the people in the photograph . . . who are they?' Carlisle quizzed.

Sir Jeremy peered over the top of his glasses. 'How did you come by this?'

'Tell me,' said Wallace. 'Was this picture taken before or after the Nottingham contract?'

'After, if I'm not mistaken—'

'And the so called client team,' Wallace pressed. 'Who are they?'

'I don't like the tone of your voice, Sergeant.'

Wallace dug his heels in. 'Would you keep records of the people who attended that day? An invitation list . . . perhaps?'

'We may well have done, yes.'

Sir Jeremy was lying, and Wallace had picked up on it. The detective gave him a look that would freeze a blast furnace. 'Such a document would be very useful,' said Wallace. 'Of course, we may wish to interview everyone involved. Those still alive, that is.'

'That's absurd,' Sir Jeremy protested.

'Not really when you consider that any one of these people may be withholding some vital piece of information. You seem to forget,' said Wallace, holding Sir Jeremy's glances, 'there's a serial killer out there and he's targeting your board of directors.'

'I'll make the necessary arrangements, Sergeant.'

Carlisle glanced at his colleague, with the kind of look he normally reserved for halfwits. 'There is, of course, the question of protection, George.'

Wallace nodded. 'Ah, protection.'

'*Protection!*' gasped Sir Jeremy.

'That's what we do best,' Wallace replied stoically. 'We protect you people from these so-called maniacs.'

That had done the trick.

Carlisle glanced at the folder in front of him, a thick, well-thumbed document. It had nothing to do with the case, but he tapped it with his pen all the same – purely a diversionary distraction. Milking it for all it was worth, he peered down at the heading:

GEORGE GRADY, OPERATION SPARROWHAWK.

And then he remembered. The case involved a horrific child sex offender, a low-life who had met more than his match inside Durham jail. Having served five months of a twenty year sentence, Grady was found dead in the showers. He'd been stabbed to death by a fellow inmate, a crazy lifer who'd lost his only son in a freak road traffic accident. George Grady's prison sentence, it seemed, had been cut short by good old fashioned criminal justice.

Carlisle opened the file – another annoying distraction.

'I've remembered the location,' Sir Jeremy said, flamboyantly. 'It was Rexroth Hall.'

'One more thing,' said Carlisle, turning to the photograph again. 'Is that not Ernest Stanton seated next to your good self?

'Yes, it is now that you come to mention it.'

'And *what* exactly was Stanton's role in this so called . . . Nottingham Flood Contract?'

Sir Jeremy rolled his eyes. 'Stanton was employed by the Environment Agency. Why do you ask?'

'And what did that entail?'

Not for the first time, Sir Jeremy's bottom lip had tightened. The mechanics of a murder investigation could be daunting, and the interview techniques no different. Prior to their meeting, both Carlisle and Wallace had agreed to spring the Ernest Stanton murder on Sir Jeremy. It was all about timing, and now seemed the perfect moment. The Chairman was floundering, and like a rabbit caught in the headlights there was no hiding place.

'Stanton was involved in global warming initiatives,' Sir Jeremy went on. 'His particular interests lay with the European Flood Directives and his involvement in RAP. That's the Risk Assessment Panel, if you're not familiar with the title.'

Wallace made a note of it and lifted his head. 'And what was Stanton's involvement in this so called . . . RAP?'

'He was a government advisor, that's how he became involved with the Risk Assessment Panel in the first place. Stanton's main responsibilities were to oversee the contract tender bids.' A rare smile cut across Sir Jeremy's face. 'All in the best interests of government, of course.'

'Yes, of course,' Carlisle nodded, knowing they'd touched another raw nerve.

'I don't want to give you people the wrong impression here,' said Sir Jeremy, flamboyantly gesticulating with his hands, 'but Ernest Stanton was a bit of an enigma as far as Gilesgate was concerned. Besides, these gatherings were purely a corporate hospitality exercise, and nothing else.'

You're lying, Carlisle cursed. Stanton was a slippery bag of worms at the best of times. He knew how to manipulate people, extract their money. Honesty and integrity played no central part in Ernest Stanton's work role. Money talked, it influenced people's decisions and was fundamental to the way Stanton had operated. It was time to cut to the quick.

'One further question if I may,' Carlisle said, pointing down at the photograph again. 'The person whose face has been partially scratched out, who is he?'

'That's Derek Riley,' Sir Jeremy sighed.

'Wasn't he a sheep farmer?'

'Derek Riley was a speculator, Mr Carlisle, and as such, he played no active role in the running of this organisation. These people are purely financial investors . . . they're what's known as Sleeping Partners.'

Sir Jeremy was merely making a broad sweeping political statement, but foremost in Carlisle's mind was: he's lying through his back teeth. He thought for a moment. 'So that would account for Riley's involvement in . . . Lowther Construction?'

Sir Jeremy's jaw slackened. 'I thought that this was a murder inquiry?'

'It is, Sir Jeremy, and one involving three of your directors,' Wallace explained.

The chairman's face darkened. Having told countless untruths, Sir Jeremy had exposed himself for what he really was – a true Charlatan.

'On Monday it was our financial affairs, today it's contractual agreements. Tell me, Sergeant, just how far your people are intending to go with this—'

Wallace cut him short. 'It's our job to solve a murder crime, Sir Jeremy, and in doing so, we intend to use every means at our disposal.'

'This is absurd.'

'You may not be aware of this,' said Carlisle, 'but this photograph was taken from the wall of the killer's flat. You could say it's his calling card, a method and means by which he selects his next victim.'

A moment's hesitation shot across the chairman's face. 'You're not suggesting these people are in grave danger, are you?'

'Those of you still alive are.'

Sir Jeremy's hands were shaking. 'And this is how he selects his victims?'

'I'm afraid so!' Wallace grinned. 'Which means that every board member still alive is now a potential target?'

Carlisle's looked at Wallace. 'What do you think, George?'

'I'm not a betting man,' Wallace shrugged, 'but the odds seem pretty crap to me.'

Sir Jeremy shut his mouth and seethed. There was tension between them, unease. The chairman hesitated, still wary of where this was all going.

'This is ridiculous, gentlemen. What kind of monster is he?'

'I wouldn't go there if I were you,' Carlisle insisted.

'So why has he chosen . . . Gilesgate?'

Carlisle observed the man's concern, closed the green folder, and then said. 'That's a very pertinent question, and one that leads us to believe that someone in your organisation may hold the answers to. Perhaps the killer has a personal grudge against one of you. Who knows? Whoever he is, he will not stop until he's eliminated every single board member. These are very dangerous times, Sir Jeremy. I'm sure you're aware of that.'

Sir Jeremy's eyes filled with terror.

'The newspapers say you've uncovered his hideout, I——'

Carlisle didn't need to listen to the rest of his story; he'd already made up his mind. He watched as Sir Jeremy pulled out a silver watch from a waistcoat pocket, tapped the face with his fingers, and held it to his ear. Beneath the underlying twitches and nervous facial contortions, the old fox was definitely up to something. Whatever it was, his was a dangerous game he was playing.

Half an hour later, after dropping off Wallace, Carlisle continued to drive south. Still deep in thought, nothing seemed straightforward anymore. Even Sir Jeremy's political morality was now in question. There again, it wasn't too difficult to find a bent politician nowadays. That much he was certain of.

No, it was something else that was bothering him. To catch a psychopath was always going to be a major challenge. Carlisle knew that. Even under stress these people showed little or no remorse towards their victims. Most psychopaths he'd ever met in the interview room were quick to blame others for their crimes. It was never their fault, and it was always all about them. Now, even more than before, he was convinced their killer wasn't a Gilesgate director. If not, then he had to be someone else – someone close to these people with a personal hate grudge.

But who? Carlisle asked.

The answer to that was proving more difficult.

Chapter Thirty-Six

Henry Fraser had deliberately chosen an alternative route that morning, just in case he was followed. It was 9.22am. With plenty of time on his hands, he called in at his favourite corner shop and picked up a dozen cold beers. Cramming them into a battered cool bag, he checked his surroundings and climbed back into the waiting taxi. A stiff south-easterly breeze was blowing in off the North Sea, when his cab finally drew up alongside North Shields Fish Quay. Apart from a few dog walkers, the place looked deserted. He stood for a while, and stared up in bewilderment at Cleveland's tall masts. Over thirty metres high, they carried upwards of a dozen sails when fully rigged out. Amazing, he thought. At one-hundred feet long and modelled on a Baltimore clipper, when riding on a good trade wind, she could average speeds of around sixteen knots. She was an impressive ship, but one he had no intentions of ever sailing in.

'Welcome on board,' Cleveland's Master called out.

Greenfingers Armstrong was a small man in stature, mid-fifties, balding, with harsh blue eyes that sat squarely behind thick rimless bifocals. His real name was Peter Armstrong, but amongst his other talents, he was a dab hand at growing his own strain of cannabis. A likeable character, Greenfingers had always managed to stay clear of trouble. Not anymore. Less than a hundred metres away, above one of the many local fish restaurants, a lone undercover surveillance officer had trained his binoculars on the early morning proceedings. Henry Fraser was the fifth Gilesgate board member to arrive at the Fish Quay that morning. Something was afoot, and the police were determined to get to the bottom of it.

Moving to the quarterdeck, Fraser was met by the rest of Gilesgate's executives. Acknowledgements were minimal, each preferring to leave the talking to the other. The thud of Fraser's cool bag hitting the ship's wooden deck made everyone jump. He knew then, he was back in control.

'Henry . . .' said Tony Harper, extending out a hand.

Harper was unreliable, and so were the others. Fraser trusted no one, not even his granny. That's why everyone's mobile phone was laid out on the table in front of them.

'I'll be brief,' said Fraser, mopping his brow for the umpteenth time. 'There have been a few new developments.'

Greenfingers Armstrong looked genuinely surprised.

'What developments are these, Henry?'

'Did I say something?' said Fraser, thumping his huge fist into the table.

Everyone knew why the big man was here, and what was to be done, but questioning him was a different matter. As yet, a plan still had to be hatched, and that was down to the big man. For the past twenty years, Henry Fraser had always handled Gilesgate's muscle. That was his thing; he was good at it, especially at resolving other people's problems. Financial matters were not his speciality; besides, it was the faceless backroom boys who always took care of his hard earned cash – investing in non-traceable assets. That's how the system worked, that's what set Fraser apart from the rest of the organisation.

The big man splayed his huge hands out in front of him, a threatening gesture that brought an instant response. 'The hit on John Matthew has been called off. And, before anyone asks, it's for technical reasons.'

'Called off, I——' Greenfingers' voice tailed off.

Someone's mobile phone vibrated on the deck table, but no one dared answer it.

Fraser shook his head. 'So, what is it you people want to know?'

Fred Sharkey, a veteran board member in his late sixties, stared anxiously across at him. 'If the contract on Matthew has been called off, who's handling Riley's killer?'

'It's already been taken care of,' Fraser assured him.

'Anyone we know?'

'All you people need to know is Matthew is now in police custody.'

'So, the pigs finally caught up with him?' said Starkey, puffing out his cheeks. 'I always knew the man was an arsehole.'

Fraser tapped the side of his head, a puzzled look. 'Yeah, but they've charged him with attempted murder. You're forgetting, Fred, he was working for us.'

'Murder!' gasped Greenfingers.

Fraser shifted his position. 'You're beginning to annoy me, little man.'

Greenfingers turned to the others for support, but none came. His voice barely a whisper, and eyes like frightened little birds, he slowly plucked up courage. 'What about the hospital guards?'

'That part of the operation has been closed down,' said Fraser. 'It wasn't Matthew who killed Derek Riley; it was this maniac, the Wharf Butcher.'

Benny Woodall leaned over the deck table. His pock-marked face twitched but his lips barely moved. Always the height of fashion, Benny loved to dress snappy. Wearing an Yves Saint Laurent grey pinstripe suit, blue silk shirt and Church New York Oxford brogues, he looked immaculate. His gold oyster perpetual Rolex watch not only looked expensive, it was expensive. It was Benny's pride and joy, and he thrived on the attention it brought him.

'So,' said Benny. 'Why the sudden shift in direction?'

Fraser flexed his huge biceps. 'That's a good question, Benny. There's a rumour doing the rounds, it was this Wharf Butcher who slit Ernest Stanton's throat.'

'But that was ten months ago.'

'Don't play on my words, Benny. It doesn't suit you.'

Greenfingers' jaw dropped in numb disbelief. The mere sight of Fraser's huge fists had dampened the little man's appetite for conversation.

'This Wharf Butcher moves too fast for my liking,' said Benny Woodall. 'What assurances do we have that he's not working for another organisation?'

'Cos he's not,' said Fraser.

'So why is he targeting the board?'

Fraser stared down at his empty beer can and sighed. The big man loved nothing more than being the centre of attraction. He thrived on it, and right now he was centre stage. 'He's eliminating you one at a time, Benny, and he's thorough with it. It's my guess that somebody has upset him, and whoever that is, he intends to get even with them.'

'He's making me feel nervous,' Benny Woodall shrugged. 'God knows who his next victim will be.'

Stony faced, Fraser leaned over and unzipped the cool bag and took out another cold beer. He was thirsty: it was a beautiful day and he was bored with small talk. Close to the river estuary, between the two piers, his interest levels had been drawn towards a small flotilla of sailing boats. Having rounded a series of bright red marker buoys, the lead boats were racing towards the finishing line. Following in their wake, the choppy seawater was throwing up huge plumes of spray. Mesmerized, Fraser slid his massive frame along the galley seat, stretched his legs, and peered over the starboard rail to watch the unfolding finale.

He wasn't alone.

'What's your problem?' said Fraser, turning sharply.

'Just curious,' Greenfingers replied.

'Curious . . . curious about what?' demanded Fraser.

'Why you never sail in her.'

'It's not my scene,' said Fraser, taking another huge gulp of his beer and leaning heavily back against the handrail. 'Besides, I've more important things to do with my time.'

Fraser turned his back on him, and continued to watch the small racing flotilla as it ran for the finishing line. He frowned on small talk; it achieved nothing. Time was precious and the demands much greater. Talk was about bargaining, saying the right things. 'You were right about one thing though, someone has infiltrated our ranks and whoever he is, he's walking a tight line.'

'I've had my suspicions for weeks now.'

'I know you have.' Fraser stepped back a pace, and spun to face him. 'Keep your ears to the ground, and see what you can find out. The minute you hear something . . . anything, you're to contact me. If the word leaks out, then I'll know where the noises were coming from.'

'You can count on me, Henry.'

'You bet I can.'

Greenfingers' face nervously twitched. 'It's the crew I'm worried about. There's talk of a power struggle at the top, and the men are on edge. If you ask me, shifting sands are dangerous, especially now that John Matthew is behind bars.'

The tide on the ebb, Fraser caught sight of a small piece of driftwood as it bobbed up and down in the water. Bored, he threw his empty beer can at it. 'Stop making judgements; others will do that for you. The rules are straightforward. We close ranks . . . move around the fringes so to speak. Any contact from above, will come directly through me.' Fraser turned sharply to confront him. 'Tomorrow you're to hold a crew meeting. Whilst that's taking place, your ship will be bugged.'

'*Tomorrow!*' gasped Greenfingers.

'Did I mention any other day?'

'You're asking too much, Henry. It's impossible to pull a crew together with such short notice. Besides, five of my men are already on shore leave.'

'Make sure it happens; if not you'll join the rest of them at the bottom of the North Sea.'

A troubled expression corrugated Greenfingers' brow. Everyone knew what happened to those who'd overstepped the mark.

Fraser stepped aside, and felt the cool breeze against his face. 'Everyone will attend. Those who don't will face the consequences. I want names. This Wharf Butcher is killing his victims to order, and he's carving his way through the organisation as if it was a slaughterhouse waiting room.'

'But how do I explain that to my crew?'

'With a mouth the size of yours, I'm sure you'll think of something,' said Fraser grinning as if to show off a new set of teeth.

Fraser leaned over and retrieved another cold beer from the cool bag. Tugging on the ring-pull it exploded with a loud bang, sending Greenfingers' nerves into overdrive. 'Try keeping it simple for a change, let's see what tomorrow brings. If the killer isn't a member of your crew, we move on. Look elsewhere. At some stage or other this maniac will eventually surface, and when he does—'

Fraser smashed a huge clenched fist into the ship's handrail.

Greenfingers winced. 'Goodbye, Mr Chips . . .'

Ignoring him, Fraser tucked the cool bag under his arm, and walked ashore across the gangway. He was a huge man, and an easy target for the police undercover surveillance team.

Chapter Thirty-Seven

It began in the temporary control room. Then spread throughout the entire network, before finally ending up on Jack Mason's computer console.

'*I do enjoy a good funeral, Jack; we must meet up again sometime.*'

The Wharf Butcher's audacity had not only shocked the backroom technicians, Jack Mason was furious. Just five days into uncovering the killer's hideout, he had somehow managed to infiltrate the Northumbria police multi-million pound computer security system.

Heads would roll.

The Police Central e-crime unit was onto it like a flash, tracing the culprit terminal to an online internet café on Westgate Road. Close to Newcastle's busy city shopping centre, and within easy walking distance of the Central Station, the location had been carefully chosen. Popular with locals, the interior was nothing flash – somewhere you could grab a quick bite to eat and stay in contact with the rest of the world. The café had a different character at night-time; it was that kind of place.

Jack Mason was in no mood for time wasters. Having pinned the proprietor up against the wall, the open flap of his jacket revealed the butt of his Smith & Wesson model 36. The humour had gone, and with it his patience.

'How often has he visited the place in the past fortnight?' Mason demanded.

The proprietor pushed back from the counter; there was genuine concern in his voice. 'I've told you all I know, Chief Inspector.'

'Is he a regular?'

'No. I've never seen him in here before.'

Mason's face was scarlet. He took another deep breath, before releasing his grip on the proprietor's arm. 'You let that little piece of chicken shit get away.'

'How was I to know who he was?' the proprietor replied.

Glancing around the room, Mason could not believe his bad luck. Two hours earlier, his killer had sat here, drinking coffee, surfing the internet. It felt incredibly unreal that someone could simply slip in and out of society at will. Now a major crime scene investigation, the warren of narrow streets that sprawled out from Westgate Road were now in lockdown. From what Mason could gather forensics had got there first, even before the Crime Scene Manager had arrived on the scene. Kitted out in their white disposable coveralls, they were now about their business. God it was chaos. It reminded him of one of those scenes in a silent Keystone Cops movie where incompetent police officers played out pandemonium on the streets of downtown New York. He counted at least a dozen police vehicles parked up in Westgate Road – with more arriving by the minute. It wasn't always like this he cursed, surely not?

Seconds later, he watched as Luke James climbed out of his patrol car and ambled towards the internet café. Mason could hardly contain himself, let alone think straight.

'The bastard has slipped through our fingers again, Luke.'

'How long ago was this, boss?' asked Detective Sergeant James.

'Thirty minutes ago according to this maggot.' Now hovering over the serving counter, Mason's face was as black as thunder. 'He paid his bill and coolly slipped back into the street unnoticed.'

'Do we have a description?'

'Yeah, he's your typical Mr Average.'

The sergeant shook his head in disbelief. Sometimes, Mason thought, it was all too easy to underestimate the traits of a serial killer's cunning. There were no witness statements, no eyewitness accounts, nothing. It was as if their suspect had simply vanished from the face of the earth. In all the years he'd worked as a copper, he'd never quite come across anything like this before. It felt like he was cradling a cat in his arms. All the while you kept thinking to yourself, those terrible claws, they can rip you apart in the blink of an eye. Not that it was ever going to be easy, he realised that. Nowadays Westgate Road was a notorious multicultural melting pot where almost anything could happen, and usually did. This time felt different though; the person responsible for this malicious prank was probably a notorious serial killer.

The next fifteen minutes were spent checking the surrounding properties. Whoever their suspect was, he certainly had a good understanding of the area. Still no further forward, Mason glanced at the buildings opposite. People were hanging out of the second floor windows, as if puzzled by all the commotion. Further afield, at the bottom of Westgate Road, huge crowds were gathered. Not the best of starts, he thought.

'If this is the Wharf Butcher's doing,' said James, 'then he's made a grave mistake in my opinion. This is a notorious drugs catchment area, so we should have plenty of CCTV coverage at our disposal.'

'You're right Luke; he may not be as clever as I first thought.'

The Detective Sergeant removed his police cap, and wiped the sweat from his brow. Of all the things that could have gone wrong that morning, this had to happen. James was married with two doting teenage daughters, but his Caribbean wife had recently been diagnosed with breast cancer. Having undergone a course of chemotherapy at the Freeman Hospital today was her last course of treatment. James was beyond himself.

'He must have sussed this place out long before he sent you the e-mail, boss.'

'I know. It's Sod's law he was wearing some sort of protective gloves when he used the café keyboard to log into my e-mail account.'

'You've got to hand it to him,' said James. 'Carlisle always said he was local. In my view, he couldn't have chosen a better place had he tried.'

'He's local all right, and no doubt working within his comfort zone.' Mason shrugged. 'What about local pubs, Luke?'

'I'm not so sure about that, but there must be a million CCTV cameras covering the area.'

'Yeah, but how many of them work?'

'We must have something on him boss, surely?'

'Maybe, but from what I've seen of some of the footage lately, the quality is crap.'

'Perhaps we should concentrate more effort around the local Metro stations.'

'Really . . .'

'Why not, at least we can question everyone who walks with a limp.'

Mason shot him a glance. 'And what the fuck do I tell the human rights activists when they accuse me of showing prejudice towards disabled people?'

The sergeant gave him a puzzled look.

God, Mason cursed. James had a point. So why was he shouting at him? The trouble was, most of the CCTV footage he'd ever come across could never be used as permissible evidence in court. It was his one big pet hate at the moment, and it annoyed him intensely.

A familiar voice suddenly boomed over the Sergeant's radio.

'It sounds like Ken Morrison has another TWOC on his hands,' said DS James. 'How the hell he does it, I'll never know. That's the third Mondeo he's pulled this morning.'

'Let's hope it's one of our police bait cars.' Mason shrugged.

'Chance would be a fine thing, boss.'

James' radio suddenly crackled into action again; the driver of the stolen vehicle, a well-known shoplifter, was now under arrest. What a pity, Mason cursed. There must be at least a dozen bait Mondeo's parked up outside Metro stations – surely one of them would take the killer's fancy?

'Ask Morrison to keep me informed,' Mason said, pointing down at the sergeant's handset.

'Will do, boss.'

As another unmarked police vehicle screeched to a halt outside the internet café, Mason gritted his teeth. How many more police officers would it take? Westgate Road was fast turning into a police parking lot and if the press picked up on it, they'd be having a field day. What's more, the surrounding area had been thoroughly searched in a grid pattern – that too had thrown up nothing. The more he thought about it, the angrier he became.

Back inside, Luke James stared in puzzlement. 'I hear Henry Fraser has been involved in another nightclub security incident. He certainly has a fierce reputation amongst the hard-core criminal fraternity,' said James. 'If he *is* working for Sir Jeremy, then it can only mean one thing . . .'

The Sergeant was right; it had taken a long time to set the investigation in motion, but Henry Fraser was fast becoming his number one target. Having spent two years in Frankland Prison for grievous bodily harm, his criminal record wasn't exactly squeaky clean either. No thanks to a sharp defence barrister named Tom Pollard – the big man had somehow managed to steer clear of trouble. Fraser was a muscle man, a leveller, someone you wouldn't want to get on the wrong side of. All the same Tom Pollard was a right pain in the arse, if not a damn good barrister. Too good if the truths were known.

Stretching his arms behind the back of his head, Mason was having another bad day. There were times, and there had been many of late, when Luke James' relentless gossip gave him a headache. The man meant well, but he could talk the hind legs off a donkey in his opinion.

'How's the wife, nowadays?' he asked, casually.

'Today's her last visit to the hospital, boss. Hopefully they'll give her the all clear, but you can never tell with cancer.'

'I thought her appointment was yesterday, Luke?'

'No, it's today. Two o'clock at the Freeman Hospital.'

Mason checked his watch: 11.20am. Realising that there was little more any of them could do, it was pointless him hanging around. What to do he thought?

'You should have told me earlier, Luke.'

James nodded. 'The job always comes first, boss.'

Mason forced a smile. 'My ex-wife always used to say that to me, every time we went on holiday together. You can never relax, she would say, you check out hotel guests as though everyone is a potential criminal. She was right of course. Once a copper, always a copper, I'm afraid.' Mason grinned. 'Get your miserable arse out of here, and give my regards to the missus.'

Luke James' face lit up. 'Cheers boss, it's much appreciated.'

The Sergeant tipped the peak of his cap as he made off towards his police vehicle.

'Let me know how you get on,' Mason said.

Despite his vigorous protests, the media were still out in large numbers. News travelled fast; too fast, in Mason's opinion. Someone was feeding them inside information; if not; these people were damn good at their jobs. Informants, whistle-blowers, call them what you will, Mason was sick of them. Where would it all end? Even governments were caught up in it. What with the Freedom of Information Act, and the pursuit of transparency, nothing was sacrosanct anymore. No thanks to the power of the computer and the mobile phone camera, censored material could be downloaded at the drop of a hat. The speed of sensitive information transfer was alarming. And that reminded him: it was time he brought the Assistant Chief Constable to heel. His interference in the case had cost them dearly.

He stood for a while, knowing just how crucial the next twenty-four hours would be. Get it wrong, and the wolves would come knocking at his door. Still, he wasn't going to let it get to him. Just how he was going to catch the Wharf Butcher, he had no idea. Something would turn up; it usually did. If not, then he would soon have some serious explaining to do.

His mobile phone pinged.

Chapter Thirty-Eight

It had just turned eleven-thirty when Mason finally ambled into Starbucks, in the heart of Newcastle's city centre. Carlisle preferred the layout, the place had a cosy atmosphere; besides, the coffee was good. It was Friday, and every available seat in the house was taken. He watched as Jack Mason stepped aside to allow a tall woman with a black buggy squeeze past him. The kid inside it was throwing a tantrum. Thrashing its arms as if the world was full of nasty grownups, it was screaming the place down. Mason just stood there, motionless, observing in silence. Nearby, a young teenage waitress was busy clearing a table already occupied by the next set of customers. Everything seemed a chore to her, as if the end of her shift couldn't come fast enough. Not a good sign, thought Carlisle.

By now, everyone and his granny knew that the Chief Inspector had received a threatening e-mail that morning. What they didn't know, not even Jack Mason, was that the killer had probably written it days ago. No doubt he was watching the detective's every movement, and laughing at him every time he tripped up. His was a dangerous game of cat and mouse that only had one outcome.

'You missed all the fun,' said Mason, pulling up a seat. 'Our friend has made contact.'

'So I hear!'

Mason took a sip of his coffee. He'd not shaved in days, giving the impression that he'd stopped up most of the night. 'The cheeky sod even had the audacity to hack into my e-mail account.'

Carlisle thought about it. 'Tread careful, Jack. He's trying to ruffle your feathers after you've torn his flat apart.'

'He's got a bloody nerve, if you ask me.' Mason puffed his cheeks and blew out a steady breath. 'It's annoying to think we pulled the wrong guy in.'

'So that's what this e-mail is about . . . he did turn up at the funeral.'

'It would appear so,' Mason mumbled.

'There must be loads of police video footage of Annie Jenkins funeral service, Jack?'

Mason's look was puzzled. 'There is, but we believe he turned up in disguise.'

'He's definitely playing mind games with you, Jack. Be careful.'

Mason shot him a withering look, but said nothing.

They spent the next fifteen minutes analysing the possibilities. And yes, just as Carlisle said they would, Mason's investigations into Sir Jeremy had thrown up a whole new raft of complications. According to intelligence reports, the Gilesgate Chairman now had the press in his pockets. Not only that, he'd built up an impenetrable ring of legal advisors around him, who were now at his beck and call twenty-four-seven. In Carlisle's mind, Sir Jeremy was using his political position to his utmost advantage. Proving it was another matter, but any investigations into his private life would be extremely difficult, if not impossible.

There was a noise of crockery breaking, which caused Mason to jump.

'Did you know Sir Jeremy was once accused of child abuse against his only son?' Mason said casually.

'What?'

'When his wife got wind of it and reported it to the local authorities, she got absolutely nowhere.' Mason tapped the tip of nose. 'I've been doing some digging around, putting my feelers out. According to old case files, there wasn't enough evidence to lay charges against him. In the end, the case was thrown out of the courts.'

'When did this happen?'

'The mid to late nineties—'

'God, that's a bloody long time ago, Jack'

Mason stared at him. 'Maybe, but it shows you what we're up against.'

Carlisle thought a moment. 'What if this never happened?'

'It happened all right. Shortly after, his wife divorced him.' Mason lowered his head as though speaking from past experience. 'It was a messy affair by all accounts, but these things usually are. Apart from suffering severe bouts of depression, his wife made several suicide attempts on her life.'

'So what happened to their son in all of this?'

'He was farmed off to live with an aunt.' Mason took a huge bite out of his sausage roll, and fiddled with the greasy wrapping. 'What's more, none of this ever made the local newspapers which is interesting to say the least.'

'No doubt his legal advisers were involved?'

Mason sighed. 'More than likely . . .'

Infuriated, Carlisle could barely contain himself let alone concentrate on what Mason was now telling him. This kind of stuff never sat comfortably in his mind, and never would. The legacy of child abuse triggered off all kinds of mental trauma inside young people's minds, and they suffered terribly because of it. Then he remembered. Back in the eighties, all sorts of scandal was taking place behind closed doors. Most of it was either dismissed as utter nonsense, or swept under the carpet as pure fantasy. Thirty years on, and it was all coming back to haunt them.

'You need to look into it, Jack,' said Carlisle. 'The people who commit this type of crime should never be allowed to get away with it.'

Mason gave him a smile that unmasked unease. 'That's why I'm bringing him in for questioning.'

'I doubt he'll talk.'

'First things first,' said Mason, with more than a hint of revulsion in his voice. 'Before we go throwing the book at him, let's find out what his business interests in Gilesgate are.'

Mason had a point, and the cold steel glint in his eye told him that someone's feathers were about to be ruffled. But there lay a problem, as most of Mason's evidence was hearsay. Any charges laid against Sir Jeremy would need to be watertight. If not, his lawyers would make mincemeat out of him in any courtroom.

'So, what happens now?' Carlisle asked.

Mason raised an eyebrow whilst staring into his cup. 'I haven't a clue . . . but I'm working on it. You seem to forget, my friend. I still have this problem of the ACC hanging over me.'

'Blimey! I'd almost forgotten about him,' Carlisle confessed.

Mason's eyes narrowed. 'Now there's a man who is definitely up to no good.'

'But that doesn't implicate him, surely not?'

'My mind's made up,' Mason said, taking another huge bite out of his sausage roll. 'What's more, I'm toying with the idea of bringing them both in together. Let's see if their stories match up. If nothing else, it will certainly put the cat amongst the pigeons.'

'Is that wise?'

'Who cares,' Mason shrugged, indicating the matter was already decided.

Carlisle knew better than to say anything; he just sat there and nodded.

'Wait till you hear this,' said Mason, cramming the last of the sausage roll into the corner of his mouth. He was in no hurry. 'A friend of mine, called Sid Holloway, has been looking into the Global Warming contractual agreements for me. When it comes to number crunching, Sid's a whiz kid.' Mason brushed the last of the crumbs from his jacket as if it was the natural thing to do. 'To cut a long story short, Sid's found a loophole in one of the European Council's contract clauses. There's a section in the fine print which states, that no one contractor can conduct more than fifteen per cent of the overall EC's budget. According to Sid, it was put there to protect the smaller companies from being frozen out on price. In other words, everyone gets a fair crack at the whip.'

Carlisle placed his coffee cup in front of him, and waited for the punchline.

'This is no ordinary system we're dealing with here,' Mason went on. 'It's rigidly run, tightly controlled, and kept under close scrutiny at all times. In a nutshell, when all the sealed bids are in, it's down to RAP to oversee the selection process.'

Carlisle thought a moment, and then the penny dropped. 'Isn't that the Risk Assessment Panel, and wasn't Ernest Stanton involved in that?'

'God, you've got a sharp memory. It took me a whole damn weekend to figure that one out, and Stanton's was the last name that sprang to mind.'

'So how does the system work?' he asked.

'Think of it as a large pot of money . . . evenly distributed amongst its European counterparts. Once a company has exhausted its fifteen per cent quota, it's automatically frozen out from any further bidding.' Mason's eyes narrowed. 'In other words, it must look elsewhere for its business.'

'Ah. I smell a rat,' Carlisle said.

Mason almost laughed. 'On the surface the rules are pretty straightforward. Once you've exhausted your fifteen per cent quota, you're out of it, unless—'

'Someone has access to the sealed-tender bids,' Carlisle interrupted.

Mason's grin broadened. 'Hole in one, my friend.'

'So that's how Ernest Stanton was able to bend the rules?'

'Yeah, I always knew that bastard was up to no good, and now I know why,' said Mason. 'That's how Gilesgate are able to continue bidding . . . through a system of fictitious Sleeper Companies.'

He watched as the detective chewed over his next statement. Mason was no fool. Had Vic Miller not stumbled across countless contract files, then everything else would have faded into insignificance. It was a clever scam, and one that had netted a significant amount of European Grant money. Mason, it appeared, now had more than enough evidence to press charges. But would he go ahead with it?

His mobile rang, but he chose to ignore it.

'On paper Gilesgate's accounts are squeaky clean . . . Charles Anderson always made sure of that. According to Sid, Sir Jeremy has far too many fingers in the pie to be an effective politician. Tell me,' said Mason, as if to enforce a point. 'Where do you find an honest politician nowadays?'

'Maybe he's genuinely concerned about the environment, or—'

'It's sod's law there's no one on the European Council who can help us.' Mason rolled his eyes. 'Let's face it: the ACC and Sir Jeremy are a formidable partnership to be up against.'

Carlisle grinned. 'So that's how Derek Riley got involved in Lowther Construction.'

'Too damn right it was,' Mason acknowledged. 'The trouble is now, how many more people are involved in these so called Sleeper Companies?'

It was still a clever scam, but proving it would be extremely difficult, he thought. 'So where do we go from here?' Carlisle asked.

'My primary aim is to catch the Wharf Butcher,' Mason replied. 'And I've got everyone and their granny trying to do that.'

'So how do we deal with Gilesgate in the meantime?'

The DCI tapped the tip of his nose again. 'Never interfere with the enemy when they're making a mistake, just let them get on with it. When the timing is right, we'll hand all this over to the Fraud Squad. Let them deal with it.' Mason's eased back in his seat, as if his mind was already made up. 'The last thing we need to do is to ruffle the killer's feathers. Do that and he'll simply go to ground.'

'Umm, that's easier said than done.'

Mason paused as a young waitress homed in on their empty cups.

'Cast your mind back to the seventies,' said Mason, 'and the Yorkshire Ripper case. Do you remember a hoaxer called Wearside Jack?'

'Who could ever forget that?'

'This e-mail stinks of it,' Mason nodded.

'Be careful, Jack. He's getting to you.'

'Nah, I'm convinced it's a prankster.'

Carlisle collected his thoughts. An internet café was the last place he would have imaged a serial killer play out his fantasies. Maybe Mason had a point. There again, what if he was wrong?

'Have you given any more thought to stepping up your surveillance operations?'

'Don't go there, we don't have the available resources,' Mason grunted.

'What a pity.'

'Cut backs, my friend, they're the bane of everyone's life.' Mason rose to his feet. 'In the meantime, let's hope the bastard doesn't decide to strike again.'

The town was busy when they stepped out of Starbucks, and walked the short distance to Greys Monument. As the first spots of rain hit the pavement, they made their way down into Grey Street.

They were not alone.

Chapter Thirty-Nine

Earlier that Morning

Grey Street was in confusion. People scurrying for shelter as a light drizzle had turned into a heavy downpour. After a long time – how long Lexus had no idea – his suspicions were finally rewarded. Jack Mason was not alone when he stepped out of Starbucks and into Newcastle's busy shopping precinct. The profiler was with him. Curious, Lexus decided to follow them. It was Mason he feared most, and he knew he must stay vigilant. The Detective was incredibly unpredictable, and capable of getting up to anything. He had no ambitions to harm him, not at present that is, but he was working on it all the same.

It was truly amazing how many organs a body would offer up before it finally shut down. A nightmare: bucket's full of blood. He loved to play God, and the thought genuinely excited him. Not everyone knew he was so unbelievably talented. There were those, not many, who believed he was totally mad. He wasn't, of course, how could he be, everyone knew he was a genius – how could they possibly think otherwise?

Despite his alertness, the two police officers he was following had vanished into Grey Street. It was a stunning area, a slice of Newcastle: granite stone faced buildings, with dark slate roofs against the backdrop of an overcast sky. Parked cars lined the side of the road, and the architecture was stunning. At least to him it was.

Then the voices returned.

Where are you?

'I'm here, numpty.'

Aren't you supposed to be following these people?

Lexus stared vaguely into space; his mind was in turmoil. He could barely think straight, let alone decide into which doorway the two police officers had now vanished. Each day was becoming more demanding, he felt. Nothing was real anymore. Everything was deception, filled with the illusion of make-believe and fantasy.

He turned his collar up against the rain, and searched in his head for answers. It was lunchtime, and Gregg's sandwich shop was alive with pretty young girls arriving from the local banks and nearby estate agents. They were laughing and joking with one another, and talking about their weekend plans. Then, just as he imagined she would, she pulled up alongside of him. She was a pretty young thing, petite, with long black curly locks and ice blue eyes that twinkled like diamonds beneath the soft shimmering strip lighting. It was funny how she unnerved him, not that he cared, but he was fearful of just how much of his uncertainty she might uncover. It was a terrible thing to have your mind taken away from you; insecurity was a daunting state to be in. But hey, he was much bigger than this; besides, wasn't she the one who was flirting with him.

Lexus often wondered if he would ever fall in love. And what it would be like. She glanced at him with eyes that seemed to burn the colour of sunlight on water, at least to him they did. As he peered down the top of her blouse, the scent of her body excited him. Her eyes, full of fear, she took flight across the wet slippery pavement and hurried down into Market Street. Why he wondered? What had he done wrong this time?

Then the anger surfaced.

Bitch!

'And she was so . . . pretty.'

The pretty one, who knows she is pretty, is probably not pretty at all.

'You're such a genius,' he smiled.

Under the cover of the Central Arcade, he now faced a more daunting challenge. It had stopped raining, and the two police officers – the ones he was following – they were hiding somewhere. Where, he had absolutely no idea, but he was working on it all the same. Then, on the corner of Hood Street, an elderly couple squeezed out of the back seat of a taxi and set foot onto the wet slippery pavement. Gripped by fear, and a whole lot of suspicion, he ducked back into the shadows.

He checked his surroundings.

How did you spot that? You're so amazingly talented.

'I know,' he replied. 'I even knew they were coming.'

Never mind that – just look who's here!

Perfect, the two of them together at last.

It was the profiler that concerned him now. He was unpredictable, and capable of reading into other people's minds.

'Can people really do that?'

Yes they can, but not into your mind, of course.

'Are you sure?'

Oh yes, I'm certain of that. You're a genius – remember?

As the profiler moved north, Jack Mason descended into the bowels of Monument Metro station. He was alone now, just him and the profiler. Even so, Lexus was wary.

There, standing in front of him, was an armed police officer. He was a tall man, with distinct bushy sideburns and protruding eyes that glared back at him as though he was invisible. He wasn't of course – but he could have been – everyone knew that. Then, as another squad car dashed headlong towards another unknown destination, his mind was thrown into turmoil again. There was work to be done, important work, and he knew he must attend to it. Close to the Bigg Market – in a quieter corner of the city – he spotted what he was searching for. It was a MK3, with reclining leather seats and such an amazing dashboard panel. And guess what, it was filled with an array of clocks and fancy gadgets.

He glanced through the window.

'Is it a trap?'

Only a genius would know that – the voice in his head replied.

'So why has the previous owner abandoned it?'

It could be a gift—

'What for me?'

Why not, they knew how important it was to you.

Thirty minutes later, opposite the North Shields Fish Quay, Lexus pulled up onto a shallow piece of waste ground and checked his surroundings. Set back from the river was the boathouse. It was a tall structure, isolated, with high windowless walls and a long flat roof that ran the entire length of the building. He was closer now, much closer than ever before. Inside the building's wooden structure, was Trevor Radcliffe's yacht. He knew that, he had seen it before, many times.

The only thing that bothered him now, was space. There wasn't any, not for what he had in mind.

Then the voices returned.

Stop worrying, you've planned this for weeks now.

'I know, but I can't help it.'

Yes you can, you're almost home and dry.

Then, Trevor Radcliffe appeared and a new excitement gripped him.

He was a frail man, unsuspecting, and totally oblivious of the dangers that now surrounded him. His death would be a clinical ending, concise, and not over indulged. There had been others of course, only Jack Mason knew that. Just how many he had no idea, but unquestionably more than a few. He checked the boathouse.

How do you feel right now?

'Excited,' Lexus replied.

Me too!

Chapter Forty

The tide was on the turn when DS Wallace and DC Bower parked their undercover vehicle onto a small piece of waste ground, and switched off the car's engine. Wallace sat for a while – both hands firmly gripped around the steering wheel – and surveyed his new surroundings. To Wallace's reckoning, and to his relief, the boatyard was little more than a hundred metres away. With clear unobstructed views, it was the perfect location to protect Trevor Radcliffe from becoming the Wharf Butcher's next target. He would need to stay vigilant, he realised that. One false move and it would all end here.

Wallace detested undercover surveillance operations; eight hour shifts, cooped up inside his undercover Ford Focus Sedan. It was unnatural, soul destroying, besides interfering with his social life. Fed up to his back teeth, he grabbed his Bushnell high- powered binoculars and zoomed in on anything that might grab his attention. It was mid-afternoon, and apart from the odd tourist mooching around town, North Shields Fish Quay was quiet. Then, at the mouth of the river he spotted a small fishing boat, as it made slow headway between the two harbour piers. Following in its wake, a flock of Fulmars were quarrelling over a few fish scraps being tossed over the stern of the incoming vessel. In search of easy pickings, a lone predator swooped low over the water, dived, and took off again with a fish head in its mouth. Before the others had realised what was happening, it was long gone. It was the highlight of Wallace's day, a small piece of action that had helped to relieve the boredom.

He watched as DC Bower set off to get them both fish and chips. Wallace was hungry; he hadn't eaten in hours now. Opposite, on the small stretch of waste ground, several cars were parked. The place had an eerie presence. One of the cars, a green Astra, belonged to one of the trawler men and it had definitely seen better days. Certain that it posed no threat, Wallace checked his watch and panned towards the boatyard for anything of interest. Apart from a few empty oil drums, an old rusty anchor chain, and pile of discarded wooden pallets, the place appeared deserted. Refocusing the lenses, he suddenly spotted the top of Trevor Radcliffe's balding head.

'Bugger,' he cursed. 'It's you again.'

Why anyone would want to kill someone as lacklustre as Trevor Radcliffe was beyond his wildest imagination. But they did, and a killer was out there somewhere, hell bent on causing mayhem. Wallace could not recall the last time he'd felt as irritable as this before. He wasn't alone, the whole undercover team were sick to death of Radcliffe's monotonous routine. It was like reading the same pages of a book a dozen times over, infuriating and totally uninspiring.

He took out his mobile, fiddled with the buttons, then checked back through the digital displays for any missed calls or text messages. There weren't any. Switching the thing off, he tossed it onto the passenger seat in frustration. Seconds later his police radio crackled into life, and spewed out some undecipherable message before falling silent again. Bored out of his mind, DC Bower not having returned, Wallace sank back into the driver's seat and tuned into his favourite music channel.

★

It was a ship's foghorn that jarred DS Wallace from a light sleep. A cross channel container ship, bound for Copenhagen. Straining to follow its movements, it suddenly dawned on him that Trevor Radcliffe wasn't alone anymore. He picked up his binoculars, and hastily zoomed in on the boatyard. All he could see, at a glance, was Trevor Radcliffe's assailant. He was a tall man; lean, early thirties, dressed all in black with fair short-cropped hair.

Then he spotted the knife.

Nothing could have prepared Wallace for this. Radcliffe's body was strung up like a broken swastika, and dangling in mid-air like a bird in flight.

'Shit!' Wallace screamed.

Bracing himself, he slammed the undercover car into gear and took off under a cloud of dust. He knew every inch of this waste ground . . . every bloody inch. As the car slid to a halt in front of the boatyard, he flung back the door and fired off two quick shots.

'Drop you bastard!'

As the assailant ran for the shelter of the boathouse, Wallace's heart sank.

Now covered in blood, Trevor Radcliffe's hands and feet had been nailed to a makeshift timber cross. His face was cyanotic, eyes glazed, and the tongue protruding beyond his lips. It was then he noticed the large gaping cavity in Radcliffe's chest, a deep red crater where the flesh had been rolled back and the upper rib cage prised apart.

There was nothing he could do for him now: Radcliffe was dead.

Fumbling for his handset, he pressed the call button.

'Oh Jesus . . .' he cried, in a voice little more than a whisper. 'I need backup . . . and right away.' The next thing he noticed, glancing around, was the fresh blood trail.

Had one of his shots struck lucky?

He crept forward, the gun pointing ahead of him. 'Police, come out with your hands up, you're completely surrounded.'

Inside the boathouse the air felt oppressive, filled with an overpowering stench of kerosene fumes. Then it struck him: he was sitting on a powder keg and about to be blown into kingdom come at any second. Panic gripped him. His hands were shaking, and the rest of his body had locked solid. The moment his foot caught the wooden trestle, he was sent sprawling to the floor. Terrified, Wallace scrambled to his feet – his gun still pointing ahead of him.

All he could hear was a door creaking, nothing else.

'Move another inch you motherfucker, and I'll blow your brains out,' Wallace screamed.

Silence followed, only the wind playing on the door latch could be heard.

Following the blood trail, at midpoint along the slipway, everything came to a stop. There, at eye level, Radcliffe's cardiovascular organs had been skewered to a jetty post. Physically sick and unquestionably shaken, Wallace dropped to his knees. He'd failed miserably, and the killer was nowhere to be seen.

And then, the sound of a wailing police car siren.

'Oh No!' the detective sergeant gasped.

Chapter Forty-One

It was Saturday afternoon, and Jack Mason was relaxing with Sky Sports TV. The television pundits were running back over the latest team selections, and on paper, today's rugby match between Leicester Tigers and London Wasps looked a mouth-watering fixture. Both sides were evenly matched, and apart from injuries, the game was finely balanced and looked as though it could go all the way to the wire. For as long as he could remember, Jack Mason had always enjoyed his rugby. Not that he was ever any good at it, as he was never selected for any of his school rugby teams, or any other team for that matter. Nowadays he was more of an armchair critic, and considered himself good at it . . . or so he would have everyone believe.

His mobile phone rang.

The voice on the other end of his phone sounded guarded. 'What's up, boss?' said Luke James.

'I'm watching the rugby on the television, why?' Mason replied.

'Don't tell me you're still following that crap.'

Mason could think of dozen things to say, but chose not to answer. This had been his first lieu day off in weeks, and he was determined to sit back and escape from the stresses of everyday life.

'You still there, boss?'

'Yes, Luke—'

'I don't want to spoil your day, but there's been another development.'

Mason picked up the remote control, and turned down the TV volume. Not one to shy away from a problem, he sensed hesitation in Luke James' voice. With one eye on the television and the other on the clock, he was in two minds whether to cut their conversation short. 'Can't it wait till Monday?' Mason asked.

'I'm not so sure, boss,' James replied hesitantly. 'There's been another murder over by North Shields Fish Quay. This time it's Trevor Radcliffe.'

Mason took a deep breath. 'When did this happen, Luke?' he said, softening the tone in his voice.

'Around two o'clock this afternoon.'

'I thought we had twenty-four hour surveillance covering Radcliffe's place?'

Mason's mobile fell silent. Then he heard a police car siren wailing in the background. 'We did,' said James. 'Like I say, it's still early days.'

'Who's the duty Scene of Crime Officer?'

'Stan Johnson . . . he's only just arrived.'

Mason sighed in relief. At least something was stacked in his favour. Stan Johnson was a good man to have around at a homicide scene. Besides being level headed, he was thorough, and knew how to keep a tight lid on things.

'Who's the duty doctor?' he asked.

There was another long pause on the other end of his phone.

'It's Doc Hindson, I'm afraid,' the Detective Sergeant sighed. 'I realise you don't see eye to eye with one another, but—'

Mason swore quietly to himself. 'It's not your problem, Luke, but thanks for the heads-up anyway.'

'No problem, you grumpy old sod,' James chuckled down the other end of the phone.

'You need to get hold of David Carlisle. Ask him to meet me there.'

'Will do, boss.'

With that Mason hung up and got ready. Having set Sky to record, he gathered his keys, locked the house door, and clambered into his car. With any luck, he would catch up on the Rugby later. There again, past experience had taught him not to hold his breath on that. There were any number of things could go wrong at a homicide crime scene, and, Sod's law, usually did.

★

The drive to North Shields took Jack Mason a little under thirty minutes. The traffic was heavy, but on approaching Union Quay, he felt a ripple of excitement. Stopped by an eager young constable intent on giving him the third degree, he flashed his ID, and was immediately directed towards a small car park opposite the New Dolphin public house. The whole area was in lockdown, and everywhere crawling with police. Ignoring the No Entry sign, Mason pulled up behind a parked police transit van and sat for a while.

Time to garb up, he thought, as he wormed his way into a hooded white over suit. Climbing the short rise to the harbour, he stood for a while savouring the views. The North Sea seemed choppy, a stiff breeze cutting directly across the Tyne estuary. To the south stood the Groyne pier; its distinctive red lighthouse always reminded him of a space ship out of one of those 1940s sci-fi movies. Close to North Shields Fish Quay, and parked up on waste ground, he spotted the familiar yellow command truck. His eyes staring resolutely ahead, he slipped back into police mode, and ambled towards the crime scene.

Ducking beneath the police line tape, he was met by Stan Johnson who quickly brought him up to speed.

'If you're looking for a body,' the SOC officer smirked, 'there's one over by that yellow machine hoist contraption.'

'Ah, now I see it . . .'

'It's not a pretty sight, mind,' said Johnson.

'Is there anything I can do?'

'Not at the moment,' Johnson replied. 'Uniforms are checking up on a couple of witness statements, but until Forensics have finished, there's not a lot any of us can do.'

Great, Mason thought. He checked his watch. It would soon be kick-off time, and with any luck the police doctor would have already established the cause of death. If not, then he would need to wait for the home office pathologists to complete their findings. There again, if the victim had been poisoned first, a full toxicological examination would be required. 'Damn,' Mason cursed eager to get going; this was the last thing he needed. These things took time, he realised that, but suddenly nothing seemed straightforward anymore.

From what he could gather, the whole area was now a hive of activity and a lot had already been set in motion. On nearing the river he saw several forensic officers, including Peter Davenport. Camera in hand, the SOC photographer was standing in a sea of yellow crime marker flags and grappling with the fading light. Running a murder scene was a job Jack Mason loved, it came natural to him. He'd always been fascinated by homicides, ever since he first entered into police training school. Today was different, today he was struggling.

Agitated, he spotted the portly figure of Henry Hindson – peering down at him from the top of a set of high step ladders. They exchanged glances, but neither spoke. Not the best of starts, Mason thought, as he glanced up at the gaping dark red cavity in the centre of Trevor Radcliffe's chest. Strung up like an art form, his body had been nailed to a wooden cross and hoisted six feet above the ground. He'd seen plenty of evil in his time before, but nothing compared to this.

Suddenly he felt his stomach lurch.

'He was manually strangled, then hoisted above the ground,' Dr Hindson said.

'Strangled first, eh?'

'I'm certain of it,' the doctor replied in his usual laconic manner.

'Do we know the approximate time of death?'

'The victim's body temperature suggests barely three hours ago. It was a pretty ferocious attack, and judging by the amount of blood loss, there should be plenty of footprint evidence.'

All the while Radcliffe's glazed eyes bore down at him.

'Was he killed here?'

'It would seem so.'

'Then he was hoisted up?' said Mason, scribbling down some notes.

'Looking at the extent of the damage, I'd say it would have taken him all of forty minutes to carry out this amount of butchery.'

He noticed the doctor's eyes – they were bloodshot and the pupils dilated. The old sod had obviously been drinking again. Nothing much changed there, thought Mason.

'It's not looking good, Doc?'

'His work's pretty crude in my opinion, Jack. Rest assured he's certainly no cardiovascular surgeon.' A faint smile passed over the doctor's face. 'Mind, I've seen worse.'

Mason took a closer look at Radcliffe's body, and began to mull over the doctor's statement. Forty minutes didn't seem long enough time to open up Radcliffe's chest cavity, remove the heart, and then crucify him. Besides, without medical knowledge where the hell would you begin?

Not a good sign, he cursed.

'Do we know where he was strangled, Henry?'

'No,' the doctor replied. 'Wherever it was, there's plenty of trace evidence under the finger nails.'

'He obviously put up a struggle,' Mason said gloomily. 'Let's hope we get a DNA match this time.'

'I'll be frank with you, Jack. Your killer's a strong bugger and pretty quick about his business. I'd say this bears all the hallmarks of Annie Jenkins' murder. And, another thing, it looks like he's used the same type of hammer-head nails again.'

Mason searched for answers. If the doctor's statement was correct, then Trevor Radcliffe's murder had turned out just as David Carlisle had predicted it would. Every slaying followed a pattern, but the speed and ferocity of the kill was staggering. With so much blood spread over such a wide area, the killer's clothing must be saturated in it.

Seconds later, they were joined by Luke James. Fully kitted out in protective clothing, he was carrying something of interest in a plastic evidence bag.

'Thanks for the call, Luke,' Mason nodded.

'I was in two minds,' said James. 'I guessed it was your day off.'

Mason acknowledged his approval with a sweeping hand gesture, before turning to the doctor again. 'When can we lower him down?' he asked.

'We can't ...' the doctor snapped. 'Someone's tampered with the hoist controls, and I'm waiting for an engineer to arrive.'

Mason swore. 'The sick bastard certainly knows how to draw our attention towards his handiwork.'

'If that's what you can call it!' the doctor replied.

Mason huffed. 'Who found the body, Luke?'

'George Wallace, boss. The first thing he recalled was seeing Radcliffe swinging from the marine hoist. It was over before it had begun, so to speak. The minute he approached the crime scene, the killer made off towards the boathouse.'

'Where's Wallace now?'

'He's with DC Bower in the Command Control Truck. They're both being debriefed by the duty investigation officer.'

Unlike Wallace, Mason mused.

'What else do we know?'

'We've managed to grab a couple of eyewitness statements from two trawler men.' James cleared his throat. 'After they heard gunshots, they reported seeing a tall man making off towards the Fish Quay. Two minutes later, he was spotted again near the Ice Factory by one of the maintenance men there. Stan Johnson has a couple of uniform lads over there now.'

Mason felt his eyebrows rise. 'Gunshots—'

'Yes,' said James. 'Apparently Wallace managed to fire off a couple of shots at the assailant as he tried to make his escape.'

'At least he did something right,' said Mason. 'Where was DC Bower in all of this?'

James lowered his head in embarrassment. 'He was taking a piss, boss.'

Mason pictured the scene, and it didn't take a rocket scientist to work out the rest of the story. He was fuming. 'Do we know how our suspect got here?'

'Another stolen Mondeo . . . the one over there,' said James, pointing across to the waste ground where several parked cars now stood. 'And before you ask, someone has already carried out a PNC check on it. This one was stolen to order from Clayton Street yesterday afternoon.'

Mason hunched his shoulders, still furious. 'Is it one of ours?'

'I'm afraid not,' James replied.

Mason swore again. Having strategically placed a dozen police bait cars specially-equipped with GPS tracking devices in and around Newcastle, he was hoping the Wharf Butcher would take one. Not this time seemingly.

He checked his notes. 'What are we doing about the local Metro stations, Luke?'

'It's already been taken care of, boss.'

'And the ferry crossings – what's happening there?'

'Both landing sites are covered,' James replied. 'But it's my guess he'll probably stay low until it gets dark.'

Mason sighed as he flipped through the pages of his notebook. It was then he eyeballed Peter Davenport. He was taking photographs of one of the jetty posts.

'What the hell is Davenport up to now?'

The doctor grimaced, as he stared down from the top of the step ladders. 'You don't even want to go there, Jack.'

'Oh and why not?' Mason replied.

'Cos that's where he nailed Radcliffe's organs to the jetty post!'

Mason swallowed hard. '*Jesus!*' he yelped. 'This place is fast turning into a bloody chamber of horrors.'

'He's certainly not squeamish, if that's what you're getting at,' the doctor confirmed.

Mason had seen enough. Besides, there wasn't a fat lot he could do until the so-called experts had finished their investigations. Suddenly, the task ahead seemed daunting.

Moving towards the river bank, he felt a distinct nip in the air. The sun now low in the sky, the technical teams were already setting up floodlighting. Seconds later he was joined by Vic Miller from the Northumbria Armed Response Team. Trailing in his wake was Eric Taylor, the man in charge of the covert operation.

'Ah, the very man,' Mason said, desperately trying to compose himself.

'What the hell happened to my twenty-four seven surveillance operation?'

Taylor gave Mason a withering look. 'I believe two of your team were covering it, Jack.'

'Covering what?'

'Trevor Radcliffe. It's—'

'From what I've seen so far, the killer had enough spare time on his hands to carry out his own private post mortem.'

Taylor's head dropped. 'I heard – well, I've only just arrived. It's—'

'How reassuring, perhaps I can help.'

Taylor nodded, but said nothing.

'You cocked up, and big style,' said Mason. 'I'm now left with another stiff on my hands, and a whole lot of explaining to do.'

'I'm sure there's a simple explanation, Jack. It—'

'There may well be,' said Mason, sucking in the air. 'But I need answers . . . and quickly. Make sure I have a full written report on my desk – first thing tomorrow morning. Are we clear on that?' he said, stepping aside to allow the two police officers to carry on with their duties.

The shadows lengthening, Mason watched as a lone police launch began another sweep of the northern riverbank. Closer to home, a team of uniformed police officers were checking out on a derelict warehouse building. Soon it would be dark. Even so, nothing was being left to chance. Everything that could be done was being done.

The question was where the hell was he?

Chapter Forty-Two

Sliding his hand around the butt of his trusty Smith & Wesson 36, Jack Mason gently eased it from its holster. Extending his right arm out across the river, he began to take aim. As the front sights came into view, he gently squeezed the trigger. Suddenly he felt an enormous sense of power, even though the gun wasn't loaded.

'*Bang, bang!*' he whispered.

'You can get arrested for that,' a familiar voice from behind him rang out.

Lowering the gun, Mason spun sharply to face David Carlisle. It seemed a lifetime since he'd last fired a gun in anger, but his twenty years with the force had taught him there would be no hesitation. 'Just keeping my hand in,' Mason replied, trying to stifle a yawn. 'I'm glad you could make it. When did you arrive?'

'Only just, I came over on the first available ferry,' Carlisle replied.

Mason shuffled awkwardly, his shoes crunching the hard gravel underfoot. 'There's not a lot I can tell you in all honesty,' he said. 'Not until the so-called experts have finished their investigations.'

They talked a while before moving towards the boathouse.

'When will he stop,' said Mason, pointing up at Radcliffe's lifeless body.

'It's becoming too much of a habit,' Carlisle replied.

Mason shook his head. 'Tell me about it. Each time he seems to take it a step further. What's going on?'

Carlisle gave a little grimace, as though the killer's handiwork had struck another chord with him. 'He's becoming more ambitious, I'm certain of that. It's as if he's reached the point of no return, and he's rushing towards the finishing line. Sadly he'll stop at nothing until he gets there. In his mind it's a matter of elimination, and his victims are mere pawns in a reign of terror against the person he loathes. The more violent his killings, the greater the terror he hopes to spread. It's his way of showing off his power over the person he despises.'

'This one's totally off his head, if you ask me.'

'It always appears that way, I'm afraid. There are days when even the Wharf Butcher doesn't understand his own thoughts . . . and that's worrying.'

Mason's expression masked unease. 'I'm getting bad vibes about this one, David. He's gone a step too far this time, and that concerns me.'

'It was never going to be straightforward, Jack. These people have the ability to get inside your head. Radcliffe wasn't a victim of chance; he was a victim of choice. He's planning the risks, and working it all out.' Carlisle took a step back and stared blankly out across the river. 'Tell me, have you had anymore feedback from Monday night's "Crimewatch" appeal?'

Mason pondered his statement; it had been a busy week. After heated discussions with several Crimewatch television producers, rather than a full on five minute reconstruction, they'd plumped for the *Wanted Faces board*. He'd been well advised. Following Monday night's live broadcast, the police had been inundated with phone calls. Two leads in particular were of great interest to him, plus a further dozen follow up calls. No thanks to the profiler, his three minute live appearance with Sophie Raworth – one of the lead *Crimewatch* presenters – had raised more than a few eyebrows amongst the top brass.

'We've had a positive response,' Mason replied cheerily. 'Sadly, this incident isn't going to help us any.'

'Let's hope he never watches the show, eh.'

'Now there's a thought!' Mason shuddered.

It was dark when Mason finally reached the Mobile Command truck. The lights were still on, and the place was jam-packed with coffee drinkers. He recognised the suited and hooded figure of DI Swan. Holding a video camera in his left hand, he was pointing to a large map pinned to the back of the Command Truck. The man he was talking to, a short, ruddy faced duty SIO called Dick Broderick, was taking down some details. No doubt the press would be hanging around for a statement, but it was still early days as far as Mason was concerned.

'A mug of coffee, sir?' a young female police community constable said.

'No thanks.' Mason nodded in appreciation. 'I must be off.'

'What shall we tell the media?' asked Harry Baldwin, the police liaison officer.

Mason though a moment. Trevor Radcliffe's murder was as near as possible a carbon copy of the way Annie Jenkins' body had been found.

Only this time, and as Carlisle had pointed out, the killer had gone a step further. Newcastle had seen its fair share of murders, but this time it was different – as if the killer was hell bent on exhibiting his handiwork. Besides, the last thing he needed right now was badass press. Even so, the community still had a right to know and he would need to think carefully about it.

Mason shook his head feebly, and then turned to Baldwin. 'Tell them we're holding a press briefing at ten o'clock tomorrow morning. That should do the trick.'

'I'll do my best, boss, but those cockroaches have been pestering me all evening.'

'No doubt they'll find something to print, Harry.'

Harry Baldwin stared sullenly across at him, stretched his mouth and gave him a lopsided grin that showed off a mouth full of nicotine stained teeth.

'Not just a wee statement, Jack.'

The silence seemed to go on for eternity, before Mason answered. 'No. Not tonight, Harry.'

Just out of habit, he checked in on Stan Johnson. There were a number of factors to consider, and most of them surrounding Gilesgate. Another board member added to the killer's shopping list was the last thing he wanted right now. Sometimes it was all so predictable, as if the killer had rehearsed his murders beforehand. The fact the Wharf Butcher could slip through the police net as though he were invisible, didn't bode well in Mason's opinion. He felt unsettled by it all – strangely nervous.

Now dark, there wasn't a lot he could do anymore. There were reports to fill in, and procedures to set in motion. He thought for a moment, and tried to get his head around it all.

'So, where the hell is he, Stan?'

The SOC officer gave him a vacant smile. 'God knows, Jack. He's probably miles away by now. Let's hope someone has spotted something suspicious.'

Then, David Carlisle appeared in the doorway. His hands were filthy and his shoes were covered in mud. It was the look on the profiler's face that caught Mason's eye.

'Yes, David.'

'Sorry to interrupt, gentlemen,' Carlisle said, holding up a forensic plastic evidence bag. 'But I found these down by the Fish Quay.'

The room fell silent.

Chapter Forty-Three

How bad is the pain?

'Dreadful . . . I can barely breathe.'

Where does it hurt, my child?

'Everywhere . . . really bad . . . what am I to do, mama?'

You will think of something, the voice inside his head replied. *You always do.*

Then, from an upstairs bedroom window a young woman appeared. She was petite, late thirties, with long shoulder-length hair and a smooth pale complexion. He sat for a while, confused, his eyes hunting through the darkness. She made him smile, and Lexus had never seen anyone more beautiful before.

What do you want? She asked.

'Don't you remember me?'

She stood for a while, as though reading his thoughts, then beckoned him inside. He thought he could hear voices, children's voices, and there was music coming from another part of the building. The room felt cold, despite a huge log fire that burned fiercely in a large open fireplace. Everything was surreal, unnatural, as though he was living out a dream.

'Is that you . . . mama?'

She smiled and her hand reached out and tenderly touched his thigh, but the pain in his side was unbearable. He tried to switch his mind to other thoughts, but the voices kept telling him to turn away. He froze, still bleeding profusely from the gunshot wound in his thigh. This was more serious than he had ever imagined; his was a desperate situation. Then it dawned on him. This wasn't Trevor Radcliffe's blood he was staring down at, this was his blood and he was slowly bleeding to death.

'What am I to do . . . mama?'

You're a genius, my son; you will think of something.

Then he remembered: had he taken his medication? Not today he hadn't. Not that it made any difference, to him at least. Up here amongst the dead, the whole world was assembled at his feet. It was an awesome sight, a million candles that flickered like glow worms in the dark night sky. And wasn't he so incredibly talented for spotting it? At least he thought he was. Then, his eyes suddenly shot open again as he struggled to cope with the truth.

'Are you still there, mama?'

Yes, my child . . . what is it you want now?

'They've shot me, mama, and it wasn't me those evil policemen had fired at . . . it was Trevor Radcliffe. He was the wicked one, the vile beast they were trying to kill.'

Surrounded by darkness, Lexus writhed on the ground in agony. The pain was relentless, excruciating, sapping his strength until he could barely breathe anymore. This was all his depraved, evil father's doing; he was certain of that. Wasn't it his despicable actions that had driven him to the lowest depths of despair? His pulse quickened, and he threatened to end it all by throwing himself into a place where all light ends and eternal darkness begins.

Then, in the pitch-black darkness of the night, he sucked in the air and tried to clear his mind of all wicked thoughts.

'How will it all end . . . mama?' he begged.

You must talk with God, only he knows how to help you now, my child.

'I know, and he talks to me the entire time.'

Inside The Ship Inn, a rundown, derelict public house long since boarded up, Lexus' mind was in turmoil. Everything was unreal – unnatural, as though he'd fallen into a pit full of writhing demons. Then, as another squad car tore headlong into the night, he crashed to the floor in agony. His shirt felt wet, and unbearably sticky.

Then the voices returned, only this time more forceful.

Death is final, but life is full of possibilities, my child.

'Is this a dream . . .?'

Do you feel pain?

'Yes, I do. I really, really do,' Lexus cried out.

Then this is reality, my child.

Chapter Forty-Four

David Carlisle watched as the water droplets rippled down the windscreen. It was late afternoon, and the rain was drumming down and bouncing off the pavement. He sat for a while, staring at the derelict building opposite and tried to get inside the Wharf Butcher's head. This place certainly felt right; he was convinced of that, but the killer was playing mind games with his thoughts and jumbling things up.

Someone clambered out of a patrol car opposite, turned his collar against the driving rain and scurried towards them. Lowering her car window, DC Carrington let out a long exasperating sigh as the police officer bent down and stuck his head in through the opening.

'Do you want us to check the building out?' the sergeant asked.

Carrington stared at him, drumming her fingers on the steering wheel. 'Is there a problem, Sergeant? I—'

'No,' the sergeant replied, the rain bouncing off the peak of his cap and sending water droplets in through the open window. 'I just thought I'd save you the bother . . . that's all.'

'Maybe I should have flashed my tits off and stimulated your brain into action.'

The officer touched the peak of cap in salute, and stepped back a pace.

'Oh, come on,' Carrington shrugged, still staring up at him. 'You don't think for one minute I was going to do that, surely not.'

'Not while you're on duty, ma'am,' the sergeant grinned. 'Another time perhaps . . .'

Carlisle ran his hand over a two-day stubble, and tried not to laugh.

'What the hell was all that about,' she sighed, as the sergeant trudged smug faced back towards his marked patrol car. 'A fat lot of bloody good the two of us sat here on surveillance operations, when some dick head RTO decides to blow your cover. What a Pratt!'

Seconds later the police patrol car pulled away from the curb and swung west, back over the road bridge and towards Wallsend. As the vehicle's red tail lights trailed into the distance, Carlisle sat back and studied the old Ship Inn opposite. Its windows and doors now boarded up, there was a large gaping hole in the roof where the tiles had been removed. Further afield, beyond the overgrown car park and derelict waste ground, was emptiness. If anyone wanted to lie low, this was the perfect place, he told himself.

'So,' said Detective Carrington, turning to face him. 'Do you still believe the Wharf Butcher is holed up inside the building?

'It's definitely his kind of place . . . and he's predictable.'

The young detective gave him a mistrusting look. 'This sounds like I'm about to get my bloody hair wet,' she groaned. 'Maybe I should have got that dick-head Sergeant to check it out for us in the first place.'

Adjusting to the dark, Carlisle worked his way through what was once the downstairs bar. The Ship Inn – a once popular drinking hole with local shipyard workers – was now in a sorrowful run-down state. The vandals had moved in, and most of the fixtures and fittings were missing, and water was pouring in through the roof. The place had a fusty smell and stank of stale urine. Then, in a corner of the room, he found what he looking for – a makeshift bed. Whoever was holed up here was obviously intending to stop a while.

'This place gives me the creeps,' Carrington said, shining her torch beam beyond the wooden staircase and into the upper level of the building. Seconds later, Carlisle stumbled across a heap of discarded blood soaked rags and bent down to take a closer look.

'Someone's in big trouble,' he called out.

Detective Carrington shone her torch beam down at his feet.

'*Shit*,' she gasped, as if rooted to the spot. 'Those look pretty new to me.'

'And similar to the ones I found near North Shields Fish Quay,' he replied.

'You were right all along. He was here.'

It was then Carlisle spotted the sketches, not too dissimilar to ones found in the Wharf Butcher's flat. He studied their content; they were unquestionably the killer's handiwork. All the signs were there, the little idiosyncrasies that drew them ever closer towards one another.

It had to be him.

'What is it?' whispered Carrington, her face now pallid.

'We're closer than we ever dared to imagine.'

'How can you possibly say that?' she questioned. 'You're spooking me, David.'

'Sometimes you get so close to these people, you eat and sleep at the same times as they do. You become as one.'

The young detective stared at him in utter disbelief. 'Please tell me you're joking.'

'I've never been more serious. Psychopaths are very grandiose, and their world is all about them,' Carlisle replied. 'They believe they're smarter than anyone else, more powerful. This one stays close to his kill zone. He's territorial, and he's feeding off it.'

'Just as a salmon returns to its spawning ground . . .?'

'Hmm. Something along those lines.'

Her words, and the manner in which she spoke them, were a new revelation to him. Carlisle shone his torch beam into the old pub lounge, and swore he felt a presence. Where darkness concealed the dangers, the young detective hovered close to his heels. Deep down Carrington appeared physically shaken by it all.

'Are you sure it's him. I mean . . . the Wharf Butcher?' she whispered. 'Could it not just be kids using this place as a play den?'

'No. It's him all right. I'm one-hundred percent certain of that.'

They searched the building together, but found nothing more. Then, the young detective pulled out her cell phone and rang Jack Mason.

Seconds later she turned to face him.

'Bugger!' she groaned. 'My shift ends in twenty minutes and Jack Mason is already on his way over. Let's hope your hunch pays off, David, as the old sod sounds in a real foul mood.'

They did not wait long. First to arrive was George Wallace, quickly followed by DC Manley. The moment the burly Constable poked his head in through the open pub doorway; Carlisle caught a whiff of Humbugs. That was it: no turning back. Over the next fifteen minutes, one by one the rest of the team arrived. Then, finally, the frosty faced figure of Jack Mason appeared in the doorway.

'What have we got, Sue?' said Mason, his cold penetrating eyes touring the building and taking in the detail.

'Whoever he is, he's badly in need of medical attention, boss.'

Mason took another look at the collection of faces now present.

'Well! Anyone got any bright ideas as to where he might be?'

'He can't be far away,' Carlisle said, pointing down at the pile of blood stained rags now scattered about the floor. 'By the look of things, I'd say he's not long moved out of here.'

'How did you find the place?'

'Intuition,' Carlisle shrugged. 'I guessed he'd stay close to home.'

Someone's mobile rang, but it was quickly silenced.

With all the media hype in the case, it wouldn't be long before someone would come poking their noses around the area. Everyone knew that. Hands in pockets, head hunched slightly forward, Mason was deep in thought. 'If he is in dire need of medical attention,' said Mason, 'we'll need to warn the medical services.'

'Tread carefully, Jack,' said Carlisle pensively. 'If he feels trapped in any way, he'll want to end it all.'

He watched as the DCI took a step back, and furrowed his brow.

'So where the hell is he?' Mason huffed.

Carlisle rolled his eyes and tried not to think about where this was all heading. The way the killer's mind was working right now, he would need to feel in control. If not, then he would simply go to ground. It was a fine balancing act, a game of chess where one false move would end in checkmate.

'After each attack there's a cooling off period,' Carlisle said, thinking out aloud. 'Then the fantasies take over again, and that's when he feels the urge to kill. He's cold, calculating, and right now full of terrible rage. It which case, he's a major threat to anyone who chooses to challenge him.'

Mason stood transfixed. 'What are you trying to say?'

'He's been badly wounded, Jack, and his ego has been severely dented.' Carlisle hesitated. 'If he's running out of time, it can only mean one thing.'

Mason shook his head. 'The bastard is about to strike again.'

Carlisle acknowledged the somewhat obvious comment with a faint nod. 'Whoever drove him to kill in the first place is now in the firing line. I'm certain of that. His thoughts and the feelings he is now experiencing are way beyond his fantasies. He's reliving his childhood past, and he's so full of rage and hatred it's tearing him apart. He's out there, Jack, and he must be stopped.'

'Bugger,' Mason shrugged.

'If we don't spook him, we have every chance of catching him,' Carlisle said, addressing the rest of team. 'He's a wounded animal, so he'll need to stay low for a while.'

Mason's grin broadened. 'And when he does surface, I'll be ready and waiting for him.'

Easier said than done, Carlisle thought.

★

News travelled fast and the crowd of journalists had grown. Several outside broadcast vans were already parked up in the area, their satellite dishes brushing the tree line. Detective Carrington said very little as she strode past the cameras and microphones that were pushed in her face. Carlisle sensed her displeasure, but refused to comment as they climbed back into the undercover vehicle.

It had stopped raining, but the ground underfoot was still damp when they eventually pulled up outside the Powder Monkey public house. Halfway between Police Headquarters and his South Shields office, the sign outside the pub door read: TWO MEALS A TENNER.

'Fancy a quick pint and a bite to eat?' the young detective asked.

The pub wasn't busy, but still had welcoming appeal. The clientele – a mixture of pensioners and young couples with children – made for a homely atmosphere.

Carlisle ordered drinks, and then glanced at the menu.

'Thanks for sharing our find back there,' said Carrington. 'There are those on the team who would have taken all the credit for themselves.'

'Think nothing of it,' Carlisle nodded.

They stood at the bar for a while, before grabbing an empty corner table close to the window, and overlooking the main street. It was weird sitting down to a meal with another woman. Sue Carrington was the first since Jackie's passing. Although not an unattractive young woman, the though suddenly crossed his mind that she was at least ten years his junior. What the hell, he thought.

'How long were you married?' Carrington asked.

Carlisle thought about it before answering. 'Almost six years; why do you ask?'

'Are you able to talk about it still? I mean—'

'No, it's OK,' Carlisle replied.

Jackie's sudden death had cast a constant dark shadow over Carlisle's life, and he was only too pleased to talk it over with someone. Unlike other women, who were shallow and only interested in exploring the morbid details, this felt different? Touched by the young detective's caring approach, he felt comfortable in her presence.

'Jackie's been dead over a year now,' he said thoughtfully. 'She died in a freak accident whilst we were on holiday together in India.'

'I'm sorry,' she added.

There was genuine understanding in her face and voice.

'It's OK,' he acknowledged. 'I'm slowly coming to terms with it.'

'What happened?'

How direct was that? Carlisle thought, but restrained himself from saying it. 'It was one of those last minute bookings,' he replied. 'You know how these things go, we were both trying to get away from it all, I—'

A memory tugged him.

Her face clouded for a moment, and her eyes rested upon his. 'Sorry. I have a nasty habit of opening my big mouth at all the wrong times,' the young detective said, lowering her head in embarrassment. 'When I was younger, my mother used to tell me I would need to know the far end of a fart about everything. Some things never change, I guess.'

He hesitated, and took another sip of his lager before placing the glass back down on the table in front of him. Oblivious to their surroundings, the old couple sat opposite were deep in conversation over some financial problems or other. He watched as the old man's weather beaten face contorted, as if disapproving of his partner's comments. Somehow the timing felt right, as if the dark clouds that had hung over him for months now, were slowly being pulled apart.

'Jackie was itching to travel on the local river ferry that morning. She always wanted to see the real India . . . to be amongst its people. She never cared much for the tourist attractions; it wasn't Jackie's thing.' Their meals arrived, along with a knife and fork wrapped in a paper napkin. He collected his thoughts again. 'The quayside was crowded when we arrived there that morning, thousands of people all jostling for position and wanting to catch the same ferry. It was quite something, I can tell you. We could see there was a problem, but no one gave a damn. Overcrowding, it seems, is an everyday part of life in India. That's how these people move around, thousands of them, travelling between cities and all desperate to get to their next destination.'

Carrington fluttered her eyelashes at him. 'I've seen pictures of people sitting on the roofs of trains before. Is it really like that . . . India, I mean?'

'That's the real India,' he smiled. 'And that's the part of India that Jackie always wanted to explore, she—'

'Are you sure you're OK to talk about this?'

'Yes, of course.'

'Sorry, it's just—' she hesitated. 'Please do go on.'

It was obvious Carrington just wanted to sit and listen to him. He could tell by the look in her eyes, and the tone in her voice. She knew the world he was talking about, its people, its cities, and its vastness; and yet her knowledge of them was that of the blind. He gathered a few chips on the end of his fork, and popped them into his mouth. 'Boats and ferries are a common form of transport in India's remote rural regions, but the safety standards are appalling.' A memory tugged him. 'We understood the risks we were taking, but we still went ahead with our journey. There we were, the two of us looking over the ferry handrail when this great big lorry appeared at the dockside. You should have seen the vague look on the other passengers' faces – nobody took a blind bit of notice. Somehow, and I don't know how, they managed to squeeze this beaten up old wreck of a lorry onto the back of the ferry.'

'Gosh!' Carrington gasped. 'It sounds horrendous.'

'I know, and the more I think about it now the more ridiculous it all sounds.' He paused for a moment, and wrestled with his emotions. 'Barely five minutes into our journey and there was this terrific jolt . . . seconds later . . . and it could only have been seconds, the ferry rolled over and capsized. The noise was deafening, and everything was thrown into utter confusion. And that was the last time I ever saw Jackie alive.' He sat in silence for a moment. 'The next thing I remember, after being plucked from the water, was this sweet old Indian lady staring down at me. She had the face of an angel, and I will never forget her kindness.'

The look on the detective's face told him everything he needed to know.

'Life's shit,' she said. 'It's unfair, and you never know the moment.'

They talked a while, but Carrington never broached the subject again.

The sea was remarkably calm when she finally dropped him off on South Shields' promenade. The wind had got up, but he still felt the need to clear his head. It was weird how some things turn out, and how just talking to someone could cut through the mental barriers. For the first time in months, it felt as though a huge weight had suddenly been lifted from his shoulders and life was worth living once more.

Chapter
Forty-Five

David Carlisle watched the morning press conference unfold from his iPhone. Beamed live across the major News networks, Jack Mason opened with a brief statement concerning the brutal murder of Trevor Radcliffe. The Detective Chief Inspector appealed to the general public for any information regarding a black MK3 Ford Mondeo – seen in the vicinity of Wallsend during the early hours of September 15th. He closed by saying the police were satisfied the net was closing in.

The reality, of course, was very different.

After grabbing a cup of coffee from the dispensing machine, Carlisle made his way towards the operations room. Met by DC Harry Manley, together they chewed over the latest developments. Having moved to her new moorings on the Quayside, Cleveland had seen more than its fair share of Gilesgate boardroom directors of late – too many in Manley's opinion. Something was afoot, and whatever it was the police were determined to get to the bottom of it.

Jack Mason's timely arrival brought with it the usual good-humoured banter, and after a brief exchange of words, Carlisle was ushered into Mason's office. The DCI's mood seemed relaxed, and it wasn't long before they got down to the business in hand. Following Monday night's live 'Crimewatch' TV broadcast, an anonymous viewer had phoned in with new information regarding the Wharf Butcher's identity. Sceptical of hoax calls, a few discreet enquiries soon uncovered the caller might be telling the truth.

Mason gave him a contemptuous look. 'You don't seem convinced.'

'Serial killers' identities never surprise me anymore, but the motivation that drives them to kill and the reasons behind their killings certainly do.'

Sipping coffee and eating a KitKat whilst jotting down a few notes, Mason was deep in thought. The one thing that Carlisle had learned about hard hitting coppers was never to underestimate the reasoning behind their feelings. Mason was annoyingly tight lipped, withdrawn, and at times lost in his own little world.

'Thanks to you, and Sue Carrington, we now know our killer is suffering serious gunshot wounds. Even so, he still hasn't surfaced and that worries me.'

'He's territorial, Jack.'

'You have a very specific way of thinking about things, my friend, but unfortunately we have more pressing matters to deal with.' Mason shook his head, and flipped the pages of his notebook. 'I recently put it to Sir Jeremy's that his son could be responsible for these killings. Naturally he denied it. Not only that, his legal team advised that unless I intend to press charges against their client, he is under no obligation to answer any further questions.'

'That's a bit strong.'

'Nothing surprises me anymore,' Mason shrugged. 'His solicitor was a right pain in arse, but he needed to be. Those maggots certainly know how to play the system.'

'That's politicians for you.'

'The guy's a hypocrite, if you ask me,' Mason shrugged.

The noise of laughter ebbed and flowed from the ops room. Distracted, he watched as Mason pushed back in his seat. His jaw was set tight, and the tiny muscle in his left eye kept twitching. Behind the occasional grunt, he detected a deep resentment towards clever-arse solicitors. Mason hated legal jargon at the best of times, and could never get to grips with it. As his story began to unfold, the more Mason elaborated, the more resentful he became. Reading between the lines, Carlisle's concerns over the Wharf Butcher's upbringing had been well founded. After their marriage fell apart, Maria Agrioli – Sir Jeremy's ex-wife – had been given custody of their only son. Half Italian, as the name suggested, amongst other things that Maria possessed was a volatile temper. A single-minded woman, she soon began to place unreasonable demands on young Samuel. Unable to cope herself, she not only subjected him to terrible emotional, physical and verbal abuse, she was extremely violent towards him. A disruptive youngster, young Samuel had spent the best part of his childhood in a youth offenders' institution. Why his mother had singled him out for such harsh treatment was anybody's guess; even so, the courts had failed miserably in their duty. In the end, it was left to Social Services to pick up the pieces, and in doing so young Samuel was eventually placed into foster care. When that didn't work out, that's when he finally went to live with his aunt.

Several concerns flashed through Carlisle's mind. If the Wharf Butcher was indeed Sir Jeremy's only son, he couldn't have written a better script had he tried. The emotional scars ran much deeper than anyone could have imagined. His was a classic case of schizophrenic paranoia, and there was no getting away from it.

'So why did Samuel leave his aunt?' Carlisle asked. 'Surely she was the only person that showed any affection towards him.'

'Good question!' said Mason, hands in pockets, now staring out through the office window. 'With the help of Social Services, we managed to trace her to an address in Wallsend. Some years ago, she was diagnosed with Alzheimer's disease. Having been placed into a Residential Care Home, she died there shortly after.'

Different scenarios played out in Carlisle's mind. He'd seen its like before, parental rejection manifesting as hatred. Had the loss of his aunt tipped Samuel over the edge? Could that have been the trigger that had turned him into whom he now was?

'So what became of the boy?'

Mason took another sip of his coffee, and bit a huge chunk out of his KitKat. 'After his aunt went into a residential care home, young Samuel simply vanished from the face of the planet.'

'What about Social Services, surely they must have something on him?'

'Nah, we drew another blank on that enquiry.'

They mulled it over for a while, both reaching the same conclusion. In Carlisle's mind, young Samuel's upbringing bore all the makings of a serial killer. Socially isolated and ignored as a child, he'd been brought up in an unstable family environment. Abandoned by his domineering mother, abused by a perverted father, there was little wonder he'd turned out as he did.

'Take a look at these,' said Mason, tossing a large green folder towards him. 'They're young Samuel's offender records. It's all there . . . his early psychiatric problems, childhood offending patterns, even the accusations aimed against his father's abuse.'

Although never proven in the courts, it wasn't long before Carlisle began to form his own opinion over the whole sordid affair. If young Samuel had been abused as a child, then this whole damn case smacked of a professional cover up.

'What do you make of it?' asked Mason.

'It's a classic case of child abuse, it's what sparks these people into doing what they do,' Carlisle replied sharply and a tad aggressively.

Mason screwed his face up. 'Malice springs to my mind.'

'He's definitely driven by narcissistic fantasy,' said Carlisle. 'Sexual abuse as a child is one of the key elements in creating a serial killer. It's more likely to have formed part of Samuel's thinking process, and that's why he's hell bent on tearing his father's boardroom apart. It's his only way of getting back at him.'

Mason just sat there and stared at him, not saying a word. It wasn't just coincidence that the Wharf Butcher had chosen to target Gilesgate's board of directors. He'd said all along their killer was determined to destroy someone else's world. Now Jack Mason had the proof.

'You're beginning to unsettle me,' said Mason, staring into empty space.

'You said all along he's becoming more ambitious, Jack.'

'Maybe, but that's the last thing I want to hear.'

'This is all about retribution. I'm convinced of it.'

'God help us all,' Mason sighed.

There followed an awkward silence between them.

'He's gaining in confidence,' said Carlisle, 'and filling in the gaps. It's his way of dealing with it, and nothing will get in his way.'

'So what does that tell me about his current mental state?'

'Whatever his state of mind, he'll need to surface at some stage or other.'

Now deep in thought, Mason gazed down at his laptop. 'Sadly, we still don't have enough concrete evidence to lay charges against Sir Jeremy. And, if we do bring him in for questioning, do we run the risk of this maniac son of his going to ground?' Mason rose to his feet, scraping his chair back from the desk. 'Let's push those thoughts to one side for a moment. The question is this, how do we find a way of getting Sir Jeremy to talk?'

Christ, what a nightmare this was turning out to be, thought Carlisle.

'There may be a way, Jack.'

Mason spun to face him – as if he'd been prodded in the back.

'Let's hope this isn't another one of your hare-brained schemes?'

'I'm not so sure about that,' Carlisle replied, thankful they were at least on equal terms for once. 'But I do have some rather interesting scandal regarding Sir Jeremy's nocturnal activities.'

'I thought as much,' Mason said, as if taken aback. 'You've been talking to your reporter friend at the Shields Gazette.' Mason never took his eyes off him. 'So what's he after now . . . money no doubt?'

'Not this time, Jack.'

'What then?'

'He's looking for an exchange of information, *quid pro quo.*'

Mason loosened his tie, and gathered a few papers together. The pieces of the jig-saw puzzle were nicely coming together, but the important pieces were still missing. 'What the hell? Sooner or later the press will pick up on it, those maggots never fail.' Mason sighed, shaking his head. 'Tell me, what is it your friend is hoping for?'

'He's looking for an exclusive, Jack.'

'Hmm . . . a headline breaking story, eh.'

'Yes. And all he asks in return is when we finally do catch up with the killer; he's amongst the first to know.'

Mason fell silent for a moment. If there was one person he despised above all others, it was Sir Jeremy. He loathed the man, and everything he stood for. Reaching into his pocket, the DCI took out his notebook and placed it on the table in front of him.

'OK. You have my undivided attention,' Mason grinned.

Carlisle grasped the opportunity.

'Six months ago my friend was covering a sports celebrity function at one of Newcastle's big hotels. Whilst there, a porter friend tipped him off that Sir Jeremy had checked in earlier that evening with a young Asian girl under his wing . . .' Carlisle stopped to emphasise a point. 'He was later caught in bed with her.'

Mason eyed him inquisitively. 'And—'

'He was caught naked and tied to the bed by a pair of tights. His little Asian friend meanwhile was whipping him with a thick leather strap.'

Mason's expression hardened. 'What kind of exclusive do you call that, for God's sake?'

'She was thirteen!'

Mason sat stunned.

'*She was what!*'

'Thirteen!'

'Christ! It doesn't come much better than that,' Mason said, trying to stay calm.

'It does when I tell you they were filming everything on a home-movie video camera.'

Mason slammed his hand on the desktop, making his plastic coffee cup shake. 'That's the second piece of good news I've received this week.'

'Oh! And what might the other be?'

'The IPPC has taken a dim view of the Acting Chief Constable's involvement in Gilesgate, and they've finally decided to press charges.'

'On what grounds?' he asked.

Mason's desk phone rang, but he chose to ignore it.

'They're looking at allegations of fraud, and one involving gross misconduct. The ACC, it appears, has been abusing his position as a senior police officer.' Mason leaned back in his seat and closed his eyes. 'Twenty-two years of unblemished service, what a bloody mess.'

'So what happens now?'

Mason just stared at him, letting the silence grow between them. 'He'll probably be suspended on full pay pending the outcome of the IPCC's enquiry.'

That had clinched it. With the Acting Chief Constable and Sir Jeremy now in the firing line, it meant the team could now get down to the real business in hand. Reaching into his bottom desk drawer, as a magician pulling a rabbit out of hat, Mason handed him a large brown envelope.

'Take a look at this.'

Teasing back the flap, Carlisle slid the photograph from the envelope. Neatly pencilled across the back, was the name: FLATLANDS FLOOD BARRIER. He sat for a moment, and tried to make the connection. The name sounded familiar, but where had he seen it before? Then, the penny dropped: it was the name on the file that Lewis Paul had carried with him during their meeting at Gilesgate's Operational Headquarters.

'I'm impressed,' said Carlisle. 'So, this is the Flatlands Flood Barrier team?'

Mason looked at him sceptically. 'All is not what it appears to be, my friend.'

'Oh and why not?'

'Hell man, the UK Environment Agency still hasn't drawn up any project plans. Take another look.'

Carlisle swung his spectacles onto the top of his head, and moved closer to the light. A dozen familiar faces, tightly bunched together, amongst them, Sir Jeremy, the ACC, Trevor Radcliffe and the towering figure of Henry Fraser. The sheer size of the man was terrifying.

'So, what's your problem?'

Mason clicked his teeth; the intellectual side about to surface. 'In a nutshell, the Flatlands Flood Barrier is purely a proposal to improve the North East's coastal flood defences. It involves building a secondary line of flood barriers in order to combat tidal surges. The existing structures, seemingly, no longer provide adequate protection.'

'This is all very well, Jack, but what the hell has it to do with catching a serial killer?'

'You need to hear me out first,' said Mason. 'Considering the project is still in the infancy stages, it certainly puts everything into context. Gilesgate has already exceeded the CEF's fifteen per cent quota, we know that, and to the tune of eight-hundred million pounds.' More thought. 'What we didn't know was just how many other people are involved in the Sleeper Company scam.'

'True,' said Carlisle, 'But isn't that another matter.'

There followed another shrug. 'We're looking at massive fraud here, and one which includes prominent household names. Proving it is one thing, besides taking up a lot of my time. That's why I've called in the Fraud Squad to deal with it.'

About bloody time, Carlisle thought. Profiling was one thing, but trying to catch a serial killer whose father was an unscrupulous politician was another. They spent the next twenty minutes going back over the detail. With so many balls up in the air, it was difficult to keep track of them all. Several thoughts ran through Carlisle's mind. The motive of financial reward was plausible, but it defied the laws of reasoning since serial killers seldom kill for monetary gain. The truth was there were three major elements to the killer's modus operandi: that of victim selection, access and opportunity.

It was time to make his point.

'He's close to home, Jack, and it's only a matter of time before he surfaces again. It's time we carried out a door to door search of the area. Let's see if we can't flush him out of hiding. Someone out there is sheltering him. If not, he's probably lying low somewhere.'

'Nah, there's still plenty of low-life out there only too willing to sell me a piece of their information.'

'I'm not convinced about that either,' Carlisle sighed.

Mason stood for a moment before shutting down his laptop computer.

'What if I tell you our killer's street name is . . . Lexus?'

Carlisle sat stunned.

Chapter
Forty-Six

The following day started bright and cool. Apart from an eerie, low swirling mist that clung to the River Tyne, Cleveland's masts stood tall and firm against the familiar backdrop of Newcastle's Tyne Bridge. Having moved to her new moorings on the Quayside, the Baltimore Schooner's presence had certainly conjured up huge public interest. Not since the Tall Ships race had so many people viewed a sailing vessel before. If nothing else, the public's insatiable interest was certainly assisting the police in their undercover surveillance operations.

Lurking in the shadows of St Anne's Quay building, DS Miller adjusted the lens of his high powered telephoto camera and fired off several more shots. It was a perfect location, with clear unobstructed views of the immediate surrounding area – and Henry Fraser. Ignorant of any police presence, the big man peered in through one of Cleveland's many hatches and into the bottomless black hole below. Adjusting to the light, he placed a large size twelve shoe onto the first rung of the ladder, and squeezed his enormous frame backwards through the tiny opening. His movements were sluggish, and as his head disappeared from view, the ladder creaked and groaned under the enormous strain of Fraser's colossal weight.

Watching from below, Greenfingers Armstrong stared up at the huge ungainly figure now descending towards him. He was a giant of a man, and one that no ship's designer would have ever considered in their plans.

'Watch your head on that low cross beam, Henry.'

'This climbing sucks,' Fraser protested. 'Everything about this fucking ship sucks.'

On nearing the deck below, Fraser unfolded his long legs and dropped down the last few rungs with a flurry of confidence.

'We'll make a sailor of you one day, Henry.'

'Not in your lifetime, you won't,' Fraser cursed. 'The sooner you're out of here, the better.'

'And when will that be?'

'When I tell you,' Fraser snarled, still trying to recover his breath after his clumsy descent into the bowels of the ship.

With barely a second's pause, Greenfingers fired off another searching question. 'Have there been any more developments since you people bugged my ship?'

'The crew's fine, it's you I'm more worried about.'

Greenfingers drew back. 'What. Me!'

'Yeah you ...' Fraser's lips tightened. 'Let's keep this conversation simple for once. Nine months ago, Gilesgate faced one of its major competitors in the law courts. It was over a technical glitch relating to some high value land reclamation deeds involving a lot of money. The case was nip and tuck, and went all the way to the wire. Thanks to a guy called Ernest Stanton, and a few hefty backhanders, the case was thrown out of the courts.' Fraser raised his bushy black eyebrows, and stared at him. 'Gilesgate's rivals went bust; the legal costs alone were a staggering two million quid.'

'Wow!' Greenfingers gasped. 'That's a serious amount of money.'

'You bet it was, and it probably cost Stanton his life.'

'I don't ever remember the case,' Greenfingers confessed. 'There again, I was probably at sea when all this took place. So, what happened to this Stanton fella?'

Fraser gave a slight shake of the head. 'The day of the court case, he ends up dead with his throat cut. It was a nasty business, and what's more ...'

Greenfingers listened intently as the rest of the story began to unfold, with a few optional extras thrown in. Behind the placid exterior, there was an astute, very intelligent man, whose sharpness Fraser was all too well aware of. Ever since joining the organisation, things had never quite worked out as Greenfingers Armstrong thought they would. Deep down, he was ill at ease with Gilesgate's secretive levels of hierarchy. Although well paid for his services, he still despised being fed second-hand information. It unnerved him, and it was a weakness that Fraser now played on.

'The person we're looking for is called ... Lexus,' Fraser chuckled.

Greenfingers' interest levels gathered pace.

'Does this Lexus go by any other names?'

'Yeah, the Wharf Butcher.'

'What!'

'You heard. When I catch up with him, I have a little job for you.'

That settled it. That's how Henry Fraser normally dealt with his problems – no questions asked – a one way ticket to the bottom of the North Sea.

'Lead weights and feet first, Henry?'

'Whatever!' Fraser sniggered. 'One thing for sure, the organisation is willing to pay good money for your services.'

'Cash in hand?'

Fraser nodded. 'Yeah, crisp new readies.'

'When?' said Greenfingers licking his lips.

'Never mind when, it's important we dispose of him clinically.'

Greenfingers' face began to twitch. 'So why are you telling me all of this?'

'Cos . . .' Fraser despaired. 'Everyone's sick and tired of looking over their shoulders nowadays. Nobody knows where this butcher's knife will strike next. That's why Sir Jeremy is prepared to pay good money for his disposal.'

They were standing now, looking out over the starboard bow of the ship. Below deck the smell of chargrilled fish wafted through the air, catching Fraser's nostrils. It smelt good, and Fraser felt hungry. It had been two long hours since he last ate. Four eggs, six rashers of bacon and a tin of beans, to be precise!

'So what are your plans for me?'

'I'm waiting for Sir Jeremy to get back to me. When he does, I'll let you know what the arrangements are. Until then, you're to sit tight.'

'And do what?' Greenfingers replied.

Fraser stared hard at the ship's captain; his eyes were cold and detached.

'Over the next few days, four important guests will be joining your ship, and when they do, they're to be made comfortable.'

'Do we know who these people are?'

Fraser rolled his eyes, tired of Greenfingers' relentless questioning. 'Make sure you have enough supplies to get them to South America.'

'South America!' gasped Greenfingers.

The big man turned away.

'Colombia—'

Stepping from the gangway, Fraser filled his lungs with a fresh intake of sea air. With the cool bag slung loosely over his shoulder, he retraced his footsteps back along the Quayside. It was a beautiful day, not a cloud in the sky. Close to the Tyne Bridge, he took one last lingering look at Cleveland. She was a fine looking vessel, and one that the north-east public had certainly taken to heart. It was strange how some things panned out. Somehow the view always seemed much better from dry land, and that, Fraser reassured himself, was the way it was going to stay.

★

Fifteen minutes later, and Newcastle's Quayside was busy. Apart from a few tourists, the majority of people were now heading for work. Fraser stood a while, outside the old Fish Market building, before making an important telephone call. It was then he noticed the stranger. A tall man, early forties, wearing a long black trench coat and a black Beanie woollen hat pulled down over his ears. Who was he, and what was he up to?

Fraser hung back, and sat for a while without appearing obvious. Board members were rapidly becoming a rarity, and this wasn't his time. Not today it wasn't. He felt for the gun, the one he'd carried with him ever since Trevor Radcliffe's untimely ending. Prompted by the stranger's unnatural antics, he pushed on. For once, Fraser felt vulnerable. The adrenaline was pumping, and the lump in the back of his throat threatened to choke him. Taking no chances, he ducked into one of the many back alleyways, and prepared for the inevitable. The moment the stranger drew level with him, he sprang into action. One arm wrapped around the stranger's neck, the other swiftly brought the muzzle of the gun to his temple.

'Give me one good reason why I shouldn't blow your fucking brains out?'

'Shoot me, Henry, and the whole damn quayside will be swarming with police officers.'

Fraser hesitated. His hands were shaking, and his grip on the gun handle had slackened. All those meetings on Cleveland, just when he thought he'd got away with it. Caught in two minds, seconds earlier he was prepared to blow the stranger's brains out. Not anymore. Now it was different.

'Keep your hands where I can still see them,' Fraser insisted.

Shabbily dressed, there was no mistaking that this was an undercover detective. The question was – *how long had he been following him?* His grip on the gun handle tightened, and for one split second their separate worlds stood still.

'Easy . . . Henry,' the stranger said, nervously.

Fraser saw the opportunity and seized upon it. 'Show me some ID.'

The detective flashed his warrant card, causing Fraser to flinch.

'Can I ask what you're doing in the area, sir?'

'Visiting friends and killing time!' Fraser said.

The stranger remained calm, remarkably calm. 'Let's start by you putting that toy gun away. It doesn't look good you waving that damn thing around in the middle of Newcastle.'

Fraser faltered then snapped out of his shell again. When he spoke his voice was assertive. 'Purely personal protection, officer, it's supposed to scare the living shit out of people like you.'

'You do know it's illegal to threaten a police officer with a weapon, sir?'

'Yeah, but it's just a kid's toy.'

'That may well be the case, but you waving that toy about can cause a police marksman an awful lot of headaches.'

For an undercover detective he was remarkably wet behind the ears, and Fraser was having none of it. But was it too late? It was time to find out.

'How long have you bastards been tailing me?'

'We prefer to call it low key surveillance, sir.'

'Surveillance!' gasped Fraser.

'That's right. This whole area is plagued by drugs problems, and we're stamping down on it. When my gaffer saw you leaving that boat back there, he naturally put two and two—'

Fraser cut him short. 'Is that so?'

'Just for the record, may I see inside your bag, sir?'

'Sure! Take a good look, officer.'

As the cool bag hit the pavement with a clunk, Fraser wiped the back of his hand across his lips. His hands were shaking, and the palms felt clammy. Then, as a precautionary measure, he took another step back. The moment the detective's fingers latched onto one of the cold ice blocks, his face turned white.

'What the—'

'I forgot to tell you,' Fraser chuckled.

'I've been bitten,' the detective gasped.

Fraser drew back, the tears streaming down his face.

'Shit happens. Will that be all, officer?'

'Yeah, for now . . .'

The moment Fraser disappeared; the undercover detective reached into a pocket and pulled out his mobile phone. Punching in a pre-selected number, the discernible change in the officer's voice told another story.

'Contact is armed and heading north towards the Copthorne Hotel.'

'*Copy that,*' came back the reply.

'Request backup.'

'*Backup declined . . . on no account are you to follow him.*'

The phone went dead.

DC Manley leant back against the wall and heaved a sigh of relief. Thanks to Fraser's hesitation and his own quick thinking, he'd managed to avert a catastrophe. It was a close run thing, a few seconds more and he could have ended up as tomorrow's headlines. Reassured, he popped another humbug into his mouth, flexed his aching limbs and took off in the general direction of Newcastle's Quayside.

Manley did not need any more encouragement.

Chapter Forty-Seven

The ten o'clock team briefing trumped up all the usual faces, thought Mason. The only oddball was an unkempt, bleary-eyed David Carlisle, who, having stayed up into the early hours of the morning listening to an old *JJ Cale* concert, looked decidedly the worse for wear. From where he now stood, Mason sensed a distinct buzz in the room – a new found enthusiasm. Determined to put Sir Jeremy behind bars, Mason had set up a small investigative team to deal with the sordid details of the corrupt politician's nocturnal activities. If nothing else, Sir Jeremy's sleazy social life had raised more than a few eyebrows in the corridors of Westminster. Shunned by the general public, his long-standing association with the press was over. Having finally turned their backs on him, he was now facing the more serious charges of an active involvement in a paedophile ring. It was headline breaking news, and his lawyers were having to work flat out in an effort to salvage his name. Mason was loving every minute of it. No longer posing a threat, Sir Jeremy's political career was all but over and his business empire in free fall.

Having opened up a whole new raft of enquiries, uncovering the Wharf Butcher's whereabouts was proving more difficult. Luke James had likened it to searching for the Holy Grail. How true that statement had turned out to be. Activities surrounding Cleveland had also been stepped up a level. It was due sail on Friday's early morning tide, and Mason had kept a watchful eye on the ship's passenger list. To date, none of Gilesgate's board members had shown their hand. With only a few days remaining, surely one of them would break cover. It was a fine balancing act, a game of cat and mouse that was severely testing Mason's patience. His initial thoughts were to sit tight, and allow Cleveland to slip her moorings before impounding her in territorial waters. It was a risky plan, he knew that, but it was the only option that appealed to him.

It was a single gunshot that halted the morning's proceedings, a muffled sound reminiscent to that of gunfire in an enclosed environment. With lightning reflexes, Mason had already cleared the occupants of the front two tables, long before they'd even realised it. Not too far away, he thought he could hear low rumbling noises coming from beyond the corridor. His heart raced, and the eerie silence that followed swept throughout the rest of the building as though struck by a nuclear blast.

There it was again.

Motionless, Mason just stood there and stared. His hands were shaking, and his mouth felt dry. Then he heard voices, and ran towards the distant echoes of fast approaching footsteps. He did not run far. Seconds later he was confronted by a distraught receptionist, ashen faced and petrified. Making no efforts to console her, the terrified young woman swept past him as though he had never existed. Palms sweating, his heart pounding, he pushed on.

Moments later, what he saw caused him alarm.

'Out!' he screamed, herding a group of onlookers back into the corridor.

Slamming the office door shut behind him, he stood silent for a moment. Stunned, he noticed the back of the ACC's head had been blown away. The remains were scattered about the ceiling and walls. From the angle and position of the body, Mason quickly deduced what had happened. He would need to work fast, as there were those beyond the corridor who would soon outstrip his authority. He searched for clues, and there were plenty. Then his eyes dropped to the corpse. The arms were dangling; the body slumped forward over the desk. It was not a pretty sight. Death had come quickly, it seemed, a single bullet through the mouth. It was a painless demise, decisive and swift, but nevertheless messy. Skirting the body, he searched for that one vital piece of evidence that would tell him everything. His foremost thought was the integrity of the police force. Suicide, he told himself, was never straightforward; it was always embroiled in complexities or entangled in doubt. Whatever his reasoning, the ACC's ultimate intention had been to blow himself into the realms of kingdom come. Who could doubt that achievement?

Then he heard shouting, but not before latching onto the blood stained envelope. Lowering the body, he wiped the blood from his hands and turned to open the office window.

Seconds later, he was confronted by the Head of Security.

'What in hell's name is going on in here?' asked Colin Bradshaw.

Mason pointed to the body.

'What the—'

'It looks like a tragic accident.'

The Head of Security looked him in the eye and then down at the body again. 'It appears anything but an accident, Detective Chief Inspector. It looks like suicide to me, even I can see that.'

'True, but we cannot be sure at this stage.'

'Why did you find it necessary to shut the door?' Bradshaw insisted. 'What in God's name were you thinking of?'

'It was—' think fast, 'purely security reasons.'

Mason slipped the blood-soaked envelope into his trouser pocket, and felt a cold shiver run down his spine. His head was pounding and his hands were sweating profusely. Most senior officers would attempt to talk their way out of a problem, choose their moment, and all too quickly lay blame on others. That's how the system worked. That's how most senior officers had reached their invariable positions in the first place. It was necessary to strip away the delusion, react first, and think it through later. Right now he needed an excuse, and any excuse was better than none. Whatever he said in the next few minutes would need to sound convincing. Besides, he was here on secondment – an outsider – easy prey for the local boys to close rank on him. Then he noticed the corpse was directly in line with the open window.

Now was his moment.

'I'd stay well clear from the window,' Mason said, anxiously pointing to the building opposite. 'Someone may have popped a shot off at him.'

Bradshaw drew back, and for one dark moment it seemed as though the game was up. Then he caught the hesitation in Bradshaw's body language.

'Sorry, Jack. I'm not thinking straight.'

As if witnessing his first gunshot incident, Bradshaw took a closer look at the ACC's lifeless body. 'My God, it's left one hell of a mess,' he said, shaking his head in profuse disgust. The Head of Security expelled a long drawn out breath. 'What an utter waste of a career, Jack.'

'It's not good, is it?'

Mason stepped aside as Bradshaw popped his head out of the open office window and checked the building opposite. Turning sharply to face him, his posture demanded attention. 'This is a nasty business, Jack. We best keep this under wraps for the time being. I can't imagine what the press will make of it all, once they find out what has happened.'

'You're right. This kind of incident never sits well at the best of times, especially one involving a senior police officer. We both could have done without this.'

'I agree, but I'll need a full written statement all the same.'

'Yes, of course,' Mason nodded.

'Good man.'

'It's not a pretty sight,' Mason said, turning to leave. 'Mind, I've seen its likes before. It's not uncommon for a police officer to play around with a gun at some stage in their career. It's a man's thing, I'm afraid.'

'Yes. Yes, of course. Let's hope for his family's sake that this was a dreadful accident. But I'm still not convinced.'

'We'll need to get ballistics involved. Let's see what they make of it all.'

'It's suicide, Jack, nothing else.'

'You're probably right, but the only person who can tell us that for sure is now dead.'

That had done the trick, and there was doubt in Colin Bradshaw's glances.

'Best leave this one with me,' Bradshaw insisted.

Mason slipped quietly from the room and into a corridor full of curious onlookers. Mission accomplished, he told himself. Having cast the seeds of doubt in the senior officer's mind, he was hoping for enough breathing time to sort things out. Accident, he chuckled, like hell. The ACC had blown his brains out rather than face the music.

He felt for the envelope . . . still there.

As he turned the corner heading towards the back of the building, he was almost beyond himself. It was insane to think that someone could end it all this way. What about his wife, thought Mason. What about his kids? Not to mention the fragments of bone, teeth and brains splattered about the place. What a waste, he shuddered.

Seconds later, he pushed back the toilet door, slid back the bolt, and sat for a while. Nerves jangling, he put his hand in his pocket and pulled out the blood-stained envelope. What dark secrets it was holding he had no idea.

He tore back the flap.

Chapter Forty-Eight

A warm wind had whipped up through the streets of Ponteland, as Carlisle pulled into the car park at Police Headquarters. By the time he reached Jack Mason's office most of the shouting was over. George Wallace sat flushed, surrounded by a team of fellow dejected detectives. Something was afoot, and whatever it was, he was about to find out.

'One of my Mondeo's has turned up at a property in Forest Hall,' said Mason.

'When was this?' Carlisle asked.

'Late yesterday evening.'

He had walked slap bang into the middle of a heated discussion, with Jack Mason taking centre stage. The atmosphere was strained, and had every reason to be. From what he could gather, one of Mason's police bait cars had been stolen close to the Wallsend Metro Station. Left unattended with its doors unlocked and ignition keys thrown onto the passenger seat, it had been easy pickings for some unsuspecting thief.

But was this the Wharf Butcher's doing?

'Do we have an ID?'

'He's male, 6'2", aged approximately thirty-five and walks with a limp. What more do you need to know . . . he fits the description perfectly.'

Carlisle trod carefully. 'So what's your problem?'

The team of detectives stared at one another.

'We need some advice,' Mason finally admitted. 'If this is the Wharf Butcher's doing, then how do we best approach him?'

Mason was right. Despite the myth that serial killers want to get caught, only a few had ever turned themselves in. This wasn't an easy decision, he realised that; they were sitting on a powder keg and the fuse had already been lit.

'What can you tell me about the property?'

'It's an upmarket four bedroom detached, with large surrounding gardens,' Mason mumbled. 'There's a team over there now, and they've set up a makeshift surveillance room in one of the properties opposite. Let's hope our suspect doesn't spot them. If he does, then god knows what will happen.'

'And the occupants of the house, where are they now?'

'On holiday in Australia, and they're not due to fly back for at least another month.'

Carlisle did a quick mental calculation. 'What else do we know about the neighbourhood?'

'It's secluded, quiet, and very upmarket. The people who live there are loaded with money.' Mason let out a long lingering sigh, as if to release some innermost tension. 'They're so far up their own arses; they don't even know when their next door neighbour's property has been broken into. What a fucking shambles.'

The other detectives remained silent, preferring to let Mason do the talking.

'I'd tread careful, Jack. Whoever's occupying the property may have overridden the house security system.' Carlisle stared at the others. 'And we all know he's good with electronics.'

Mason shook his head. 'That's a good point.'

'Who's keeping an eye on the property while the owners are away?'

'We've made a few discreet door to door enquiries, but that's about it at this stage.'

Carlisle was silent for a moment. 'So, where is your suspect now?'

'He left the house around seven thirty this morning, and was followed to the High Street in Wallsend. That's the last we've seen of him.' Mason shook his head in despair. 'He's a cunning bastard; you've got to hand him that.'

'Who's following him?'

'DC Carrington,' Mason lowered his head. 'I've instructed her to stay with the stolen Mondeo, on the off-chance he'll return to it. If he doesn't, we're sunk.'

The one thing Carlisle had learned was never to underestimate a serial killer's cunning, as they were masters at their game. If this was the Wharf Butcher's doing, and he had no reason to believe otherwise, the team would need to take advantage of every opportunity. He sat in silence for a moment. This was a big breakthrough, and the tension was already beginning to show. They would need to tread carefully, bring a sense of order to the place. Easier said than done, he thought.

'The trouble is this, Jack. These people are good at playing Jekyll and Hyde. They have the ability to move in and out of society at will. Never underestimate their actions. You'll need to stay close, blend into the background so to speak. One thing for sure, he'll be watching you every step of the way.'

Mason sighed, and scratched the side of his head. 'Yeah, but will he return to the Mondeo? That's my biggest concern right now.'

'If he is who I think he is, then yes.' Carlisle turned to the others. 'There again, if he's active, then that's an entirely different matter.'

'What's his state of mind?' said Mason, pacing the office.

'Psychopaths are very grandiose; their world is all about them. Right now he believes he has the power over life and death. In which case, our best option would be to play him at his own game. Think as he does.'

Mason just stared at him. 'Which is?'

'How does a spider catch a fly, Jack?'

The DCI stood for a moment. Carlisle could almost hear the cogs going around in his head. 'We set a trap,' said Mason. 'Put a stop to his movements. Is that what you're saying?'

'Yes and no, it all depends on what kind of trap you're thinking of setting?'

'First things first,' Mason shrugged. 'We need to get a fix on the property.'

'Fix! What kind of fix?'

'I'm looking for a DNA match, fingerprints, anything that points us to the killer. The last thing we need is to go in heavy handed only to find it's not him. I've been there before, and I've certainly no intentions of going there again.'

Stirrings and mumblings came from the team.

'Be careful, Jack. He may have set traps. This one's clever with electronics, remember?'

'Did you hear that, lads?'

At least Mason was thinking rationally for once.

'May I suggest no marked police cars or uniforms are seen in the area?' Carlisle advised. 'Anyone on duty there should be dressed in plain clothes. If he is active, and I believe he is, then he'll need to move around freely without the feeling of being watched.'

Nursing a mug of coffee, Mason stared blankly out of the office window. Seconds later, he banged the empty mug on his desktop. 'This is beginning to sound like a plan. If this does turn into a lengthy stake-out, which it may, we need to be prepared for every eventuality.'

'Who else is involved in following the Mondeo?' Carlisle asked.

The question had caught Mason off guard.

'No one is, why?'

'If he is active, then DC Carrington will need to be on guard. The last thing we need is a dead female police officer on our hands.'

Mason stared at him dumbfounded. 'If I didn't know you better, I'd tell you to sod off. Carrington's wired up, she only has to call in for assistance.'

A memory jogged him.

'This surveillance property,' Carlisle said, remembering how the killer had slipped through the net at Annie Jenkins' funeral, 'how secure is the place?'

'Why don't we take a look for ourselves,' Mason sighed.

Aware that the suspect's mind had a bad habit of going into dark places where ordinary people's minds didn't go, the DCI appeared on edge. For the first time in weeks, Carlisle began to realise that Mason never had a plan in the first place. Maybe he was operating on pure adrenaline alone, which was usually the case. Despite all that was going through his head, it was still the same old Mason. Behind his hard-cop carapace, there was a certain inevitable vulnerability. Spur of the moment tactics, and back of the fag-packet plans had their place, but now wasn't the time for either. Mason was floundering, and running short on ideas. Not the best of situations to be in, especially when a serial killer was out there.

Before leaving, the DCI dished out a new set of instructions, and made a few discreet phone calls. The minute they pulled out of Police Headquarters, the first spots of rain fell on the car's windscreen. Another bad omen, thought Carlisle.

Chapter Forty-Nine

Stepping from the battered white transit van, Carlisle adjusted his sunglasses and glanced at the four-bedroomed house opposite. Why the killer had chosen this property above all others in the area, was beyond him. This was egotism gone mad. The house had great style and character, fabulous architectural features, attractive brickwork and a contrasting slate roof. His first impression was that this was rich man's territory. The people who lived here certainly didn't struggle with their mortgages.

'What do you make of it?' said Carlisle.

Mason took a step back. 'I couldn't afford the council tax, let alone the deposit on one of these properties.'

It felt strange working on an undercover stakeout again, but little had changed. As ever, Jack Mason was still the true master of disguise. Wearing an orange high-visibility jacket, grubby white T-shirt, blue denim jeans and a pair of mud-spattered boots, his colleague looked anything but a senior police officer now engaged in a hunt for a serial killer. Formalities over, the DCI reached down inside the driver's door and picked up a clipboard and pen.

'Snap out of it,' Mason insisted. 'It's time to look busy.'

'I am.'

Mason shook his head in a show of contempt, and climbed into the back of the transit van. Seconds later he dragged a huge industrial high-pressure jet washer towards the van's rear doors.

'Stick this on the driveway, and try putting your back into it.'

'I thought this was an undercover distraction?' answered Carlisle.

'It is, and you're the labourer.'

'This is bloody ridiculous, Jack.'

'What the hell are you whingeing about now?'

'This contraption,' he said, pointing down at the jet washer. 'It weighs a bloody ton.'

The banter between them was flowing thick and fast, just as it had in the old days. Then without warning, the DCI suddenly leapt from the transit van and began laying out an impressive line of road cones. Perfect, he thought, he couldn't have done better himself. Within minutes, the whole area had taken on the appearance of a major construction project in progress.

'Tell me . . .' said Mason, poking his head into an open man-hole drain. 'What kind of crazy are we dealing with here?'

'He's back to his old tricks and working within his comfort zone, I'd say.'

'But why this area, what's going on inside his head?'

'Good question. He probably sees himself as bit of a celebrity, and he's making a personal statement. It's a familiar pattern with these people. They're egotistic, full of their own self-esteem.'

'Don't tell me he's planned all of this?'

'He probably has.'

'You're joking!' Mason said, shaking his head.

'That's what we're up against, I'm afraid.'

Then, from a neighbouring upstairs window, Carlisle caught a chink in the curtains.

'Don't rush it,' Mason said. 'Remember, we're here to fix the service drains. Try to look natural, without that stupid grin on your face.'

Carlisle was enjoying himself. It reminded him of the old days, when they'd worked together in the Metropolitan. There were times, and there had been many over the years, when they'd been caught in some hair-raising schemes. Drawn together from different social classes, theirs was a strange personality clash. Even so, they still had great respect for one another's individual qualities, and that's what held them together. As Mason had once said – *friendly disputes are healthy, you need to embrace them.*

How could he ever forget that?

'And that's another thing,' Carlisle said, pointing to the side of the white transit van. 'Someone's spelt maintenance with *'e'* instead of an *'a'*.

'What!'

'Those were my exactly sentiments. It's brains you need round here, not brawn.'

Clipboard at the ready, Mason strolled towards the rear of the surveillance house. Seconds later, they were inside and moving down a long narrow hallway. At the top of a short flight of stairs, the landing turned back on itself and brought them to the front of the building. The first bedroom, the smaller of two, was empty and void of all furnishings. It had a musky smell, and reminded him of an antique shop crammed full of old books. The second room, the master bedroom, was teaming with sophisticated police surveillance equipment. Not surprised, the air inside stank of Chinese takeaways – a sure sign that a round-the-clock surveillance operation was in place. Taking centre stage, a high definition professional camcorder was pointing directly down at the property opposite. It was then he noticed a large net screen hanging just a few feet back from the window. He'd seen its like before, a tool used by the military. Although partly restricting the light, any internal movements would not be spotted from outside of the building. Another clever weapon in the team's armoury, noted Carlisle.

From a distance, the undercover detective cut a dash. Wearing a black polo shirt, tracksuit bottoms and a pair of black trainers, his slicked back, black hair, had been cropped short on the sides.

'What's happening, Donaldson?' Mason asked.

'He's still occupying the property opposite, boss.'

'What about his movements?'

'It's difficult to keep a track of him, as he's in one minute and out the next.'

'Where is he now?'

'He took off around six, and hasn't been seen since.'

Mason checked his watch. 'That's almost four hours ago?'

The surveillance officer nodded, determined to keep his eyes peeled on the property opposite. 'This is the longest he's been away.'

'What about the stolen Mondeo. Has he taken it with him?'

'Yes,' Donaldson nodded. 'But we believe he's disarmed it, as we're not picking up a tracking signal.'

'Shit!' Mason cursed.

From where he now stood, Carlisle could see the gardens opposite were well maintained. Someone, obviously, was keeping an eye on the property. The front lawns had been freshly cut, and the driveway kept neat and tidy.

Mason leaned over to take a look for himself.

'When was the building opposite last checked out?'

'Shortly after six, boss.'

'Did they find anything?'

Donaldson spun round, both hands still firmly fixed on the camcorder.

'Sergeant Holmes reckons the suspect's computer was bugged. Fortunately, he stumbled across a couple of rogue leads attached to the back of the server. Had he not, I guess this whole operation would have gone up in smoke.'

Mason turned to Carlisle, and nodded. 'You were right about traps, my friend. This one's a cunning bastard.'

'According to the shift log,' said Donaldson, turning a huge piece of pink chewing gum over in his mouth, 'his actions are unpredictable, and there's no set pattern to his movements.'

Carlisle looked at Mason, and felt the knot in his stomach tighten. If, as the surveillance officer was suggesting, the killer's movements were erratic, it could only mean one thing. The Wharf Butcher was active.

Mason spoke first. 'Who else is monitoring his activities?'

'As far as I know, everyone is.'

Mason turned to face Carlisle. 'What do you think?'

Carlisle straightened, his nerve ends tingling. 'He's badly injured, and full of terrible rage. It's not redemption he's seeking, it's revenge. I don't want to sound alarmist here, but in my opinion his next victim will be the person who sparked off his killing spree in the first place. He's running out of time, and he needs to see it through.'

'You make it sound so bloody simple, Goddammit,' Mason cursed.

'Harsh reality is always better than false hope, I'm told.'

They spent the next twenty minutes running back over the detail. Then, from an inside pocket, Mason handed him a crumpled blood-stained envelope. Carlisle drew back, where the light was much better.

He began to take in the content:

Dear Brett,

If you are reading this letter, it means that I'm now dead. The act of taking my own life isn't something that I do without a lot of thought. Sadly, there are no other options left open to me, and I can no longer come to terms with the appalling mess that I now find myself in.

Four years ago, I invested my life's savings into a company called Gilesgate Construction. Assured of a good return, I thought no more about it. On reflection Gilesgate is a well-known, highly reputable multi-national conglomerate, who deal in global warming initiatives – or so I was led to believe. Not until attending my first annual board meeting, did I learn that my initial investment had reached a staggering one hundred fold their original value. Not only that, once my dividend had cleared my bank, I found I was contractually bound into the system - ad-mortem – until death. Naturally suspicious, I began to take a closer look at Gilesgate's activities. Nothing could have prepared me for what I was about to discover. Gilesgate Construction, it seems, has managed to infiltrate the ranks of the European Environment Agency. Having devised an ingenious system of bribes, its Chairman, Sir Jeremy Wingate-Styles, is able to use his political influence within the European Council's decision-making plans. It's a water-tight scam, and one that has netted a staggering £3.5 billion Euros from the Central European banks.

As you can well imagine, these past few months have been a living hell for me. Not only that, I have placed my entire family in an untenable position for which I can never forgive myself. My only request, dear friend, is that you deal with my affairs as best you see fit. Everything I know about Gilesgate's illicit activities has been documented and locked away in my safe. Should you or any of your colleagues wish to pursue this matter further, you have my sincere blessing.

Goodbye and God bless
Gerald.

There was nothing more to say, the letter had said it all as far as Carlisle was concerned. 'How did you come by this?' he asked.

'I found it under his body.' Mason cleared his throat. 'Brett Jones was his legal adviser, besides his being a close friend of the family.'

'It must have come as a real shock to them.'

'How would I know?' Mason shrugged.

'*What!* You mean you've—'

'Goddamn it! The ACC should never have reduced himself to such indecision. The moment he knew something was wrong, anything, he should have pounced on it.'

They were standing now, facing one another across a narrow landing.

'What happens when the IPCC puts two and two together? They're bound to—'

'Who cares?' Mason shrugged. His voice was stressed, but his determination never faltered. 'He got what was coming to him. Let's face it: the old sod was driven by pure greed.'

'All the same he—'

'Think about it,' Mason interrupted. 'The honour and integrity of the force are at stake here. God knows what the press will make of it all, if they ever found out.'

Nothing would happen until Monday, of course, and that's when the IPCC hearing would take place. In the cold light of day the ACC's greatest fear wasn't death. If it had been, then he couldn't have committed suicide in the first place. No, thought Carlisle, his greatest fear was the disgrace he'd brought upon his own family. Mason was right. The moment the Independent Police Complaints Commission had begun to look into Gilesgate's financial affairs, the Acting Chief Constable would have known the game was up.

Then the penny dropped.

'No wonder he ordered you to stay well clear of Gilesgate,' Carlisle said, and smiled.

'Too damn right,' Mason retorted. 'The old sod knew he was finished, the minute the Fraud Squad was involved.'

'Conscience can be a funny thing, Jack.'

'Thankfully he documented everything down. And now we know why.'

Mason looked at him, physically shaken, and there was bitterness in his voice. No wonder he sounded agitated. There were so many scenarios, so many imponderables; it was difficult to work out. Not only were Mason's resources stretched, the killer's unpredictable antics were putting undue strain on the rest of his team. If that wasn't bad enough, the odds were now heavily stacked against him and he didn't know which way to turn.

Back inside the surveillance room, DC Donaldson was in the middle of adjusting the camcorder.

'Anything . . .?' Mason asked.

The surveillance officer grunted some inaudible muttering, and continued with what he was doing. From what Carlisle could see, very little had changed. The house opposite was still empty, and there wasn't a Mondeo standing on the driveway. Not a good sign, he felt.

'It's not looking good, Jack.'

'Tell me about it,' Mason sighed.

'There must be a way out of this mess, surely.'

Mason raised an eyebrow. 'What if we bag this maniac, and the rest of Gilesgate's board all in one fell swoop?'

'Great idea, but how do you propose to do that?'

'That wasn't my question,' Mason groaned.

'But we're fast running out of time, Jack.'

'I realise that—'

Oh, shit, thought Carlisle, still trying to think positively. Not the best of situations to be in, but there again, he'd been in a lot worse.

'You do realise he'll stop at nothing until he gets what he wants.'

Mason eyes narrowed, but he refused to comment.

'I can't speculate,' Carlisle went on, 'but he's out there somewhere and closing in on his next target.'

'Get to the point!'

Still deep in thought, it seemed as though Mason had completely run out of ideas. What to do next, thought Carlisle. Then it came to him. 'The Mondeo . . . we need to stick close to it,' he said excitedly. 'It's the one key tool in his armoury. Without it he's lost.'

'So he does have an Achilles heel after all,' Mason grinned.

'Yes, and he needs it to finish the job.'

Mason's face contorted and twisted in concentration. There were times when he looked seething and mean, and others, when he looked calm and calculated. Right now, Mason bore the look of indifference.

'That gives me a terrible dilemma.' Mason sighed. 'If I move against Gilesgate now, then I'll take away the killer's next target. What to do?'

Carlisle sensed the logic, but the answer came naturally to him. 'If it was me making those decisions, then I'd stick to my original plans. Our suspect's mind is focused on a tried and tested system. As long as we don't spook him, your plans have every chance of succeeding.'

'So we stick with the Mondeo?' Mason shrugged.

'If it were me, I would.'

Mason's look was mean. 'In which case we sit tight, and sweat it out.'

Chapter Fifty
Later that day

Henry Fraser ran an index finger around the lip of his glass, his eyes fixed firmly on the circular movements. 'This Jack Mason knows far more than he's letting on,' Fraser said. 'He's been pushing his nose into our affairs again, and he's asking for trouble.'

The sparkle was gone. Ever since the Assistant Chief Constable's untimely suicide, Sir Jeremy had barely slept a wink. The net was closing in, and it was only a matter of time before the police would come knocking on everyone's doors. The Chairman's face looked mean, as if hungry for answers.

'How much does Jack Mason know?'

Fraser screwed his face up, enjoying the limelight. 'I'm told the Fraud Squad is now involved.'

'What are they after now, I—'

'Tell me,' Fraser interrupted. 'Why did the Commissioner blow his brains out?'

Sir Jeremy seemed to wait for Fraser to elaborate, but he didn't.

'I have absolutely no idea, Henry.'

'I don't like what I'm hearing, you were closer to him than any of us and yet you know nothing?'

'Who knows why he chose to end it all, perhaps he had no other option.'

Fraser brushed aside the chairman's indignation, knowing full well he was clutching at straws. The future looked grim, and plans were afoot to slip out of the country on board Cleveland. Apart from him, that is. Fraser had other ideas.

'I've formed my own opinions as to why he pulled the trigger, and you lot don't want to go there,' Fraser said. 'Once a copper, you're always a copper in my books.'

Sir Jeremy peered over the top his spectacles. 'Everyone's entitled to an opinion, Henry. But it still doesn't resolve our problems.'

No doubt about it, Fraser thought, the man certainly had balls.

Fraser eased back in his seat and spread his enormous hands on the boardroom table in front of him. The cuffs of his shirtsleeves were turned up, his huge biceps preventing him from turning them further. 'I presume you guys are still planning to skip the country tomorrow?'

Sir Jeremy flashed him a stern glance. 'What are you suggesting, Henry?'

'I'm not. I'm merely making a point, that's all.' Fraser's eyes narrowed dangerously. 'If these paedophile charges were to stick, wherever you go you'll be hunted down. You know that. Those types of crimes never sit well with the criminal world. These people have a specific way of dealing with paedophiles, and it ain't good . . . I can assure you.'

'What the hell are you trying to say?' Sir Jeremy insisted.

There was menace in Fraser's eyes.

'These rumours I'm hearing, it ain't looking good—'

Sir Jeremy raised a hand to cut him off. 'The police still haven't charged me with anything, and the main witness is a raving mad lunatic. What do you have to say about—'

But before, Sir Jeremy could finish, Fraser had retaliated.

'It's making me uncomfortable, it ain't right.'

'But it's true,' Sir Jeremy protested.

The tension between them was mounting, and Fraser wasn't sure who he could trust anymore. Where others saw problems, Fraser saw opportunities and it was this aspect he was now working on.

'This whole damn charade is media driven. Believe me; those bastards certainly know how to milk a good story.' Nods of approval gathered pace. 'I know I'm right,' Fraser went on. 'Fortunately I'm not on the receiving end of the Wharf Butcher's knife. You guys are, and you need to shake out of it. Tomorrow you'll all be out of here, and sailing into warmer climates.'

'Is there an alternative?' Sir Jeremy nodded for Fraser to elaborate.

'No. I just thought I'd mention it . . . that's all.'

'I'm convinced Mason's no nearer to catching this maniac than you are, Henry.'

Fraser sensed Sir Jeremy's predicament, but refused to be drawn in by it. Fear, it seemed, had leached into the boardroom like a virus. Talk was cheap, and it was time to move on.

'In my books, it's the Wharf Butcher who holds all the trump cards. And that's another thing,' Fraser said, tapping an index finger on the boardroom table. 'I'm convinced Jack Mason is trying to lure his killer into a trap.'

Having remained silent throughout, Mike Findley lit another cigar, eased back in his seat and exhaled a huge cloud of cigar smoke. The ex-stockbroker was on more than just speaking terms with Fraser. They were regular drinking partners, and as such, were often seen together frequenting the local gambling clubs. Mike Findley knew a thing or two about investments, and had always kept Fraser's financial affairs in order for him. In return, if anyone gave Mike Findley a problem, it was Henry Fraser who usually sorted it out for him. It was that kind of relationship.

'Tell me,' said Mike Findley. 'What's Mason up to now?'

'The man's a dickhead as far as I'm concerned, but he's not as daft as he makes out to be. He's playing a dangerous game of cat and mouse with you all, and none of you can see it.' Fraser made a little sweeping hand gesture. 'Sooner or later he knows this maniac will come looking for one of you, and when he does, Mason will be sat in the side-lines and waiting to pounce.'

Mike Findley's face had turned a pallid colour. 'Don't tell me he's using us as human bait, surely not?'

'I couldn't have put it better myself, Mike,' Fraser chuckled.

'If this hunch of yours is true,' said Sir Jeremy, 'it seems we've all gravely underestimated Mason's understanding of the situation.'

'I could be wrong, of course,' Fraser replied, holding up his huge hands.

'I doubt it, Henry,' Mike Findley said. 'You always speak at lot of sense.'

Fraser sat unmoved for a moment, conscious of the things unsaid. The last meeting had been a difficult one – for Sir Jeremy at least. The big man leaned over in his seat, and made a show of checking his watch. 'Let's hope this Wharf Butcher moves sooner rather than later. In the meantime, you guys need to relax and let me do the worrying.'

Sir Jeremy hesitated, and then said, 'What if we get to this Wharf Butcher first?'

'I'm still working on it,' Fraser shrugged. 'Tomorrow you'll be carrying an extra passenger on board.'

'Like who?' Mike Findley said, nearly choking on the stub of his cigar.

'This one only has a one way ticket, Mike. It's to the bottom of the North Sea.'

Nervous titters of laughter broke out around the table.

'How confident are you?' Sir Jeremy asked.

Fraser hit back. 'Never doubt my ability, Sir Jeremy. Besides, I now know who's behind these killings.'

Fraser was playing with his words, attention-seeking. It was his way of dealing with the problem, his way of staying in control. The only high point, if you call it that, was the look on Sir Jeremy's face.

'These plans of yours,' Mike Findley said. 'They're obviously financially driven.'

'That's the deal, Mike. That's what you people pay me to do – any objections?'

The room fell silent again.

Chapter Fifty-One

It was 10.02am

The engine still running, Lexus steered the stolen Mk3 Mondeo over the kerbside and viewed the house from a distance. He was hungry; he had not eaten in fifteen hours now. There was nothing but calm when he rolled down the driver's side window, and inhaled the cool morning air. From his position, everything seemed in order. There was new mail in the letter-box, and the small upstairs window – the one he left open last night – was still open. Even though the house appeared empty, what untold dangers lay within, he had no idea. Not everything had gone to plan, at least not today it hadn't. Besides, this whole area gave him the creeps. He preferred the roughened edges, where the challenges were far less predictable.

He checked his rear mirror.

Then he heard voices!

What do you think of your new home?

'It's perfect, maybe I should keep it for my own.'

Why not, you've earned it.

He paused, as a young woman in a blue Nissan saloon drove past him on the opposite side of the street. The car was at a snail's speed, and barely ticking over. Bemused, and riddled with self-doubt, he spotted a small child strapped into the backseat of the car. It was fast asleep and dreaming in la-la-land, just as it should be at this time of day. Then he realised, the young woman was driving on the wrong side of the road. Panic gripped him, and he was thrown into utter turmoil again. Who was she, and why was she driving on the wrong side of the road? Swearing quietly, he hesitated, filled with indecision and the fabric of uncertainty that threatened to draw him ever closer towards the trapdoor of insanity. 'Does reality really exist?' Lexus asked.

Only in the darkest corners of your mind, the voice in his head replied. Lured into false security, his inner thoughts moved ever closer towards the dark side. He was eight years old, with big blue eyes and a lily-white complexion to match his long blonde curly hair. As the illusion intensified, so did his sense of judgement. If this wasn't a dream, could the silver cloud he was riding on be real? There, beneath his feet, stood a beautiful white house. It was awesome, as if his past life had unravelled before him. Drawn in through an open bedroom window, he tried to focus his mind. In his dream he was lying face down on the bed, and the image of his perverted father standing over him. Gripped by darker forces, he lunged out, towards the ghost like apparition that dared to call himself his father. Tears trickled down his cheeks, and his mind played tricks with him. There was nothing he could do to stop the merciless beatings and vulgar acts of abuse that were taking place before his very eyes – nothing.

He reached out, infuriated with rage. Both hands firmly wrapped around his father's throat, he glared at him. 'Was there ever a creature left abandoned as much as I was, Father. Was mine a life lost? From the moment I was born you despised me. Shut away like some animal, only to be brought out and abused as a plaything. You are the beast that created me . . . you, not me. How dare you call yourself my father?'

Squeeze tighter, Lexus.

'I am,' he cried out. 'I am, and with all my might.'

You must squeeze tighter, Lexus. This monster must never slip through your fingers again. Do not let it happen.

'It won't . . . I promise you.'

Only then did his eyes shoot open.

Only then did the truth unfold.

There, playing on the car's windscreen was an eerie red spectral of light. He sat for a while, transfixed, as it danced as a firefly hovered over a still pond. Then he spotted movement. His eyes narrowed and the muscles in the back of his neck tightened. Fear gripped him, and the knot in his stomach intensified. Tighter and tighter until he could barely breathe anymore. Not twenty feet away stood a solitary figure. He was bolt upright, tall, with a strong jawbone pushed out from beneath a black woollen balaclava. Motionless and standing beside him was a large German Shepherd. Panic ripped through him as never before.

Then, the inner voices returned.

You still awake?

'Yes, numpty, a genius never sleeps.'

Really! Isn't that the devil's beast now standing before you?

Only the cushion of darkness lay between truth and sanity – a bleak world full of evil writhing demons, and terrible nightmares. His head was pounding, and his heart threatened to explode inside his chest. Overcome with rage, Lexus beat his fists against the dashboard in a final act of revulsion. This was no dream, this was reality, the here and now gone mad.

Then, in the darkest corners of his mind, a wave of fear washed over him.

'What should I do, mama?'

You will think of something, my son.

'Like what? I can't think of anything anymore?' Lexus cried out.

You must, before the evil beast devours you.

Chapter Fifty-Two

It was ten-fourteen when Luke James finally set foot on the driveway outside the surveillance house. How much longer Jack Mason's plan would hold up was anyone's guess. Shielding his eyes against the bright morning sunlight, he glanced across at the stationary Mondeo now sat opposite him.

Its engine still running, its driver still at the wheel, James stood transfixed. An observant man, he could see the blue Nissan saloon as it slid effortlessly towards him from the end of the street. Right on cue, the young Detective dipped her headlights as she drove past him. Strapped into the rear seat of the vehicle, he recognised his daughter's favourite doll. God, it looked so real, even he could have sworn it was a young child. It was perfect. They weren't out of danger yet. One false move and it could all end in disaster. Even so, thought James, nothing could move in or out of the cul-de-sac without the police knowing about it.

Earlier that morning, many of the local residents had been evacuated from their homes. What had started as a low-key stake-out was now a major tactical firearms operation. Security was tight, watertight, James believed. With every available police officer now drafted into the area, Forrest Hall was in lockdown. All that it needed was for the Wharf Butcher to make his move. Only then could Jack Mason's shoot to kill policy be put into operation. A single twitch would be enough, regardless of any human rights, moral values or any other ethical principles that could be thrown at the police. That's how it would end – out here on the streets and away from the prying eyes of the media circus.

Stepping from the shade, Luke James suddenly caught sight of a thin white plume of smoke trailing from the Mondeo's exhaust. It wasn't much, but it was enough to make his pulse race. Then he caught movement.

★

The moment the car shot backwards, the windscreen exploded into a thousand tiny fragments. It had barely moved. Close to the line of fire, Jack Mason moved his body sideways swinging his handgun with the vehicle's slight movement. Less than ten metres away, a lone marksman had trained his Heckler and Koch assault rifle onto the slow moving target.

Mason gave the signal.

Seconds later, a short burst of automatic fire tore through the driver's side door. Though the Mondeo had stopped, an alert firearms officer dashed to the front of the vehicle and unleashed another devastating cacophony of automatic fire. Whoever was inside never saw the bullets coming.

'Cease fire,' Mason commanded.

'Hold your positions,' another shouted.

The eerie silence that followed was broken only by the hissing of hot steam escaping from the Mondeo's punctured radiator grill. After what seemed an eternity, Mason rose from his position and approached the vehicle with caution. His movements were deliberate, almost robotic as he dropped to one knee and checked his surroundings.

'Cover me,' he mouthed to the nearest police officer.

With lightening reflexes, the DCI pushed the nose of his Smith & Wesson in through the window opening and fired off two quick shots. The man who appeared to have more lives than a cat, had finally run out of luck.

Nobody moved.

Seconds later, Mason took a step forward and gently teased back the driver's door. Sick in the pit of his stomach, he found the Wharf Butcher lying prostrate across the front seats of the Mondeo. Part of the back of his head had been blown away, and he was lying face down in a pool of blood. Breathing heavily, Mason mentally prepared himself for the unexpected. Prodding the lifeless body with the muzzle of his gun, he flinched. Then, in a last act of defiance, the Wharf Butcher's left arm slid ignominiously to the floor.

It was over.

Blood leaking everywhere, the killer's lifeless body was dragged from the cab of the vehicle, and unceremoniously dumped in the middle of the road. Face upwards, for all to see, even in death the Wharf Butcher's facial expression bore an implacable smile of innocence. Straddling his suspect's body, Mason shifted his stance. Around the serial killer's neck hung the trophies of his appalling campaign of terror. Watches, rings, earrings and personal trinkets, all snatched from his victims' dead bodies as a permanent reminder of the people he'd so horrifically mutilated.

Why, Mason kept asking himself. Why do these people do such terrible things?

'You need to check this out,' someone called out, from the rear of the Mondeo.

Mason froze, gathered his wits, and swung to face the young Constable.

'What is it, Griffiths?'

'Take a look at this, boss.'

Mason slid the Smith & Wesson back into its holster and trod cautiously towards where the young constable was now standing. How his patience had held as it did, he had no idea. Yes, he had made a few rash decisions, and yes the outcome had turned out even better than anticipated. But for the brilliant mind of David Carlisle, none of this would have happened. Still numb with shock, Mason was conscious he was walking unsteadily.

Get a grip, he cursed.

The young constable's face had a pallid look, and his answer, when it came, seemed to take forever. 'Here, boss,' said PC Griffiths, pointing down into the boot of the Mondeo.

Mason just stood there, and stared at the grisly torso now confronting him. The flesh, ice cold at a touch, appeared as though it had been embalmed and kept in a fridge. Grotesque as it was, the face bore a remarkable resemblance of waxed preservation. Hacked to pieces, the hands and feet were missing, but the victim's facial features were clearly recognisable.

'Who is he?' asked PC Griffiths.

'His name is Sir Jeremy Wingate-Stiles.'

'Not a pretty sight, boss.'

'Most murder victims never are,' Mason sighed.

All of a sudden the car's radiator exploded under a cloud of hot steam, sending debris in every direction. Mason drifted for a moment. Eyes glazed, as he stared at the rest of the carnage. The air, filled with diesel fumes and the smell of burnt gunpowder, had a strange comforting effect on him. It was over, that much he was certain of, and people's lives were no longer threatened anymore.

Then, out of the corner of his eye, he spotted Harry Manley as he approached from one of the house gardens. The Detective's face carried a mischievous look, and there was devilment in his glances.

'Happy days eh, boss,' said Manley, pushing his head into the boot of the Mondeo.

Mason regarded him quizzically. 'That's what happens when you go poking your nose into other people's affairs, Harry. There's always somebody out there who wants to chop you down to size.'

No sooner had he said it, than the rest of the team fell about laughing. Mason had seen enough, and began dishing out orders.

His mobile phone pinged – it was the confirmation he'd been waiting for. News travelled fast, Cleveland had been detained inside British territorial waters and was on her way back to the River Tyne. All that remained now was to deal with Henry Fraser. The rest, as they say, would quickly fall into place. He was certainly looking forward to his interview with Henry Fraser, but that was not until tomorrow. So far Fraser had said very little, but he had good reason to keep quiet. His lawyer, Tom Pollard, was plea bargaining and trying to reduce his client's charges.

An hour later, and much to Mason's relief, he was driving south along Whitley Bay Promenade and towards his favourite Mexican restaurant. He'd not eaten in hours, and his stomach was rumbling. The moment he pulled onto the curb side, his heart sank. The restaurant blinds were shut, and the place had a deserted look. Then, he noticed the hand written sign sellotaped to the restaurant window:

SORRY – CLOSED FOR RENOVATION.

Mason was furious.

Chapter Fifty-Three

Henry Fraser sat facing Jack Mason across the interview table, at Market Street police station in Newcastle. It had been a long drawn out session and the DCI was exhausted. The only positive, if there was any, was Fraser's defence lawyer. An astute, intelligent man, who had taken copious notes throughout their interview. Up to now he had said very little, but there again he had every reason to do so. Although the evidence was overwhelmingly stacked against his client, there was still room for manoeuvre. But there lay Fraser's problem. In offering the police some vital piece of information, there was a slim chance the charges against him may be reduced.

Mason, silent as a stone, reflected on Fraser's last statement.

'So you're looking for a deal, Henry?'

'Yeah . . .' Fraser grunted. 'But it depends what's on offer?'

'Right now,' said Mason. 'I'd say at least thirty-five years.'

'*Thirty-five years!*'

'That's about the size of it,' Mason grinned. 'In my books, that will make you eighty something when they finally open the cell doors to your freedom again.'

Mason sat back in his seat, trying his best not to laugh.

'That's bloody ridiculous.'

'I know, Henry. But that's how the system works unfortunately.'

Mason was choosing his words carefully, playing around the edges with an icy cold precision. He watched as the big man swirled the remnants of coffee in the bottom of the plastic cup, as if the enormity of it still hadn't sunk in. Fraser was trapped, and didn't know which way to turn.

'How do I know we can trust you?' Fraser said.

'You don't.'

'As we stand it's only promises across a table.'

'Of course you don't have to deal with me,' Mason reminded him. 'Perhaps someone else might offer you a better deal. There again, how do you know you can trust them?'

Fraser swallowed hard. 'This all stinks of the same shit to me, I—'

'No promises, Henry' Mason said, raising his hands in submission. 'It depends on what you tell me.'

Fraser's voice softened. 'So what are we looking at?'

Mason tapped the folder in front of him with his pen, as if to attract Fraser's attention towards it. 'The more you tell me, the more we reduce the sentence. It's that kind of deal. Not the best arrangements, I know, but it's a lot more than your cell mates are being offered.'

There was a long pause, before Fraser's lawyer nodded his approval.

'What do you want to know?' Fraser asked.

Mason pressed the concealed button hidden beneath the interview table, which started the video recording. He cherished the moment, knowing that several senior officers were also listening in on their interview. He was in no hurry. It was just a matter of dotting the i's and crossing the t's – and Mason was good at that.

'Why not start by you giving me some names?' Mason said with a wry smile. 'Take your time; you've certainly got plenty of that on your hands.'

Fraser folded his arms across his chest, a defensive stance. The big man looked humble, almost resigned to his fate. He had to dig deep, and Mason could sense the hurt. Fraser certainly knew how to handle the physical side of trouble, but how good was he at handling the mental pressure. That, Mason hoped, he was about to find out.

'Tell me, Jack,' said Fraser, 'how much do you know about Sir Jeremy?'

'It all depends,' Mason shrugged.

Fraser drew breath through his teeth. 'Let's skip the paedophile stuff for a minute, and talk about Gilesgate's setup,' Fraser said. 'The organisation is built in the form of a pyramid. The higher up the pyramid you ascend, the higher your stake in the profits. It's a bit like playing the stock market, come to think of it. There are different types of shares that come with different conditions and rights – if you know what I'm saying?'

Mason gave him a dubious look, but the explanation seemed reasonable. Now wasn't the time to ruffle the big man's feathers. 'So,' said Mason, 'where do you see the Board of Directors in all of this?'

Fraser eyed him with suspicion. 'It's the board who run the day to day operations at Gilesgate. They're the people who oversee the budgets, and ensure the contracts are finished on time.'

'And what about Sir Jeremy, where does he fit in all of this?'

'That's a good question,' Fraser said, growing in confidence. 'Sir Jeremy may head up the board, but he's not the top man in all of this. No. It's the other guys who pull the contract strings. That's how the system works.'

Mason nodded. 'So, Sir Jeremy acts as a go-between?'

'Let me put it another way,' Fraser explained. 'Whilst the board are dealing with the operational side of things, it allows Sir Jeremy to use his political influence. He knows people, important people, and that's how these contracts are won over.'

'I see,' said Mason.

Still babbling, Fraser pushed back in his seat. 'Like I say, Sir Jeremy can get awfully close to these people. He's good at what he does, and knows how to win these people over.'

'Which people are these, Henry?'

'You know who I'm talking about. The people who dictate who's spending what, where, and when of the taxpayers' money.' Fraser's face twitched with displeasure. 'Believe me; these guys hold the purse strings to some of Europe's more lucrative global warming contracts.'

'You mean Government Officials?'

'Yeah, but don't quote me on that,' Fraser shrugged.

Mason drew back in his seat and turned to face him. Palms held open, shoulders slightly hunched. It was his way of teasing out the information, his way of making the subject feel inferior as if they already knew what was coming next. 'The problem is, Henry, you're playing around the edges and dressing the story up so to speak. If Sir Jeremy isn't the man at the top, then who the hell is? And another thing, this pyramid you talk of – are you saying that Gilesgate is being run from elsewhere?'

'Don't fuck with me, Jack. You know I can't tell you that. You should talk to Sir Jeremy about that.' Fraser forced a rare smile. 'Tell me, when did you last hear of a trustworthy politician?'

Still unaware that Sir Jeremy was dead, Fraser was playing into his hands. He was trapped, and lies wouldn't save him now. Mason thought a moment on how best approach it. He took another swig of his coffee, and tilted his head back in thought. 'We're talking massive corruption here,' Mason went on. 'Tell me, is Sir Jeremy using his political clout to skirt around the CEM's fifteen-per cent monopoly ruling, or are we talking something entirely different here?'

Fraser jerked back in his seat, as if stunned by a Taser gun. 'How the fuck did you know about the fifteen-per cent monopoly ruling? Who told you that?'

'I know a lot about a lot of things.' Mason shrugged. 'The problem is this, after this interview my superiors will be talking with the Crown Prosecution Service about your current charges. They'll want to know how I got on. Not very good, I'll say. The suspect is refusing to cooperate. Do you see where I'm coming from, Henry?'

Fraser squirmed.

'You're putting undue pressure on me, and it's making me nervous.'

'That's what I'm paid to do, Henry. That's how these things operate. Just give me a few names, and I'll ease my foot off the pedal.'

'It's not that easy, and you know it.'

His back to the interview room door, Mason began to think about this. If Sir Jeremy was using his political influence to win over contracts, then who were these faceless people at the top? Better still, who was authorising the contracts? He made a mental note of it.

'I take it Sir Jeremy pays these people good money for their services?'

'That's what politicians do, isn't it?' Fraser mumbled. 'You only have to watch TV to see they've all got their snouts in the trough.'

'Not all politicians are bent, Henry.'

Fraser shrugged in disbelief. 'As far as I'm aware, the organisation is throwing huge sums of money in Sir Jeremy's direction. He sees to it that Gilesgate picks up the more lucrative contracts, the ones that pay big dividends . . . continuous expansion programmes, coastal sea defences, diversionary canals, that kind of stuff. It's big business and the CEF are willing to pay top dollar for the privilege of Gilesgate's services.'

'I see.' Mason leaned forward on the interview table. 'And who else is involved?'

Fraser dug his heels in. 'That's asking too much, Jack.'

'That's unfortunate, Henry, as most of the crap you've been spouting . . . I already knew.' Mason was lying, but Fraser was falling for it. 'Unless you can come up with names, how do I know you're telling me the truth?'

'Naming these people is a different matter, Jack. Even you know that.'

Mason was testing the water, and Fraser was coming along nicely. They'd covered a lot of ground, and the big man had revealed far more than he'd ever dared bargain for. Murder was one thing, but corruption in higher government office was a completely different matter. No doubt the Fraud Squad would be keen to get their hands on the interview tapes. But hey, who cared – right now Mason was having a ball.

Fraser looked him in the eye. 'So what exactly are you wanting from me?'

'I need proof, Henry. I need names. Who else is involved in the scam?'

There followed a short pause, then Fraser said, 'I suggest you start with the Agricultural Minister's department or maybe the Secretary of Overseas Affairs' office. These foreign diplomats carry an awful lot of political clout in the European corridors of power. Mind, they don't come cheap,' Fraser said, pointing a finger in the air. 'Money talks, it has a big influence on these people's decision making.'

'Anyone in particular spring to mind?'

Fraser was becoming more agitated. 'You need to talk that over with Sir Jeremy – find out what he has to say?'

'That's not possible,' Mason said, purposely lowering his voice. 'Sir Jeremy's jumped ship, and left the rest of you to stew in your own shit.'

Fraser's defence lawyer remained unruffled; he just sat there and smiled. Mason knew then he should have been more forceful – more direct.

'You look surprised, Henry.'

'How come you people know all this shit?'

'Well,' said Mason, thinking back to his conversation with Vic Miller on Wednesday. 'Sir Jeremy was certainly on Cleveland's passenger list last night, but when she sailed on the early morning tide, he was nowhere to be seen. I've had my suspicions about that little shit for weeks now. Never trust a politician, cos they'll always come back to bite you.'

Fraser shook his head. 'The bastard—'

Mason stared back at him.

'What can you tell me about his son . . . young Samuel? We know John Matthew made a bad job of taking him out – pity he lost an arm in the attempt. Tell me, Henry, when did you first find out young Samuel was killing Gilesgate board members for fun? Did you guess it was him, or did someone tip you off about him?' He suddenly caught the anger in Fraser's glances and decided to throw him a lifeline. 'There is of course the question of Sir Jeremy's sexual exploits with young children. Never liked paedophiles myself, they always leave a nasty taste in my mouth. Perhaps that's why he did a runner?' Mason shrugged. 'God knows what his cell mates will make of it all when they find out he's a paedophile.'

Fraser almost laughed. 'They'll string the little shit up.'

'It's a nice thought, Henry, but what if he mentions your name into the bargain?'

Fraser hesitated, stood, and then walked to the back of the interview room. He was angry; Mason could see it. The next twenty minutes proved invaluable, and it wasn't long before Fraser began to unravel the facts with the devotion of a priest attending confession.

All he needed now was a name, something to get his teeth into. But the fish was refusing to bite, and it was annoying him intensely.

'Who else is in on it, Henry?'

'You're moving too fast, Jack,' Fraser answered. 'I need assurances, or there's no deal.'

There followed an awkward silence between them, broken only by Mason's reluctant intervention. 'Let's talk about this "Flatlands Flood Barrier" contract. How do these EU deals filter back down through these Sleeper Companies? Who are the principal players, Henry?'

Fraser's confidence suddenly grew in stature. In the end, he'd almost reached the point of bragging about his own personal involvement in Gilesgate's business affairs. Names followed companies; companies followed structure and before too long, the pieces of the jigsaw puzzle finally fell into place. Pleased with his findings, Mason now had enough evidence to bring the whole of the Gilesgate organisation to its knees – along with a dozen top European executives.

Tiring of Fraser's repetitiveness, Mason leaned over and flicked the video recording switch to the OFF position. It was then that Fraser realised he'd been betrayed.

'What the fuck—' Fraser screamed. 'You promised no tapes – we had a deal.'

'Deal, what deal was that, Henry?'

Fraser flayed his arms out across the interview table. 'You two-faced son of—'

'What a pity,' said Mason, shaking his head from side to side. 'Greenfingers was right all along – he warned me you had a volatile temper.'

'*Greenfingers!*' Fraser screamed, jumping to his feet.

Slamming the door behind him, Mason made a beeline for the front desk. The last thing he heard was the interview room furnishings bouncing off the walls. Henry Fraser was all he'd imagined him to be, a born loser, a twenty-five stone spineless overgrown baboon who could only throw his weight about when the odds were heavily stacked in his favour.

Thirty-five years, Mason grinned. What will I be doing then?

274 MICHAEL K FOSTER

Chapter Fifty-Four

The following day, David Carlisle entered Northumbria Police Headquarters full of trepidation. The Wharf Butcher's death had told him nothing. Such a violent ending had left him with far too many unanswered questions. What was it that unlocked the moral safety catch that could turn a person to perform such barbaric acts? That question had intrigued him from the moment he first clapped eyes on his victim's disfigured bodies. If nothing else, he wanted to learn from it. Who this man was, and what made him tick. These were the questions that had pushed him to the very limits of his own mental boundaries. It was the driving force that went to the very heart of criminal profiling. Psychological input was valuable to the investigations of all crimes, not just those that caught the newspaper headlines. It was all part of the learning curve.

Avoiding a heavy media presence, Carlisle entered the building through one of the many side doors, where he was met by a small delegation of senior police officers. These were the Special Crime Attachments – the SCA, the faceless think tank – whose extended hands were now telling him his part in the police operation was over.

'It turned out just as you predicted it would,' Mason said, squeezing his way through a crowd of senior police officers.

Carlisle took his arm; the curiosity of the Wharf Butcher's final moments still with him. He'd always imagined he would meet face to face with the killer, exchange confidences, reach out into the killer's mind and unravel the mystery that controlled his impulses.

Sadly, it wasn't to be.

'How did it end?'

'He was blown away in a hail of bullets.'

'Decisive?'

'Instantaneous, more like,' Mason bragged.

Carlisle gazed at the others; their faces were familiar, but they were far too full of their own self-importance to be listening to what they were talking about. So this is how these people operated, he reminded himself, full of hot air and arrogance.

Carlisle gathered his thoughts. 'I take it you didn't get to question him?'

'For Christ's sake, he was far too dangerous to bring in alive. Even you know that.'

'It sounds like you didn't even try.'

At that point Carlisle was half expecting Mason to pull out his little black notebook, but he didn't. Instead, he backed away, still looking suspicious. Deep down, he wanted to understand the reasoning behind the Wharf Butcher's motives – an unsolved mystery that only the killer could answer.

'It's over, my friend. The Wharf Butcher is behind us now,' Mason confirmed, as if that was the end of the matter. 'He was far too emotionally detached. Besides, he showed absolutely no empathy towards his victims. Goddammit, you said yourself there was no cure for psychopathy. That's why I ended it as I did.'

Mason pointed towards the foyer, the others now in tow.

'It's not often you get the chance to talk to a serial killer, Jack, they're not everyday people. These individuals differ from the rest, they possess very complex personalities.'

Mason shook his head. 'Why must you always find a need to dissect everything? These killings have stopped, it's over, and that was my number one priority.'

'And mine.'

'So deal with it, for God's sake!'

Carlisle's mind still running amok, they dropped into silence again. It was Mason who spoke first. 'Fortunately, this isn't going to be a long drawn out enquiry.'

'Dead suspects don't stand trial?'

'Dead suspects are less paperwork,' Mason said, fixing his gaze. 'I trusted in your judgement and believed you got really close to him in the end. Fortunately, you have a very specific way of dealing with these things. When you said he'd return to the house, I simply increased my numbers and waited for the Mondeo to show up.'

'He was far too predictably organised to do otherwise.'

Mason looked at him, bemused. The DCI had no further interest in understanding the workings of a serial killer's mind, he realised that.

Homicide was homicide, in Jack Mason's book. The quicker he got to his target, the fewer body bags he would require. His was a simple game of numbers.

'This fraud scam is causing me a political headache,' Mason cautioned. 'The people involved are all senior European politicians, apparently. Needless to say, the Home Office are now involved.'

Typical, thought Carlisle. Like it or not, he would need to come to terms with it no matter how hard he fought it. The Wharf Butcher was dead and that was the end of the matter as far as everyone else was concerned.

Mason eyed him with suspicion before pulling him to one side. 'What I'm about to tell you is strictly confidential. If this leaks out, it's probably more than my job is worth.'

Carlisle nodded his agreement.

'The Wharf Butcher was born out of wedlock; his real mother's name was a young woman called Emily Haley.' Mason smiled thinly. 'By all accounts, she first clapped eyes on Sir Jeremy at a political fund-raising rally, and after a short fling, she fell pregnant by him. To cut a long story short, when young Samuel was born, that's when Sir Jeremy's ex-wife agreed to adopt the child.'

'Christ! It's little wonder things turned out as they did,' Carlisle pointed out.

Mason breathed in deeply. 'It seems Sir Jeremy's perverted child exploits were widely known in higher circles after all. What's more, some Senior Police Officers now admit to a cover-up, and that's why he was never brought to justice.'

Carlisle didn't need to listen to the rest; this had been a lethal time bomb waiting to happen. All too often, the boundaries between fantasy and reality get lost in a love-hate relationship between the killers and their parents. At least there was a perfectly reasonable explanation behind it all.

Moving towards the lift, Mason allowed the others to board before them. As the rest of the story began to unfold, it soon became apparent that Sir Jeremey had made more than enough money from Gilesgate's corruption scam. Having bribed his way into Europe's corridors of power, no wonder the Home Office was involved. Fraud, child sex abuse, and corruption were a volatile concoction that had finally cost Sir Jeremy his life.

Mason went on. 'Thinking back, I get the distinct impression that this all kicked off during the Ernest Stanton trial. Within hours of leaving the courtroom, he ends up dead with his throat cut. It's funny old world.'

The monster that finally turned on his creator, thought Carlisle. He'd never considered spontaneous killing before, but it had a nice ring about it. It seemed logical. What's more it was probably the start of things to come, the motive that drove young Samuel to kill in the first place? It would certainly have taken a special kind of mentality to do that; there again, his father's illicit activities had probably sparked off a whole host of emotions inside young Samuel's head. Wham bam, before anyone knew it, the ticking time bomb had suddenly clicked into place. Perhaps that's why young Samuel chose to cut off his father's hands, believing that crucifixion was far too good for him. If nothing else, the dates and timing were right.

'If Stanton was his first,' Carlisle said thoughtfully, 'Young Samuel most certainly acquired a taste for it. Let's face it; he certainly knew how to go about destroying his father's empire. That's what usually happens with these people unfortunately, humiliation can spark off all sorts of hatred inside these people's heads.'

'Well, there you have it,' Mason shrugged. 'You've answered your own questions regarding the Wharf Butcher's personal motivations.'

Carlisle gave him a half-hearted smile. 'All the same, it's a pity I couldn't get to question him. Now that he's dead, we'll never know.'

'Probably not,' answered Mason.

Silence hung in the air; broken only by the closing of the lift doors.

On reaching the top floor, they were joined by Colin Bradshaw, the Head of Security. After issuing a brief press statement to the gathered media, Mason, it seemed, had already turned his attentions towards other unfinished business.

'So what was the significance of the Longshore Group photograph?' Carlisle asked.

'Purely academic,' Mason replied, pointing towards the empty corridor. 'The killer's computer was crammed with any amount of Gilesgate material. Group gatherings, profiles, background details of those who were involved in the scam . . . you name it, young Samuel had meticulously documented everything down. He even kept dossiers on their private lives. Where they lived, what they ate and drank, even their socialising habits.'

'I always said he was organised.'

'Too damn right he was.' Mason clicked his tongue. 'I often wondered what went on behind closed doors . . . now I know.'

'What about the absence of medical records?' Carlisle quizzed.

Mason swung sharply to face him. 'Let's not go there! The bastard had a nasty habit of tapping into other people's computer systems, including mine.'

They entered into a small side room; Mason offering him a chair opposite.

'Thanks to you, my friend, we've finally nailed our man. All that remains now is for the Home Office to put the rest of these people behind bars. Now that we've recovered the rest of the ACC's documented evidence, that shouldn't be too difficult. Such a pity he had to blow his brains out, but there you have it,' Mason shrugged.

'So what will happen to you, Jack?'

'They've asked me stay on, offered me a new position on the Serious Crime Squad. The funny thing is,' Mason smiled, 'I've fallen in love with the area. I like the people up here; they're genuine, and easy to get on with.'

'Oh. So what do you intend to do about it?'

'I'm working on it, my friend.'

Could Mason finally be mellowing with age, he wondered; probably not. Jack Mason was the last in a long line of special enforcement officers; they broke the mould the day he joined the force. That's why he was nicknamed – *The Bulldog*.

Chapter Fifty-Five

Only time would tell, thought David Carlisle. Close to the city centre, a watery November sun was flooding down into Grainger Street. Despite the recent setbacks, these past few weeks he'd felt a totally different person. Never far from his thoughts, Jackie would always remain close to his heart, he realised that. Even so, he was slowly coming to terms with his loss. Life, it seemed, was certainly more bearable nowadays, and he was beginning to feel good about himself again.

Leaving the A1, he turned east towards his father's house. It wasn't the perfect day to go fishing – overcast with the odd few splodges of rain. Nevertheless, there were important matters to attend to. It was Saturday, and he'd been looking forward to the weekend. The moment the car pulled up outside his father's bungalow, the old man was stood waiting for him. Wearing a worn woolly hat, heavy green windproof jacket, and thick tweed trousers, he was carrying his favourite fishing rod.

'I guess the traffic was busy, son.'

'Just a bit, Pop.'

His father bore that resolute look of a boxing champion about to defend his corner at all costs. Around his feet were his favourite tools of combat, fishing basket, catch nets, umbrella, folding seat, along with a large wicker hamper basket crammed full of all kinds of unknown goodies.

'Today's the day, son,' his father smiled.

'Let's hope Herman doesn't spill you into the river again.'

'Not today, he knows better than to pull that little stunt on me again. Besides, I'm prepared for him this time.'

'It sounds like we have a cunning plan up our sleeves?'

His father sounded deadly serious. 'I have, but I'm keeping it a secret.'

As the last of the fishing tackle was loaded into the boot of his Rover, Carlisle allowed himself a rare smile. No doubt another tall story was about to surface from the depths of the River Coquet. Not surprisingly, Herman the fish and Lexus the Wharf Butcher were one of a kind. Both steeped in fantasy, both elusive to catch.

Carlisle's mobile phone rang.

He hit the missed calls button, and Jack Mason's number suddenly popped up on the display screen. Seconds later, the DCI's voice message sounded distinctly rambunctious.

Call me when you're free, my friend.

Curious, he slipped the phone back into a trouser pocket and tried to make the connection. There again, Jack Mason hadn't made contact in weeks, so why was he phoning him now? He stood for a moment, confused, still searching for a reason.

'Who was that, son?' his father asked.

'Nobody,' he replied.

'Your face tells me otherwise, son.'

Carlisle smiled wistfully. 'Just another one of those nuisance calls.'

'They're damned annoying,' his father protested. 'Once they get hold of your number, they never let go.'

He watched as the old man stared at him blankly. Something was amiss, and whatever it was he sensed his father's angst.

'What is it now—'

'My house keys,' his father said, fumbling around in his pockets. 'I put them down somewhere, and can't remember where.'

'But you've only just locked the front door with them.'

Then he heard them jingle. Age, it seemed, was fast catching up with the old man. Although still in good physical shape, his mind wasn't all it was cracked up to be. Carlisle placed a reassuring arm around his father's narrow shoulder – a manly gesture.

'Best be off then.'

'Right—'

'We've got a fish to catch, remember.'

No sooner had the car swung north to sounds of *JJ Cale,* and '*Playing in the street,*' his father had fallen asleep. Would this be the day of reckoning? He thought.

Probably not!

You've turned the last page.
But it doesn't have to end there . . .

If you are looking for more action packed reading in the DCI Mason and David Carlisle crime thriller series, why not join me at **mike-foster.me** for news, behind the scene interviews, and latest updates.

Satan's Beckoning, the next DCI Mason and Carlisle crime thriller – is due for publication *Summer 2016.*

Printed in Great Britain
by Amazon